THE BEST OF
ALL FLESH

ZOMBIE ANTHOLOGY

Other anthologies edited by James Lowder:

THE BEST OF

ALL FLESH

ZOMBIE ANTHOLOGY

EDITED BY JAMES LOWDER

2009

CONTENTS

ACKNOWLEDGMENTS

Anthologies are intensely collaborative projects, and several people deserve recognition for this one: George Vasilakos of Eden Studios, for publishing the original Books of Flesh anthologies and clearing the way for this volume; Alex Jurkat, for editorial support and encouragement on the original trilogy; William and Deborah Jones of Elder Signs Press, for making *The Best of All Flesh* a reality; the critics and award juries who were so kind to the Books of Flesh series, in particular Edward Bryant for his thoughtful *Locus* review of *The Book of More Flesh*; the readers, for supporting each new release and helping spread the word to fellow zombie fans; and, finally, all the authors who participated in the Books of Flesh anthologies, for allowing me the honor of publishing their words.

INTRODUCTION

THERE WAS A TIME, NOT so long ago, when zombies did not rule the world—the world of publishing, at least. Before the turn of the millennium, customers could wander the aisles of the local bookstore or scan the websites of their favorite online book retailer free from fear of the walking dead. No zombie hordes clambered with unholy glee onto the *New York Times* bestseller list. No shambling corpses pestered Jane Austen's heroines, devouring all the eligible bachelors and interrupting the wittiest *bons mots* with their tortured groans. If you wanted stories about zombies, you had to peruse the pages of genre magazines for the occasional new tale or search out reprint anthologies for long-lost voodoo yarns resurrected from the pulps.

In 1999, when I first pitched the idea of an original zombie anthology to George Vasilakos of Eden Studios, competing books were scarce. The groundbreaking Skipp and Spector splatterpunk zombie-fests, *Book of the Dead* (1989) and *Still Dead* (1991), were almost a decade old and hard to find. Slightly more recent, but equally elusive for book buyers, were Stephen Jones's *The Mammoth Book of Zombies* (1993) and Byron Preiss and John Betancourt's *The Ultimate Zombie* (1993). If bookstores carried any titles featuring the walking dead, they were probably S.D. Perry's novelizations of the Resident Evil video game series. It's telling that the highest profile zombie books at the time were game tie-ins. Games provided the primary outlet for new zombie-themed entertainment in the latter half of the '90s, with the Resident Evil and House of the Dead franchises bloodying arcades and home consoles around the world.

With 1999's *All Flesh Must Be Eaten*, Eden Studios unleashed some undead mayhem of its own onto the tabletop gaming market. The game, billed as "zombie survival horror roleplaying," offers players the chance to create characters that battle the walking dead in a wide variety of locales and eras. Unlike RPGs such as *Vampire: The Masquerade*, or the Resident Evil video games, *AFMBE* doesn't rely upon a single setting. The game's "deadworlds" can include everything from sword and sorcery fantasy to post-Apocalyptic science fiction to horror-steeped alternate history. The zombies are as diverse as the background worlds, sometimes conforming to the role of the familiar, Romero-inspired gut-muncher, oftentimes manifesting as something entirely new. This made the All Flesh line ideal for a collection of first-rate zombie-themed fiction. Because there was no company-controlled setting, no specific rules for the living dead to obey, writers could be free to follow their undead muses in whatever direction they shambled.

It took a year of discussions before we set the first book in motion, but once it became clear that Eden's fans were open to a fiction collection, things moved quickly. I decided early on that I'd run an "open call" for submissions. This meant that anyone and everyone could send their work my way. The response was terrific. While the table of contents for *The Book of All Flesh* lists twenty-five stories, I received more than ten times that many for consideration—and stories of remarkably high quality, too. The slight trepidation I felt about finding tales with a novel approach to the zombie theme vanished within a week. By the time the first anthology saw print in 2001, I was convinced that there were enough good zombie stories out there for at least one more book, if not more. That turned out to be true, as we proved with *The Book of More Flesh* in 2002 and *The Book of Final Flesh* in 2003.

From an editor's perspective, open call anthologies are a risky proposition. Reviewing the flood of manuscripts they generate can be tedious. A fair number of the submissions will not be quite ready for professional publication. Still, every envelope holds a potential gem, a surprising change of pace from a veteran writer or a story from an author with whom you've been hoping to work or, better still, a completely unheralded and startling tale from someone who has yet to break into print anywhere. In the end, the Books of Flesh anthologies included works from well-established pros, familiar names such as Tom Piccirilli and Ed Greenwood, and a large number of stories from authors who were just starting to make names for themselves and have since gone on to much greater prominence in the horror field. A full third of the stories published in the three anthologies were first professional sales, and several of those debuts are included here.

Selecting the stories for this collection was no easy task. I valued all the entries in the original volumes enough to publish them in the first place, after all, and deciding which stories not to incorporate here was rather like choosing which three fingers to chop off each hand before a piano recital. Still, I tried to craft a table of contents for *The Best of All Flesh* that includes roughly equal representation from all three volumes and reflects the terrific variety of tones and styles found throughout the series. I attempted to strike a balance, too, between longer and shorter works.

I chose not to include a few notable stories because they are currently and readily available to readers outside the original books. For example, Matt

Forbeck's wonderfully inventive, Origins Award-winning superhero tale "Prometheus Unwound" (from *The Book of All Flesh*) can be found both in the anthology *Of Dice and Pen* and on Matt's own website. Similarly, Darrell Schweitzer's "The Dead Kid" (from *The Book of More Flesh*) is available in the excellent zombie-themed reprint anthology *The Living Dead*, edited by John Joseph Adams. Readers would be well served to look up both those stories, or perhaps even track down the original trilogy, rare though some of the books may now be.

Eden Studios and I have discussed adding a fourth, entirely new anthology to the series. (We should have known better than to include the word *final* in the title of the third book.) By the time we get around to that new volume, zombies may have worn out their welcome elsewhere. Even if the media's trendmeisters turn their attention to some other genre fad and the walking dead no longer rule the world of publishing, they'll continue to have a place of honor with me. I know from experience that there are plenty of unique and compelling stories out there, just waiting to be told. And despite the unearthly wailing and the occasional misplaced rotting limbs I find lying around the office whenever a new zombie book bursts onto my schedule, I'll always consider myself most fortunate to play some role in shepherding the living dead to print.

— James Lowder
August 2009

WHAT COMES AFTER

KRIS DIKEMAN

READE GLANCED UP AS THE cruiser rolled past the outermost barricade, into the countryside proper. It was a perfect, clear September day, a crisp taste of fall on the breeze, but the blue sky stretching above the car only made him feel vulnerable and exposed. The National Guard had done a good job of cleaning up, but the wrecks and burned-out cars scattered along the gravel shoulder on both sides of the road made him nervous. They provided ample cover for anyone—anything—waiting, like a wolf in a fairy tale, to gobble up unlucky passersby.

In the road ahead, a deep, raw gouge cut into the blacktop where the bulldozer had moved the battered wreck of the school bus onto the shoulder. The bus was back upright; it was filthy with mud and soot, one side horribly crumpled. It sat on its deflated tires in a drift of debris: gravel, slivers of chrome, bits of plastic, paper, and broken glass, lots of broken glass. "Crash dandruff," Sheriff Howell used to call it. All the little bits of crap that accumulated, as if by magic, whenever there was a wreck.

Reade turned his face away from the bus as the car passed by, tried not to look at the smashed windows and the emergency exit door torn almost off its hinges, streaks of clotted blood and gore spattered across the sooty yellow paint. He put his foot on the gas, willed the car to take him away from this place, this bad place—*crime scene, call it what it is; it's a crime scene*—and saw a child's sneaker, a black high top, close to the road's edge. The dirty laces stirred and flapped idly as the cruiser shot past.

Goddamn those guardsmen anyway, he thought. *Why the hell couldn't they have picked that up?*

He knew his anger was irrational. The soldiers had done their best—done things he didn't like to think about—but the heat of indignation helped push back the queasy feeling in his stomach. With the wreck getting smaller in the rearview mirror, Reade remembered how Sheriff Howell had sneered when the Guard had shown up.

"Weekend warriors, Georgie," Howell had said, hitching his belt buckle up over his gut and reaching for his spit cup. "Soft boys in suits, pretending to be soldiers."

But they had turned out to be more, even Howell had admitted later. How much more had been made clear the night the innermost security fence had given way. The dead, pale and gray in the glare of emergency lights, had poured through the breach by the dozens. Reade remembered the look of calm control on the face of the Guard captain as he fired the flame thrower into the vanguard of the zombie mob. They had gone up like kindling, their burning bodies lighting up the night.

The Ransom place was coming up on his left. The windows and doors were still tightly boarded up and, except for the overgrowth of weeds and high grass, the house looked in good shape. John Ransom and his wife had moved into town one week before martial law had been declared. Reade had come out and helped John board up windows, drain the pipes, and get the house ready to stand empty. While they'd nailed sheets of plywood into the window frames, Ransom's wife Lorraine, her face ashen, had silently carried boxes of clothes out to their minivan. The previous day, a zombie had come up behind her son Jason as he was picking tomatoes. Jason had been plucked himself, there one second, gone the next.

"I saw them things on the news, Georgie," John Ransom had said, pulling another ten-penny nail from the jar on the porch and setting it against the plywood. "But I threw that fat fool boss of yours off my land when he told us to come into town. And now my boy is a monster, and his mother's heart is broken . . . ."

A sudden movement in front of him jolted Reade from his reverie. Adrenaline surged through him as the cruiser slowed.

A dead raccoon moved across the road before him in a crabwise shuffle, the track of the tire that killed it clearly visible on its flattened midsection. The animal glared up, eyes shining, teeth bared, misshapen body tensed to spring. Reade veered as the car reached it, closed his eyes as the thing crunched under the left front wheel. All the while he told himself that it was not possible for him to hear the *pop* of its brain pan under the tire. He looked in the rearview mirror and saw the dark stain on the road twitch and quiver, teeth spilling out as the ruined jaws snapped mechanically.

He had almost reached his destination. And just beyond it, the cemetery.

The house was almost completely hidden by a high chain link fence, like the perimeter fence that encircled the town. As he pulled up to the gate and put the cruiser in park, Reade saw that the electricity was off. He took an enormous key ring from his pocket and searched until he found a key with a little piece of white tape and the words *Buren Fence* in Howell's fussy printing. Reade checked the rearview mirror, then the sides, put his hand on the door handle, and took a few quick deep breaths, like a swimmer preparing for a race.

There's no need for this nonsense, he thought. The Guard had sanitized the graveyard; there hadn't been a sighting in days. But when he touched the door handle, he flashed back to Bob Kerrigan, the town's mayor, being yanked out of his Ford pickup.

"I'll just be a minute, Georgie," Bob had said. "I left something on the kitchen ta—" And then the stinking, putrescent arm reached in and grabbed Bob by his hair and yanked him backward out of the truck, and he was gone. Reade had sat, frozen, and listened to the screams getting fainter and the slurping sounds getting louder. *Who's gonna sign the paychecks now?* he had thought foolishly. And then he saw the keys dangling in the Ford's ignition and next thing he was tearing down the road back to town, to the shocked and unbelieving townspeople, to the sheriff's black fury.

"You were supposed to look after him." Howell had thundered. "I can't run this whole goddamned town by myself, you know!" And Reade had stood, head down, miserable, overwhelmed. Out of his depths. That's what his mother had called it whenever he got himself into a situation he couldn't possibly handle.

Now he fought to keep his breathing under control until the familiar panicky feeling receded. He climbed out of the car and unlocked the gate, keys jangling in his hand only a little. He suppressed the urge to glance behind him, slid back into the cruiser, and pulled the car into the driveway. As he re-locked the gate, he tried to keep his back straight and his hands steady. He turned slowly when he heard the front door open. Sheriff Howell's star was a ponderous weight on his chest, the gun awkward and heavy on his hip. Reade wondered for a bleak moment if he looked as ridiculous as he felt.

Mrs. Buren stepped out on the porch. "Hello there, Georgie," she said. "I'm glad you're here."

"Hello, Mrs. Buren."

Her dress was clean and freshly ironed, her hair set in a familiar tight bun. She looked like what she was—a retired small town schoolteacher—and Reade could feel something in his chest loosen a little. She had deep circles under her eyes, and in the unforgiving light of midmorning he could see the lines around her mouth had deepened considerably since he'd seen her last. But her eyes were focused and clear, none of that glazed, faraway look he had seen so much of lately.

She's made of sterner stuff than that, he thought, and felt an unexpected surge of affection for this woman who had terrorized his childhood. She had been the strictest teacher he'd ever known, with high, exacting standards. He had barely kept his head above water in her classes—been "out of his depths" there more often than not. Now she smiled at him, and Reade realized she had been assessing him, too, checking to see what kind of stuff *he* was made from. That smile, so open and genuine, meant she had not found him wanting. He was surprised and a little amused to find that her approval—so hard to win in the past—still meant a great deal to him.

"Well now, Georgie," she said. "Come on into the house, why don't you. I've made tea."

He came up the steps, and as he reached her she slipped her arm under his, like a lady being escorted to a fancy dinner. She gave off a fragrance of lavender and spray starch. Reade felt disoriented; in the jumbled memory of his childhood, Mrs. Buren was a towering presence. This faded, delicate old woman barely came up to his chin.

Mrs. Buren pointed him to an overstuffed wing chair. "Pardon me, dear, while I put pot to kettle," she said, and went into the kitchen. The tea things were already set out on a small rolling table: crustless sandwiches, china cups, silver spoons. The room was immaculate. There were ceramic figurines on the mantle, a grandfather clock ticking calmly in the corner, an assortment of pictures in antique frames arranged on a lace doily across the piano. He settled into the chair more deeply, closed his eyes, thought how it was nice to sit in a room without boards on the windows or bloodstains on the floor.

"It's a comfortable chair, isn't it?" asked Mrs. Buren as she stepped back into the room. Reade jumped up and took the silver tray with the steaming teapot from her, set it down next to the little trolley. She picked up a cup and poured him out some tea. "That was my husband's favorite chair. That young captain from the National Guard liked it, too. He made himself right at home here." Mrs. Buren frowned. "He certainly enjoyed giving me orders. He forbade me to set foot out of this house until you arrived. There's no milk, but will you take sugar?"

"No, thank you, ma'am." Reade took the teacup and saucer, and balanced them on his knee, mindful of the faded Oriental rug. "I imagine those fellows from the Guard just wanted to keep you safe, Mrs. Buren. They caught h—uh, they got a lot of criticism for even letting you stay out here in the first place, after martial law was declared."

Mrs. Buren gave a small, tight smile of satisfaction as she poured his tea. "Martial *rule*, Georgie, depends for its existence upon public necessity. Necessity creates it, justifies it, and limits its endurance. The captain and I had quite a few interesting discussions on the subject. In the end, he saw the sense of my staying here."

"Yes, ma'am." Reade took a sip of tea to hide his smile. He remembered the Guard captain sitting with Sheriff Howell in his office, a map of the county spread out across the battered oak desk between them.

"*You* tell the old bag she has to move out," the captain had said. "Every time I mention to her that she's living next to a graveyard, that fuckin' *dead people* are digging their way out of the ground at the rate of about two per day, she gets this stuck-up look on her face and starts in arguing with me. 'The civil law cannot be displaced, young man. And let us call things by their right name—it is not martial *law*, but martial *rule*.'"

The sheriff had tipped Reade a sly wink as he commiserated with the captain on the frustration of dealing with an old lady so well-versed in the intricacies of the law. But after the guardsman had left, Howell's laughter had rung through the office.

"He's a fair shot with a flame thrower, Georgie, but he's no match for that old biddy. I'd sooner face a roomful of the dead than cross her m'self," Howell had said, wiping tears from his eyes. And Reade had laughed, too, though secretly he felt sorry for the captain, who was clearly used to people jumping up when he yelled frog. Unfortunately for him, Mrs. Buren was also used to giving orders, and it would take more than the end of the world to change that.

Now she passed Reade a plate of sandwiches. "Once those young men learned to respect my privacy, and not help themselves to things they shouldn't, the time passed quickly enough. Some of them turned out to be quite useful. I was almost sorry to see them go."

Reade looked over one of the dainty sandwiches. The bread was the same government issue whole meal everyone in town had been eating for weeks, though this had the crusts neatly trimmed. The filling was a single leaf of lettuce and a thin slice of pink meat. He took a small bite and chewed carefully. Spam.

"It's the Guard's leaving that's brought me out here, Mrs. Buren," he said, and took another sip of tea. It had a strong, smoky flavor.

She leaned back in her chair. "You want me to come into town."

"I do." Reade set down his teacup and looked her in the eye, hoping he sounded more authoritative than he felt.

"I'm afraid you've wasted your time, Georgie." She looked at him more closely. "I should be calling you *Sheriff* Reade, shouldn't I? You are the sheriff now. And with the mayor gone, as well, you're all the town has by way of an authority figure. Poor Bobby Kerrigan. He was such a good student, and a fine mayor. You were there when he was killed, weren't you?"

Reade struggled to keep his voice steady. Getting angry now wouldn't accomplish anything. "You know I was." *But I'm not ten anymore*, he thought. *I won't let you get the upper hand on me all that easy.* "And since I am the sheriff now, I may as well say what I've come to say. I need you to pack up some things and come into town. All of this is far from over. Your house is completely isolated. The idea of you staying here alone is just crazy."

To his surprise, Mrs. Buren's face quickly went dark with anger. "That is an inflammatory and imprudent thing to say, Georgie. I thought I taught you better than to speak so carelessly."

Reade flushed. "I'm sorry, Mrs. Buren. Of course I didn't mean—I meant to say, now that the Guard has left, I've had to make a decision. I'm responsible . . ." He hated the way the tone of her voice shot him back across the years, turning him into a frightened, floundering child again.

To his relief Mrs. Buren smiled at him, her anger gone as quickly as it had come. "Of course you are. You just spoke without thinking. I know you're doing your best, all on your own. The guardsmen certainly cleared out in a hurry. Drink your tea, dear, before it gets cold."

Reade took another sip. They were both silent for a moment, then Mrs. Buren stood up and pushed the tea trolley back. "This house has been in my family a long time. Since things are getting back to normal, I don't see why—"

Reade stood up, too. "Nothing is normal. Now that the National Guard has left, it's even more important to be careful. I can't guarantee your safety all alone out here. Everyone else has moved into town—" He sat down heavily, feeling drained. He pointed to her chair, and Mrs. Buren sat down.

"No one can predict what will happen," he said, "or what won't happen. Like the graveyard out here. Everyone thought it was going to be a real mess. No one could figure out why they hadn't—why you hadn't been . . . hurt right away. Plenty of other graveyards in town gave up their dead, all the churchyards, even the old potter's field. No one gave any thought to how stony hard the ground was out this way. So they rushed all those guardsmen here, and it turned out to be a kind of turkey shoot, with the dead coming up so slow, it was actually pretty easy—"

Mrs. Buren looked away. Red spots of color bloomed on her cheeks.

Reade cursed himself and started again. "That's a dumb way to describe it, and I'm sorry. I know some of the people in that graveyard belonged to your family." He hesitated. "At least your husband wasn't there."

"There were quite a few of my people out there," she said, a little hoarsely. "But I was spared that, at least."

Mrs. Buren's husband had died in the Korean War, his body never recovered. Reade hated that he knew that. He could point to any person still alive in town and say where their dead relatives were buried, or at least where they should be buried. It was an awful thing to know more about the dead of his town than the living.

"Mrs. Buren, not all the dead come out of graves we know about. We put men on shifts to watch the cemeteries, but there are family plots all over the place—on farms, old estates. Unmarked graves. Not all of them registered with the county. And then there's the other ones, hidden bodies that nobody knew about—"

She looked up sharply, and for the first time he saw a trace of fear in her expression. Reade was encouraged; perhaps he could convince her yet.

"Hidden bodies?" she said. "What are you talking about?"

"Do you remember Jennifer Collins?"

"Remember?" she said, her eyes wide. "Oh, oh, no . . . ."

"I know she was a favorite of yours."

"A teacher should never have favorites, but I truly thought I could help that poor girl." Mrs. Buren lowered her eyes to the floor. "Growing up without a father can have such an enormous impact on a child. And then, last year, that man she was living with ran off, abandoned her and their little boy. It was like a curse, passed down the generations. She turned out to be no better than her mother. What a waste," she said, her anger flaring up again. Reade wondered what she thought had been wasted: Jenny's life or her own time.

"She killed the boy's father."

"Oh, Georgie, what an awful thing!"

"Everybody knows he slapped her around, and I guess he went too far. Maybe she was scared for the baby. She killed him and hid his body in the privy out behind their mobile home. That must have been tough, shifting a big man like him, but she managed it . . . ."

I shouldn't be telling her all this, he thought, but he found he couldn't stop. In his mind he saw Jenny Collins's little boy, barely a toddler, blue pajamas covered with blood and slime. The baby had launched itself at Reade, right across the shattered, stinking remains of its father. Sheriff Howell had pushed Reade aside and the baby had battened itself onto Howell's leg, a feral animal in footie pajamas. Howell had actually given out a startled laugh—until the child's tiny teeth pierced his skin. Then he screamed. Reade had been the one to pull the boy from Howell's leg. When he'd finally torn it away, the baby still had a goodly chunk of shin in its mouth and its round cheeks were filthy with blood. Its squirming body had been so horribly *cold.*

He didn't want to talk about it. But all the awful things Reade had seen and done in the past months were building up in him, filling him up like poisoned water in a well. If he didn't speak, he'd drown . . . .

"One night the body of Jenny's husband woke up. It got Jenny, and the little boy, and about a dozen other people down in the trailer park. Then they rose up and set off on a rampage, and there was hell to pay. We lost a lot of people. As for Jenny and the baby—well, Sheriff Howell actually burst out laughing—"

"Jenny was punished." Mrs. Buren's voice was a whisper, but the venom in it shocked Reade out of his recitation. "Her sin came back to her. It was no better than she deserved, but the baby, that innocent child—he never even had a chance. He deserved a chance . . . ."

Mrs. Buren put her hand in front of her face, shooing away the rest of Reade's words like flies, and the sheriff cursed his own selfish stupidity. He got down on one knee in front of her, almost like a suitor, and gently pulled her hands away from her face.

"You have to listen to me," he said. "I *can't* let you stay out here by yourself. They sanitized that graveyard out there, but there could be unmarked graves. There could be bodies we don't know about, making their way up. That soil is stony, and that makes it hard going for them, but there's something in it, something that makes the older dead ones more . . . preserved than normal. We had one come out of the church graveyard that was over a hundred years old, and it did a lot of harm before we could stop it. It doesn't matter how long ago they died. If there's even a scrap of bone and muscle left, it hungers, and if the head is intact, it'll hunt."

Mrs. Buren pulled her hands out of Reade's, stood up again, and walked to the window. "You don't have to tell me these things. My people certainly are out there. We heard them at night, scratching their way up. Out there in the moonlight, the bones clicking against the earth reminded me of castanets. My husband and I took a trip to Spain once. That was just after we were married. Really, I think that was the happiest time of my life." She stopped for a moment and looked down at the floor.

"Two weeks after the soldiers arrived, I woke early and walked out to the fence to take in a breath of morning air. And standing on the other side to greet me was my dear cousin, Annabelle. She was just fifteen when she died. I was twelve, and hadn't been allowed to go her funeral. Influenza, they said. But now I know the truth. She was there at the fence to greet me. And so was her unborn baby."

"My God . . . ." Reade sank back in the chair. Had he really thought of this house as safe? Had he worried about frightening this woman? It was a miracle she was still sane.

"She stood there, her arms wrapped around her stomach, cradling her poor little bastard, her tattered burial gown swaying in the breeze. They buried her in white. That's funny, don't you think? She tunneled out of that hard ground, and the baby burrowed out of her. It yowled at me from her torn belly, with its horrible little puckered-up face. It was hungry."

Mrs. Buren walked back across to the tea tray and picked up her cup. "I think she killed herself. Or perhaps she simply died from the mortification of it. Either way, it was her shame that killed her. But the truth comes out. It comes up. Secret things don't stay secret forever. Like that soldier that ran away. Sooner or later, he'll be found."

One of the guardsmen had gone AWOL just before his unit had been reassigned, taken some food and his gun and left the house during the night. The captain had come to see Reade about it the day they shipped out, as worried as he was angry and embarrassed. Reade had promised to keep an eye out, told the captain he'd keep in touch. On the desk between them was Sheriff Howell's revolver and badge. And down the hall, the zombie that had once been Sheriff Howell raged and shrieked, throwing itself against the cell bars.

"Do you want me to do it?" the captain had asked, and Reade had said no, no thank you; he would manage.

Mrs. Buren saw the concerned look on the sheriff's face and gave a shrill laugh. It was an unpleasant, brittle sound. "You think your old teacher is going to go crazy out here, don't you? Oh, Georgie Reade! That is funny!" And through her laughter, Reade saw that black anger bubbling up again.

"Lots of people have had problems coping," he said. He thought of Lorraine Ransom, with her pale face and empty eyes. The night they burned her son's body, she threw herself on the pyre. Reade had caught a glimpse of her, cradling her zombie boy in her arms, just before the flames roared up to consume them.

He ran a hand through his unwashed hair and slumped down in the chair, suddenly feeling very tired. "I haven't been sleeping so well lately," he said in response to the concern he thought he saw in his host's eyes. "I can't catch the knack of sleeping more than an hour at a time anymore."

"You'll sleep now, dear. For a while, I think." Mrs. Buren's voice sounded as if it came from some great distance. Reade looked up at her, and it took a moment for him to realize he was on his knees again. There was one more brief moment of lucidity before he pitched forward onto the carpet and darkness took him.

He woke up slowly, head pounding, a taste in his mouth like century-old grit. Masses of dull silver duct tape secured his wrists to the armrests of a heavy, straight-backed wooden chair. His legs were strapped solidly to the chair's legs in the same fashion. Dim light filtered in from the high rectangular windows set close to the ceiling. He was in the basement. The cinderblock wall before him had been whitewashed recently, the red earth floor around him neatly swept. The air was thick with the terribly familiar stench of dead flesh, cut with a strong smell of disinfectant. The Oriental carpet from the living room was piled in an untidy heap next to the chair. *That's how she got me down here,* he thought. *She wrapped me up in the rug and dragged me down the stairs.*

To his right stood a small table covered with a bloodstained tea towel. On the towel rested a roll of duct tape and a copy of *Gray's Anatomy*, with a small boning knife laid across the pages to hold the book open at a color illustration of a dissected biceps.

"You're awake, Georgie. That's good. I was worried I let your head hit the steps one time too many." Mrs. Buren stepped in front of him. Her hair was disheveled. Smudges of earth and something dark stained the front of her dress. Behind them, Reade could hear movement.

He cleared his throat and tried to speak. "Mrs. Buren." It came out as a harsh whisper. "Whatever it is you've done, we can talk about it. Please, just cut me loose."

"I'm sorry," she said, and her eyes were oh, so far away. "But I can't leave this house. He needs me. And we need you."

"Did one of the soldiers hurt you? Did you do something to them? If they hurt you, whatever you did was self-defense." He forced himself to try and think clearly, past the steady throbbing in his head. He could feel blood trickling through his hair. But his gun was still strapped to his hip.

Mrs. Buren looked at him with pity. "You don't understand, Georgie. I've done so much wrong. I've sinned, and suffered for it, as sinners should. But now I've been given another chance." She reached out and tipped his chair back on one leg, spinning Reade in neat pirouette away from the wall to face the basement's other occupants.

The soldier was taped to his chair in the same manner as Reade. Large sections of flesh had been neatly stripped away from the meaty parts of his arms, thighs, and chest, leaving precise rectangular holes. His heart peeked out from a dark mass of rotting viscera and coagulated blood. The arms and seat of his chair were black with gore. Reade knew that the dead didn't bleed that way; the soldier had still been alive when the flesh was stripped off him. He had crossed over and risen up—that was clear from the gray, grainy texture of his skin and the feral way his teeth gripped the wad of duct tape securing his head and neck—but he posed no threat now. His head was gone from the bridge of his nose up, the skull scooped clean of it contents.

Just behind the soldier was a mattress piled high with quilts and blankets. In the center, hands and feet trussed with more tape, huddled a zombie child. Reade thought it might have been about five when it died. Its flesh had the hard, desiccated look of a body that had been underground for some time. Next to the mattress lay a stinking pile of rags, bits of bone, and chunks of dried flesh. Farther back, close to the wall, two holes—one large, one small—gaped in the cellar floor, with stony earth heaped around their edges.

Mrs. Buren nodded toward the pile of rags, bones, and flesh, all that remained of a brutally demolished corpse. "She came here after my husband died. Horrible woman. She said the child was my John's, that John was going to leave me and marry her, that she would be a truer wife to him, because she had given him a son. She said she wanted money, or she'd tell. So I gave her some tea, just like the tea I gave you, only stronger. Much stronger. And I gave the boy some lemonade. Then I brought them down here and buried them. I waited for someone to come looking. But no one ever did."

Reade tried to speak and found he couldn't. The shock of it all was too great.

"We've lived here together, the three of us, all these years. They were my secret. And then the dead began to rise. I came down here every night. I waited, and I prayed. And one night, when those awful men were off in town, I heard a noise, no louder than a mouse scratching for food. But oh, it made my heart light. He was finally coming up, coming back to me."

She gestured at the pile of flesh. "I didn't regret killing her—that slut, that whore. But the child, that had been wrong. Bastard or not, he was all that was left of my dear husband. Killing him was a terrible mistake, one I regretted bitterly. But when I heard them coming up I knew I've been given a second chance."

"The Guard," Reade managed in a gasp.

"They searched the cellar the day they came. 'Securing the perimeter,' they called it. That was before the boy came back to me, so the guardsmen didn't find anything. But one of them did help himself to a jar of my best preserves. I pretended to be angry about that and made them put a lock on the cellar, and then took the key. They had a good laugh at the foolish old lady, but they kept out after that, just to keep me quiet." She chuckled at her own cleverness. "By day, I watched those men destroy what was left of my kin. At night, I came down here and listened. And when the time was right, when I knew they were ready to break through, I told one of them."

She pointed to the remains of the soldier.

"He was the greediest—I've always been good at spotting the weak ones, the greedy ones. I told him they were here, and I needed help destroying them, because they were a secret. I offered him money if he'd come down when the others were out in my garden, swilling beer, smoking God knows what to celebrate their last night. And he came down. He took care of that—" she jerked her thumb again at the pile "—and then I took care of him. He turned out to be very useful. He lasted much longer than I'd expected."

She smiled down at the boy, her face radiant with affection, and in a distant corner of his mind Reade thought he had never seen her look so happy. She stepped over to the soldier's corpse and tore a dangling strip of flesh from his shoulder, then dropped it in front of the child. Its head came up immediately, and cellar dirt trickled from the empty eye sockets. It wriggled forward toward the flesh, sniffed it with its ruined and rotted nose, and moaned in disappointment.

"But now my little boy doesn't want him any more, do you dear?" The child moaned again, and she made a little shushing sound. Then she leaned forward and gently squeezed Reade's biceps, testing its firmness. Reade remembered that moment on the porch, her sharp look of assessment, her sudden smile of approval. It'd had nothing to do with how he carried his badge.

"Mrs. Buren," Reade said as calmly as he could manage, "don't do this . . . ."

He struggled for breath, hunted for the words that would reach this woman. But even as he spoke them, he knew that they were wrong. He was, once more, out of his depths. "He is not a child anymore," Reade sputtered. "He—*it* is a monster. For God's sake, think about what you're doing. Please, I don't want to die this way!"

She stepped past him to the table. "But you won't die, Georgie. At least not right away. I've learned a great deal about how much to take, and from where. I'm sure you'll last much longer than the soldier. And I'll be here to help you, dear."

She glanced at the anatomy book, just as Reade had seen her consult her lesson plans at the start of a class. Then she gave a short nod, picked up the knife, and stepped toward him. Reade moaned. The zombie boy mewled with excitement. Mrs. Buren smiled.

"If you're ready, Georgie, I think we will begin."

SIFTING OUT THE HEARTS OF MEN

WARREN AND LANA BROWN

OUR DEAR MOTHERS AND OUR wives would not like to know the truth of life in this alien country, so when my brother soldiers and I have written home, we have been careful to tell them only how different and how longingly the same the country looks, the extent of the few kindnesses the local people have been willing to offer, and that, tired, we have slept well at night.

I wonder, though, if our mothers and our wives and our fathers and our sisters and, God forbid our children, have learned yet, have somehow got an inkling, of the horror.

When the rebels started up, there was no question that our Union would whip them right soon. Our families now know the folly of that hope. More than four years later we have whipped them not enough, and they us more than we ever expected, and the situation has grown bleaker than I think my family, in their gray house in the city, could picture from their dreams alone.

I pray they still need their dreams to picture it; I pray they have not seen it close. Probably, I think, they have not. The dues of war surely are paid first and most horribly in the field. I'm headed home. I pray to leave this behind.

I thought, when I killed my first man at Bull Run, and was not killed myself but saw so many killed before me, when I first smelled the rotting bodies, bloating in the sun when we could not get them in the ground fast enough, or at all, that war was something different from what any woman could imagine. I thought, when I heard legless men screaming to be killed, when I saw the doctors do no better to the boys than the rebels at their worst, I believed no mother could, as my mother did, admonish her son to war.

But killing is the least of war. You stop wondering at the killing, at having killed, that you will kill again, when you worry more that your belly is empty and your shoes worn through or stolen from you. You want a biscuit more than you do salvation. A drink of rye more than to go to heaven. You forget what Heaven is supposed to be like, because you are in Hell and the two do not marry.

I am going back now. Gus and I talked it over and we think the two of us together might make a go of it. The rebellion has died out, and Billy Yank and Johnny Reb no longer hate each other, but watch their brother soldier's back. Like so many men, Gus and I have stopped caring about the Union, or the honor of our names. We have stopped worrying that women will not greet us on the street if we have not fought like men.

To be a man is not what it was.

I thought, when I first killed a man, and when I first went hungry, that war was the deepest hell you could go to. But there's worse things than death and pain, worse things than killing another's kin. There's coming back after.

At first we couldn't even tell one from the other. The boys are so dreadful pale and sickly, their skin a rash of sores, their clothes in such rags, so many of them wounded here or there but still staggering, that the first ones got too close.

Our company had been marching all day and half into the night, tired, wet, and so boiling was the heat the sergeant had allowed we could march without our shirts. I had lagged behind some, considering if I should chuck my kit right there and fall down asleep, as I was sure I could. *Who would miss me?* I asked myself. But they shot deserters in those days and I took one more step, then another, then another.

I heard something behind me. It was dark, the moon covered in the clouds that had worked to drench us all day. I saw one of the boys, one I didn't recognize in the dark, and he walked even more bone-tired than I. I stopped and reached a hand out to him, as you did a fellow soldier then, but something about his face made me look twice, and I pulled my hand away. His uniform bulged at the belly as if too small for him, an unlikely sight among foraging troops; and then I saw the devilish mass below his neck. His chest was torn away as I had seen so many times, his lifeless heart burst forth unnaturally. I did not know what to make of it in my mind, but I screamed, Gus tells me, and I ran, thank God, for he was reaching for me and surely I would be one too now if I hadn't. He lurched forward as the boys turned to see what new horror could possibly make an 1860 man cry out, and he got hold of Samuel Miller's arm and bit it clean through, and Samuel's screams were added to the night.

The night was horror like none since, for none knew then to shoot them clean through the head, and he trampled on and tore two others despite our shots, until one of us hit him between the eyes on pure luck. But that night was the last that the men breathed sound; for once he fell, we thought the misery was done. Samuel and the others cried a merciless long time until they died, and by morning we knew the plague was Hell indeed, for they rose up again, and we murdered our soldier brothers without a thought, except to save ourselves.

The officers, bound by that epithet to carry on and carry us too, ordered us to bury the men and strike out again. But they could not look at us straight. Hours to days and days to a week, we gleaned there were hundreds of the risen, all through the countryside. We had but one message from a passing rider, that there was no help in the direction we were going; we received no orders at all. By week's end, we determined to save the precious ammunition we had for the dead, and let the rebels alone.

We went on this way six more days, marching to no particular place, for there was no particular place that would receive us safely. We killed perhaps two hundred of them, and ran from a thousand more. We found they could not climb a tree after a man, but that a man would be trapped forever if he tried the trick. On the sixth day, Gus found himself so much accustomed to the target that he killed the major, who had been missing since dawn, with a single shot at fifty feet. There were but twelve of us left then, all the officers gone, and Thomas Greanley said we had a better chance each man for himself. No man had very much to say in dispute, and it was decided. As near as we could calculate, we were not far from the ocean, and many of the men saw in that direction some hope of help, or final reckoning. Gus and I determined to pair up, as we both wished to head dead north.

I hoped that the plague had not reached the cities, or if it had they had found some way of curing it. My family—mother and father and sister, and my dear wife Ruth and little son Jack—were in the Union capital, and I placed my bets on that city, where our able president had dealt so nobly with the danger of disunion. If any man could save his people from this calamity, Abe Lincoln could.

For a time Gus and I made good progress, in one day traveling better than twenty miles where the land was flat and dry and the woods thick enough to hide us but well passable. Perhaps our spirits once lifted at the thought of home lifted our strength also, but for how long can raised spirits endure in the fear of Second Coming, or the coming of Lucifer himself? Our pace soon flagged with our strength. The land had grown more inhospitable, offering rocky ground and ravines in our path, which in the drizzle and overcast skies seemed sometimes like the mouths of Hell from which the walking dead had sprung. We had hoped to locate mounts to carry us north, but horses have vanished from the land, or are found only as carcasses, alive with bluebottles and maggots. I think that our fatigue is so great sometimes that we would gladly leap astride the rotting beasts if they too should rise as the human dead have risen and urge them like riders of the Apocalypse toward our homes and loved ones. But the plague seems visited upon man and man alone. For a fact we hoped this was the literal truth before we came upon the mother in the road.

We were five days into our homeward trek, and had stayed the night in a derailed boxcar, its doors barricaded against the terrors of the night. Our meager rations of hardtack and jerky had been consumed, and we had set snares for rabbits or partridge, or whatever small game might spring the trap. Our plan as always had been to alternate the night watch, but hunger and fatigue took their toll and both of us slept, slept that is until the wailing of the babe broke the quiet of the early dawn. I awoke after Gus, in time to see him, Navy Colt in hand, sliding the door aside with his great arm. Quick to follow him and making sure a cartridge filled the breech of my carbine, I descended to the ground and beheld yet another thing that no man should behold.

It had not been a baby's wail that had awakened us. A babe there was indeed, pressed to its mother's breast where they stood in the road, the light of the rising sun making them a master's portrait of life and love, a glowing hope that all our dreams had not fallen into blackness. But the picture burned away as we saw that the scream was delivered from the young mother's lips, that her girl child even gray in death suckled with cold delight at the blood that flowed from the rent flesh of her mother's breast. Of all we had endured thus far, this scene exceeded the worst. So much so that Gus, a hard strong man, fell to his knees and sobbed as the young woman wailed again, clutching her dead but living child even closer in a hopeless embrace. I could not bear it and raised my Spencer to end the mother's pain only to find Gus before me, the cold eye of his revolver staring at my own face.

"You will not shoot a living woman, Tommy Barnes, before my having shot you first."

His manner was straightforward and without bluster, and I knew that for a brief moment he was mad, and I knew also that he would kill me dead.

"She will not be a living woman long, Gus. You have seen enough to know it."

"I have seen men take bullets meant for other men too. And I have seen men carry others across battlefields on their shoulders when they had no chance."

We stood looking at each other, and as my piece was cocked I am ashamed to say I considered feigning my consent, then shooting my friend in his madness when he presented the chance. But he was my friend and I lowered my Spencer and we went to her and used all the strength we both had in us to separate her from the baby. We watched her for an hour, and in her delirium she spoke enough to tell us that her name was Amy Chester, that she had folks in Baltimore and would we please let them know she and the baby were all right. We promised her we would. It was only when she slept that we did for it, and only when she awoke with empty eyes, approaching us in unclean hunger, that Gus himself killed her.

It is now three days since we buried poor Amy Chester and her child. Our progress north continues slowly, but we have had good luck with game. I cannot help but think as we eat the rabbits and birds that maintain our strength that we ourselves are the game of the carnivorous dead who were once our brave comrades and our equally brave enemies. If in sacrament we take the bread as the body of Christ, have we his children somehow now become the sacrament of the damned, our own flesh taken to celebrate the reign of the Legions of Hell? Such thoughts can not be borne by sane men. And Gus and I do ponder in our despair whether our wits have departed us.

He carries the locket of Amy Chester wrapped in a Confederate dollar upon which is written the particulars of her people. He has shown me a likeness of his own wife, Rebecca, taken by cholera a year before the outbreak of the war. The resemblance between the two women is strong, and explains in part I think his adamant defense of Amy. He had not spoken much of Rebecca before, and never shown her picture.

On Tuesday we came upon a large group of Negroes close by the side of the road. Men, women, and children there were, set in a neat camp with several wagons, and mules to pull them. The men were well-armed, some with Henry rifles, and drew down on us as we approached. In our ragged state it took us some convincing to show them we were not Confederates, but their leader, who went by the name Benford Blue, was a reasonable man who accepted us for what we were, and pulled from his kit a corporal's insignia, holding it next to mine.

"So you two boys sick of the fighting too?"

I could see that Gus did not well approve Blue's manner of speaking, and before I could stop him he was bound to reply.

"And I think I have seen things that would make the whites of your eyes go whiter, and stared them down too, you darkey son of a bitch."

Several of the men approached closer at this and I thought we would fare no better than rebels at their hands at that moment. But Benford Blue waved them back. He stood before Gus and raised up his buckskin shirt to reveal a livid rough-healed scar.

"A Confederate bayonet did that, Union man." He turned to show a net of slash marks on his back. "And a sergeant on the Union side did this when I was a green recruit and a white man said I was a thief. The rebel is dead and the liar is dead too. They both saw it was Benford Blue who killed them, saw him face to face, as you see me now." He lowered his shirt, and raised one leg of his pants. "And the man who did this was already dead, soldier." Benford Blue smiled down at the scabbed red sore. "Now he's dead for good."

I was overcome by terror, though my mind told me the Negro was not one of the dead himself. But how could it be? How could he survive what no other had? Gus had begun to back away; I could see he was ready to run. I started after him, but something told me these Negroes were our hope. If Benford Blue had survived, he must know how to answer the horrible punishment God had inflicted.

I leaped upon my friend, tumbling us both to the ground. "They're alive, Gus," I whispered as he struggled with me. "This place is safe."

The Negroes shared their mess with us and even Gus was grateful. The women held the children back from touching us or playing near. I could see from their dress that some were freedmen and others must be recent slaves. They had banded together, as had we with our rebel brothers, to arm against the unexpected enemy. As to Blue's miraculous survival, it resulted, as he explained with what I believe was no small satisfaction, that his people had discovered no secret, only a mystery. No black man or woman or child that they knew of had been afflicted. They hid in fear just as did we whites, but only as they would from wild animals. They were safe from the living death.

We beseeched them to shield us, and I reckon we weren't the first. Benford Blue would have none of it. It strengthened our case not at all that we could not have been afflicted, that we showed no sores or wounds that would bind us to rise after death. Blue said he could not be sure of it, because we were white men.

After a night they sent us on our way, standing guard so we would not be tempted to turn back, though we were in spite of it. But we walked on just the same.

We were some two days walk north from Benford Blue and his band when we found ourselves on the bank of a mist-covered river we judged to be the Rappahannock.

Having taken such pains to avoid towns and their mass of people in our journey north, we were at something of a loss to determine exactly where we were. But we agreed that it would be best to follow the river northwest, skirting Richmond, which lay somewhere north of the river. Neither Gus nor I had any desire to meet up with a body of Union soldiers, who this far to the north might not look kindly on our desertion of our duties regarding the now almost forgotten war.

We had seen few of the walking dead for some days, and I dared hope that the plague had indeed confined itself to the battlefields we had left behind. With these thoughts of affirmation and accompanying visions of my dear loved ones, whom I prayed waited in a neat clapboard house in the capital, I put my hand on Gus's shoulder.

"I think we will see the Potomac before too many days more journey, my friend."

He replied with something of a smile, "I believe you are right, Tommy."

It was then the monster came at us out of the mist. Its dark bulk loomed into view eerily silent, like some Leviathan come from out of the depths to join the risen dead. We had been too subject to queer and monstrous sights of late and had become quick to fight or run. Before I knew what had happened Gus had raised his revolver and let fly a shot at the thing, the report of his Colt so close by it nearly deafened me.

The huge shape defined itself now and we beheld an immense ironclad very like the Confederate *Virginia*, against which the Union's *Monitor* had prevailed off Hampton Roads. That this ship wore the Union colors suggested she had been captured from the rebels and turned to the use of our Navy.

We could hear the huff of her engines now, and could see the smoke from her stack as she churned the water toward us. I expected at any moment she must turn to follow the curve of the river, but instead she continued toward us and we sprung away as her prow drove into the bank and she came to rest with a horrible rending sound as a full third of her length reared up on shore with a force that ripped her funnel from its fastenings and brought it crashing forward onto her deck. A great hiss of steam escaped from amidships and the sound of her engines lapsed into silence.

Gus and I stared at each other.

"Where is her crew?" I asked when I could speak.

He shook his head. As if in answer a steel hatch begin to rise on her deck, slowly, as if the man below had not the strength to push it to.

"They must be in a bad way," Gus said, hastening toward the great hulk, then finding a handhold on a stanchion and hoisting himself up onto the deck.

"Hang on, Gus. You don't know what you'll find there," I called to him.

He grinned at me. "Dead men can't run a ship, Tommy."

He pulled the hatch cover open and shouted a hello into the depths. A pale arm reached forth and gripped his ankle.

"To Hell with you," he said, and leveled the Navy Colt and fired.

"Guess I was wrong, Tommy," he shouted, slamming down the hatch cover. It was the last thing I ever heard him say, for at that moment the ironclad seemed actually to take a great breath. Then I was lifted into the air and the world filled with thunder.

When I awoke I could find only pieces of the ironclad, and pieces of men. The boilers had taken Gus from life and the grisly crew from death. Driven barrel-first into a tree trunk like Excalibur into the stone was Gus's Navy Colt. Try as I might, I could not get it free.

I was almost compelled to cry at being all alone in this godforsaken world. I realized now that Gus was my tether to a willingness to go on. I fell to my knees, not to pray, for surely no prayer had been answered since the beginning of the plague, but to give myself up to the destiny of living death.

But as I sobbed on the riverbank, I thought again of my kindly young wife and our little child. I could not know, might never know, if they were safe or dead, or in that horrible purgatory in between, but I could not fail to try to reach them. I staggered to my feet again, and wandered northward.

I could not sleep and feared to lie down and try, so I walked all night, and just as dawn broke I saw a town ahead. I no longer cared what I might meet there; I had no choice but to march as straight as my body would bear, and that I did.

Like the countryside in which it abided, the town was in that stage of panic that at first glance might be mistaken for the laziness of a Sunday afternoon. No one was in sight. The stores were boarded up and no sound escaped from within. I was afraid, more than of the dead, that there would be no one at all. I walked the boards next to the shops and saloon, and crossed the square to check the stables. As I stepped in front of the church doors, I heard a stifled cry: "Mister!"

I stopped and stared, and could make out no movement. But then the door came slowly open and a man whispered loud, "Hurry!" and waved me to him. I ran as well as I could in my condition, and was escorted inside, where perhaps twenty townspeople still held out hope. They looked me over closely and, accepting that I had not been infected, asked me if I had ammunition, and told me I could stay. They did not ask my story. I did not have to ask theirs. God had made our stories all the same. We had forged new gods: the carbine, the Gatling gun, and the cannon. The dead we made, and now we could not look away from them.

As I took my futile post at a window of the church, I looked my nameless companions over, for they might be the last of the living I would ever know. I saw in them more than the muted and dazed fear I had grown used to in my own face, reflected in Gus's. One woman held a newspaper and sobbed, and several others gathered round her. The men looked each other in the face with despair. I walked to the woman and took the broadside from her, and read that our beloved Abe Lincoln had been murdered.

Shot through the head. The great man. Could it be? The report said the event took place in a theater; did that mean our capital had not been afflicted, that the face of society was yet aswirl with pretty girls and honored gentlemen? Did they not know what horror the war had turned to?

Or was our captain himself a victim of God's retribution?

It seems only hours ago I was drinking rye with Gus in camp, winning seven dollars from Ben Stuart with a queen-high straight, and he was cussing me and we were complaining about the cold and heat and other discomforts a man finds on the periphery of war. Now I hold my rifle on the windowsill in anticipation of the most brutal kind of killing that I have been called upon to do. To kill not the man himself, but his living soul, that would not give up because he fell.

And I wait for the final moment, to place a hole in my own brain. I know now I cannot spare my wife and child the torments of earth or Hell. I can only spare the world the specter of my sin.

SUSAN

ROBIN D. LAWS

I T HAD TAKEN HIM UNTIL his fifth trip to the loading dock of the old sugar refinery before it finally came to him what the smell reminded him of: alligators. Saint Augustine's Alligator Farm, in St. Augustine, Florida. His parents had taken him there when he was a little kid. And in turn he'd taken Maggie and the kids during their own trip down there, just three years before The Rising. How could he have forgotten that smell? Thick, damp, loamy. Thousands of alligators lolling around, packed together in mossy water, shitting and pissing and screwing and fighting over chicken carcasses. Grinning up at you as their reek rose into the humid air. Like they knew their stink was going to stay on your skin and hair, root its way into the fabric of your polo shirt and your cut-off jeans and stay there for as long as it could. They might be penned up and put on display, those alligators, but they could still fuck with you. A little, last gesture of impotent reptilian malice. Well, this place smelled like that. It hit you as soon as the guy opened the big corrugated metal door. Forster was glad to have finally pegged the thing that had been nagging at him all this time.

Forster reached for his wallet to pay the guy but Tim, who'd come in behind him, put a restraining hand on his shoulder. The guy waved the two of them through with no payment exchanged. This was a new arrangement. Tim had paid the hundred bucks for Forster last time, but now he seemed to have some kind of comp privileges. It did not surprise Forster that Tim might be providing some kind of *quid pro quo* service for them.

Even if he'd been able to rouse himself to curiosity over this minor detail, he knew better than to ask. If it was interesting enough to come up in idle conversation, Tim might drop a mention of it. Forster had established himself as worthy of trust.

They headed toward the steps that led up to the top level of risers. Tim liked to survey things from on high. Observe the bettors as well as, maybe even more so than, the competitors. The first couple of times, Forster had preferred to get closer to the action. Now it was fine by him to sit beside Tim.

On the way up the stairs, Forster stopped his hand just short of getting a big splinter from the railing. It, like the rest of the bleacher structure, was chunked together from raw, unfinished lumber. The first time he'd been there it was all fresh and new, like it had been put up the previous day. Now it was starting to get grimy.

"Watch out for splinters," he said to Tim.

"Thanks," said Tim.

They were hardly at the top of the stairs when one of Tim's regulars was on them, panting like an aged sheep dog. Large, wide, bald face, distinguished mostly by his big comb-over and silver-framed aviator glasses. He wore a cheap brown suit, the polyester fabric pilling up at the knees. Matching brown tie, lighter brown shirt. Forster had him down for a government employee of some sort.

"Hecuba's gonna freakin' kick freakin' righteous ass tonight," the regular said. He put extra emphasis on the word "ass." "I can feel it. It's gonna be her biggest night yet."

Tim leaned his long body casually up against the railing and reached for the cigarette he'd tucked behind his ear. He didn't light it or anything, just played with it, tapping it against his left palm.

"Think so?"

"Know so."

"That kind of certainty . . . I don't know. What kind of odds we want to talk?"

Forster sidled past them toward the usual spot on the third-last bench from the top. The odds-making process was of little interest to him. He wasn't here to bet. He'd burned out on gambling a long time ago.

He lowered himself onto the hard bench and looked down at the other people. Immediately below him, a white-haired man spoke in a high, flutey voice to a broad-shouldered guy in a plaid flannel shirt. At least a generation separated them and something about the ease with which they sat together said to Forster that they were father and son. Directly over, a very obese young woman with stringy hair and a big white sweatshirt with a picture of border collie puppies on it unrolled a paper bag and took out a rattling package of cheese doodles. Down front was a row of Tamil guys, all of them in ski vests. The Portuguese, Chinese, and gangbanger delegations were also present in force. They waved fistfuls of hundreds at each other. Forster saw Tim's leather cowboy hat down there among them; he was weaving between the groups, making notes with his stylus on his knock-off Palm Pilot.

The place was fuller than it had ever been before. Word was really getting out. Forster was surprised that the organizers were willing to let so many in. Too many people knew now for this to go on for much longer. The cops would get tipped off and come in the middle of the night with the heavy-duty Gauzner sprayers. They wouldn't bust in during an event, with the bleachers full. Too big a chance of things getting out of hand. No matter how much they'd have liked to track down each and every spectator and see them slapped with ten-to-fifteen for criminal facilitation, illicit custody of PMAs, first degree.

Forster closed his eyes. The insides of his eyelids burned. He needed more sleep. He wished he could close his nostrils, too. Identifying the smell had done nothing to make it more tolerable; just the opposite.

He must have nodded off, because he started when Tim, sitting down next to him, leaned on his shoulder.

"Good action?" Forster asked, by way of conversation. Tim nodded. Forster thought maybe there might be a hint of a grin on him somewhere, but with Tim you couldn't always tell.

The P. A. made itself known with a squeal of feedback. Tim shuddered, but Forster did not. Every freaking time they had the mike pointed into the speakers. He'd come to expect it.

The voice at the mike did not trouble itself to rouse any extra anticipation or excitement in the crowd. It was an unconfident teenager's voice, occasionally cracking and inevitably rising toward the end of each sentence. "Everybody get ready for tonight's bout," it said. "Tonight we have the new challenger, Orkon the Eviscerator." The crowd greeted this news with a ritual booing. Orkon was here as meat, just like all his predecessors.

Heavy blue drapes parted down on the left side of the pit, and out came two men in bulky padded suits, the kind used for attack dog training. Riot helmets made them look like they had bug heads. They wheeled in Orkon on an industrial-sized upright dolly. Six wide leather belts, each with a huge rusty buckle, secured the zombo to it. They had a big fake Viking helmet with tinfoil-covered horns plunked on his head. Orkon looked like he had some fight in him; he hissed and snapped his half-missing teeth at the ring men as they wheeled him to his corner. He wriggled and strained at the belts, but they didn't give. It would be good to start the match when he was still pissed, so they left him in place and hustled across the ring and through the drapes on the other side.

Forster could see a wave of doubt ripple through the guys nosed up to the plexi-shielding in the front row. Maybe this one was ready for Hecuba. Some bills changed hands. But then the voice announced the arrival of the current all-time champion, and the small crowd surged to its feet, stamping and whistling. They began to chant "He-cu-*ba*, He-cu-*ba*, He-cu-*ba*." Forster half-heartedly chanted along at first, but then left off, not sure who he actually meant to root for.

The ring men came back with the second dolly, this one bearing the shorter, stouter corpse of a woman. Forster had spent a certain amount of time thinking about her, wondering who she'd been before she got bit. There was something about her pear-shaped figure, her wide thighs and the vestiges of sandy, permed hair on the top of her head that, to Forster, said supermarket checkout clerk. Possibly a Wal-Mart greeter. Definitely something from the lower echelons, like that. Well, she'd found a distinction now she'd never had when she was breathing. More money had changed hands on her in the course of a couple of matches than she'd probably earned in her whole living existence.

Unlike her opponent, Hecuba was not moving at all. Those little lizard-smart eyes of hers were darting back and forth, but that was it. "Conserving her energy for the fight," Forster heard the white-haired dad say to his son, giving him a rib-nudge. The son must have been the newbie, Dad the old hand. Forster had listened to many of the bettors go on about how Hecuba knew exactly what she was doing, that she recognized somehow she was competing. She had that something extra, the motivation that made for a champion. Forster had not stirred himself to disagree but had seen nothing in her, other than the usual insensate, predatory stimuli-and-response behavior. She was just faster and meaner than the others, that's all.

The audience was clapping rhythmically now, the sound building itself up into a big crescendo. The organizers weren't much in the way of show-men, because they didn't wait for it to peak or anything. The announcer did nothing to build or shape the crowd's anticipation. Forster had to admit, though, that this actually gave the thing an air of authenticity, that he would have soured on it even sooner if it had been all faked up. Maybe they knew what they were doing after all.

The handlers casually reached into a toolbox that had been sitting center-ring the whole time, and withdrew from it a pair of plastic Super Soaker squirt guns, one bright neon green plastic, the other pink. Both were stained red-brown. Each ring man stepped back, took aim at one of the zombos, and let loose, drenching his target.

The guns held human blood. Zombos could not, under normal circumstances, be induced to attack each other. They could sniff out live from dead. The only way to make them go apeshit on their own kind was to spray them with the fresh stuff from a live victim. After witnessing his first match, Forster asked Tim where they got it, but Tim refused to speculate. Which answered the question, more or less.

The ring men retreated and, from backstage, one of them hit the remote switch that blew the micro-charges on the belts. Little plumes of smoke rose up from the dollies as the zombos staggered forth. From the way Orkon struggled with the restraints just a few seconds earlier, a bettor might have put his money on him being first to free himself and to capitalize on that freedom. But the bigger corpse staggered around, batting at the rising puffs of burned powder, as Hecuba crouched down, hissed, then made a run at him. She tackled Orkon, knocking him off his feet, and began to claw at his eyes with her jagged, extruded fingernails.

Tim leaned forward, biting his lip. One of the Portuguese guys got up on his bench and executed a little dance of exultation. Orkon squirmed out from under his attacker and flailed wildly at her head. As he lunged for the side of her throat, she scrabbled backward on the particle board flooring. He dove at her. She thrust herself upward and back, to a crouching position. Orkon rose to his feet, too.

The Viking helmet had fallen off in the melee's first moments. As part of the whole warrior theme, the ring men had strapped a belt, scabbard, and sword to Orkon's otherwise naked waist, and for a moment it seemed like he was going to pull the sword and go hacking at Hecuba's head with it. But instead, he tore the belt off and tossed it aside. Then Orkon threw his head back and shrieked; his gray tongue flopped past his chapped and peeling lips. Hecuba held her ground, pawing the flooring with her splayed left foot. Forster noticed there were a couple more toes missing than last time.

Hecuba braced for Orkon's charge, and he came at her headlong. She back-swatted him with her hand, though the force of the blow hardly seemed to register with him. He howled again, then thrust a punching hand deep down into her chest. Even Forster couldn't help but wince at the sound of cracking bone. Orkon kept his hand inside her, his shoulder muscles working like he was groping around for something. Another distinct snap followed. Finally Orkon withdrew his bile-smeared arm. He held something long and sharp-ended in his quivering fist: one of Hecuba's ribs.

The room went quiet as the bigger zombo took a step back, raised up the rib like a dagger, and then stepped forward to drive it down through Hecuba's left eye socket. Leaping from the flooring to put all of his weight behind the blow, the challenger knocked his prey down. Hecuba's limbs flopped like trout on the floor of a boat, then stopped. Orkon pushed his face deep into her gaping chest cavity, to feed. Moments later he staggered back, shaking his head from side to side as he spit chunks of unsatisfyingly dead meat from his jaws.

Then he did the thing every victorious zombo did, the thing that the organizers relied on to control their fighters. He smelled the sweaty, agitated spectators, and leaped like a frog onto the reinforced plexiglass. Blue sparks ran up the metal stanchions separating the clear panes. Embedded filaments too small to see carried the current to the zombo at every point of his contact with the barrier.

Orkon convulsed three or four times, then fell motionless to the ring's floor, face up and spread-eagled. The ring men dashed out and rolled their victor into a canvas tarp, which they pulled tight with what had to be several dozen sets of belts and buckles. By the end of the procedure, Orkon had opened his eyes and was irregularly blinking. The ring men hastened their buckling, and soon he was completely unable to move. They finished off by gingerly wrapping a ball gag around his slowly jawing mouth. A tentative-looking assistant, also fully geared in padded armor, piloted a gurney onto the stage. The ring men casually hefted the bagged zombo and flipped him onto the gurney, which they quickly wheeled off through parted curtains.

Forster could hear the blood rushing past his ears. Not a sound in the entire freaking place. He looked at the men across from him, saw their dropped jaws and checked his own to see if it was also swinging back and forth like the head of a drinking bird. It was not.

The serene expression on Tim's face as he rose to make his rounds through the arena showed that his money had been on Orkon.

Down front, a short, buck-toothed man wearing a fur cap sat staring at Hecuba's opened corpse, tears rushing down both of his capillaried cheeks.

Tim sat across from Forster in their habitual coffee shop, his arms splayed across the red fake leather covering the backs of the booths. He had laid his hat down beside him, revealing his receding hairline, a feature accentuated by his habit of gelling his hair tight to his pointy-crowned skull.

"I had opportunity to smell-test Hecuba a couple days back," he said. "Much as they tried to mask it, you couldn't miss the formaldehyde. I mean, just count back the months to her first match. She had to be getting pretty squishy."

"I think I'm bored with this shit, too," Forster said.

"Don't tell me."

"I hardly felt anything at all this time."

The waitress came with their coffees. Tim ordered an open-face turkey sandwich with mashed potatoes. Forster glanced at the menu for the first time, scratched his neck, and said he'd have what his friend was having.

"What has it been? Just six times? And it's already paled on you."

"The process of my beginning to feel nothing seems like it's accelerating. It's the same curve, just faster now. Like I could plot it on a graph." Forster fished a ballpoint out of his coat pocket and began to draw a curving line, like the dorsal surface of a whale, on the diner's all-white place mat. "First is the fear—I feel my heart pumping—and from then I can begin to feel other things: elation, fury, a sense of connectedness to the people around me. Then the fear dies down. Revulsion comes in to replace it, and that's fine, too. That's feeling something, after all. I'll settle for revulsion, I think. Then thorough self-loathing. Even more unpleasant, but still feeling. Then this begins to leach away, too, leaving just this sort of flat . . . grayness. Like the people around me are actually a million miles away."

"Present company excluded, naturally." Tim inspected the cigarette he'd been fidgeting with, broke it up into three pieces, and deposited it, unsmoked, in the amber-colored ashtray.

"The drugs were the first, and they lasted the longest of all. There were so many different ones to try. And part of the experience is the people you're around when you're on them, and the things that happen. But the end of that curve was when I couldn't get a buzz off anything. All just maintenance. Big deal. The good time period: that lasted, what, eighteen months? Nearly two years?"

"Sounds about right. Plenty of people party-heartying then."

Tim would know; he'd been Forster's dealer from the start. The two of them had been in grad school together, way back. Now here they were again. Each was the only person the other could fully talk to. Tim had to dumb himself down around the lowlifes he worked with. References to Foucault or Godard strictly off-limits. The post-Rising labor market tolerated many quirks, but certain things you didn't discuss in the break room.

"Then the hooker thing," Forster continued. "That overlapped, but all told lasted me maybe a year. Little less."

"Lots of people find that alienating."

"The various fetish scenes—I know you don't want me to get into the details—"

He could see Tim tense up. "Yeah, keep it to vague allusions. That one time I asked . . . ."

"Each of those was its own separate curve. Things I never thought I'd ever see myself doing, then quicker and quicker, I was not only doing them but had gone through them. They were dead for me, passé.

"Okay, the S/M scene, that's so all-encompassing. That did last longer than some of the things before it. But still, same pattern. Part of me was hoping that this deathmatch thing. . . . It wasn't sexual, it wasn't bodily, it would be different. The spiritual purity of the degradation, it would last longer. And the first time—"

"A classic match. Hecuba's first."

"Thought I'd shit myself, I was so scared going in. Scared of a raid. Of it being a scam, of getting robbed and beaten. Of how I'd react when I first saw one of them again. Of maybe one of them getting loose, biting somebody, starting a cascade."

"And jeez, when the head went flying into the crowd . . . ."

Forster remembered his coffee and took a big drink of it before it cooled too much. "Yeah, maybe that was part of it. That first one was so . . . so . . . intense that from then on in, it was all downhill. If that third match—that awful drawn-out one where they just wouldn't go for each other—if that had been my first one, if it had built up more, maybe I'd still be feeling a jolt. But the whole time tonight, I kept waiting for it to kick in, and nothing."

"Yeah, that night, that was a classic, all right."

"But tonight, it was all just the same old dull feeling—the same non-feeling. And the people around me, I didn't feel like I was part of them, a member of their race, or even in the same room with them. Like I'm watching via a grainy, black and white security monitor. The only thing that got my blood pumping at all was first contact with that smell, and even that was only for the first few moments. You can get used to fuckin' anything, that's what I've learned."

"Ever given any thought to Africa? Or New Orleans?" Tim was referring to places where the syndrome still raged. Most of the Third World writhed with it; their governments couldn't afford the full array of Gauzner technologies. They had plenty of the bombs but not enough spray units. Various outside funding proposals were snarled in the U.N. for the third year running. New Orleans was still under military quarantine, with only the most determined death's-heads getting through. The whole coastal region of Louisiana kept breaking out, for reasons the experts never managed to pinpoint. Urban legend held forth on the subject of a Gauzner-resistant strain, but proof remained elusive.

"Those places don't interest me. I keep telling you, it's not a death wish. I want to feel the opposite of dead. If I wanted to top myself, I'd just head out to the viaduct and jump. To expose myself to the infection again—you know what that would betray."

"Yeah. Of course." Tim pursed his lips. "I didn't mean to—all I was saying is, the gladiator thing, I was really hoping it would last longer for you."

"Yeah. Me, too." The waitress brought the food. Forster stared down at it, unhungrily. Tim dug in. The matches always gave him an appetite.

"Look," said Tim, between oversized mouthfuls of mash potato and gravy. "I knew this time would come, though not so soon. And you know I sympathize with your malaise. And admire the headlong way you pursue it. There for the grace of god and all that.

"So."

"There's this thing. I been keeping it in reserve for you. I'm only in the preliminary stages of hooking it up. The people who handle this, they're not my usual circle. You'd say they're several circles away, okay? So what I'm saying is it's all chancy. Can't guarantee anything. And if it does go through, these are some crazy, nasty mofos and I can't extend any kind of my usual dispensation. If things go wrong, it's all on you, right?"

Forster sat forward. He felt like his heart had started up again.

"It's really freaking sick, okay? And if this doesn't do it for you, I tell you, my wad is shot. There's no further frontier I'm capable of pointing you toward. But, jeez, if you're into it, it should last you more than six lousy times. Now I know you know the kind of discretion I expect of you. So don't be insulted if I repeat that this has absolutely, in no circumstances, not a word breathed to anyone except for me. This is not like the thing tonight, where they're inviting in half the world and its uncle. Okay?"

"Come on. Tell me."

Tim looked around for eavesdroppers. "Like I say, it's preliminary. It might not come off."

"Come on."

He leaned forward and spoke *sotto voce*. "How would you like to fuck one of them?"

He walked home from the subway, rock salt crunching under his boots, his breath illuminated by orange streetlights. The very idea of it had given him a hard-on, his first in months. The bitter chill of the air invigorated him. He strode up the concrete steps toward his building's foyer, reaching into his pocket past the freezer-bagged supply Tim had sold him, to his keys. As he unlocked the front door, he saw, through its glass, a slim figure wearing a hooded coat. Forster could not see her features, but knew her frame. Sephronia. Her presence utterly deflated him, threw him back into the gray again. He resigned himself and opened the door.

She stepped toward him. "John, I've been waiting for you, hoping you'd—I'm sorry, but this is the only way."

Forster stood before her, paralyzed, not knowing whether to stand there and take it or shove past her wordlessly.

She took another step his way, and lowered her hood, revealing the harsh pink and unwholesome smoothness of the scar tissue that covered her face and entire skull. She'd left off her wig. The gesture was one of remonstrance. Forster knew he should be feeling bad, but had forgotten how.

"I need you to see me," Sephronia said. "To look into my eyes."

He had done this to her, tenderly, over a period of weeks, with a portable acetylene cutwelder. She had consented to the act, sure, but in the expectation that he'd keep her around. That it was a sealing of the permanency between them.

"Please, at least say something."

"If I could think of something to say, I would."

She made a third step toward him. He thought he might flinch from her, get backed into the mailboxes, but found himself standing his ground.

"I've been thinking," she said. "That you didn't see the degree of commitment I had ready for you. That you needed to see how far I am willing to go for us."

She pulled back her coat's fake-furred left cuff to reveal, at her wrist, a freshly cauterized, naked stump. "I did this to show you."

Forster finally found what it took to brush past her. "That's sweet, honey, and I wish I could care." He slid-clicked the lock on the interior door and slipped through. She tried to catch it and hold it open, but he closed it quickly. He headed to the stairs without looking back at her. As he walked up toward his apartment door, he tried unsuccessfully to make himself feel guilt for what he'd driven her to, or, if not that, at least empathy for her state. Most elective amps started with their off-hand, but Sephronia did everything with her left.

She'd find someone. The amp lifestyle was one of the fastest-growing out there. She'd get over him and settle down with some young, apprehensive stump-lover anxious to abase himself before her every crippled need. Maybe if he knew she'd end up worse off than that, he'd be able to conjure up the proper remorse.

Forster looked again at the slip of paper with the address on it. He'd expected another disused industrial site, like the one where the fights were held. But this was an old restaurant with papered-over windows. "New Harmony Restaurant," said the sign that hung overhead. "Delicious Meals," with the word delicious in quotation marks.

His hard-on was back, after having deserted him again. The anticipation had made him feel real, for the first couple of weeks. By week three, with still no phone call from Tim, it trickled away. With anyone else, Forster would have concluded he'd been taken in by a line of bull, but he trusted Tim better than that. Tim had made clear that his arrangements might not come through. By the time the call came, Forster had given up on the whole prospect. Yet here he really was, he told himself, really standing in front of the place where he was going to get to fuck a zombo.

There were three doorbells, and he'd been told which one to buzz, and how many times to hit it. As he followed his instructions, it occurred to him that the sex of the subject had never been mentioned. He thought it would be better if it were female. Despite his expanded experiences of the aftermath years, he hadn't completely shaken his preference for women.

They kept him standing there for a while, stamping his feet against the sharp cold. Finally a small tear opened up in the butcher's paper that lined the glass door. Dark, heavy-browed eyes appeared.

"Yeah?" said a voice muffled by the glass.

"You got some videos for me to return?" replied Forster, providing the prearranged response.

The door opened. The man behind it was mountainously tall and fat, wearing a food-stained khaki T-shirt stretched too tight across his belly and man-tits. His long beard and shaggy dark hair were all of a piece. He didn't step aside to let Forster in until Forster took a step toward him. He glowered suspiciously down. Forster understood this as the intimidation necessary to the arrangement. Still, a little talk from the guy could at least indicate what was expected of him next. He looked around at the interior of the building. The restaurant fixtures had been completely torn out. Busted pieces of gyp-rock lay on the floor amid a dusting of plaster. Most of the golden wallpaper had been torn off the walls, but a few pieces remained, and they were stained the color of rust. Could well have been blood; the place might have been a massacre site. This had been one of the city's worst-hit neighborhoods.

Two men appeared from what was probably the former kitchen. One wore a Juventus soccer jersey over gray wool slacks and had a heavy gold chain-link bracelet around his hairy wrist. The other was skinny and looked like he should be working in tech support somewhere, with a white dress shirt, bushy carrot-colored hair, thick-framed glasses, and an overbite.

Juventus-jersey did the talking. "You're Forster?"

Forster nodded.

"Cash up front."

Forster reached casually into his coat, pulled out the roll, and tossed it to Juventus, who plucked it from the air and, without looking at him, passed it back to Tech Support. "Count this," he said. Tech Support rolled away the thick rubber band, dangling it off his thumb as he riffled through the bills nearly as fast as a machine would. Juventus pocketed the entire amount and left the room.

Man-Tits lumbered forward and pointed toward a wooden door, painted white. "She's down there." Forster had been in some pretty brusquely run brothels before, but this was the epitome. It was perfect.

Tech Support evidently felt the lack of amenities and beat Forster to the door, opening it wide for him. He gestured for Forster to precede him down the dark stairs. For a moment, Forster's shoulders tensed up, ready for a conk from behind. But he'd already given up all but pocket change. They had no good reason to cack him.

Forster heard a switch flicked behind him. A utility light hung from a wooden ceiling beam. The staircase led down into a dingy corridor. There were more rusty stains on the whitewashed walls. Under the stairs stood a row of unplugged refrigerators.

"So," came Tech Support's voice, "do you, uh, live in the city, or have you come down maybe from somewhere else?"

Forster was uncomfortable with them even knowing his real last name. The guy had to be fishing for clues they could use in an after-the-fact blackmail operation. "No offense, but I'm not really in a frame of mind for chitchat."

"Right. Sure."

Forster reached the end of the staircase, expecting Tech Support to follow and point him toward the room where she'd be waiting. Instead the guy sat himself down on the second-last step. He brushed some lint off a pant leg. "Look, the others only care about money. For you to do your business and go." He had some kind of subtle speech impediment, but Forster couldn't narrow down exactly what. "But there's a right way and a wrong way to, uh, go about this." He stopped, clearly struggling for the exact right phrase. "Look, you've got to treat Susan in a certain way. You can't assume just because of her condition that she isn't feeling what's happening to her."

Tech support's eyes were watering up. He stuck a finger in past his glasses to rub at an eye. "Try and be—I know gentle sounds funny. It's not the right . . . I guess try and be receptive to her mood, to the kinds of movements she makes." He swallowed hard. "Don't just force yourself and pump, pump, pump. That makes Susan very unhappy, very unsettled for days afterward. For you, this is just a one-time thing. In and out. Just try to understand and don't be a jerk." He looked searchingly up into Forster's face, presumably looking for a nod of assent or something.

Forster gave him nothing. The guy was creeping him out. He'd felt fine until this. "Which door do I go through?"

Tech Support stood, pulled on his sleeve. "It's not just for her sake I'm asking. It's much better if you let Susan take the lead. You'll like it a lot better, I swear. Really."

"Which door?"

Tech Support pointed to a door at the end of the hallway. Forster walked down to it. He looked back and saw Tech Support looking at him forlornly. The guy was draining his jolt. Forster turned around.

"You aren't going to be standing outside the door, are you?"

"Well, uh, I'm supposed to . . . in case there's a problem."

"But there won't be a problem, will there? Everything is well secured, right?"

"Yes, yes." He started to approach. "I've readied her. You won't have any problems. Just be—"

"Because, no offense, but I don't want to be aware of your presence. Right?"

Tech Support nodded quickly, up and down. "Right, right." He pivoted and scampered up the stairs.

Forster waited until he heard the upstairs door close. He turned back toward the door at the hallway's end. He stopped to take a deep breath, to try to refocus himself, to get the awareness of what he was about to do surging through his body again. He took a big snort of air like it was coke. And another. He put his hand on the door handle and stepped into darkness. It smelled both like alligators and like formaldehyde. Immediately a noise started up, a low punctuated growl, like a cat struggling to choke up a hairball. He reached out and groped for a light switch. Fluorescent lights flickered and then grudgingly went fully on.

She lay face down on what looked like a hospital bed, pastel green paint chipping off its metal frame. They'd spread her out, strapping each leg to one of the bedposts. To accomplish this, they'd twisted both of her ankles severely. Her skin was paler than the specimens Forster had seen at the zombo matches, making obvious a complex of purple bruises around the restraints. As he stepped closer toward her, her growling upshifted into a sort of frenzied pant. He could see her trying to lift and turn her head to see him. A brittle mass of peroxide hair wildly haloed her head, hardly moving as she thrashed. As far as Forster could tell, she'd have been an average-looking woman in life, tall and thin-boned but no particular beauty. The bleached hair was out of character with the rest of the corpse: undoubtedly a post-mortem addition. She shook the bed frame but could not budge it from its moorings; it had been bolted into the concrete floor. There was some give in the bolts, though. He wondered if they knew. He would tell them afterward. The presence of a little risk made it better.

Forster took another step forward. He slowly moved his fingertips toward the back of her thigh. He left them in the air for a moment before bringing them brushing against her ashen flesh. It felt rubbery and not ice cold, but cool. Her flailing intensified and he pulled his fingers away. He leaned in to study the surface of her skin. White lines crisscrossed it, and Forster was curious to know what they were. On close inspection, they seemed to be bloodless, open, scabless cuts, perhaps made with a thin blade like a box-cutter's. Maybe they were just artifacts of handling.

A pair of black fake-satin panties had been put on her; they were at least a size too small, and her dead flesh puckered at the waist and leg holes. Forster's hand went out toward them. Then he stopped, and remembered to look around the room for holes in the walls or ceiling. Starting with the places that would afford the best view of his face, he quickly spotted a drill-mark, and checking it out close, a pinhole lens. He withdrew a deck of Post-It notes from his jacket pocket and fixed the gummed edge to the wall, just above the hole. He glanced back at the door, saw that it had a cheap brass slider to bolt it shut. He slid it. Forster turned back toward Susan and her black panties. Without looking too closely, he shoved them to the side. He was rock-hard.

He unclipped his sleek gold-and-silver belt buckle and unzipped his fly. She had stopped her screaming and thrashing. He looked again at Susan. He stepped back. He bit his lip. He checked himself; he was still hard. He zipped up his fly and buckled his belt.

He sat down on the cold cement floor.

Well, Forster thought, *who'd have thought? I've found it. I've found the place. The place below which I will not go.*

Well. It had been well worth the money. He breathed in deep. He would remember the air he was breathing. He ran his hands together. They felt real and solid for the first time since the night when it all happened. He ran his fingers over his face. That felt real, too. He felt that he was inside himself. Not above or outside, but inside.

He walked over to Susan and moved her panties back into place. The contact started her to shrieking again. He backed off, startled. He had to look away from her. He sat down again. His chest felt like he was back on speed.

Wow. A place below which I cannot go. Wow.

He unbolted the door and opened it. Juventus and Man-Tits were standing right there, with Tech Support off to one side.

"You didn't take too long in there," Juventus said, expressionless.

"You know what? I've discovered I'm not up to it. I thought I would be but I'm not."

Juventus rolled his tongue thoughtfully under his closed upper lip, his eyes still empty. "Then we have a problem."

Forster felt dampness at the collar of his shirt. He knew that to get through this, he would have to fake the very detachment that had just fallen away from him. "I'm not asking for my money back. I've just decided I don't actually want to fuck the zombie, that's all."

Juventus shoved him back into the room. "You're going to fuck that zombie."

"What? What do you care? You have my money."

Juventus shoved him again. He pointed to the Post-It note on the wall.

"You'll excuse me," said Forster, wishing his voice wasn't rising so high, "if I decided I didn't want streaming video on your website of me porking a zombo."

"But you haven't porked jackshit," Juventus said. Another shove. "Raising the question of whether you're a cop. So to prove you're not a cop, you're going to fuck that zombie and I'm going to stand here and watch."

Forster momentarily took his eyes off Juventus and looked behind him, at Tech Support. He looked very unhappy, too. Afraid this would be tough on Susan, no doubt. She was hissing and dry-retching again. Forster glanced down and saw that the bolts holding down the bed were even looser than before.

"You can't just make a guy fuck something. I mean, if you don't got the wood, you don't got the wood."

Juventus smirked. "We got an injection to help you in that area. For twenty-four hours, you'll be a rebar." He made a vague waving gesture; Tech Support opened a plastic case and handed a syringe to Man-Tits.

Forster leaped up to try and grab Juventus by the ears. Juventus punched him hard in the gut and he doubled over. Forster duck-walked backward and sank to his knees at the head of the bed, gasping. Man-Tits advanced on him. Forster reached over to the belt holding Susan's left hand to the bedpost and wrenched open the buckle. She bolted upward, her freed arm arcing over to the other wrist.

"You crazy motherfuck!" Juventus said, wide-eyed and frozen. "Get the sprayer!" he yelled.

Susan ripped the other belt in two and wrenched herself upward, heaving the bed out of its moorings. It flipped up with her and its head-beam clipped Man-Tits on the temple as she lunged for him. She and the bed landed on Man-Tits and shook around. He howled as the bed bounced up and down and blood began to pool out onto the floor. Tech Support was gone from the hallway. Juventus reached for an ankle holster, pulling a small pistol and firing shots into the bed, probably hitting Man-Tits as well as Susan. Then her claws snaked out and grabbed his leg, pulling him off balance and onto his ass. She clawed into his thigh, opening an artery. Juventus groaned and clamped his hands over the wound. Susan slashed away the bindings on her ankles, wriggled from under the bed, and began to gnaw on his crotch. She sank her fingers into his skull and banged his face repeatedly into the concrete. When Juventus went motionless, she whipped around to face Forster, crouching as Hecuba had.

Tech Support appeared at the doorway, holding a gleaming, unused Gauzner sprayer out before him like an assault rifle. His face was beet red, his nose leaking snot. "Susan!" he yelled. "Susan!" Until she finally turned around.

"Susan, you got to listen to me," he said. She wove in the air before him, like a cobra before its charmer. "Susan, please. I don't want to have to use the sprayer. You do understand the sprayer, right? Just calm down. Everything can be all right. Just us now. No more others. You've taken care of these two. That's all you need to do."

She darted forward and ripped his belly open. She clamped one hand around his jaw-line and lifted him up over her head and against the wall. She banged him against it just like she'd smacked Juventus against the floor. Tech Support hadn't died yet and was pleading with her the whole time, though with her grip on his windpipe Forster couldn't make any of it out. She began to keen, almost like she was singing a note. Forster circumnavigated the crumpled bed and Man-Tits's already-shuddering corpse to grab the sprayer. Gauzner designed it to be operable even by a small child in emergency circumstances. Forster pointed it at Susan's back, pulled its big trigger, and watched the blue liquid hit her, slackening and melting the muscles of her back. She fell like a sack. He sprayed her some more, then pointed it under the bed to douse Man-Tits. Then he did Juventus and Tech Support, before they even started moving.

Forster dropped to the floor himself, when it became clear the lot of them were topped. He sat there gulping, and thought about what had happened during The Rising, when the intruder bit Maggie, who then passed it on to the kids. How when they came for him his instincts had taken over, the pick-axe in his hand. How he'd dug it into their skulls, instead of doing what he'd later wished he had done: let them take him, too.

He'd piece out the exact reasons later, but right now what he knew was he'd come alive again. Silently, he thanked Susan for the resurrection.

FAMILIAR EYES

BARRY HOLLANDER

WHENEVER SHE RETURNED, HE KILLED her.

She lurched from the woods again. By the time he grabbed his aluminum bat, she was fumbling with the back gate. By the time he slipped out the front door and rounded the house, she had given up on the gate and crawled over the chain link fence, leaving behind scraps of rotting cloth and pale flesh. He hid behind an overgrown azalea, watched for something familiar in those eyes.

All he saw was a zombie's empty stare.

Her next challenge: the wooden steps leading up to the deck and sunroom door. With a foot on the first step, she hesitated, as if considering the daunting nature of the task she faced. He held his breath, hopeful. Maybe this time. Maybe she would recognize the house, the deck where she spent so much of her time coaxing plants to life, where she loved to sit in a chair at the end of a long day, sipping tea and reading some trashy romance novel. He'd seen hints, no matter what the experts said, hints that she was more than a walking piece of dead meat.

Another step, then her hand gripped the rail, almost caressed it in recognition. Blank eyes scanned the yard. She knew. Somehow she realized he had moved from inside the house to where he now stood, sensed that he hid nearby. Tired of the game, he stepped from behind the bush, bat concealed behind his back. He didn't want to use the thing, not again, not unless he absolutely had to.

"Hello, Margaret."

Vacant eyes met his, orbs offering no spark of recognition, only the mindless hunger of a zombie.

His zombie.

The deck forgotten, she made an awkward, stumbling fall off the steps, arms outstretched for a deadly embrace. He danced back, tried again.

"Margaret. It's me . . . ."

She took another step, and he backed away farther.

"It's John . . . ."

She gathered momentum, her legs finding their pace, their rhythm.

Avoiding tree roots, he kept a safe distance between them.

"Please, Margaret. I know you're in there. You have to remember."

Fingers clutched empty air. He ducked a second swipe of her broken, dirty nails. He didn't want to feel that cold touch. Not again.

"Please." He almost choked on the words. "I can't keep doing this."

Another sweep. Icy fingers brushed his cheek, and his skin crawled at her touch. He thought of the flower garden, angled that way, but she cut him off and forced his back against the fence. It was too late. As she staggered forward, fingers clawing for his face, he brought the bat from behind his back, felt its weight seem to grow into an anvil's as he realized what had to be done. With a shift left to draw her off balance, he swung the bat in a wide arc to meet her head. The impact made a dull metallic *thump*.

She crumpled into the dew-washed grass, face upturned to the sky. Her mouth continued to work, as if chewing his skin and bones. In that movement, he thought he heard the whisper of his name. He bent closer.

"Margaret? God, I'm sorry . . . ."

Eyes focused, then were overtaken by a blank, indifferent stare.

John pulled a dripping beer from the ice chest and handed it to Frank as the man joined him on the front porch step. The summer evening turned purple, fireflies winking in the shadows. A bat flitted across the cul-de-sac as a streetlight sputtered to life, luring insects to the feast. Frank popped open the can, took a long, hard drag, then another, and wiped his mouth with an arm.

"She came again, didn't she? Third time? Fourth?"

"Third." He watched the Georgia night come slow and sweet, hurting all the more to be out with a beer on such an evening, him alive and alone, Margaret's body covered by a plastic sheet in the backyard. They stared at the darkening sky, drank quietly.

Frank sighed. "Dealt with the body?"

"No." A cat crossed the street and disappear into a line of shrubs. "I'll bury her tomorrow. In the morning."

Frank shook his head. "It's your business. I've told you that before, and I'm not going to report you or anything, but it's a hell of a risk. You sure about this?"

John answered with a long drink, letting the beer dull the ache inside. He knew what Frank meant, even if he didn't want to come out and say it.

Fire.

Douse her with gas, toss a match, sit and watch her skin bubble and blacken until there's nothing left but ash and charred bones. Grind the bones to dust and scatter them as far as you can manage. People did that with their zombie, if the zombie didn't get them first. John shuddered, reached for another can. He popped the top, a misty spray wetting the grass.

"She can wait until morning," he said.

Frank rolled the can in his big hands, searching for wisdom on the warning label.

John looked at him. "I can't do it."

"Bury her?" His friend shrugged. "I'll do it. Won't like it, but I'll do it. I know you're not one of those nuts on TV, the ones who think the zombies have come to take us with them—what is it? Oh yeah, to a 'higher plane of existence.'" He snorted, then put out a hand. "Sorry."

"I understand. No, it's not that." John took a breath, let it out slowly. "I just can't burn her . . . not like that bastard Willard."

The old man lived on the next street. His wife had come back for him, as had one of his grown children, and he'd burned both in front of the whole neighborhood. John still couldn't believe either woman would return for such a fool, that he mattered so much to them. That he mattered to anyone. "Fried and forgotten," Willard had said, grinning while what remained of his wife smoldered in the yard, the sweet stench of cooked flesh filling the air.

"Willard might be a bastard, but he's no fool," Frank said. "Burning's the only way. If the cops find out, they'll come and do it whether you like it or not, then probably cart your ass off to jail for good measure. You know the law."

"Screw the law and screw Willard." John stood. "I can't burn her. Not yet, at least." He let his reasons hang in the air, unsaid.

His neighbor hadn't moved, just looked up at him from the porch step. "Not everyone uses fire. Shirley Martin didn't."

A few weeks after her husband Sam died, Shirley Martin lucked into spotting him as he reeled toward the house. She got in a lucky blow to the head—that always dropped the zombies cold for reasons scientists couldn't begin to explain—and stuffed him into an old wire dog cage they kept in the garage. The best anyone could figure, she'd hoped to talk sense into the man, if only she could force him to sit still and listen, as if being a zombie were no different than him coming home after a few too many beers. That night, as she slept, Sam pried apart the metal bars with his bare fingers.

He didn't eat her all at once. Zombies never did.

Later, some neighborhood kids spotted a bloated Sam wallowing in the street like a snake after a big meal. Where he would have gone next was anyone's guess. John knew you could never tell with zombies. After killing their most important loved one, some went after a second, but others just called it quits and clawed their way back into the hole from which they'd come, dragging a thin blanket of dirt back on top of them as if they were embarrassed by what they'd done. The late-night TV shows were full of gags on the subject: the zombie husband who ignored his wife and killed women from his various affairs, or the wife who chased her zombie husband in hopes of being the one he wanted, or the bachelor who rose from the grave only to find himself with no one to kill, not even his mother. He just sat there, body parts falling off while he tried to come up with someone, anyone, he loved well enough to eat. Sick stuff, but no worse than the industries that had popped up around the zombies' emergence. If religious beliefs didn't allow burning, you could, for a hefty price tag, bury the dear departed in a high-security cemetery. Crematories, of course, were now almost as plentiful as McDonald's.

Burning. It always came back to burning.

The neighborhood teenagers chased Sam down with bats and rocks, beat his body to a mushy pulp, and started a bonfire in the middle of the street. They danced around what was left of him as he burned.

Frank crushed his can, sat it with the other empties. "Thanks for the beer."

"I'm sorry, Frank." John put a hand on the man's shoulder. "You did what you had to do with Kelly. I understand that. I'm just not ready. Not yet."

Frank nodded. "It's your call, but it's not her, John. Not any more. No matter what she looks like or sounds like, even if she manages to mumble a few words like they sometimes do." His bones creaked as he stood and stretched. "Just get her in the ground as quick as you can, like you've done before. You know what can happen if you don't."

"Yeah, I know."

He couldn't sleep. He ended up in the sunroom, staring out the window at the dark lump in the yard. The sheet was a waste of time, but he couldn't stand the thought of her out there, exposed to the night like some pile of dirt. She deserved better.

Kelly and Margaret had died together when a drunken jerk in an SUV ignored a red light and plowed into Kelly's compact car, killing both women. The drunk walked away with a few bruises and long list of criminal charges. After the funerals, he and Frank had spent the next few weeks plotting ways of torturing the guy, once he got out of prison, eventually settling on a plan to strap him into a compact car out at the junkyard and slowly crush it.

It had to be slow. On that much they agreed. The man had to scream.

The zombie risings had only just started, though no one could explain why. No comets had blazed across the sky. No weapons of mass destruction had erupted in a third world country. There was no reason at all for the resurrections that anyone could identify, though several religious sects claimed responsibility once it became clear what was happening. A few dead people crawled out of the ground, then more, and after a short time, people figured out that the zombies tracked the person they loved the most in life. Get in its way and a zombie on the hunt might take a swing or two, maybe give you an infectious scratch, but that was often the worst of it. So long as you weren't the loved one of choice, that is. The dead seemed eager to take those special few back to the grave with them.

The government ordered everyone to report zombie sightings, and special units armed with flame throwers patrolled the larger cemeteries. Backhoes dug up graves, and the disinterred corpses were piled and burned. At night, the fires glowed in the distance and with the breeze came the smell of burning meat. Later, people learned that a blow to the head would stun the zombies, but it didn't keep them down. Zombies reburied after being stunned often rose up again a short time later.

Leave the body out too long in the open air, they also discovered, and the zombies became almost impossible to destroy, even with fire.

At the time of Margaret's death, John hadn't cared one way or the other about the undead plague, he missed her so much. They'd never had children of their own, couldn't have them because of Margaret's childhood illness. Friends had kids, watched them grow and go off to the college, and through it all he and Margaret had smiled and quietly promised that they would always have each other. No matter what else, they would have each other. John never considered that she would come back, not as a zombie. Not her.

Until she did.

He remembered how he woke early that morning, before sunrise, made coffee, happened to glance out the kitchen window and see a shape moving among the trees. Margaret, wearing the dress she had been buried in, worked from tree to tree, hugging each for support as she neared the house. Without a thought, he rushed out the back door, calling her name. The moon had dropped beneath the pines, yet some of its ivory light leaked through the needles and branches. She turned to him, eyes like black buttons. Again he called her name, tried to reach the woman behind the blank face. Instead, she groped her way toward him and he quickly found himself with his back pressed against the deck, his dead wife moving closer.

He'd seen the news, the video of zombies as they roamed the landscape—but Margaret? She reached out, grabbed his arm, sent ice into his veins. He ducked a sweep of her hand, pulled her along with him across the yard, aiming for nowhere in particular, just trying to get away and stay close at the same time. He jerked free, stumbled his way into the flower garden grown wild, the weeds now competing with blooms for space—another sign of her being gone. Backing into the tangled growth, he tripped on a shovel and fell. He grabbed the wooden handle on impulse.

Dead eyes took in the garden and, for a moment, John thought she connected somehow with that place she had spent so much time tending. The world stopped: The morning birds fell silent in the trees, the low hum of traffic from the highway a half-mile away quieted.

"Margaret?"

She looked nothing like the woman who'd driven away that afternoon, laughing with her friend, nothing like the woman in the casket, solemn yet at peace. Her clothes were stained red by the Georgia clay. A clump of grass and leaves hung in her hair. A vacant stare greeted him now. Her starved mouth moved as if chewing him in advance.

And even now, when he thought back to her first return, he remembered the sudden, shameful relief he felt.

"At least you came for me," he remembered whispering as she gathered herself, pushed through the flowers, groping for his flesh. For him, not the man from her first marriage, who'd left her for a younger woman, one able to bear children. "At least I have that."

She did not acknowledge his words. Instead, she reached for him hungrily.

"Please," he begged. "Don't make me do this."

Fingers clawed at his face. He jerked left, saw the way she responded, noted that she stumbled a half-step in that direction. He tested it again to the right, saw the same response. Slow, to be sure, but every move he made she countered, trying to cut off his escape. He stepped left, brought the shovel swinging from the opposite side, felt the dull thud as it struck her cheek.

Later that morning, Frank came to see him.

"God, I never thought it would happen to her." Frank put his hands in his jeans pockets, glanced back over his shoulder at his own empty yard. "Do you think. . . ?" He let his voice trail off.

All John could do was shrug. He had spent the morning in tears.

Frank sat next to him. "You have to destroy the body. That's what they are saying. Do it fast." He waited for an answer. "John, either destroy the body or report it to the cops so they can do the job. I know it's hard, but that's not Margaret."

Maybe it wasn't, he remembered thinking.

Maybe it was.

Let her come back, he decided. He'd bury her, but at least then she'd be able to come back. There had to be something of her left inside, the real Margaret. And they'd have each other again. She'd promised that, after all. And she had recognized something about the garden, he was sure of it, no matter what the experts said about the way the dead perceived things.

He dragged her out to the woods behind the house, that first time. Her mouth moved once, but nothing came out. It was the eyes, the cold eyes, that hurt the most.

Those he covered first.

A week after Margaret's first appearance, Kelly came looking for Frank and almost got him.

A deep sleeper, he woke just in time to see his dead wife bouncing wall-to-wall down his hallway. He had a gun at his bedside and put six shots into her before she made it to his bedroom door. She staggered back a few steps as if slapped, the bullets doing little more than create a few holes and slow her momentum, but it bought him enough time to grab a bat from behind the bed and take care of the rest. He telephoned, asked John to come over. By the time he'd arrived, Frank had dragged Kelly's body into the backyard. A gallon of gasoline waited nearby.

Frank handed him a beer as he approached. "Drink," he said.

Frank tossed his own can into a pile of empties. "I'm not going to make her go through this again," he said. "*I'm* not going through this again."

John hadn't said anything. What could he say? Even then, he knew that they saw things differently. Frank and Kelly had three grown children, a couple of grandkids. He had someone else.

So he stood silently by as Frank filled the air with the sharp smell of gasoline, lit a piece of paper with his cigarette lighter, and dropped the flame onto his dead wife's body. John looked away, but he stood next to his friend and they choked together on the stinking smoke that seemed to shift in their direction no matter where they moved, as if Kelly were insisting upon one last, horrible memory of her passing.

After Margaret's first appearance, John had spent hours on the Internet, researching what people knew—or thought they knew—about the zombies. Some experts argued that there was a pattern in the appearances and wanted to study it further, but the government, pushed by religious leaders, clamped down on any such proposal. State and federal law required the destruction of any zombie, regardless of who they were or where they were spotted. John read what little he could find on patterns, tried to reason out the truth from what scientists and New Age nuts and Goth gurus offered to a frightened public. A warped mythology dominated most discussions, a strange mix of hard fact and Revelations-inspired fear. One woman on CNN had insisted the dead followed a biological cycle of rebirth, that they only wanted to return to those they loved and shepherd them to a new level of existence. When the newscaster pointed out that the zombies also wanted to eat their loved ones, she sniffed and explained that consumption was their only method of incorporating "the other" into themselves, into the lives they now enjoyed.

"It's all about love," she said, her voice calm and serious. "It's all about return and renewal."

Her interview had been followed by the story of a young mother who'd come back and eaten her own children.

A few fringe groups claimed that, given enough time, the "returned" could be brought back to actual life. They had loaded up their dead and taken them to compounds designed to allow the zombies to rise. Then they would "put them down" as gently as possible and let them rise again, in a continuous series of deaths and resurrections. Police raided a few such places on public safety grounds, dragging out a jumble of kooks and, in those instances where a zombie had slipped out unnoticed and found its target, half-eaten bodies.

"I'm not one of those kooks," John told himself every time he came across such a story. "I'm not."

But he was becoming more and more convinced that, just maybe, he could reach Margaret. Maybe the crazy people were on to something that the Feds didn't want known.

Armed with baseball bats and all the information he'd been able to gather, he waited for Margaret to return a second time. Now, he'd be ready. There was a motion detector near her new grave, out behind his house, with a wire that ran back to the sunroom. It was there that he slept, on the creaky couch she'd always threatened to throw away.

A beeping seeped into his skull.

He made it to the grave as she was still scraping away the soil, trying to free herself from the sticky clay. His teeth chattered despite the warm night. It was Margaret, he told himself, not some monster.

Her eyes searched the darkness, found his.

He stepped clear of the tree behind which he'd been crouching. He called her name, tried to explain what was happening, even as she stumbled forward like some creature from an awful late-night horror movie. He kept the tree between them, begging and dodging, allowing her to get close enough once to grab his shoulder and send the cold of the grave through the shirt and into his bones. Then he fell over a root, and crawled through briars and pine straw until he made it to the open gate to his backyard. Always in his mind lingered the idea that she would recognize something, anything, of the place she loved so well. That, he hoped, would bring her back to him.

He never had the chance to test his theory.

Margaret knocked him down halfway into the yard, fingers tearing at his clothes to rip them free and expose what lay beneath. He kicked her off, felt her hand grab an ankle as he stood, fell hard again. She came up on one knee, began to reach for his face, so he swung the bat sooner than he had hoped would be necessary. It slammed into the side of her face.

She fell, tried to rise.

"Stay down," he sobbed. She pushed herself to stand, so he hit her again—then listened, hoping to hear his name, to hear anything at all. She lay there, quiet.

In the morning he woke, dragged her to the same hole from which she'd crawled a few hours earlier. Before he could roll her into the grave, her mouth formed a word. Some said zombies could talk, a word or two at most, but the skill never lasted and their utterances never qualified as real conversation. They spat out random sounds, usually, at best phrases spewed from the depths of their calcified brain like an animal twitching even after it was dead.

Still, John risked the danger of putting his ear to her open, drooling mouth. But he heard nothing. She did not speak again. He waited as the sun climbed over the trees, waited as long as he dared, then rolled her into the grave and covered her face with dirt.

And now, she had come a third time.

John drank coffee, ate a piece of dry toast, then walked into the yard and pulled the plastic sheet back from his dead wife's body. He waited for her to speak, of course, and heard nothing at all. Maybe Frank was right. Maybe they all were right—the government types who said zombies were nothing more than animated meat. He was fooling himself.

He grabbed her arms and dragged her out the back gate, across the ravine that ran like a spine through the neighborhood, up the slope, and into the scattering of pine and oak where the hole, the same hole, gaped ready. His shovel leaned against a tree, as it had since after her first appearance. He dropped her arms, leaned on the shovel, and listened to the day: the birds and the traffic, the quiet of his neighborhood. Some people had left, had moved to safer, gated communities that promised zombie-free living. But the promises never panned out. Whatever invisible tether existed between the zombie and their loved one could not be broken so easily.

With his shovel, John cleared some of the loose dirt from the bottom of the hole, making sure it was deep enough to keep the animals away. He had just stepped out of the grave when he heard it.

"John?"

The word sounded more like "Thawn," but he knew what she meant. John closed his eyes, took a shaky breath, and steadied his grip on the shovel. Fire. In his mind, he pictured a cleansing fire.

"Hush, dear," he finally said. "I'm nearly finished."

Silence for a moment, then: "Again?"

It sounded like "Athen?"

He couldn't bring himself to reply this time, so he blinked back the tears and continued digging. He had almost finished when she spoke a third time.

"I'm trying, John."

Clear as a bell this time. He looked hopefully at her face, saw only her blank stare directed at the sky, one eye askew.

"I miss you," he said.

Silent once more, Margaret gazed through the trees, seeming to watch the few puffy clouds passing overhead. John sighed, took her by the arms, and started to roll her into the hole. Then he stopped and bent over to lift and cradle her body, so light and fragile, so like a baby's.

"Until next time," he said, gently lowering her into the grave. He straightened, took the shovel, and scooped up a spade full of red clay.

She stared up at him with familiar eyes.

Those he covered last.

GODDAMN REDNECK SURFER ZOMBIES

MICHAEL JASPER

P EOPLE STOPPED COMING TO THE North Carolina coast when the dead returned to the beach after four decades away. Got to the point where folks couldn't sit outside their own beachside trailers with a case of Bud without some rotting corpse staggering up and asking for directions to the cemetery or the bars or the bait shop, the whole time smelling like spoiled tuna. They killed us for most of the entire tourist season before we realized what they were up to, and actually did something about 'em. Goddamn zombies.

Back at the season's start, like now, I spent most of my days down at the end of the pier, the longest one in the state, where the stink of fish innards cooking in the sun never got to me like the reek of dead-person guts in some walking corpse does. If you come out to Long Beach—which you *should* do, even now, with the zombies and all—to fish and swim in the bath-warm water during the day and eat seafood and drink cold ones with us at night, you'll find me there at the farthest tip of the pier, past the signs saying *No Spectators Beyond This Point* and *King Mackerel Fishing Only*. If you give a shout for Big Al, I'll come over and say "hey" to you, long as the kings aren't biting.

Anyway, before things got messy again, I caught my limit most days by noon, smoking and drinking with the other old men with skin like leather and just enough teeth to hold their Camels in place. After the doc threatened to cut a hole in my neck, I stopped with the cancer sticks, but I still like a cold Bud while I watch my lines in the salty, hot Carolina air.

High point of those days came late in the afternoon, when the pretty girls came up and visited with us after a day of sunbathing and gossiping. Oh Lord, to be young again. Their tanned stomachs were tight and their long hair was salty and wet from the Atlantic, and they acted like they wanted to learn about fishing. We all knew they weren't interested in any of that. They were up there on the pier with us for protection.

Because every afternoon, when the tide started to head out, the dead came lurching out of the brush on the other side of the dunes and headed for the waves. The girls didn't want to be alone on the beach wearing just their bits of bikini as the zombies walked past, dragging their coffin lids behind 'em. Couple of the girls even recognized their grandparents, stripped down to their birthday suits, showing off their pale gray skin. That shook 'em up pretty good, let me tell you.

Far as I could tell, the girls didn't have nothing to worry about. These zombies were here for one thing only—they wanted to *surf*.

Some of us thought the zombies were attracted to the waves because of the pull of the tides. Mort and Lymon had their nicotine-and-six-pack theories about the moon's effect on the graveyards and the bodies buried in 'em. "Tidal forces from the moon," Mort said in his gravelly voice. "Pulls 'em up outta the ground just like it makes the waves come in and out. They put that cemetery too close to the ocean, that's what. Yeppers. Tidal forces."

We all just laughed and tried not to look at the naked corpses falling off their coffin lids like the newbies we called "grommets" back in my surfing days. Ten of the dead were out on the water that day, flinging their rotting and bloodless bodies toward the next wave. I recognized Alfie and Zach, old buddies from high school (flipped their car into the Intracoastal Waterway one Saturday night in '59 and drowned in three feet of water) along with my own mother (lung cancer, '82) surfing next to four-decades-dead Purnell Austin, forever twenty-one.

They took some tremendous tumbles, like the time Purnell was launched off his lid by a wave and slammed headfirst into the lid of the rotting girl next to him, sending pieces of nose and teeth flying. That one was so bad I caught myself moving out of my chair toward the water. But the surfing dead don't need any kind of first aid, not any more. Purnell climbed back onto his coffin lid, twisted his head with both hands to the left once, hard, and got ready for the next wave with a laugh. Lucky he didn't lose his head on that one.

The zombies' laughter was like the cough of a lifelong smoker, and it made the hairs on my arms stand up. Must've been hard, laughing when you didn't need to breathe any more.

Quiet old Bob Mangum nodded his bald head toward the undead surfers. "It's the beginning of the end times, 'at's what it is. Nothing to do with no moon or no tidal forces." He hobbled back to his cooler of shrimp bait and his five fishing lines. "Keep an eye out for Jehovah 'n' the horsemen," he added.

Now, I've always been one to just let things be. Long as the zombies left our people alone and no one went missing like last time, I was fine without getting into some sort of hassle with 'em. Cops didn't care about the zombies either, so long as no one was hurt. Still, there were more and more of 'em every day, almost to the point where they'd taken over the whole beach. And someone must've told the reporters this time, 'cause for a while there, they were almost as thick around here as the zombies.

Luckily, the film crews didn't last long, not after we started telling 'em it was all a hoax and they learned that the surfing dead didn't photograph well. All the zombies left were gray smears on film that looked like they'd been faked to even an old fart with bad eyes like mine. We told 'em they were wasting their time and their film, but who ever paid attention to a crusty old man like me? They were gone within a week with no story and a pile of worthless film.

Tourists were another story. Of course, they were scared shitless by the walking dead, whether they thought it all a big put-on or not. Us locals can adjust to 'most anything, long as it doesn't get in the way of the fishing, but most tourists ran off the instant they caught sight of some old zombie woman limping up the beach, tits hanging to her belly button, dragging her surf lid behind her like the train to a wedding dress. Even worse were the dead young 'uns, the teens killed in drunken car wrecks that went 'round as if they were showing off their missing arms and legs. Made it hard to concentrate on your John Grisham lawyer novel, or your gushy, Fabio-on-the-cover romance paperback, I'm sure.

The tourists that did stick around, wasting their film with more damn photos, didn't last too long. The zombies were "quaint" at first—swear to God I heard one of the Yankee women say this, heard it all the way up on the pier—but when their stink filled the air and the chunks of dead flesh started washing up onto the beach, they skedaddled real quick.

While packing up the kiddies and their plastic shovels and expensive umbrellas and chairs, some of the housewives showed another side of things. I saw some of 'em suck in their soft bellies when one of the fresher, not-dead-for-*too*-too-long male zombies whizzed past on his surf lid, as if those mamas had some sort of chance with a rotting old redneck boy whose last memory was red ambulance lights or a doctor beating on his chest a handful of years ago.

Now, I didn't mind getting rid of loud and rude tourists—most of 'em were Yankees anyhow, moved down here for their high falutin' tech jobs a few hours away up in Raleigh—but my buddy Lou at the Surf 'n' Suds Pier Restaurant and Angie at the Wings store needed the cash that those tourists brought. They couldn't handle another bad season, not after three hurricanes in the past five years, including the near miss from barely a month earlier that had left half the beach underwater. It was hard enough getting folks to come to Long Beach the way it was, and then the goddamn undead showed up.

I've lived here all my life, and I've watched the landscape change as the ocean ate away the sand dunes and made the new hotels the developer fools built sink and dip like leaking ships, and in that time I saw the same sort of tourist come down to our beaches. They'd pack up the brats, soak up the sun 'til it burned 'em, spend their money in our shops, and try to catch fish off the shallow sides of our pier. Like clockwork, they'd leave one week later, not to return until the following year. At the end of summer us locals cleaned up their mess and got back to our own business. That was the way things went.

The only disruption in the pattern was back in '60. That was the summer I came back to Long Beach to find the cemeteries from here to Southport empty, and the dead walking the streets.

I'd been surfing for a decade by that point in time. I'd started with my older brother's board when I was 'most ten years old, most times falling off it like a grommet before a wave ever picked me up. But I stuck with it and spent most days surfing instead of in school with the other kids. I always figured one of these days I'd go back and get my diploma, but then my sixtieth, then my seventieth birthday snuck up on me, and after that I just didn't see the point of it, really. I get all I wanted in life with fishing.

That summer of 1960, when there weren't waves big enough to go surfing, I learned all about pier fishing. I figured if I made friends with the fishermen on the pier, at the least I'd get fewer sinkers thrown at me on those days that I surfed a bit too close to their lines. Surfers and fishermen hardly ever see eye to eye, dealing like they do with the ocean from two very different angles. But bribed with enough smokes and brews, the fishermen warmed to me and taught me all I'd ever want to know. After that summer I never got hooked by a cast or smacked with a thrown sinker.

And then the zombies came calling. It all started on a Monday morning in early September, right after Hurricane Donna blasted through. I was half-buzzed by ten in the morning, nursing my fifth beer, when the first body flopped onto the flooded beach west of the pier. Looked like a damn fish thrown onto the sand by a rough wave, except the ocean was dead calm for a change. The body was shedding its pasty white skin, along with the occasional body part, with each spasm. An eyeball rolled back into the surf like a stray golf ball hit by an idiot tourist golfer.

Me and the boys were down there in five seconds. In spite of all our bad talk about the tourists, none of us wanted to see one of 'em die. And no fisherman or surfer wants to see a corpse on their beach. That's what we all figured this was, judging by the white skin of the man flailing on the sand: a near-drowning.

He wouldn't let us set him up to help him breathe, even though Bob was positive he couldn't get a pulse. For a mostly dead fella, he had the kind of strength I'd never felt before. I grabbed his arm, nearly sicking up my beers at the cold and loose feel of his flesh, like the skin on uncooked chicken. He lifted me right off the ground with that one arm.

It took us an hour to figure out what he was. His face had swollen up, but I swore there was something familiar about that crooked nose and that anchor tattoo on his shoulder.

Luckily the Oleandar Drive-In in Wilmington had been playing a horror triple-feature earlier that summer, and my buddy Marty had seen all three flicks, including *I Walked With a Zombie*.

"That's Jack Johnson!" Marty shouted. "Swear to God! He's one'a those zombers!"

The dead guy opened his one remaining eye and gave Marty what looked like a pissed-off glare. That's when I knew it was Jack, because of those Paul Newman ladykiller eyes. Or eye, I should say. His right one was floating up and down in the surf like a bobber. Jack was polite and didn't say anything about Marty's mangled terminology. Jack Johnson had drowned a week ago, caught out in the hurricane trying to save his boat.

"Ain't no such thing as a zom*bie*," Bob said in his quiet voice as we helped Jack to his feet. Bob had been old even back then. If I was a fool like Marty, who died in 'Nam when he fell over a trip wire after three hits of acid and blew his face off, I'd be wondering if ol' Bob wasn't a "zomber," too.

We didn't know what else to do, so we handed Jack his eye, which he popped back in its socket, and let him be. The fish were biting, that's all I can say in our defense. Marty left us to go surfing, and Jack walked off in the opposite direction of the pier.

We'd pretty much forgotten about him until we heard the screaming coming from the Dairy Queen up the road.

Purnell Austin, one of the biggest guys I knew back in school before I dropped out, had been stuffed into a garbage can outside the DQ. Both his legs had been broken, and they dangled out of the garbage can like dead flowers. But that wasn't the worst of it. When we pulled him out of the can, his head was split in two, and over half of his brain was gone. The top half of his head sat on a pile of bloody newspapers, looking like a hairy pottery bowl.

Before I sicked up my Budweiser breakfast, I saw two things that will stay with me until my dying day, and probably beyond even that.

The first was the teethmarks that had been left in the pinkish-gray brain matter of Purnell's battered skull.

The second was Jack Johnson's sky-blue eyeball, staring up at us from next to the garbage can.

When the dead started showing up this time, 'most everything was different. The corpses on the beach were just as bad as the crew from four decades ago for stinking and losing body parts—but at least this time no one living has gone missing. Back in '60 we'd lost almost a dozen folks before we could get the situation under control. We'd been able to keep the reporters and the other authorities away. Only Sheriff Johnson knew about the zombies back then, and he hadn't been keen on letting anyone outside of the Long Beach community know that his brother Jack was a "zomber" with a taste for brains. We kept it hushed up, for our own good.

Seems to have worked out alright. This time no tourists have turned up dead, with their heads cracked open like walnuts, missing most of the gray shit that makes up people's brains. At least not yet.

The zombies came this time just for the surfing, and nothing more.

I take full responsibility for that. I was the one who taught 'em how to surf. Goes to show you *can* teach an old dog new tricks, even if that old dog is dead. Or undead—however you wanna call it.

Nobody else was having any sort of luck keeping the zombies under control. You could shoot 'em or stab 'em with a filleting knife, but they didn't even flinch. If you were close enough to stab at 'em you were probably a goner anyway. We didn't figure out until it was almost too late that we should've been aiming at their heads the whole time.

After four of us young punks got killed by the zombies, and I'd taken the worst beating of my life from Marty's Great-aunt Esther (dead of a stroke in '38), we had to regroup and find some other way to keep the zombies from chowing on our brains like undead stoners with the munchies. If the outside world heard about this, the town would shrivel up and die, and we'd be good as dead then ourselves.

It was me who came up with the idea of surfing. I loved it, I figured, so why wouldn't the dead? If there was a heaven, I figured it had clear skies and monster waves all day and night.

So we taught the zombies to surf. They took right to it, even though their bodies were never as coordinated as they'd been while they were alive. At least we didn't have to worry about anyone drowning.

Old Bob had the idea of collecting the brains from the fish we caught off the pier to give the dead to eat, sort of a goodwill gesture, and they went along with it. For the rest of fall, nobody else went missing or showed up with a scooped-out skull. The zombies surfed up to the start of winter, until another tropical storm blew up in November. They made one last surf as the storm passed over, and then they went to rest again back in their waterlogged graves, settling their coffin lids and surfboards back on top of them like blankets.

This has been the summer for surfing, that's for sure. The waves have been unbelievable, bringing with 'em the biggest fish I've ever caught. Just last week I pulled in a fifteen-pound king mackerel from off the pier and nearly pissed myself. I was getting ready to fillet it up after Lou took my picture with it when I smelled the stink of zombie on the fish. I tossed it over the side of the pier, hoping no one saw me do it.

I should have known then that the dead had overstayed their visit once again. I continued to ignore 'em, I really did, but they were affecting my livelihood now. A man's got to fish, and a man's got to eat.

Some of the other guys were noticing it, too. Most of the fish we caught went back over the side after a quick weighing and measuring. The too-sweet stink of rot was on our hands, and we couldn't get it off no matter how much we wiped 'em on our shorts and shirts.

Like I said before, I've always been one to let things be. If I got hungry enough I could cook the hell out of the fish I caught and choke down the zombie-tainted meat. If I had to. In fact I'd almost resigned myself to this two days ago when I heard a gaggle of our young girls on the beach. They were all screaming and pointing at the ocean.

Now, let me explain something to you about a man and fishing. If his concentration is just right, with the sun keeping his head warm and the fish keeping the muscles in his arms tense, you can drop a nuclear bomb on the bait house behind him and he'd only check his lines and maybe blink once or twice. So I'm not too surprised that I'd never noticed it had gotten so bad with the zombies.

Anyway, after hearing the commotion, I set down my reel like I was in slow motion, like it was the last time I'd ever see it, and I turned to look at the beach, where the girls were still screaming.

The ocean was *thick* with the goddamn redneck surfer zombies.

They were perched on top of their coffin lids, leaning into the waves from the back half of the lid, just like I'd taught 'em decades ago. It was as if they had some sort of Stick-Em keeping 'em attached to their lids, because not a single one fell off.

And that was when I noticed that all the zombies were aiming in the same direction, their surf lids pointed toward a circle of blood fifty yards beyond where the waves broke.

Old Bob was already running down the pier toward the beach, with Mort and Lymon busting a gut trying to keep up. I dropped my line, grabbed the pneumatic spear-fishing gun from the crow's nest upstairs, and did the best swan dive off the side of the pier that a seventy-six-year-old redneck could do, right into the salty waves. I thought I'd broken my neck until I resurfaced, eyes stinging and head reeling.

"Shoot 'em in the head," Marty had told me all those years ago. "It's the only way to take 'em out . . . ."

We'd been smoking and drinking all night on the beach, watching the corpses surf in the moonlight. Marty was leaving for Fort Leavenwood the next week for basic training, and then he'd be off to Vietnam a few years later, waiting for his encounters with acid and the tripwire.

"Blow their brains out, huh?" I finished off my bottle of beer and launched it at out at dead Purnell out there surfing. He was barely a month dead. It smacked him in the chest and knocked a chunk of gray flesh into the waves with a soft *plop.*

"Yeah. Go for the head," Marty said, nodding. "Spread their brains out all over the place, so they can't put 'em back together."

Years later, after catching a midnight showing of *Night of the Living Dead,* I'd wondered if that George Romero fella had been out to Long Beach that summer, checking out the situation, maybe even talking to Marty. In any case, Marty had been right about the head shots. They stopped the ones that wouldn't leave the locals alone, and motivated the rest to pick another hobby. The zombies were much more interested in learning to surf once we blew off a few rotting heads.

As I swam through the waves after taking my dive off the pier, my old heart pounding in my ribs, I thought about Marty and all the others from Long Beach, including those of my friends who were now zombies. I wished there had been enough of ol' Marty left for 'em to ship back to us. He always loved catching a good wave.

Half a minute later I was there, outside a ring of thirty surf lids, each holding one zombie apiece. They were surrounding the bloody froth, watching the struggle with dumb, blank faces.

"Get back," I shouted, raising the gun and aiming it at the closest zombie. The coppery stink of blood was in the air, mixed with the zombie's odor of rot and the salty spray of the waves. I dog-paddled my way to the middle of the coffin lids and saw that the struggling had stopped. I lowered the spear gun and waited. Just like that, a zombie's head and shoulders lifted from the water, followed by the lifeless body of Janie Winters, covered in blood.

"Bastards!" I screamed as I pulled the trigger of the pneumatic gun.

I probably would have taken off the head of the zombie holding Janie, sending her under again, if the zombie closest to the two of 'em—Purnell Austin, actually, of all damn people—hadn't thrown himself in front of the spear and caught it with the back of his head. The spear got stuck in his skull, but still managed to scattered most of his face. The zombies closest to him were showered with whitened bits of brain and dried strips of brown flesh.

"Daaaa-aaamn," Alfie, the car wreck zombie, said in his guttural voice. "Why'd ya do thaaaa-aaat?"

Just like the summer of '60, it made me want to retch, having to kill someone who used to be my neighbor. But just like last time, they'd left me no choice. Or so I thought.

I dropped the gun when Janie moaned. A jagged gash ran the length of her thin arm, and that's when I realized how close I had come to making a huge mistake.

Blinking saltwater and sweat out of my eyes, I saw what had really been going on. The corpse of an eight-foot-long shark floated behind the zombie holding Janie, its side peppered with bloody, fist-sized holes. Four of the zombies had been torn to shreds fighting off the shark, which had gone after Janie, but they'd survive.

Well, maybe *survive* isn't the right word. But you know what I mean.

We made an agreement, the zombies and us living folks. They can come surfing every couple of years during the low season, long as they leave when we ask 'em to and stick to eating fish—not human—brains. Otherwise, us humans will start digging up graves and blowing off some zombie heads.

To our shock, they agreed, even though I could tell it was killing 'em—ha ha ha—to leave the waves behind for the year. The surfing is *that* good 'round here.

And hey, if they're willing to keep the waters shark-free for their surfing pleasure, that's fine with us.

Janie is doing better, and is likely to get most of the movement back in her arm after the shark bite heals. She stays on the shore all the time these days, concentrating on her tan instead of swimming or surfing.

Meanwhile, I keep a close eye on the cemeteries from here to Southport, as well as the Weather Channel. You never know what the next hurricane might stir up, and I can't say I'm partial to cooking my fish until the taste of zombie is fried out of it.

But, at the same time, I know I'm getting on in years, and I'm sort of looking forward to surfing again someday soon.

Got a coffin lid all picked out, too.

TRINKETS

TOBIAS S. BUCKELL

GEORGE PETROS WALKED DOWN THE waterfront, the tails of his coat slapping the back of his knees. An occasional gust of wind would tug at his tri-cornered hat, threatening to snatch it away. But by leaning his head into the wind slightly, George was able to manage a sort of balancing act between the impetuous gusts of wind and civilization's preference for a covered head.

The cobblestones made for wobbly walking, and George had just bought new shoes. He hadn't broken them in yet. Still, the luxury of new shoes bought the fleeting edges of a self-satisfied smile. The soles of his new shoes made a metronomic *tick-tick-tick* sound as he hurried toward his destination, only slowing down when he walked around piles of unloaded cargo.

Men of all sorts, shapes, and sizes bustled around in the snappy, cold weather. Their breath steamed as they used long hooks to snatch the cargo up and unload it. George walked straight past them. He did not put on airs or anything of the sort, but he hardly made eye contact with the grunting dockworkers.

His destination was the *Toussaint*. George could tell he was getting closer as the quiet suffering of the New England dockworkers yielded to a more buoyant singing.

George detoured around one last stack of crates, the live chickens inside putting up a cacophony of squawks and complaint, and saw the *Toussaint*.

The ship was hardly remarkable; it looked like any other docked merchant-men. What *did* give one a reason to pause were the people around the ship: they were Negroes. Of all shades of colors, George noticed.

Free Negroes were common enough around the North. But to see this many in one area, carrying guns, talking, chatting, flying their own flag—it made people nervous. Ever since the island of Haiti drove the French from its shores and won its independence, their ships had been ranging up and down the American coast. George knew it made American politicians wonder if the Negroes of the South would gain any inspiration from the Haitians' visible freedom.

The crew stood around the ship, unloaded the cargo, and conducted business for supplies with some of the Yankee shopkeepers. George himself was a shopkeeper, though of jewels and not staples of any sort. He nodded, seeing some familiar faces from his street: Bruce, Thomas. No doubt they would think he was here for some deal with the Haitians.

The smell of salt and sweat wafted across the docks as George nodded to some of the dockworkers, then passed through them to the ship's gangplank. One of the Haitians stopped him. George looked down and noticed the pistol stuck in a white sash.

"What do you need?" He spoke with traces of what could have been a French accent, or something else. It took a second for George to work through the words.

"I'm here for a package," George said slowly. "Mother Jacqueline . . . ."

The man smiled.

"Ah, you're that George?"

"Yes."

George stood at the end of the plank as the Haitian walked back onto the ship. He returned in a few minutes and handed the shopkeeper a brown, carefully wrapped parcel. Nothing shifted when George shook it.

He stood there for a second, searching for something to say, but then he suddenly realized that the tables had been turned. Now *he* was the one who wasn't wanted here. He left, shoes clicking across the cobblestones.

In the room over his shop George opened the parcel by the window. Below in the street, horses' feet kicked up a fine scattering of snow. When it settled by the gutters, it was stained brown and muddy with dung.

The desk in front of him was covered in occasional strands of his hair. He had a small shelf with papers stacked on it, but more importantly, he had his shiny coins and pieces of metal laid out in neat, tiny little rows. George smiled when the light caught their edges and winked at him. Some of the coins had engravings on them, gifts between lovers long passed away. Others had other arcane pieces of attachment to their former owners. Each one told George a little story. The jewelry he sold downstairs meant nothing. Each of the pieces here represented a step closer to a sense of completion.

He cut the string on the package and pulled the paper away from a warm mahogany box lid. The brass hinges squeaked when he opened it.

Inside was a letter. The wax seal on it caught George's full attention; he sat for a moment entranced by it. The faint smell of something vinegary kicked faint memories back from their resting places, and Mama Jaqi's distant whisper spoke to him from the seal.

"Hear me, obey me . . . ."

George sucked in his breath and opened the seal to read his directions. *There is a man*, the letter read, *right now sitting in a tavern fifteen or so miles south of you. You should go and listen to his story . . . .*

There was a name. And the address of the tavern.

Who was Louis Povaught? George wondered. But he didn't question the implicit order given. Layers of cold ran down his back, making him shiver. Automatically, without realizing it, he pulled something out of the box and put it in his pocket, then shut the lid. As he donned his coat and walked out of the shop to find a carriage, he told Ryan, the shop's assistant, that he would be back "later," and that he should close the shop himself.

Hours later, the sky darkening, George's cab stopped in front of the Hawser. A quick wind batted the wooden sign over the door. George paid and walked inside. It was like any other tavern: dim, and it smelled of stale beer and piss. He looked around and fastened his eyes on a Frenchman at the edge of the counter.

Frenchman, Negro, Northerner, Southerner, English . . . to George, all humanity had seemed more or less the same after he'd met Mama Jaqi. Yet even now he could feel that he was being nudged toward the Frenchman. This is the man he was supposed to meet, as irrational as it may have seemed. George carefully stamped his new shoes clean, leaned over to brush them off with a handkerchief he kept for exactly that purpose, then crossed the tavern to sit by the stranger.

The Frenchman—who would be Louis Povaught, George assumed—slouched in his seat. He hardly stirred when George sat next to him. The barkeep caught George's eye, and the shopkeeper shook his head. When he turned back to look at Louis, the man was already looking back at him.

Louis, unfortunately, hadn't spent much time keeping up his appearances. A long russet-colored beard, patchy in some places, grew haphazardly from his cheeks. His bloodshot eyes contained just a hint of green, lost to the steady strain of enthusiastic drinking.

"I think, not many people walk in here who do not order drink," he declared. "No?"

George pulled out his purse and caught the eye of the barkeep. "He'll have another." George looked down and pulled out paper money, leaving the shiny coins inside.

"And you," Louis said. "Why no drink?"

"It no longer does anything for me," George explained. He reached his hand in the pocket of his undercoat. Something was there. Like something standing just at the edge of his vision, he could barely remember picking it up.

Now George pulled it out. It was a silver chain with a plain cross on the end. The shopkeeper held it between the fingers of his hand and let the cross rest against the countertop.

"I have something for you, Louis," George heard himself saying. "Something very important."

Louis turned his tangled hair and scraggly beard toward George. The chain seductively winked; George locked his eyes with the entwined chains and followed them down to the rough countertop. Such beautiful things human hands made.

Louis's gasp took George's attention back to the world beyond the necklace.

"Is this what I think it is?" Louis asked, reaching tentatively for it. His wrinkled hands shook as they brushed the chain. George did not look down for fear of being entranced again. He did not feel the slightest brush of Louis's fingernail against his knuckle.

"What do you think it is?" George asked.

Louis turned back to the tavern.

"My brother Jean's necklace," Louis said. "On the back of this, it should have engrave . . ." Louis waved his hand about, "J. P. It is there, no?"

George still didn't look down.

"I imagine so."

Louis leaned back and laughed.

"*Merde.* So far away, so damn far away, and that bitch Jacqueline still has talons. Unlucky? Ha," he spat. "Do you know my story?"

"No," George said. "I do not."

The barkeep finally delivered a mug of beer, the dirty amber fluid spilling over the sides and onto the bar top where it would soak into the wood and add to the dank and musky air. Louis took the glass with a firm grasp and tipped it back. It took only seconds before the mug contained nothing but slick wetness at the bottom.

Louis smacked the mug down. "Buy me another, damn you," he ordered. George tapped the counter, looked at the barkeep, and nodded.

Stories, George thought, could sometimes be as interesting as something shiny and new. He would indulge Louis, yes, and himself. He handed Louis the necklace.

"Jean was much the better brother," Louis said. "I think it broke my father's heart to hear he died in Haiti. My father locked himself in his study for three days. Did not eat, did not drink. And when he came back out, he put his hand on my shoulder, like this—" Louis draped a heavy arm over George and leaned closer; his breath reeked of beer "—and he tells me, he tells me, 'Louis, you must go and take over where you brother has left off.' That is all he tells me. I never see him again."

Louis pulled back and scowled. "And Katrina, my wife, she is very, *very* sad to see me go away to this island. But I tell her it is good that I take over the business Jean created. I will make for her better husband. My brother has left me a good legacy. Hmmm. I did good business. I made them all proud. Proud! And you know what," Louis said, looking down at the necklace, "it was all great until Jean walked into my office three month later. It was . . . I'd seen his grave! There were witnesses . . . ."

"Business was good?" George interrupted. "What did you do?"

Louis ran a thumb around the rim of his glass.

"It didn't cost much. A boat. Provisions. We bought our cargo for guns . . . and necklaces, or whatever: beads and scrap." He opened a weathered palm. There was nothing in it.

"What cargo?" George interrupted. This was the point. It was why Mama Jaqi had sent him.

"Slaves," Louis said. "Lots of slaves."

"Ah, yes," George said. Mama Jaqi had been a slave.

"I made money," Louis said. "For the first time I wasn't some peasant in Provencal. I had a house with gardens." He looked at the shopkeep. "I did good! I gave money to charity. I was a good citizen. I was a good *businessman.*"

"I am sure you were," George said. He felt nothing against Louis. In another life, he would maybe have gone with Louis's arguments. He remembered using some of them once, a long time ago. A brief flash of a memory seared George's thoughts: he'd desperately blabbered some of the same things Louis had said, trying to defend himself to the incensed Mama Jaqi.

Quickly George shook away the ghostlike feel of passion. He needed to prod Louis's story along. He was here for the story, but he wanted it over quickly. Time was getting on, and he had to open the shop tomorrow. He would have to finish Mama Jaqi's deed soon. "What a shock seeing your brother must have been," George said at last.

"I thought some horrible trick had been played on me," Louis said. "I had so many questions about what had happened. And all Jean would do was tell me I had to leave. Leave the business. Leave the island. I refused." Louis made a motion at the bartender for more beer. "I was still in Haiti when it all began. Toussaint . . . the independence. I lost it all when the blacks ran us all off. I slipped away on a small boat to America with nothing. Nothing."

The Frenchman looked at George, and George saw a world of misery swimming in the man's eyes. "In France," Louis whispered, "they hear I am dead. I can only think of Katrina remarrying." He stopped and looked down at George's arm.

"What is it?" George asked.

Louis reached a finger out and pulled back the cuff of George's sleeve. Underneath, a faint series of scars marked the shopkeep's wrist.

"Jean had those," Louis said. The barkeep set another mug in front of the Frenchman, and left after George paid for it. "Do me a favor," Louis said, letting go of the other's sleeve. "One last favor."

"If I can," George said.

"Let me do this properly, like a real man. Eh? Would you do that?"

"Yes," George said.

Louis took his last long gulp from the mug, then stood up.

"I will be out in the alley."

George watched him stagger out the tavern.

After several minutes George got up and walked out. The distant cold hit him square in the face when he opened the door, and several men around the tables yelled at him to hurry and get out and shut the door.

In the alley by the tavern, George paused. Louis stepped out of the darkness holding a knife in his left hand, swaying slightly in the wind.

Neither of them said anything. They circled each other for a few seconds, then Louis stumbled forward and tried to slash at George's stomach. George stepped away from the crude attempt and grabbed the Frenchman's wrist. It was his intent to take the knife away, but Louis slipped and fell onto the stones. He landed on his arm, knocking his own knife away, then cracked his head against the corner of a brick.

Louis didn't move anymore. He still breathed, though: a slight heaving and the air steaming out from his mouth.

George crouched and put a knee to Louis's throat. The steaming breath stopped, leaving the air still and quiet. A long minute passed, then Louis opened an eye. He struggled, kicking a small pool of half-melted snow with his tattered boots. George kept his knee in place.

When the Frenchman stopped moving, George relaxed, but kept the knee in place for another minute.

The door to the tavern opened, voices carrying into the alley. Someone hailed for a cab and the clip-clop of hooves quickened nearby. George kept still in the alley's shadows. When the voices trailed off into the distance the shopkeeper moved again. He checked Louis's pockets until he found what he wanted: the necklace. He put it back into his own pocket. Then he stood up and walked out of the alley to hail his own cab.

The snow got worse toward the harbor and his shop. The horses pulling the cab snorted and slowed down, and the whole vehicle would shift and slide with wind gusts. George sat looking out at the barren, wintry landscape. It was cold and distant, like his own mechanical feelings. He could hear occasional snatches of the driver whistling "Amazing Grace" to himself and the horses.

Mama Jaqi had done well. George felt nothing but a compulsion for her bidding. *Obey.* . . . No horror about what he had just done. Just a dry, crusty satisfaction.

When he got out, George paid the driver. He took the creaky back steps up. He lit several candles and sat in his study for a while, still fully dressed. Eventually he put his fingers to the candle in front of him and watched the edges turn from white, to red, to brown, and then to a blistered black. The burned skin smelled more like incense than cooked flesh.

He pulled them away.

Tomorrow they would be whole again.

George lifted the silver necklace out with his good hand. He set it on the shelf, next to all the other flashy trinkets. Another story ended, another decoration on his shelf.

How many more would it take, George wondered, before Mama Jaqi freed him? How many lives did she deem a worthy trade for the long suffering she had known in her life? Or for the horrors of George's own terrible past? He didn't know. She'd taken that ability away from him. In this distant reincarnation of himself, George knew that any human, passionate response he could muster would be wrong.

Even his old feelings would have been wrong.

Long after the candles burned out, George sat, waiting.

MURDERMOUTH

SCOTT NICHOLSON

F ONLY THEY HAD TAKEN my tongue.

With no tongue, I would not taste this world. The air in the tent is buttered by the mist from popcorn. Cigarette smoke drifts from outside, sweet with candy apples and the liquor that the young men have been drinking. The drunken ones laugh the hardest, but their laughter always turns cruel.

If they only knew how much I love them. All of them, the small boys whose mothers pull them by the collar away from the cage, the plump women whose hair reflects the torchlight, the men all trying to act as if they are not surprised to see a dead man staring at them with hunger dripping from his mouth.

"Come and see the freak," says the man who cages me, his hands full of dollar bills.

Freak. He means me. I love him.

More people press forward, bulging like sausages against the confines of their skin. The salt from their sweat burns my eyes. I wish I could not see.

But I see more clearly now, dead, than I ever did while breathing. I know this is wrong, that my heart should beat like a trapped bird, that my veins should throb in my temples, that blood should sluice through my limbs. Or else, my eyes should go forever dark, the pounding stilled.

"He doesn't look all that weird," says a long-haired man in denim overalls. He spits brown juice into the straw covering the ground.

"Seen one like him up at Conner's Flat," says a second, whose breath falls like an ill wind. "I hear there's three in Asheville, in freak shows like this."

The long-haired man doesn't smell my love for him. "Them scientists and their labs, cooking up all kinds of crazy stuff, it's a wonder something like this ain't happened years ago."

The second man laughs and points at me and I want to kiss his finger. "This poor bastard should have been put out of his misery like the rest of them. Looks like he wouldn't mind sucking your brains out of your skull."

"Shit, that's nothing," says a third, this one as big around as one of the barrels that the clowns use for tricks. "I seen a woman in Parson's Ford, she'd take a hunk out of your leg faster than you can say 'Bob's your uncle.'"

"Sounds like your ex-wife," says the first man to the second. The three of them laugh together.

"A one hundred percent genuine flesh-eater," says my barker. His eyes shine like coins. He is proud of his freak.

"He looks like any one of us," calls a voice from the crowd. "You know. Normal."

"Say, pardner, you wouldn't be taking us for a ride, would you?" says the man as big as a barrel.

For a moment, I wonder if perhaps some mistake has been made, that I am in my bed, dreaming beside my wife. I put my hand to my chest. No heartbeat. I put a finger in my mouth.

"I'm as true as an encyclopedia," says my barker.

"Look at the bad man, Mommy," says a little girl. I smile at her, my mouth wet with desire. She shrieks and her mother leans forward and picks her up. I spit my finger out and stare at it, lying there pale against the straw, slick and shiny beneath the guttering torches.

Several of the women moan, the men grunt before they can stop themselves, and the children lean closer, jostle for position. One slips, a yellow-haired boy with tan skin and meat that smells like soap. For an instant, his hands grip the bars of the cage. He fights for balance.

I love him so much, I want to make him happy, to please him. I crawl forward, his human stink against my tongue as I try to kiss him. Too quickly, a man has yanked him away. A woman screams and curses first at him, then at me.

The barker beats at the bars with his walking stick. "Get back, freak."

I cover my face with my hands, as he has taught me. The crowd cheers. I hunch my back and shiver, though I have not been cold since I took my final breath. The barker pokes me with the stick, taunting me. Our eyes meet and I know what to do next. I pick my finger off the ground and return it to my mouth. The crowd sighs in satisfaction.

The finger has not much flavor. It is like the old chicken hearts the barker throws to me at night after the crowd has left. Pieces of flesh that taste of dirt and chemicals. No matter how much of it I eat, I still hunger.

The crowd slowly files out of the tent. Through the gap that is the door I see the brightly spinning wheels of light, hear the bigger laughter, the bells and shouts as someone wins at a game. With so much amusement, a freak like me cannot hope to hold their attention for long. And still I love them, even when they are gone and all that's left is the stench of their shock and repulsion.

The barker counts his money, stuffs it in the pocket of his striped trousers. "Good trick there, with the finger. You're pretty smart for a dead guy."

I smile at him. I love him. I wish he would come closer to the bars, so I could show him how much I want to please him. I pleased my last barker. He screamed and screamed, but my love was strong, stronger than those who tried to pull him away.

The barker goes outside the tent to try and find more people with money. His voice rings out, mixes with the organ waltzes and the hum of the big diesel engines. The tent is empty and I feel something in my chest. Not the beating, beating, beating like before I died. This is more like the thing I feel in my mouth and stomach. I need. I put my finger in my mouth, even though no one is watching.

The juggler comes around a partition. The juggler is called Juggles and he wears make-up and an old, dark green body stocking. He has no arms. His painted eyes make his face look small. "Hey, Murdermouth," he says.

I don't remember the name I had when I was alive, but Murdermouth has been the favorite name the others call me lately. I smile at him and show him my teeth and tongue. Juggles comes by every night when the crowds thin out.

"Eating your own damned finger," Juggles says. He takes three cigarettes from a pocket hidden somewhere in his body stocking. In a moment, the cigarettes are in the air, twirling, Juggles's bare toes a blur of motion. Then one is in his mouth, and he leans forward and lights it from a torch while continuing to toss the other two cigarettes.

He blows smoke at me. "What's it like to be dead?"

I wish I could speak. I want to tell him, I want to tell them all. Being dead has taught me how to love. Being dead has shown me what is really important on this earth. Being dead has saved my life.

"You poor schmuck. Ought to put a bullet in your head." Juggles lets the cigarette dangle from his lips. He lights one of the others and flips it into my cage with his foot. "Here you go. Suck on that for a while."

I pick up the cigarette and touch its orange end. My skin sizzles and I stare at the wound as the smoke curls into my nose. I put the other end of the cigarette in my mouth. I cannot breathe so it does no good.

"Why are you so mean to him?"

It is she. Her voice comes like hammers, like needles of ice, like small kisses along my skin. She stands at the edge of the shadows, a shadow herself. I know that if my heart could beat it would go crazy.

"I don't mean nothing," says Juggles. He exhales and squints against the smoke, then sits on a bale of straw. "Just having a little fun."

"Fun," she says. "All you care about is fun."

"What else is there? None of us are going anywhere."

She steps from the darkness at the corner of the tent. The torchlight is golden on her face, flickering playfully among her chins. Her breath wheezes like the softest of summer winds. She is beautiful. My Fat Lady.

The cigarette burns between my fingers. The fire reaches my flesh. I look down at the blisters, trying to remember what pain felt like. Juice leaks from the wounds and extinguishes the cigarette.

"He shouldn't be in a cage," says the Fat Lady. "He's no different from any of us."

"Except for that part about eating people."

"I wonder what his name is."

"You mean 'was,' right? Everything's in the past for him."

The Fat Lady squats near the cage. Her breasts swell with the effort, lush as moons. She stares at my face, into my eyes. I crush the cigarette in my hand and toss it to the ground.

"He knows," she says. "He can still feel. Just because he can't talk doesn't mean he's an idiot. Whatever that virus was that caused this, it's a hundred times worse than being dead."

"Hell, if I had arms, I'd give him a hug," mocks Juggles.

"You and your arms. You think you're the only one that has troubles?" The Fat Lady wears lipstick, her mouth is a red gash against her pale, broad face. Her teeth are straight and healthy. I wish she would come closer.

"Crying over Murdermouth is like pissing in a river. At least he brings in a few paying customers."

The Fat Lady stares deeply into my eyes. I try to blink, to let her know I'm in here. She sees me. She sees me.

"He's more human than you'll ever be," the Fat Lady says, without turning her head.

"Oh, yeah? Give us both a kiss and then tell me who loves you." He has pulled a yellow ball from somewhere and tosses it back and forth between his feet. "Except you better kiss me first because you probably won't have no lips left after him."

"He would never hurt me," she says. She smiles at me. "Would you?"

I try to think, try to make my mouth form the word. My throat. All my muscles are dumb, except for my tongue. I taste her perfume and sweat, the oil of her hair, the sex she had with someone.

Voices spill from the tent flap. The barker is back, this time with only four people. Juggles hops to his feet, balances on one leg while saluting the group, then dances away. He doesn't like the barker.

"Hello, Princess Tiffany," says the barker.

The Fat Lady grins, rises slowly, groans with the effort of lifting her own weight. I love all of her.

"For a limited time only, a special attraction," shouts the barker in his money-making voice. "The world's fattest woman and the bottomless Murdermouth, together again for the very first time."

The Fat Lady waves her hand at him, smiles once more at me, then waddles toward the opening in the tent. She waits for a moment, obliterating the bright lights beyond the tent walls, then enters the clamor and madness of the crowd.

"Too bad," says the barker. "A love for the ages."

"Goddamn, I'd pay double to see that," says one of the group.

"Quadruple," says the barker. "Once for each chin."

The group laughs, then falls silent as all eyes turn to me.

The barker beats on the cage with his stick. "Give them a show, freak."

I eat the finger again. It is shredded now and bits of dirt and straw stick to the knuckle. Two of the people, a man and a woman, hug each other. The woman makes a sound like her stomach is bad. Another man, the one who would pay double, says, "Do they really eat people?"

"Faster than an alligator," says my barker. "Why, this very one ingested my esteemed predecessor in three minutes flat. Nothing left but two pounds of bones and a shoe."

"Doesn't look like much to me," says the man. "I wouldn't be afraid to take him on."

He calls to the man with him, who wobbles and smells of liquor and excrement. "What do you think? Ten-to-one odds."

"Maynard, he'd munch your ass so fast you'd be screaming 'Mommy' before you knew what was going on," says the wobbling man.

Maynard's eyes narrow, and he turns to the barker. "I'll give you a hundred bucks. Him and me, five minutes."

My barker points the stick toward the tent ceiling. "Five minutes? In the cage with that thing?"

"I heard about these things," says the man. "Don't know if I believe it."

My mouth tastes his courage and his fear. He is salt and meat and brains and kidneys. He is one of them. I love him.

He takes the stick from the barker and pokes me in the shoulder.

"That's not sporting," says the barker. He looks at the man and woman, who have gone pale and taken several steps toward the door.

Maynard rattles the stick against the bars and pokes me in the face. I hear a tearing sound. The woman screams and the man beside her shouts, then they run into the night. Organ notes trip across the sky, glittering wheels tilt, people laugh. The crowd is thinning for the night.

Maynard fishes in his pocket and pulls out some bills. "What do you say?"

"I don't know if it's legal," says the barker.

"What do you care? Plenty more where he came from." Maynard breathes heavily. I smell poison spilling from inside him.

"It ain't like it's murder," says Maynard's drunken companion.

The barker looks around, takes the bills. "After the crowd's gone. Come back after midnight and meet me by the duck-hunting gallery."

Maynard reaches the stick into the bars, rakes my disembodied finger out of the cage. He bends down and picks it up, sniffs it, and slides it into his pocket. "A little return on my investment," he says.

The barker takes the stick from Maynard and wipes it clean on his trouser leg. "Show's over, folks," he yells, as if addressing a packed house.

"Midnight," Maynard says to me. "Then it's you and me, freak."

The wobbly man giggles as they leave the tent. My barker waits by the door for a moment, then disappears. I look into the torchlight, watching the flames do their slow dance. I wonder what the fire tastes like.

The Fat Lady comes. She must have been hiding in the shadows again. She has changed her billowy costume for a large robe. Her hair hangs loose around her shoulders, her face barren of make-up.

She sees me. She knows I can understand her. "I heard what they said."

I stick out my tongue. I can taste the torn place on my cheek. I grip the bars with my hands. Maybe tomorrow I will eat my hands, then my arms. Then I can be like Juggles. Except you can't dance when you're dead.

Or maybe I will eat and eat when the barker brings me the bucket of chicken hearts. If I eat enough, I can be the World's Fattest Murdermouth. I can be one of them. I will take money for the rides and pull the levers and sell cotton candy.

If I could get out of this cage, I would show her what I could do. I would prove my love. If I could talk, I would tell her.

The Fat Lady watches the tent flap. Somewhere a roadie is working on a piece of machinery, cursing in a foreign language. The smell of popcorn is no longer in the air. Now there is only cigarette smoke, cheap wine, leftover hot dogs. The big show is putting itself to bed for the night.

"They're going to kill you," she whispers.

I am already dead. I have tasted my own finger. I should be eating dirt instead. Once, I could feel the pounding of my heart.

"You don't deserve this." Her eyes are dark. "You're not a freak."

My barker says a freak is anybody that people will pay money to see.

My tongue presses against my teeth. I can almost remember. They put me in a cage before I died. I had a name.

The Fat Lady wraps her fingers around the metal catch. From somewhere she has produced a key. The lock falls open and she whips the chain free from the bars.

"They're coming," she says. "Hurry."

I smell them before I see them. Maynard smells like Maynard, as if he is wearing his vital organs around his waist. The wobbling man reeks even worse of liquor. The barker has also been drinking. The three of them laugh like men swapping horses.

I taste the straw in the air, the diesel exhaust, the thin smoke from the torches, the cigarette that Juggles gave me, my dead finger, the cold gun in Maynard's pocket, the money my barker has spent.

I taste and taste and taste and I am hungry.

"Hey, get away from there," yells the barker. He holds a wine bottle in one hand.

The Fat Lady pulls on the bars. The front of the cage falls open. I can taste the dust.

"Run," says the Fat Lady.

Running is like dancing. Maybe people will pay money to see me run.

"What the hell?" says Maynard.

I move forward, out of the cage. This is my tent. My name is on a sign outside. If I see the sign, I will know who I am. If I pay money, maybe I can see myself.

"This ain't part of the deal," says Maynard. He draws the gun from his pocket. The silver barrel shines in the firelight.

The Fat Lady turns and faces the three men.

"I swear, I didn't know anything about this," says the barker.

"Leave him alone," says the Fat Lady.

Maynard waves the gun. "Get out of the way."

This is my tent. I am the one they came to see. The Fat Lady blocks the way. I stare at her broad back, at the dark red robe, her long hair tumbling down her neck. She's the only one who ever treated me like one of them.

I jump forward, push her. The gun roars, spits a flash of fire from its end. She cries out. The bullet cuts a cold hole in my chest.

I must die again, but at last she is in my arms.

If my mouth could do more than murder, it would say words.

I am sorry. I love you.

They take her bones when I am finished.

SITTING WITH THE DEAD

SHANE STEWART

I T'S NOT UNTIL HE HEARS the padlock seal itself that he notices that everyone is gone. The noise startles him, pulling him from a brief slumber as he sits in the old folding chair. He looks around, checks his environment. There's a table by the far wall. Sealed double doors behind him. A stack of folding chairs to the left. And the coffin in front of him.

He stands slowly, stretching the tiredness out of his joints before he turns toward the doors. He tries the handles first, finds them securely locked. He pushes the doors a few times, throwing his weight against them. They refuse to move. Satisfied, he circles the room, checking the windows. It's painfully hot, even though the sun went down a little while ago. The windows are open, with a screen on each one to keep out the bugs and let the breeze in. Beyond the screen, thick iron bars prevent escape.

He glances at the coffin only briefly, doesn't even stop to survey the occupant. He simply crosses to the table. There's a thermos, heavy and metallic, with a single coffee-stained cup. Next to the thermos there's a slender black box and a short-handled steel mallet. Next to that, a snub-nosed .38.

He picks up the revolver, checks it out once, and then slides it into his jacket pocket. If he has to go for a gun, he's not sure what he'll grab for—the .38 or the 10 mm under his shoulder. But since the funeral director didn't know about the automatic he left the .38, just in case. You never know how these things will turn out, after all.

Still, he muses, *it's good to have a backup.*

He fingers the box briefly before grabbing the mallet. He doesn't want to open it, not yet. There's too much temptation to just get it all over with, and he doesn't want to let her down, just in case. Instead, he turns back toward the chair and drags it over to the table. He cracks open the thermos and pours thick black coffee into the cup. Sipping it makes him wince.

Never figured out what they put in the coffee around here, he thinks. *But they wouldn't dare serve this at Starbucks.*

He glances again at the coffin, but still refuses to walk over there. Instead, he pulls a deck of cards from his pocket. He leans back in the chair, props his feet on the table, and begins shuffling. It doesn't take long before he starts bringing random cards to the top of the deck, quietly muttering the name of the card before he flips it over. Now and then he fans the cards, spreads them, cuts them, all the while keeping track of which card is where in the deck.

"The three of hearts."

The voice startles him. He glances outside reflexively and calmly notes how dark it's become, before looking at the coffin.

She's sitting up, smiling at him pleasantly. Her thin white hair hovers like a cloud around her head. "I pick the three of hearts," she says.

He smiles, then cuts the deck with one hand. He taps the top of the deck for flourish and peels the card away. He holds it up, face toward his audience. "What do you see?" he asks.

The wrinkled face smiles. "You did it again, Pumpkin."

He smiles thinly, puts the cards away. "Hello, Gram."

For a moment he thinks he sees light in the old, dead eyes staring at him. "I must look just awful," she says.

He stands up and stretches, then smiles at her. "You don't look too bad, all things considered."

"You mean," she says slowly, "considering that I'm dead and all."

He nods. The funeral director told him that it was impolite to remind the risen that they're dead. He's never been very polite, not since he left home at least, but he doesn't want to remind himself of her death either. Looking at her, the first thing he sees is her eyes. The pupils have spread, pushing all the color out of them. Big, black, dead eyes. He's suddenly very aware of the guns. The .38 pulls his jacket to the right, while the 10 mm brushes lightly against his side.

They stare at each other for several minutes before she glances around the room. "I've never seen Juniper's parlor so empty. I'm used to seeing at least a few people in here."

"Only one person gets to sit in here with you," he says. "The rest of the family is either at home or out in the main hall."

"I know. The old ways are the best, after all."

He shuffles, looks down at his feet.

"Nervous, Pumpkin?"

"No," he says. "Just . . . I don't know."

"Impatient, maybe?"

"No," he lies.

"They don't do this much anymore, do they? Not here in the holler, like we do. Not much call for folks to sit with the dead all night anymore. It's a shame really."

He stands motionless, resisting the urge to end this with a bullet. He still doesn't know which gun he'd go for first. He kicks at the floorboards. "I thought the floor was concrete in here?"

"It used to be," his zombie Gram says. "But there was a mudslide long about—I suppose it was six years ago now. Took some of the support right out from under the floor. The slab cracked in half and brought part of the funeral home down with it. Old Man Juniper had it cleared out, and then rebuilt it to how it is today. Managed to keep the same doors for the viewing room here though." She waves one hand at the thick double doors. "Those doors have been on this parlor since old Thomas W. Juniper first opened it back in 1853. Wouldn't be right, Eustace says, if they weren't here. And Eustace was the first person put to rest in his newly rebuilt parlor."

She looks at him, sees him staring at the floor. "I'm sorry, Pumpkin, I'm rambling again. Is something on your mind?"

"I was just thinking . . . did Eustace sit up?"

Her smile disappears. "Wouldn't really matter if he did. That no good Phillip went and hired someone to sit up with him. That weren't right, but that's just my opinion."

He laughs a little. "You've always been full of opinions, Gram."

"Maybe I have, but still . . ."

He looks up at her, tensing. "Gram?"

Her dead black eyes turn on him, and for a moment he considers grabbing the gun and shooting her in the head. Just like an off switch, he always tells himself. Just at range.

But her eyes suddenly shift, and she looks away. "I—I'm sorry, Pumpkin. I just—for a moment—I was just real . . . hungry for a second there." A faint smile returns to her undead lips. "I'm all right now."

"You sure?" he says. He still wants to draw a gun.

"I'm sure."

He stares at her for a moment before he lets himself relax.

"What was I saying, Pumpkin?"

"You were talking about your opinions, Gram."

"Oh. Oh, yes. I remember now. All those new ways to prepare the dead folk—they just aren't right. You remember Kendall Powell? He died when you were eleven, and his wife sent him off to be embalmed. Poor man sat up that night, and there was nothing left in there. His whole mind was gone. Tore out of here and started killing anything he could get his hands on. Ripped up three of our pigs before your grandfather, God rest his soul, put the poor man down with his 12-gauge. There wasn't enough of poor Kendall's head left for a decent viewing after that. They had to lay a picture on top of his neck for the viewing. And that one boy, Billy Gray, what fell out of that tree when you were in high school? You remember him, don't you? They flushed him with water 'cause that other mortician came to town to try and run the Juniper's out of business, and Billy done sat up and killed poor Bobby Mitchell and stuffed him in his coffin. Then he went and just started killing and eating folks. You remember him, don't you Pumpkin?"

"Yeah," he says quietly. "Billy was the first zombie I ever shot."

"It ain't natural to go and mess with the dead like that. Nothing good comes from it."

"Is that why you wanted it done the old way? Because you didn't want to chance coming back like that?"

"Well, yes, that's—"

"You could have opted for cremation."

The silence surprises him, and he looks up from the floor to see her staring at him. Her mouth has gone slack, and her eyes are wide and dark. He starts to reach for a gun—only vaguely aware that he was reaching into his jacket—when she speaks again.

"Cremation! Never! My brother Barnaby died not three weeks after you left home, and he had them cremate him. They put him in that coffin, and they wheeled him into the fire, and the minute he started to burn, he began to pound on the coffin something fierce. He wailed and screamed and hollered and kicked and beat on that pine box the entire time he was burning. Then the box came apart, and he started crawling for the furnace door, and he beat on that and wailed until he couldn't wail no more. No, sir. I may not know what is waiting for us when we go, but I know one thing: Barnaby met the beyond screaming in terror. That is no way for someone to go."

"So you prefer this? You prefer nailing?"

"I prefer anything," she says, "that gives me the chance to talk to my family one last time."

"I see."

"Do you remember Julie Fisher, that girl you were always sweet on?"

"Yeah," he says.

"She died last year. That Isaacs boy—what was his name, Winfred? Whipple?"

"Winter, Gram. Patrick Winter Isaacs."

"Yes, that's it. She started living with him after you left the holler. Never married him. He got her pregnant, is why, but no one thinks she had a choice in the matter."

He listens to the silence for a second. "Gram?"

"What? I'm sorry, Pumpkin. I was just . . . so hungry . . . ."

"You were talking about Julie, Gram. Julie and Winter."

"I was? Oh, yes. Anyway, she died last year. Winter beat her to death. He got tossed in jail, and that's the last I heard of him. I suppose he's still in there, maybe. If he ever gets out, her father is liable to shoot the little so-and-so."

He grinds his teeth back and forth. "Gram," he says finally, "you're rambling."

"No, I'm not. I know exactly why I brought Julie up, young man."

"Why is that?"

"She asked me to be her nailer. I was her second choice, you should know."

"Who was her first?"

"You."

His heart stops, but only for a second. "Me? Why would she want me to—?"

"Because you left. Because you said you'd come back. Because she'd been hoping that you would come back. And because she wanted to tell you that she loved you before she died."

He falls back, leans against the wall, and stands there, silent, for several minutes. "And when no one could find me, they came to you . . . ."

"Yes. And she wanted me to tell you that she loves you, and that she's waiting for you."

He looks down, fingers the revolver through the fabric of his coat. *It wouldn't take much to end all of this*, he thinks.

"She lingered for a while, hoping you'd make it home. I—I had to shoot her, with Juniper's little revolver, late the following morning."

"I'm sorry, Gram."

"So am I. That was when I decided I wanted you to be my nailer. Partly because I had to pass on Julie's message, and partly because—well, it's been so long. What's happened to you, Lyle?"

"Nothing, really," he says. He turns away from her and looks to the floor. "Just a couple of runs of bad luck, is all."

He glances over at her. She just sits there, staring at him with those black eyes. *Silence for more than fifteen seconds*, he thinks, *and she's gone. Gram will be gone, and all that will be left is me, the gun, and a starving machine. One Mississippi. Two Mississippi.*

At thirteen Mississippi, she speaks. "I'm waiting."

He rubs his eyes before he looks at her. "It all started going wrong in school. I lost my job, and tuition was due. I needed money fast, so I went to the casino. I walked up to the blackjack table with $37 in my pocket. I walked away with a little over $800. All because I'm good with cards."

He fiddles with the deck in his pocket. He tries to look away again, but he can't stop looking into those dead eyes. *I used to be able to avoid talking to her*, he thinks. *Once upon a time I could keep secrets from Gram.*

After a moment he decides it doesn't matter. *The dead tell no secrets. Neither did—does—Gram . . . .*

"I paid my tuition, then went looking for a new job. But I couldn't find one, or I'd get one and not be able to keep it. Classes started getting tough, and I thought if I had an easy source of income, I could study more. So I went back to the casino. I got escorted out by security that night, although they let me keep the $300 I'd won. I started hitting the other casinos for cash. Pretty soon I was banned from all of them.

"So, once again I'm looking for a job. I end up at this warehouse, on the late shift. I'm up all night loading trucks, and in the morning, I'm sleeping in class—if I even made it to class. My grades are suffering, and I'm thinking it can't get much worse." He smiles thinly. "Was I ever wrong."

"What happened?"

"There were these homeless guys that came by the warehouse on Tuesday nights. The foreman would put them to work, give them some money the next day. One morning last January, all four of them come in, and they're dead. One of them froze to death the week before, and he had bitten his friends and killed them before he could stop himself. They got the foreman, then they got Sam and Adam. That left just me and Johnny.

"We made our way to the foreman's office. Johnny played baseball growing up, so he picked up a two-by-four on the way. He was swinging it around while I dug through the office. I found a long-barrel .22 pistol in the filing cabinet, and some bullets. That's when they found us . . . ."

"How many did you shoot, Lyle?"

"Three. Johnny got one with the board. Then the other three got hold of him. I . . . I couldn't load the gun fast enough."

He looks away from her. "I put a bullet in Johnny next. Then Sam, then Adam. There wasn't enough of the foreman left to get back up, but I shot his corpse anyway. The police arrived not long after. They asked me questions, I answered them. When it was over, this guy walks up. Says he has a new job for me."

"I've heard," she says, "that sometimes folks die in the cities and no one notices before they rise up. And with no one to help them along, they can't get away from that hunger. And then you get packs of hungry dead folk running around."

He nods.

"I've heard that some people get paid to hunt them down."

He reaches under his jacket and pulls out the automatic. "They issue us these. We get a bounty for each zombie we drop. We get the pistol and a sack and a big knife. We shoot them, chop off their heads, and bring them in. Then we go around and collect the rest of the bodies. We can also be hired to take someone's place when they have a relative who wants to be dealt with in the traditional way."

"So you make a living off the dead now."

He nods. "Sometimes I get a few odd jobs here and there. Usually just to make things meet."

"I've heard bad things about people in your line of work."

"Some of the squads pad their quotas, supposedly, with homeless people that aren't dead. Others are supposed to hire themselves out as reasonably priced hit men."

"You don't do that."

"No, I don't," he says. "But sometimes I wonder if I would, given the chance."

"If you have to shoot me," she asks calmly, "which gun will you use?"

"I—" He looks at the floor for a moment, then up at her. "I don't know."

Several minutes pass without a sound.

"Do you have my nail?"

He looks up at her quickly. "It's on the table."

"Bring it here. I'd like to have a look at it, while I still can."

He retrieves the slim black box and walks over toward the coffin. He stops and looks at her. Her eyes are black and sparkling, and her smile has some faint, sinister bend to it. "Gram?"

"Hmm? What?"

"How are you doing?"

"I'm tired, dear. And—well, hungry, too."

He looks at her for a moment. Then he reaches into the box and pulls out the nail.

It's long, although he can't quite tell how long. Little more than a foot, he'd guess. Fifteen inches, maybe. The head is wide, and the point is broad, like an arrowhead. He knows the clinical aspect of the nail, its purpose. The broad point cuts at the brain and, if inserted properly, will allow the risen to fade away and move on. And if the blow isn't precise enough, the nail still serves a purpose—holding the risen down in their coffins, where they'll stay, until rot finally claims them. Some of his associates on the squad purposefully nail people down wrong, then cut the spinal cord so the unfortunate can't move or make any noise. They're supposed to finish the risen off with a bullet through the temple. Most of them consider it a waste of ammunition.

Gram looks at the nail with a mixture of—what, exactly? He has a hard time reading the dead black pits her eyes have become. If he takes away the eyes, the look on her wrinkled face is calm, almost gentle. *Is that admiration?* he wonders. *Appreciation?* There's supposed to be some sort of greater significance to the nail, but he forgets what.

Finally, she speaks: "It's a good nail."

He nods.

"Have you ever—?"

"No," he says. "This is my first time."

She smiles. "Thank you for agreeing to be my nailer, Lyle."

"Your welcome, Gram." He takes the nail and holds it loosely in his hands. "Gram?"

"Yes?"

"Did people always come back like this?"

"I don't know, Pumpkin." She sighs, more out of expectation than anything else, he figures. She hasn't drawn a breath since she sat up. "I should be going now, I think. Before I start getting hungry again."

He nods, then walks over to the table to retrieve the hammer. He looks at the automatic in his hand, then lays it down on the table. He takes the .38 out of his pocket, too. When he walks back over, he carries only the hammer and the nail. She is smiling.

"Goodbye, Gram."

"Goodbye, Pumpkin."

She lays down in her coffin, folds her arms over her chest. He steps forward and places the tip of the nail against her forehead. She closes her eyes. He holds the hammer over the head, then brings it up for the first blow. Calmly, quietly, she starts to sing.

"Amazing grace, how sweet the sound . . ."

Tink.

". . . Th-that saved a-a wretch li-ike meee . . ."

Tink.

". . . I-I once wassss losst, b-b-but n-n-ow I'm fff—ff—"

"Found, Gram."

"Ffff-found." Her lips tremble slightly. "Ff-finish . . . i-it, P-p-p-pum . . ."

He draws in breath as the hammer lifts. "Was blind . . . but now . . . I see . . . ."

Tink.

ELECTRIC JESUS
AND THE
LIVING DEAD

JEREMY ZOSS

S TARING AT THE SOFT BLUE glow of Electric Jesus, Lawrence Schwarzenbach wondered how much longer he had to live. The windows and doors of his small house were all boarded up and barricaded, but he knew that the living dead would smash through those defenses eventually. He could hear them banging on the walls, scratching at the windows with their ragged fingernails. They moaned, and chewed at the siding. It wouldn't be long until they found a way in.

Three days ago, zombies were one of the few problems Lawrence didn't have. Now, none of his other troubles even mattered. He would gladly trade his zombie problem for all the previous crises in his lonely teenage life. An acne-scarred, overweight sixteen-year-old, he spent most of his time alone in his room, listening to bad metal music and thumbing through *Hustler*. When he tired of staring at the airbrushed, silicon-enhanced beauties and touching himself, he moved his two hundred pound frame over to his computer desk and focused on his collection of ultra-violent video games. He'd sit for hours, the pale blue light of his monitor washing over his pasty complexion and reflecting off his short, greasy hair as he blasted computerized foes into oblivion.

Now, with a horde of the living dead trying to pound their way into the shabby one-story house he shared with his mother, Lawrence wished he could smite his real-life foes as easily. Yet, he had none of the elaborate weaponry his digital counterparts carried. He had nothing special to strike out with, nothing special to protect him. The only object that offered him any hope at all was Electric Jesus.

Electric Jesus was his mother's favorite knickknack. He stood on top of their ancient console television, radiating a gentle blue light. His foot-tall, plastic-molded form froze Him in a welcoming pose, arms against His tawny brown robes and outstretched, palms upward. His head tilted slightly to His right, and a gentle smile brightened His face. Where the front and back plastic pieces met and formed a seam, a series of small slots allowed light to escape from within—a soft azure glow that emanated from the single neon-blue lightbulb housed inside the plastic Savior.

Lawrence had seen his mother praying to Electric Jesus many times since she first brought Him home from the flea market, years ago. She would get down on her knees, her elephantine belly resting on her thick thighs, and beg for Jesus to help her with her Godless son. Now Lawrence imitated the posture that he had secretly mocked for so long, hoping the statue could provide—something. Anything. He was desperate, and ready to admit it.

He buried his knees deep in the brown shag carpet in front of the TV, the drone of the automated radar weather map seeping from the tinny speakers. He folded his hands together and, with a stained, black Cradle of Filth T-shirt pulled tight across his large belly, Lawrence lifted his voice to heaven.

"Lord," Lawrence said, "I know I never go to church or read the Bible or anything, but I could really use your help. I know I told Mom that I didn't even believe in you, but I always sorta did, and I don't really know what else to do. There are zombies outside, and they're trying to get in. And my Mom went out to the store three days ago, and she hasn't come back. I'm afraid they got her."

Lawrence stared at Electric Jesus, waiting for a sign. Tears welled up in his eyes and rolled down his round cheeks.

"Help me, Lord," Lawrence begged, voice wavering. "I ran out of food two days ago. The phones are dead, and the TV and the radio don't have anything on except static and the Weather Channel. I took all the furniture and used it to seal off the doors and the windows, but they're going to get in!"

"And just what do you expect me to do about it?" Lawrence heard a smooth, silky voice say, and he practically fell on his ass.

"Jesus!" Lawrence exclaimed.

"That's my name, tubby, don't wear it out," the voice called back. Lawrence got up off the floor, waddled over to the TV, and stared at the glowing blue figure.

"You can talk?" he asked incredulously, wiping his eyes on the back of his hand.

"I am the son of God, genius," Electric Jesus answered.

"But you're plastic," Lawrence stammered. "You aren't *the* Jesus, are you?"

"You tell me, porky," the voice said, seemingly from somewhere inside the statue, since the lips didn't move.

Lawrence frowned at the figure. "I didn't think Jesus would be so mean."

"Yeah, and I didn't think the next person I appeared to would have every Cannibal Corpse album," Electric Jesus answered.

"Hey!" Lawrence yelled. "I prayed to you for help, and you aren't doing anything but calling me names!"

"You called me, I came. What more do you want?"

"I want some help, goddammit!"

"Watch the blasphemy, piglet."

Lawrence grabbed the plastic statue from atop the TV. Electric Jesus's long cord jerked from the wall and his blue light went dead. The set's console shook and a framed picture on top tumbled to the floor.

"I could smash you to pieces, you know," Lawrence said.

"Who's gonna help you then?" Electric Jesus asked.

"Some help you've been so far."

"Okay," Electric Jesus said. "Make you a deal. Plug me back in, and I'll see what we can do."

"Deal," Lawrence said, and set the statue back down on to the TV. He took the cord and reached down behind the console, plugging Jesus back into the outlet. Electric Jesus's ghostly blue aura returned immediately.

"Aaaaaah. Thanks, kid," Electric Jesus said. "I do love the juice. Have a seat."

Lawrence plopped himself down, cross-legged, in front of the TV just as he had done so many times before. He stared up at Electric Jesus, awaiting instructions.

"So do you need electricity?" Lawrence asked. "'Cause you kept talking when you were unplugged,"

"Naw, I don't really need the juice," Electric Jesus said. "It just . . . relaxes me."

"Well, I don't want you to be *relaxed*!" Lawrence struggled to rise, reaching toward the cord again as he rolled to his protesting knees. "I want you to be alert, 'cause—"

"No!" Electric Jesus shouted. "Don't you unplug me again!"

"You do need it, don't you?" Lawrence asked, shaking his head. "You're not really Jesus. You're . . . something else."

"I don't need it," Electric Jesus protested. "I can quit anytime I want. But it helps me think, so just leave my cord alone!"

"Whatever," Lawrence grumbled.

"And I am really Jesus."

"Fine. Whatever you say."

"All right then. So, what did you say your name was, kid?" Electric Jesus asked.

"Lawrence."

"Hi, Larry. I'm Electric Jesus. Can I call you Larry?"

"I don't really like that much. The kids at school always call me Larry, even though I ask them—"

"That's just swell, Larry," Electric Jesus interrupted. "You got bigger problems right now than what kids call you at school, am I right?"

"Yeah, I guess so."

"Well, Larry, what's going on? What's the situation? Where are we?"

"You're Jesus. Don't you know?"

"Hey, I just got here. Fill me in."

"OK, here's what's going on," Lawrence said, wiping his sweaty palms on his chest. "A few days ago, I was sitting in my room playing video games, and my Mom comes in and says that we were all out of food, so she was gonna go down the street to the store to get some donuts. I told her to get me some jelly ones and I went back to playing my game. A few hours went by, and I noticed she wasn't back yet. So I went and looked outside, and I noticed that there wasn't a single person around. I thought it was weird, but no big deal. So I came inside and turned on the TV."

"I'm gonna guess that you do that a lot," Electric Jesus snorted.

Lawrence ignored the comment and resumed his story. "Every channel had on a news report about how people were being attacked by maniacs, and everyone should stay inside. I figured my Mom might be holed up at the store, so I got out the phone book and called. Nobody answered. I waited and tried again. More than once. No answer, and she never came back."

Lawrence's story was interrupted by a loud crash from outside. He froze, and waited for some further indication of the zombie hoard's status. After a few moments of relative calm, he continued.

"So, the next day, I turned on the news again. This time, all the different stations were saying that the maniacs were actually zombies, that dead people were coming back to life and attacking the living."

"Hmm. People coming back from the grave," Electric Jesus mumbled. "Never heard of that one happening before."

"Huh?" Lawrence asked.

"Oh, nothing. Continue with your fascinating story."

"All right. So on TV they were saying people were coming back to life. I wouldn't have really believed it, except they had footage of these dead people walking around. They looked just like they did in all the zombie movies I've seen. They moved around all slow, and looked all rotted and gross. But they looked real. A few hours later, a couple of the channels went dead, so did the phones. I got real scared, and so I started to board up the windows. While I was nailing a shelf to the big window that looks out over the street, I saw my first zombie close up. He was some old guy who used to live up the street. He was all yellow looking. His eyes were really black, and he wandered around like he was lost, dragging one leg behind him. I saw him, and I knew he was one of them. I boarded up the window before he could see me."

"You sure he wasn't just some guy whacked out on crack?" Electric Jesus asked.

"I doubt it. When I was boarding up the rest of the windows, I saw more and more of them. They started to gather into groups and now they're moving around together, like a pack of animals. I got the whole house sealed off, and even planned an escape route. If they get in, I'll run through the door to the garage and get into my Mom's car. Hopefully, the automatic garage door opener still works, and I'll back out and drive away." Lawrence bowed his head and muttered into the shag, "Too bad I don't know where I'll go."

"Where are we now?"

"Las Vegas," Lawrence said.

"Great," Electric Jesus groaned. "I'm in the one place on the planet where a zombie infestation is an improvement."

"It's not that bad," Lawrence offered weakly.

"Yeah, and crucifixion is just a little uncomfortable."

"Can I get back to my story now?" Lawrence asked, furrowing his brow.

"Whatever works for you, pal," Electric Jesus said, though not at all facetiously. If Lawrence hadn't been so preoccupied, he might have caught the significance of that.

"Now, where were we?" the young man mused, a bit pompously; it wasn't every day he had Jesus for an audience. "Oh, yeah. So today the zombies started crowding around the house, trying to get in—you can still hear them pounding on the walls—but I didn't know what to do. I mean, I don't have a gun or anything. And none of the TV stations except for the Weather Channel were coming in, and for some reason they aren't even saying anything about the zombies. So I prayed. Just like Mom would have done."

"And this is where I come in," said Electric Jesus brightly.

"Yeah. So are you gonna help me or not?"

"I guess I'll try—although I'm not all that happy about it," Electric Jesus grumbled.

"Why?" Larry snapped, fat face red with anger. "Aren't I good enough to help?"

"Well, your Mom prayed to me a lot, and she always asked for me to help you find religion. There are a lot of people out there that need my help, Larry. People who go to church. You didn't even believe in me until this whole zombie thing started, but you want me to ignore all my faithful flock and help you?"

Lawrence looked down at his stumpy fingers as he picked absently at the fraying shag of the carpet. "Then why did you come here?"

"Because I promised your Mom I would," Electric Jesus sighed. "You might have had your problems with her, but she was a good Christian woman at heart, and only wanted the best for you."

"Yeah, well then why did she leave me here at home with nothing but Twinkies to eat so many times, huh?" Lawrence asked, looking up at the statue. "How come she let me get so fat? How come I turned out to be such a loser, if she's such a great Mom?"

"I didn't say she was mother of the year, or anything," Electric Jesus said. "But she did love you."

"Well, I don't love her," Lawrence hissed.

"Honor thy Father and Mother, Larry," Electric Jesus scolded. "Besides, you said you were worried when she never came home from the store."

"Shut up," Lawrence said, wiping his nose on his bare arm. "I don't want to talk about this. Like you said, I have other things to worry about."

"Yeah, you do," Electric Jesus said. "Hear that?"

The pounding outside the house was growing louder.

"So what should we do?"

Electric Jesus yawned. "I don't have a clue."

"What?" Lawrence yelped, on his feet faster than he—or anyone else—would have though possible. "You said you'd help me!"

"Before we go on with this, Larry," Electric Jesus said calmly, "you really should think for a moment about the conversation you're having. Have you considered the possibility that you are hallucinating right now?"

"You mean . . . you're not really talking to me?"

"You tell me. You said yourself that you have no food left. I can't imagine you've been sleeping well. You're scared and freaked out. . . . Your mind may be playing tricks on you."

Lawrence slouched as a fresh wave of despair washed over him. "So . . . you're not real."

"Does it really matter?"

The quick, calm answer made Lawrence square his shoulders again, as much as they ever were squared, anyway. "I guess it doesn't matter." A sly smile went creeping across his face. "In fact, that would explain why you were such a prick. The real Jesus wouldn't act like that."

"If I am a hallucination, then everything I'm saying comes from you. Low self-esteem, Larry?"

"Any reason I should have *high* self-esteem? Look at me!" Larry tilted his head down toward his protruding belly.

"Well, you survived this long. That's more than a lot of people have done."

"That's true," he admitted. "I guess I have that going for me."

"Right on, big boy!" Electric Jesus exclaimed.

"So what should we do?" Lawrence asked.

"Well, partner," Electric Jesus said. "I think we should amscray on out of here. You must smell like a pig sweating gravy to those things out there. And let's face it, there's a lot of you to go around. As soon as they break in, you're a full-course Thanksgiving dinner"

"Where should we go?"

"Anywhere but here. We'll go find us some nice gals and repopulate the world."

"Even if I was the last guy on earth, I doubt I could score."

"There's that self-esteem issue again," chided Electric Jesus, this time more kindly. "But let's focus on the problem at hand. How does one survive an attack by the living dead when your only ally is a talking statue?"

"I was hoping you'd have an answer for that question," Lawrence said.

"Never fear. We'll figure something out. Now let's—"

A loud, nearby crash interrupted Electric Jesus. At the sound, Lawrence turned a shade paler and his eyes widened. "It's them!" he exclaimed. "They're going to get in!"

"They smell bacon, piglet," Electric Jesus said.

"Shut up and help me!" Lawrence yelled.

A second crash followed the first. The sound of wood groaning rolled in from one of the bedrooms.

"What do you want me to do? I'm plugged into the wall here!"

"Do something!"

"Abracadabra," Electric Jesus bellowed, "zombies go away!"

Yet the pounding continued. The sound of glass shattering filled the air, followed by the crack of splintering wood.

"They're coming through the kitchen window!" Lawrence shrieked.

"Time to get out of here, Larry," Electric Jesus said. As if to prove his point, there was a dull thud in the kitchen, followed by a series of hungry moans.

"One of them is inside!" Lawrence said, trembling at the shadow moving closer to the kitchen door.

"You gotta make your way to the garage, Larry," Electric Jesus said. "You got the car keys?"

"Y-Yeah," Lawrence stammered as he patted his pockets. "I got 'em, but where will I go?"

"I don't know, but you'd better decide quick," Electric Jesus said. "Look."

Lawrence turned to see a rotten-looking thing shamble into the TV room. Its head was cocked to one side and it held a limp left hand close to its chest. The creature's dark eyes widened as soon as they took in Lawrence, and it staggered toward him, moaning.

Lawrence backpedaled until his butt pressed against the old TV. The zombie continued forward, and soon was upon him. The young man screamed as the zombie's clammy hands pawed at him. The dead man leaned in, jaws working furiously, trying to take a chunk out of the fat face before it. Lawrence jammed his forearm across the zombie's neck to hold it off. The creature snapped at the air in front of Lawrence's nose, and the hot smell of rotting meat escaped from its throat.

"Hit it with something!" Electric Jesus shouted.

Lawrence's left hand shot out behind him and groped at the top of the television. As soon as he connected with an object, he grabbed it and pulled it to him.

He raised Electric Jesus high above his head and brought Him crashing down on the zombie's skull. The statue's hand pierced the dead man's head and stuck. Electric Jesus let out a disgusted cry. The zombie moaned louder as Lawrence pulled the statute free and clubbed the creature again. It groaned and released its grip, falling to its knees. As the creature kneeled before him, Lawrence battered it with Electric Jesus until its skull opened wide, spilling the dark mess inside onto the dingy brown carpet.

The zombie had no sooner hit the floor than Lawrence shot out off the room, Electric Jesus still in hand. As fast as his thick legs could carry him, he ran down the hallway toward the garage. He hustled through the door and slammed it behind him. His mother's car was waiting for him as he had planned. The huge, early-eighties Oldsmobile seemed like a steel savior, come to take Lawrence away from the swarming dead.

"Think you could find the time to wipe the zombie brains off my face?" Electric Jesus said.

"Once we're on the road." Lawrence replied as he opened the driver's side door and got behind the wheel. He flung Electric Jesus on the seat next to him and started the car.

"Got your driver's license, Larry?" Electric Jesus asked.

"Does it matter?" Lawrence hit the electric garage door opener clipped to the sun visor.

"I guess not," Electric Jesus sighed.

The garage door opened and Lawrence began backing out the mammoth car. As he rolled down the driveway, Lawrence saw the swarm of zombies clawing and pounding their way into his house. Somehow they hadn't noticed the huge Oldsmobile pulling slowly away.

"Seatbelts save lives," Electric Jesus noted, and Lawrence dutifully pulled his shoulder strap across his round belly and clicked it in place.

"I meant me," said Electric Jesus.

Lawrence set Him upright on the seat and pulled the lap belt tight across His plastic torso.

"And plug me into the cigarette lighter while you're at it," Electric Jesus added.

"God, you are the pickiest talking statue I ever met," Lawrence grumbled as he attempted to fit the power cord into the socket. The prongs of the cord scraped along the inside of the metal cylinder, but kept slipping out. He gave up trying and angled the car onto the street. Electric Jesus mumbled something in disgust, but Lawrence ignored him.

"Goodbye, Mom," he whispered as he shifted into drive.

"If it wasn't for her, you wouldn't have this car," Electric Jesus said. "Or me." Lawrence nodded solemnly. "So where are we going, Larry?"

"Anywhere but here."

"Then let's get this wagon rolling!"

The car crept down the road in the direction of the setting sun. As they made their way cautiously down the street, Lawrence took in the overturned cars and ransacked houses that had once been his neighborhood.

"I bet this street has seen better days," Electric Jesus commented as the car rolled past a fire hydrant spewing water into the air.

"Yeah," Lawrence said as he brought the car up to speed. "You know, I've never been outside of this town. Too bad it took something like this to get me out."

"Think of it as an important turning point in your life," Electric Jesus offered.

"I think that's the first helpful thing you've said," Lawrence smirked.

"Well, don't get all mushy on me," Electric Jesus scoffed. "We don't exactly have time for male bonding. We still need a place to go."

"The Weather Channel was still broadcasting," Lawrence said. "We'll find out where they're at, and head that way."

"Nice to see you take charge here, Larry," Electric Jesus said. "So, why do you think they're still on the air?"

"I don't know. I'm hoping the zombies haven't gotten that far yet. I mean, they can't be everywhere yet."

"Yeah, I'm really tired of this Lazarus crap. Coming back to life used to be something special. These days, it seems like everybody's doing it."

Lawrence smiled. "But you did it before it was popular."

"Was that a joke?" Electric Jesus asked. "Good one, Larry. I'm glad to see you can get your mind off all this."

"Thanks, but call me Lawrence."

"You got it, pardner," Electric Jesus said as Lawrence guided the car around an overturned Jeep in the middle of the road.

Finally confident that he was at last far enough away from the house that the zombies wouldn't hear the engine revving, Lawrence put his sneaker-clad foot to the floor. He headed toward the highway entrance and away from the only home he had ever known.

"What do you think is out there, Lawrence?" Electric Jesus asked solemnly.

"I don't know," Lawrence said. "Let's find out."

LAST RESORT

MICHAEL LAIMO

THE DESERT NEVER SEEMED SO alive. Nothing had ever been so hard as leaving it all behind.

Jack peered over at Bryan, the boy's face anemic under the bite of the late afternoon sun, harsh rays blaring through the windshield. The nine-year-old stared back at his father for the briefest moment, then set his empty sights back across the shimmering asphalt of I-75. His blistered lips gently parted as though to say something, but nothing came forth. Silence. Jack knew better than to get his hopes up by now.

The sign for Las Vegas Boulevard came into view and Jack took the mini-van across the unmarked drift of sand hiding the road. The wheels kicked up clouds of dust as if cloaking their entrance; the stuff blanketed the cracked windshield. He turned on the wipers, chasing away only minimal amounts of sand, just as the wheels skidded harshly into a deeper drift. The mini-van fishtailed toward the side of the road, and for a moment Jack thought it might get stuck, but it snagged something solid and cleared the obstruction. At the end of the off-ramp, he looked up and saw the once-famous Las Vegas Strip, its two-mile stretch of hotels never looking more dead. No lights. No sounds. No movement. A harsh contrast to the shimmering desert plains behind.

"What do you think?" he asked Bryan. Getting an answer from his son was as much a long shot as finding a working slot machine, one no less willing to pay out. He put a hand on Bryan's shoulder; the boy flinched, eyes straight ahead, the sweat long dried up from his emaciated frame. "You think we'll find anything here?"

Bryan stared straight ahead, unanswering.

Jack turned the steering wheel, started down Las Vegas Boulevard. "Let's find out, shall we?"

A minute later they passed the familiar diamond-shaped *Welcome To Las Vegas* sign that for years had ushered in hundreds of millions of thrill-seekers to their preferred places of contribution. It stood barely recognizable, like a rotting scarecrow, half its letters circling the base of the steel post in crumbled pieces. To the left Mandalay Bay towered silently into the gray sky, a giant now set in dead stone by the darkest of all Medusas. Lifeless taxis and cars crowded the entrance, spilling mummified bodies from unshut doors and broken windows. Having never visited Vegas at its zenith, Jack could only fantasize at the gaiety and excitement that had once thrived here. The photos he'd seen, the movies, the paintings—it'd all looked as though a grand celebration were taking place. Fourth of July, but even bigger and better and more stimulating than one could ever fathom. Now it looked mournfully unremembered, as dazed and as desperate as the two of them might've appeared, if anyone had been around to see them: wounded, straying into town, stomachs crying for food, eyes in search of shelter, minds in search of solace.

Ahead, the Strip was clogged with hundreds of abandoned vehicles, some inverted, some piled three high. Slowly Jack turned left onto Paris Avenue. "Might as well find some food first," he told Bryan, staring at the road ahead and knowing quite well it didn't matter which path he took, what choices he made for them.

Winding around a number of wind-stripped cars, Jack chanced another look at his son. The boy's body trembled, near seizure, fingers clawing his chest, eyes looking through the side window at the atrophied bodies in the road and weird brown weeds growing out of those corpses not covered in sand. *Lucky me*, Jack thought, keeping his attention ahead. This stretch of road lead, virtually unobstructed, all the way to Paradise Avenue. He turned left past the shattered ruins of the Hard Rock Cafe.

Ahead a number of smaller motels flanked the sidewalk, the remnants of cars and taxis stripped, useless, at the curbs. Farther down, a few small stores lay deteriorating like defeated soldiers hurled aside in the heat of battle, their corpses picked at by vultures who themselves had no time to savor their winnings before also being devoured. Other local businesses—a drug store, a deli—were boarded over, the wood splintered in places to reveal a terrifying blackness within their husks.

To the left Jack saw a diner, its wrap-around front window fully destroyed. A sign hanging from a rusted post out front whipped about in the wind, the bitter shrill of its rusty hinges shooting across the lifeless street like the wail of a starving cat. He pulled off Paradise into the lot of the small eatery, sheets of sand thrashing Bryan's closed window. A white Buick LeSabre sat alongside the convenience store next door, its owner long gone and forgotten, perhaps rotting beside the video poker game he'd come to play.

The wind picked up again, sand billowing on all sides of the mini-van in more driven whirls. Instantaneously the sun dipped behind the soaring hotels, the cold of night racing in to spread its darkness over Jack's thin grip on faith, like massive, tenebrous wings.

Jack set the van in park and got out, walked around the front of the vehicle to Bryan's window. The boy pressed quick-bitten fingers against the glass, eyes dried of tears cast somewhere beyond Jack's presence. Absent of desire.

"I'll be back, kiddo. I'm just gonna check and see if there's any food, okay?"

Bryan panicked, hoarse voice wailing over a dry, swollen tongue, through yellow teeth. His eyes bulged, hands pounding the window then searching for the door handle that wasn't there. Jack slid open the side panel of the mini-van, removed a shotgun and pistol from the back seat. He checked to make sure they'd both been loaded, then reached over to the front seat, ribs jutting against the tattered cloth interior, and handed Bryan the pistol. The boy quieted.

"You won't need this . . . but take it just in case."

Jack shouldered the rifle, closed the side door, then stepped toward the diner. The winds surged, stronger somehow in the sun's absence. Sand battered his face, a hot sheet bringing pain, nearly blinding him. He squeezed his eyes shut and wiped away granules drawn to the moisture of his tears. Wrapping his arms around his head, he tackled the three sand-buried steps to the entrance of the diner and went inside.

The counter, stools, booths were wrecked, the glass displays smashed, dishes and utensils strewn everywhere. Stepping over a fallen stool, he peered behind the splintered counter-top. The empty eye sockets of a uniformed waitress stared back at him from the floor. The flesh had been eaten clean from her bones, only patches of mold-buried muscle and tendon remaining on her arms and legs. For a moment Jack imagined he saw something wriggling down there, something beneath the tatters of her uniform near the hollow of her stomach—something bigger than any insect he could name.

He pulled back, at once assuring himself that it was just a shadow . . . just a shadow . . . just a shadow cast by the setting sun through a shard of glass still in the storefront window frame. Jack turned away, a writhing feeling in his stomach reminding him of the thing's latent presence, promising him that it knew he was nearby . . . that it *smelled* him, wanted him. That he had much more to offer than its present host.

Swallowing a dry lump, he stepped back to the front of the diner and peered outside toward the mini-van. Bryan, still in the front seat, stared back at him, white fingertips pressed against the window. Jack's thoughts were torturesome, tears moistening his dry eyes, his once-beautiful Little-Leaguer now a poor nine-year-old pushing forty. The remnants of his mother's features had long vanished, resigned to two years of torment, of suffering, of pain. Jack held up an index finger, mouthed *I'll be right there.*

The boy stared, unanswering.

Jack turned and entered the kitchen.

The place was destroyed, glass and garbage everywhere. He pulled a cigarette lighter from his pocket, kept it in hand; he would need it soon, as only one small window in the rear provided light. Pans, empty cans, dishes littered the floor, doors ripped free from ovens, an open freezer revealing a barren interior. A microwave lay shattered on the tiles near the sink. Shelves, emptied of all canned goods. Everything coated in sand.

Again Jack wondered if Las Vegas could be *the* town harboring individuals who'd outlasted the scourge. After thirteen days out from their former sanctuary, Jack had seen no signs of life. Nothing in Dallas, nothing in Phoenix and all the small towns in between. Dead or alive.

After Phoenix, he had decided that here, in this city of sin, people of great importance—those who'd held high seats in the social stature court—might gather. Las Vegas would draw those who retained the influence to put them in touch with the select crowd, the ones collaborating to create shelter, the *smart* people who had known where to hide when it all ended.

Jack peeked out the kitchen door, across the counter and beyond the empty window frame. Bryan's fingers moved from the window to his mouth, jagged nails driven to the spaces between his rotting teeth. Jack wondered, *What could be easier than taking the gun, putting Bryan out of his misery, then doing the same for myself? A single, clean shot to the temporal lobe, ensuring paralysis of after-death brain activity. But would it definitely work?*

He'd seen corpses rise up with their heads nearly lopped off, half-moon craters leaving just a single eye for sight, a gaping void where the lower jaw once existed—signs of unsuccessful suicide attempts. Such creatures had walked the land for nearly two years, spreading disease, famine, their numbers increasing too fast for those humans still alive to make heads or tails of the plague. The risen dead fed on living flesh, an instinctual response triggered deep in the still-active subconscious mind, eating eating eating until there were no more *living* human beings left to eat. All the animals, too—the dogs, cats, birds, perhaps even the fish, though Jack hadn't yet an opportunity to test the waters.

The corpses returned to death through the ravages of starvation, cannibalism, ultimately becoming subject to myriad insect-borne diseases. With everyone and everything dead—people, animals—the swarming carcasses could no longer nurture their sparked intuitions and suddenly ceased to walk, as if some higher authority had pulled the plug.

What if Bryan and I die, Jack pondered, *only to return to the same unyielding quest for nourishment?*

Jack sifted through a foot-high drift of sand. Found an unopened can of beets. He used his hunting knife to strip the lid, speared three juicy purple disks, and sucked them down. They were hot, sour. He searched on, found nothing of value but considered taking a handful of green fuzzy things that might have once been potatoes. He ate half the can of beets, then exited the diner, leaving the green things behind.

He smiled halfheartedly at his son as he approached the van. Bryan pressed a palm against the window, face looking weird, doll-like: drawn without emotion. Jack slid the side door open, placed the shotgun on the seat, then reached over and handed Bryan the beets. He watched as the boy plucked them with his soiled fingers, opening his mouth just enough to put them in. Jack closed the door from the inside and climbed over into the front seat. Bryan's cracked lips had beet juice all over them. Jack couldn't help but think how much it looked like blood, how the boy looked more dead than alive.

How easy would it be to simply end the suffering with a pull of a trigger?

He started the car, noting the need for fuel. Before driving away he looked over at Bryan and the gun nestled between the boy's delicate thighs. Bryan sipped beet juice, then offered the can back to his father. Jack downed the rest in one gulp as he took the car across Sands Avenue, back toward Las Vegas Boulevard.

The night was dark, thirsting for Jack, Sharon, and Bryan, as the family of three went about their evening, unaware of the unconventional circumstances taking place around them. Not an hour prior, every dead and not yet buried thing—man and animal alike—had animated and at once taken pursuit of warm flesh for consumption. Dead people ate living dogs; dead dogs ate living people. No prejudices existed. If it was dead, it wanted to eat you: man, woman, child, animal.

Jack owned three twenty-four hour convenience stores. Sharon picked up Bryan from Little League, met Jack at six as he made the rounds collecting the day's receipts. The first stop proved to show no great day of business, the take nearly half the usual amount. The second stop, his largest store, was unattended, the on-duty clerk having seemingly made himself off-duty. Jack checked the schedule. David was written in for the five-to-ten shift. Damn, the new guy. "David?" he called.

And then he saw: a young woman rising up from behind the counter, blood and gristle covering her face. Sharon screamed; Bryan's jaw clenched in shock; Jack tried to yell, but couldn't understand the unconscionable events taking place in his store. The girl held up what must have been David's arm, jammed it to her mouth, savaging the bicep with her teeth. The fear-hesitation succumbed to mortal terror and Jack, Bryan, and Sharon began screaming, unable to tear their sights away from the flesh-chewing woman in front of them, the woman who reached down and ripped something else free from the unseen body, something wet and gut-wrenching, then rose back up with steaming organs slipping through her fingers, slapping the floor, the meager pieces in her grasp finding their way toward the enthusiastic gnaw of her teeth.

Jack picked up his son, Sharon frantically grasping the sweat-soaked polyester of the boy's baseball jersey, stumbling over her husband's feet as they careened outside, away from the horror inside. The door of the mini-mart slammed shut behind them, leaving them abask in the moonglow of the night. The living dead awaited them in the parking lot, more than twenty bodies staggering aimlessly about, moaning incoherently in response to the three-some's hysterical cries. Then the dead were suddenly running after them, arms outstretched, mouths gaping, tongues lolling, the whites of their eyes moving in instinctual jerks like moths fluttering about a bright light.

The family screamed uncontrollably. They returned inside the store, Jack locking the door, one then two then suddenly ten or more ashen people slapping the glass-front, staring in, banging aimlessly into each other like eager piranha eyeing a meal on the non-water side of the fishtank. Heavy breathing and crying filled the store, pounding hearts pressuring their ears. They stood there, Jack, Sharon, Bryan, all of them staring in awe at the clawing cluster of insane people pressing their wounded, colorless faces against the glass.

A scream filled the air. Sharon's terrified voice wrenched Jack's soul just as surely as the sight of the flesh-eating woman tearing a hunk from his wife's trapezoid with a swift lock of the jaws. The most influential woman of their lives fell to the floor in unfathomable pain, her shoulder gushing blood in mad spurts as the flesh-eating woman chewed her prize, gazing at Jack and Bryan. She then dropped the half-eaten lump and came for them, mouth gaping, arms outstretched, suddenly eager to collect more warm flesh.

Jack grabbed Bryan and carried him down the aisle to the coolers that stocked beer and milk and soft drinks. He released his son, then grabbed a can of insect repellent and sprayed it at the oncoming ghoul, all the while retrieving a cigarette lighter from his pocket. He flicked it, the flame emerged, and he raised it to meet the spray of the repellent. Flames shot out, four, five feet, and then more as the woman caught fire, howling as if rats were stuck in her throat. Arms flailing wildly, her blazing body knocked into the counter and sent blistering candies to the floor in a shower of color.

Jack screamed for Sharon, she limping beside Bryan as he helped her into the back room. They locked the door behind them, went down into the basement, locked that door behind them, at last falling together into a familial heap at the center of the room, crying, trembling, wondering what would happen next.

Unlike the fronts for Treasure Island or The Stardust, the canopied approach to The Mirage allowed for the mini-van to pass right through.

"Come with me," said Jack, stopping behind a stripped taxicab.

Bryan's eyes still had clouds in them, Jack noted, but it felt good to see him moving. Jack reached into the back seat, grabbed the rifle; Bryan brought the pistol he held in his lap. They stepped over bones and mummified bodies, the green felt mat with the white Mirage script out front rotting and stained with blood. The glass doors at the entrance were shattered, the shards still scattered across the marble flooring inside. Shriveled bodies lay everywhere, many missing limbs. The trees inside lived on, the branches growing above and beyond the smashed greenhouse dome. The huge fishtank behind the check-in desk remained intact, the water long evaporated, the fish turned to bone. The slot machines and gaming tables were utterly destroyed, casualties of war.

"We go to the top floor," Jack said. "That's where the important people would've gone."

They found the steps and climbed and climbed and climbed, taking breaks every three or four floors to catch their breath. On the twenty-first floor they rested longer, and Jack used this time to think of Sharon and their time in the basement of the mini-mart, his mind's-eye watching her get sicker and sicker as the wound in her shoulder festered, spread its unstoppable infection; how she stopped eating and how he and Bryan had to tie her to the pipes so she wouldn't hurt them. For she'd lost all recollection of who she was, had become an animal with no thoughts, only instincts, instincts that offered no help to her as she grew weaker and weaker, until she could no longer breath. Her body had withered to a fraction of what it once was.

Jack tried to shake away the bubbling memories, didn't want to but could not help but recollect what happened a few minutes later, when Sharon came back to life with the desire to eat suddenly upon her again. How they sat there watching her moan and wail and reach for them, how she gnawed through her own limbs like a captured shrew, intent on devouring her husband and son.

He also didn't want to remember how he had used a baseball bat to beat her head into a bloody pulp, smashed it until only her body remained, twitching for hours as the unlife seeped from it and finally released its uncanny grasp. How they stared at her body for days, then bagged it and put it on the highest shelf in the stockroom, away from the cans of food that lasted them nearly two years.

On the thirtieth floor, it appeared the entrance had been barricaded at one time, shafts of splintered wood just beyond the ajar door. Nails jutted from the jamb like thorns, hundreds seemingly inefficient in their commitment to restrain the enemy. Just beyond the entrance, Jack saw withered bodies, those full of limb and riddled with ancient gunfire. The gruesome stench here intensified, even after the whole world had gone to rot and it seemed impossible for anything more offensive to assault his nose. Father and son managed to squeeze through the available space—just as the flesh-eaters had done years ago. Dozens of motionless bodies lay twisted throughout the lengthy corridor, skin like leather taut against crumbling bones and shattered skulls.

"This way," Jack said, pointing to the left. He eyed a massive doorway at the end of the hall, a suite once fit for presidents and kings. "What do you think?"

Bryan nodded.

"Hello!" Jack called, knowing that if people were still alive here, they might assume them to be the enemy and shoot them just as they had the flesh-eaters.

They climbed over and around the head-wrecked corpses, some piled three high, unmoved since meeting their second fates. At the door. Jack tried the knob. Locked. He knocked. "Hello! Is there anybody here?"

Silence. At first. Then, a faint, painful cry.

"Stand back." Jack placed a hand on Bryan's chest. The boy staggered back, staring at the door. Jack raised the rifle and blew away the lock, making a head-sized hole. The door inched open. In a cautious way, Jack pressed his fingers on the warm door and pushed forward, slowly revealing the suite's interior.

At first he saw nothing, a room stripped of furniture, a shattered floor-to-ceiling window with tattered curtains billowing in a strong, whistling breeze, gray dusk-light seeping through and illuminating the room in wavering strips. Metal shelves lining the walls held a handful of empty cans and jars, remnants of a food supply long exhausted.

The soft cry he heard moments earlier had gained strength and volume with no door to block its reach. Once a whimper, it had become a moan rife with anguish. With hunger.

Its source appeared.

On all fours, an unclothed ghoul, skin green and craggy, crawled in from a doorway leading into another room. Its left eye was a dark, gaping socket from which fresh blood ran down and doused its lower jaw. It tried to stand but failed, both feet worthlessly reduced to shredded stumps and exposed ankle bones.

Thoughts flew through Jack's burned-out mind as if charged with an outside power. *When there's no more food, then everything dies. Even the dead. If this one's still alive, then there must be—must've been—someone alive here to feed it.*

He raised the rifle in a jerk, blew the demon's head away. Bryan didn't so much as flinch. "Let's see if there's anyone here," Jack said as he stepped over the dead thing and peered into the room.

What must have been a master bedroom suite for the rich and famous had become a playground for the devil's work. Perhaps twenty people had hid here two years past, when the dead took over the earth. And here they had remained in their shelter, a place that had once provided adequate sanctuary from the hell thriving thirty floors below, co-existing until their food supply ran out and they starved to death and started coming back to life, first one and then another. The strong killed the reanimated things off and tossed them into the hallway, attracting even more ghouls that blocked their only route to further sustenance, until they could no longer escape, until the dead outnumbered the living and made food out of them. Until only one remained, this last thing that had eaten the warm, dying remnants of the last human beings in this hotel, abandoning the mangled stew of body parts only to investigate the warm *living* human beings who had entered its domain.

"Bryan," Jack said staring at the festering mass before them. "We should try another hotel. What do you say? The MGM?"

Jack turned to face his son.

This time, the nine-year-old answered his father.

He shoved the barrel of the pistol into his mouth and pulled the trigger.

The desert never seemed so alive. Nothing had ever been so hard than leaving it all behind. Jack drove in silence, his blistered lips gently parting as though to say something. Nothing came forth. Jack knew better than to get his hopes up by now.

The sign for Denver, Colorado came into view and Jack took the pick-up across the unmarked drift of soil hiding the road. The wheels kicked up clouds of dust, as though in effort to cloak his entrance.

Once, long ago, he had read about a bomb shelter hidden deep in the mountains of Colorado, a place that would shield those inside from an atomic bomb or nuclear missile.

Surely there would be people there.

He saw the Rocky Mountains in the distance. He prayed to no one in particular with the hope of finding sanctuary there, all the while eyeing the rifle on the seat next to him, promising himself that Denver would be his last resort.

CHARLIE'S HOLE

JESSE BULLINGTON

"**G**ET IN THE GODDAMN HOLE, Private!" Sergeant Reister was bellowing now.

"No, sir," Tosh repeated.

"You miserable piece of panda shit, get in the hole!"

"No, sir."

"I'm giving you to the count of five to get your scrawny ass down there before I put you there permanently, you disrespectful faggot."

"No, sir."

I felt sure Reister was gonna lay him out right there, put a bullet in his head or maybe just beat the life out of him, but no—he just stared at Tosh, loathing emanating from his eyes. All fifteen of us did our best to pretend not to notice the confrontation, but I'm sure everyone there could see the score. Tosh had snapped, and Reister didn't give two shits.

"Five," Reister said levelly. "You are not in the hole, Private."

"I am not going down there, sir," Tosh said, as if Reister hadn't heard right the first nine times.

"Am I to understand you are disobeying a direct order?" Reister now looked perfectly calm—serene, even. His smooth face glowed in the sunlight, giving him the look of a warlord, as opposed to a grimy sergeant.

"That is correct, sir," Tosh said in that monotone voice of his. "I've gone down six holes in the last month. That's every damn hole we've come across, and I'm sick of this shit. I'm no goddamn tunnel-rat, and you know it."

"Do you know what happens if you disobey my direct orders, you yellow turd?" Reister asked real sweetly.

"Court-martial, the brig," Tosh shrugged. "I don't care anymore. Anything to get the hell away from your crazy ass."

"Court-martial?" Reister grinned. "Court-martial's for a trial. Trivial offenses only, my boy. What you're talking about is sedition."

All the chatter stopped right then, and to my horror I saw Collins slinking toward me. Collins is definitely all right, but he usually thinks with his lips instead of his brain. He might've been the best friend I've had here, but his smart mouth had gotten us the worst goddamn post possible: point. And the last thing this situation needed was a heckler. I tried to scoot away, but where could I go?

"Sedition?" Tosh yelled, finally raising his voice. "I didn't say shit about sedition and you know it!"

"Disobeying my direct orders is incitement to rebellion, and I have authority to neutralize a rebellion by any means necessary," Reister said cheerily. "At sea we'd call it mutiny, plain and simple."

At this all the other grunts ceased their chores to watch things play out, and all pretenses were dropped as Reister's hand folded up to grip the handle of his M-16. Some of the fellahs trained their pieces at Tosh. Others leaned forward, puffing their cigarettes. The shit was about to go down.

"Do it, then," Tosh shouted. "Enough of this bullshit!"

"You're going down that hole or you will be one dead dink, I shit you not," Reister spat.

I knew Tosh was gonna bite it right then and there, when Collins leans over to me, never minding the cataclysmic turn events had taken, and opens that goddamn mouth of his.

"Reister's hoping to find a Silver Star down one of these holes," the stupid fuck says as loud as day.

Did I say things were tense before? Shit. I heard a drop of sweat explode louder than a shell as it struck a leaf, and then the silence was broken. *Shattered* would be a better word.

"Fuckin' goddamn hell!" Reister's full attention had swiveled to Collins and me. "You think there's something funny about the way I run my ship, queerbait?"

He advanced on us through his disciples, and stopped ten feet away. I about shit my pants. I thought I was gonna get it, gunned down by my own sergeant. Reister looked back and forth between Collins and me. I was tempted to put my Colt in my mouth and end it all there, but I didn't.

"Eh?" I saw, with a mix of relief and dismay, that Reister was pleased. Immensely pleased. "Laugh it up, butt-buddies, 'cause you're going with him."

He turned back to Tosh, calling, "Now you got someone to hold your hand down there."

"More like his dick!" this big gorilla named Frank says, and all the grunts have a good belly laugh at our expense. Reister beamed at us like we'd just won a new car. I looked to the hole, where Tosh stood.

The mouth of the tunnel gaped at me like an open grave. It was an almost predatory opening, a gap in the floor of the jungle. Roots stuck out of its side, and I felt queasy watchin' Tosh stick his head in there. It didn't look so steep, leisurely arcing down into the earth.

I shook like the coward I was as I descended into my first tunnel, Tosh's boots kicking wet dirt into my mouth. Of all the places to lose my VCTS cherry, it had to be this damn hole? The only good thing was that it hadn't been used in a while; the flip side of this being spiders, centipedes, and worse, all on my ass. All I'd brought was my pistol and canteen, and even then it felt tighter than a nun's ass in there. I even forgot my flashlight, so all I could see were shadows cast on Tosh's butt.

With each foot I wriggled, it got worse and worse, claustrophobic as fuck. I felt like I'd reverted to the me of six month's ago—freshmeat, a pussy. Of course, we all were. Assholes, dickheads, limpdicks, dickbiters, dicksmokers, faggots, queers, girls, bitches, pussies, pukes, chickenshit motherfuckers; any insult you can think of, Reister had called us. I'd always wanted to stick up for Tosh when Reister fucked with him, but how could I? I'd been in here for twenty-three weeks and five days, and I still got teary every time I went on point. A couple of times I'd nearly collapsed with fear in the jungle, so scared I couldn't breathe.

This felt worse. Much, much worse. I had no idea how far we'd gone, wondering if gunfire would come from ahead or behind. Reister, that psychotic bastard. I suddenly hated Tosh for causing the whole mess, and Collins even more. Then I hated myself for being such a pussy.

On we went, into the mud, into the very ass of Vietnam, until Tosh stopped, and I rammed my skull into his boot.

"It's cool," he said. Twisting his waist, he squirmed forward and disappeared from sight.

I could hardly breathe, and I nearly vomited as Tosh helped me out of the tunnel and into the tiny cave ahead.

"Dead end," Tosh whispered, waving his light around the burrow.

It couldn't have been more than a dozen feet across, and maybe six feet wide, but after that tunnel it felt as spacious as any mess hall. Collins's orange head poked out of the hole and we helped him up. Even squatting so our asses brushed the soft earth, my head still raked on the ceiling. It was a goddamn miracle this place hadn't caved in.

"Thank God," Collins panted, spitting dirt and pawing his vest.

"Lucky there weren't any snakes in this one," Tosh said as he leaned back and unscrewed his canteen. "Last one Sergeant sent me down had a goddamn pit viper in it."

My breathing had almost returned to normal, when Collins lights up a joint. I swear, that mother can be a right dick sometimes. I started coughing and turned to go back up the tunnel. I felt spooked, nauseous, cramped, and was more than ready to get topside. Tosh grabbed my boot, though, and turned to Collins.

"Put that shit out before you smoke up all our oxygen," he told Collins, as he passed me his canteen.

After a few more puffs, Collins stamped out his Jay and we all just laid back for a second. It stunk like weed and mold down in that cave, and I turned to leave again.

"What's your hurry?" Tosh asked. "This hole's cool—no other tunnels."

"But Reister," I began.

"Fuck 'em," he said. "He'll just have us stand watch or some shit when we get out. Better off down here with the spiders."

"So, Tosh—" Collins said, but Tosh cut him off.

"Toshiro, man. Toshiro," Tosh grinned. "I hate that 'Tosh' shit."

"So what's with you and Reister?" Collins asked him. "He seems eager to get rid of you."

"Why do you think?" Tosh snapped with sudden intensity. "Because in his book I'm just another slope, not a Japanese-American, not an American at all."

We were all quiet for a second, but then Collins, of course, keeps prodding.

"Jesus, why don't you transfer?"

"Why don't you?" Tosh smiled weakly. "No one gets out of this squad without his okay. I've tried, but he's not down. He wants me dead out here, and that's that."

"Bastard," Collins muttered, and began chewing up the remainder of his joint.

"What's his damage?" I thought aloud.

"Former drill sergeant," Tosh answered. "Got tired of being an asshole back home, needed to come be an asshole over here. Wanted to 'see the shit,' he told us once. 'Need to get some gook blood under my fingernails.' Stupid redneck fuck."

I slipped as my boots shifted in the sloppy dirt, and I toppled backward. I didn't hit the wall very hard, but my shoulder sunk in deep, so deep I had to put my elbow in the wall to push myself up.

"So I'm the only guy who thinks Reister's nuts, at least until you guys showed up," Tosh continued while Collins turned his flashlight on me. "I can't get him court-martialed, and even if I did, I'd get fucked up."

"Oh shit," I managed, as the part of wall I'd hit collapsed, and I pitched onto Collins to avoid falling in.

"Shut up, shut up," Tosh hissed, pointing his pistol and flashlight into the gap I'd busted in the wall. Tosh scooted to it and punched out a few more heaps of clay. Between the two beams of light we could see a second tunnel running alongside the wall. It was a little larger than the first, but not by much.

"Must've been a T-intersection they blocked off," Tosh whispered as he flashed his light down the tunnel in either direction. As he did, we all heard a faint rustling, but it went silent before we could get a bead on which way it had come from.

No one spoke, but a decision was made. There was no point in arguing; we were going down there. Not for Reister; not for the greater glory of the USMC; but for our own lives, worthless though they may be. The noise told us Vincent Charles was close, and we stood a much better chance down here than in his jungle later tonight. Splitting up was our only option. If they got behind us, we were fucked.

Tosh went right, Collins and me went left. We were to meet back at the cave in one hour. That seemed a helluva long time to me, but it was slow going in those tunnels. Collins had the flashlight, so I wiggled after him in the darkness. After a few dozen feet, I managed to get around so I could look behind us, but Tosh's light had already vanished. All I could hear was the wheezing of Collins's lungs and the gurgling in my own sorry guts.

The fear washed back over me, and I started to lag behind. Once I tried to tell Collins to wait up, but he shushed me immediately. I had to stop several times to get my breathing sorted out, and I was sure we must've gone too far. After shaking off the willies for the hundredth time, I noticed Collins had stopped up ahead at an intersection. It was another T, our tunnel dead-ending into it. I scrambled through the tight hole, unable to see anything but the firefly of Collins's flashlight far ahead of me.

I'd calmed down a bit, when my already-strained nerves were snapped by a sudden burst of gunfire somewhere back in the tunnels. Three shots in quick succession, then silence, then the rest of the clip going off. The possibilities were endless, but none of them were good. I cupped my hands to call out to Collins, but paused, unsure if I should disturb the tomblike quiet that had again enveloped the tunnel.

Then I heard the screams. The echoing wails came from back the way we'd come, from Tosh. The shrieking got worse and worse, rising in pitch until it cut off suddenly.

For a while I lay still in the tunnel, feeling dizzy all of a sudden. Then Collins was waving his light in my eyes, and I lost it. I began to kick and claw the walls and ceiling, covering myself in mud.

"Get yer ass over here," Collins called out, his voice booming. "Chill the fuck out!"

Getting myself under control, I moved forward once more. Every few yards I'd have to stop and squirm around to glance back down the passage, even though I couldn't see a damn thing. I was getting close to Collins, a scant twenty-five feet away, when I heard it.

There are no words to describe the horror I felt at hearing that sound. I envied the dead as I heard that noise, and froze in mid-wiggle. It was the unmistakable scraping of someone or something pulling itself up the tunnel.

I groaned, trying to scream but too damn scared to do so. Collins must have heard as well, because he hurled his flashlight at me. It thudded off the floor, bouncing to within my reach. I frantically drew my Colt and turned the light down the tunnel. Its beam splashed over the pockmarked burrow, fading out down the passage.

"Come on, get over here," Collins said, his voice drowning out the scrape-scraping.

Then it hit me, a warm breeze fluttering down the tunnel. A sweet, charnel-house smell rode that draft, the odor of southern fried slope. I thought of a guy I'd hated in my last company, and how he'd smelled after the mortar had done its work and left him to the jungle for a few hours. That same, almost erotic smell of raw meat had hung over the crater his remains were spattered about.

The light revealed nothing but an empty tunnel. Still, I knew something lurked just beyond the beam's reach. The noise grew louder and louder, and the smell became worse and worse. I wanted desperately to crawl up the tunnel to Collins, but stayed rooted in place. Then the noise and stench coagulated into a sight, making substance from shadow at the tip of my beam, and all hell broke loose.

The thing didn't crawl so much as slither, its leathery skin sticking to the clay. I'd seen dead bodies on numerous occasions, and more importantly, I'd smelled them. Even if what came at me out of that pit had a whole face instead of that larvae-infested quilt of rotting skin, even if its chest was intact rather than split open and coated in gore; even then the smell would have been enough for me to know: The thing was dead. A dead gook—moving, for God's sake!

Its left arm ended at the elbow, the flesh worn away to reveal splintered bone and the ragged threads of nerve and muscle. The fingers of its other hand were grated and mangled. Yet they pulled its mutilated body forward. As the thing leered fully into the light, I could make out the brainpan through a crack in its decaying face. It came at me out of the darkness, and I went totally fucking apeshit.

The first few shots sank into the side of the tunnel, but the weeping flesh-blossoms opening on its face and shoulders told me I'd hit it a few times. It stopped, but only momentarily, before lurching forward again. I sobbed and spat, pulling the trigger again and again, even after the clip ran dry. Unable to take my eyes off the crawling corpse, I tried to back up, but my legs wouldn't bend.

I chunked my empty gun at the crawling thing, but it fell short. Before I knew what I was doing, I had thrown the flashlight at it, too. That fell short, too, and worse—the light landed pointing into the wall. Most everything went dark, except for a small patch of tunnel wall lit up by the beam. I couldn't see the thing, but knew it was still there. And when the hand grabbed me by the back of my collar, I thought it had gotten behind me somehow—but it was only Collins, pulling me back up the tunnel by my head and flailing arms.

He probably said something, but I all I could hear was the scrape-scraping. And the smell—oh God, the smell! I stopped thrashing as Collins hauled me backward in short jerks. *Scrape, scrape, scrape.* Inspiration hit me, and I fumbled madly at my vest. Just as Collins backed into one of the cross-passages at the intersection, the thing bumped the flashlight and the beam spun around to spotlight that oozing face. Scraps of wet flesh dangled from its mouth, dribbling blood onto the clay.

Screaming, I yanked the pin from a grenade. Collins was screaming then, too, and I side-armed the explosive at the oncoming horror. I badly wanted to see if it would hit, but Collins punched me in the mouth. Then he was shoving me up a tunnel, grinding his back into my folded knees.

The light came next, so bright I could see miles and miles down the empty tunnel in front of me—hundreds of miles of dirt and clay and light—and then I went black.

I awoke to Collins screaming, and hands clawing at my legs. Whimpering, I kicked at the arms and began to pull myself away up the tunnel. It had got us, and I dared not think what kind of shit we were in. Then Collins stopped screaming, and the hands stopped pawing.

"David," Collins gasped from behind me. "David, it's me, oh fuck, it's me, it's me . . . ."

He sounded far away down the tunnel. I wanted out of this shit, out of this damn grave I'd crawled into. I thought of the smell, and vomited onto myself.

"David," Collins was saying, "Jesus, David, help me. I can't feel my legs. They're gone—my legs, my fuckin' legs."

He began to cry, and in my delirium I crawled up the tunnel, away from the sobbing. The blast had done a number on me, and I paused to try to get a grip on what had happened. *Run*, I thought. *Get out now*. Then I remembered Collins lying fucked up in the dark. Part of me had to keep moving, but just as I resumed my crawling I heard Collins shouting my name. I couldn't leave him.

"David?" Collins whimpered. "Hey, fuckin' say something, man."

"It's me," I mumbled, uncertain how to proceed. I backed up a way, so that I lay awkwardly over Collins and could feel his arms and chest under my legs.

"My lighter," he groaned, and tried to get at his vest, but my knees were in his way. Blind and half deaf, my head grinding into the ceiling, I groped all over his muddy fatigues until I found the bulge of his Zippo. I clumsily pulled it out and squirmed off of him. It took some work, since I was shaking so badly, but I got it lit after a few tries. I fearfully waved it in Collins's direction, and began to laugh. The light was feeble compared to a flashlight, but I could clearly see that Collins lay buried up to his thighs in dirt; the tunnel behind us had caved in on him.

With some work we dug him out, and at finding his feet intact, he began to laugh like it was all some big fucking practical joke. It was miraculous he hadn't broken anything. He seemed a little shook up, but otherwise okay.

"A grenade?" Collins said. "That was fuckin' stupid."

"I'm sorry," I whispered, as those dingy old claws of fear began digging themselves into my heart again, "I'm so sorry. I didn't mean to—oh shit, we are so fucked!"

Collins went silent, and he took his Zippo out of my hands and flicked it closed.

"Turn it on," I begged him.

"No."

"Please, I can't see—I can't—I can't," I stuttered.

"Look," Collins said, his voice a helluva lot sterner than I'd ever heard it before, "we can't get out the way we came. That's obvious."

"But—"

"And if were gonna find another way out, we'll need some light. I don't want to burn the fluid until we really need to see something."

And even though I knew he was right, I couldn't stop shaking.

Buried alive, I kept thinking. *My dumbass had buried us alive. How far to the surface? Were we going up or down? What was that thing? Seriously, what the fuck was it?*

"Let's get going," Collins said, and I was squashed into the mud as he scrambled over me.

My fear didn't leave, but I beat it into submission, and followed Collins. Every time I moved forward, though, I'd sniff the air and perk my ears a bit. For shit's sake, I was scared.

All I could hear was the sound we made as we went, scraping and squishing. Rather than growing used to the dark, my eyes seemed to tint, the blackness appearing to thicken and harden. Several times we rested, our fingers just as raw and aching as our knees were bruised and sore. Once I thought I smelled the stench again, but immediately realized it was only my own stink of piss and puke and sweat. We encountered no adjoining passages, and I began to lose hope.

I had no grenades, no gun, and no flashlight—only a goddamn jackknife. The death I'd sentenced us to would not be quick. I couldn't stop thinking about the creature, and wanted to know what Collins thought about it, but he wasn't in the mood for conversation.

Collins stopped suddenly after God-knows-how-many hours, and I immediately curled up to get some shut-eye. He kicked me, and I was about to tell him to fuck off when I saw it, too: A speck of light glittered far off down the tunnel, a spot of brilliance in the catacombs.

I heard Collins un-holster his Colt, and as quietly as we could, we resumed crawling. My guts jumped about in agitation, and I had to suppress my giggles. We had finally made it, dragged our worn-out bodies through miles of tunnels all night long, and were now about to emerge into the morning jungle. After all the pain and terror and despair, we had made it.

With the light still apparently a long way off down the tunnel, Collins stopped again. I began to ask him what the score was when he kicked me quiet. I heard his Zippo flick open, and everything went white. As my eyes readjusted, I saw why we had stopped.

The passage ended not a foot in front of Collins. A smooth, reddish block—wholly out of place in this world of brown clay—was wedged into the tunnel. A hole no wider than a cigarette passed through the block, which was where the light was coming from. It wasn't sunlight either, not nearly bright enough.

Collins looked pretty rough, with blood caked on his chin and vest. He turned to me and put his index finger to his lips, the pistol concealing his face. Be quiet. No shit, Sherlock.

The tunnel wasn't any broader here, but Collins was small enough that he could swivel around in a fetal position after giving me the lighter, getting his feet in front of him. He clicked the safety off his Colt and pushed at the wall with his feet. Nothing. Killing the Zippo and pocketing it, I leaned into Collins as he gave it another go. The block shifted a fraction of an inch. With a groan, Collins heaved again, and the block moved another half-foot.

Light now trickled in from all four sides of the block. A final kick made it topple forward. Collins scooted into the light. He slid down a little way into what must have been a deeper, wider tunnel beyond the one that had brought us there, though I couldn't see any details yet. The back of Collins's head was in the way.

Suddenly Collins yelled, "Don't move, motherfucker!"

My gorge rose. We weren't alone anymore. Shit.

I nervously crawled to the end of the hole and stopped, paralyzed with awe. Not only were we not outside, we weren't in another tunnel, either. Stretching out above and below me lay an ornate temple, lit with several long candles that cast an unnatural amount of brightness on the room. The ceiling had clearly been carved from the clay, but the four walls all looked like they were made up of blocks similar to the one we had dislodged. The floor below my perch gleamed black and yellow, covered in a thin coating of moss.

I wanted to examine the carved ceiling and what appeared to be a shrine set against the opposite wall, but Collins and his new friend quickly reclaimed my attention. The man wore yellow robes, and stood in the center of the room. He looked old, like ancient fucking old, and rather amused at the pistol being waved in his face by the furious Irishman. It seemed ridiculous, but we'd apparently managed to bust out into the church of some weird gook god.

"David," Collins yelped, his back to me. "David, get down here! Oh shit, don't you fuckin' move, you fuck."

I tried clambering down, but slipped and fell, cracking my shoulder painfully. The moss felt soft and nice, though, and I wanted sleep more than anything in the world, but Collins's boot persuaded me to rise once more. I got up, supporting myself on the loose block I'd narrowly avoided braining myself on.

"Oh, man," Collins said, "what the fuck is this, what the fuck?"

I looked up again at the images etched in the clay ceiling. It was like I couldn't help myself. They were kind of a cross between a sculpture and a picture, weird spirals of black clay rearing out of the smooth earth to form miniature people and less identifiable creatures. The detail seemed flawless, right down to the ribbons of drool hanging from the teeth of the monstrosities that tore their way free of the clay. My heart beat wildly, and I had to remind myself to breathe.

Then I looked to the shrine—a tiny spring encircled by clay beasts. The spring bubbled out a pathetic stream of black water. The run-off was carried along some tiles into a fungus-coated stone pipe, an aqueduct. Scrawled over the hole where the pipe left the room were a bunch of odd letters, not Vietnamese or Cambodian, but characters from some older, weirder alphabet.

Other than the way we had come and the aqueduct, there seemed to be no exits from the room.

My canteen was dry, so I made my way to the shrine on shaky legs. The idea to do so came to me suddenly, and seemed like a really good one. When I got close, I saw that the spring was only able to sustain the small pool. The run-off barely made it a few feet down the tunnel before moss sopped it up. As I bent to drink, Collins got agitated.

"Hey—hey! What're you doing?" he stammered. "Get the fuck away from there!"

I paused, looking back at Collins and the old man. The geezer had turned so that I could see he was still smiling, but I got real confused then, because I realized that the old guy was about as Charles as me or Collins. He looked—I dunno, Middle-Eastern, maybe, because of his long beard. His scalp was shaved smooth, but it looked like his head was covered by faded tattoos or something—the skin all blue and splotchy. He had the palest green eyes, almost white, and those eyes kept staring at me as if I were the only other person in the room, as if Collins and his gun didn't exist.

"Drink," the old man said, his English clear and precise, despite an almost German accent.

At this, Collins flipped his shit.

"You fuck," he babbled. "You're helpin' us—U.S. Marines, understand? Get us outta here, you—you—hey, how many of you bastards are down here? What the fuck is goin' on, what is this shit, what is this?"

"Relax," the old man said. "Drink. Sit. You are my guests."

As he said this, his eyes sparkled, and I moved away from the pool toward Collins.

"Relax?" Collins shook, wired on fear and confusion. "Dude, you got no fuckin' idea what we been through—what we saw—so shut the fuck up!"

"It's been such a long time," the old man continued, ignoring Collins, "since I've had company. Rest a while."

The old man's tranquility must have been contagious, because Collins calmed right down. "Look," he said, his finger easing off the trigger, "how do we get out? That's all we want."

The old man didn't answer, but his smile broadened. He turned his back on Collins, and went toward the spring. Collins, pissed at the brush off but no longer raging, walked after him. I watched anxiously, feeling lost and tired.

"Hey, you old gook," Collins said. "I said you're gonna help us." And at this the geezer spun around. He didn't look so frail anymore, and his beard stirred as if a wind brushed it, only I felt no wind.

"I am no 'gook', you wretched Western slug," he intoned, his smile gone, "I care not for your petty squabbling, and will not pick sides in your hollow wars. I did not help the others when they came, and I will not help you." And he turned away to kneel before the spring.

I felt sick, not just tired or scared, but one hundred percent, death's-door ill. So I gazed back up at the ceiling, trying to find a familiar, comforting image among the strange gods. Collins kept pressing though, advancing on the old man; like I said, he never did know when to shut the fuck up. "What others—the V.C.?" he said. "Where are they? When were they here?"

"When they built that tunnel, they came through the wall. After that, they all left. Most, anyway. There are still a few, I think, in here somewhere," he looked slowly around the walls of the temple, as if peering through the blocks or at something invisible to us.

Removing a clay cup from his robe, he filled it with the dark water. He offered this to Collins, who finally lowered his gun. I was relieved by that. The last thing I wanted was for Collins to shoot the old man. I didn't really know why.

"Came through the wall?" Collins asked, sipping the water.

"They came through," the old man said, "by chance, when they were excavating a tunnel system to hide from you crusaders."

"Crusaders?" Collins snorted, finishing his water and handing me the cup. "We're USMC, not King Arthur's fuckin' knights."

"Wait a second," I said, bending back down to refill the cup. "You said they came through the wall. So you were already here. If they built the tunnel, how did you get down here?"

"Yeah," Collins seconded, moving around the side of the pool. He squinted at something I couldn't see, so I turned away and put the cup to my lips. Sipping the water, I found it to be the sweetest I'd had since home. A little thick, but definitely refreshing.

"I read of a spring in the jungles a long time ago," the old man said, "a small creek mentioned in an ancient tome. Many years had passed since the book was penned, and many more passed before I found the stream. By the time I'd arrived, it had dwindled to a miniscule trickle in the hills, which I followed down into the earth, until I located its source." He waved his spindly arm at the pool before us.

Collins had reached the wall and, ducking down, leaned over the shrine to look down the aqueduct pipe.

"Hot damn," Collins said excitedly, "bet we could follow this all the way out!"

I looked apprehensively at the narrow exit. If possible, it seemed even smaller than the last two tunnels. But I'd spent more then enough time down in that damn temple, or whatever the hell it was.

"Yes," the old man said, his smile reappearing. "Yes, that leads to the surface."

"Aha!" yelped Collins. He snatched a small leather bag he'd spotted in a crevice by the pool, then tossed it to me. The weight of the thing nearly bowled me over. Collins was waving his gun around again, and for the first time I began to question his sanity. We should not fuck with the old man; that seemed obvious.

"What's in there?" Collins hooted. "If it's supplies or food, it's ours!"

My guts began to thrash around again, and I bent to open the bag. Just as my fingers undid the complex knot, the old man appeared over me, and for no reason I can name, I silently handed him back the bag. But as he took the offering, I distinctly felt movement from the satchel, the leather pushed violently outward by something inside.

"What the shit!" Collins gasped. "David, what the fuck is your problem?"

"We don't need it," I whispered, staring at the pulsating bag.

"What the fuck is in it?"

"Nothing to help you," the old man said. "Old books. They'll do the likes of you no good at all."

"Books?" Collins demanded. "Lets see them."

"There is nothing in them that will allow you to live to see the sunrise," the old man said, and even though I could no longer bring myself to look at his face, I knew he still smiled.

"What?" Collins screeched. "What? Fuck you!"

And Collins—nice, funny, a little dumb but okay Collins—emptied his clip into the old man.

I felt paralyzed, watching him jab his gun into the geezer's robes and blast away. But nothing happened. We all stood still for a moment, silent, waiting. Then Collins dropped his Colt, which skipped away off the moss.

The old man turned to Collins, who looked back at him. Collins even met his gaze—for about a minute. Then he collapsed, wailing and pulling at the old man's robes. As he bowed before the geezer, whispering apologies through his sobs, the man looked to me again, and try as I might to look away, I found myself peering into those treacherous green eyes of his.

He spun away, depositing his satchel back in the nook and striding to the block we'd knocked down. Then he began to mumble and chant. I hurried to Collins, who was still shaking and moaning, and splashed water onto this face. He looked pale and fever ridden, but he came to his senses enough for us to get our shit together. Retrieving his gun, I ejected the spent clip, found some extra rounds, reloaded it, and tucked it into my belt.

I turned back to the old man, who once more faced us. With stomach-turning horror I realized that the half-ton block was back in place, sealing the room. Collins had stopped crying, but when he looked at that block, I thought he might start up again.

The old man towered over us, and I knew the true meaning of fear. Not the fear that compels the feet to action; but a fear of such magnitude that awe or madness or worship can be the only possible responses to it. This was the fear of God that I had never known. Real terror confronted us in that instant, in the guise of that old man. And when he finally averted his glare, we knew that he owned us, and that, for the moment, he was a merciful master.

"Go," he said disgustedly.

We fled—not out of fright, but out of respect. We walked slowly to the pipe, our eyes fastened on the old man's robes. The farther we moved away from him, the more our wonder turned to dread. Finally, we panicked. As I'm bigger, I managed to push in front and began scrambling with mad-dened intensity down the narrow confines of the aqueduct.

I should've been too tired to move, let alone pull myself by my fingertips over miles of jagged stone, but I moved with a speed bordering on the supernatural. Our flight must have lasted many hours, but I can barely remember it. Once I must have slept, as Collins woke me with a pinch to the ankle. Sometime later I shit myself, the rancid smell an unwelcome reminder of the thing in the tunnel.

Finally, after losing three fingernails and a boot, I found the rock giving way to clay, and knew we'd made it. The tunnel grew wider, opening into a cave that the aqueduct passed through. The incline leveled off as the night sky came into view up ahead, revealed to us through gaps in the vines that dangled over the cave mouth. Grabbing Collins by the arm, I started to run forward, laughing as I approached freedom. If only I'd thought to use Collins's Zippo, we might have made it.

I didn't even feel the first few strikes, and had collapsed to my knees before I understood what had happened. Collins stepped back screaming, and went down hard. The moonlight barely reached us in the back of the cave, but I could see well enough to know I was fucked. Cobras, dozens of 'em, rearing at me out of the darkness, long fangs sinking in and ripping out, over and over and over.

It didn't sting so much as burn, my whole body incinerating from the inside. I felt the snakes writhing underneath me, the fire growing and growing, and they didn't stop. They were all over me, fat coils of scales rubbing, hoods flaring, and the noise—the *shick, shick, shick* of snake sliding on snake—and the screams . . .

After a time, they stopped biting. Every few minutes one would experimentally strike at a twitching limb, but the onslaught had ended. *I should die*, I thought, *any second the fire will cool, and I can rest—sleep—die.* But I didn't. The burning intensified, the sickness so bad I could feel my skin crack and ooze as the venom rotted me alive.

Then I remembered the Colt.

It took me a spell to jam my bloated finger into the trigger guard, and as I raised it, the gun went off. At this the snakes under and on me were striking and thrashing again, but I couldn't care less. In the cave's dimness, I could see Collins's serpent-covered body still convulsing a few feet away, could hear his whimpers, soft but clear. I couldn't get up, so from where I lay I put five round into Collins's back, then put the barrel in my own mouth and pulled the trigger.

Thum-thump. Sleep. *Thum-thump.* Staring at the ceiling, can't sleep. Light enters the cave, snakes everywhere, slithering over and under and through us, out into the sunshine. Watch the light on the wall through my ruined face, feeling cold metal in my throat, hearing the damn heartbeat sound, louder and louder, and I'm dead. But I'm not. Heartbeat getting louder until I can't think, all I want is to die but I can't and it hurts, the fucking thundering heartbeat, and I'm clawing at my chest, digging through purple layers of poisoned meat until I find the bastard and put my fingers through it and tear at it until most of it comes off in my swollen fist and I squeeze until it's dribbling gore—and I realize it's not my heart that's making all the racket. Now I'm moving, ripping at Collins's breast, and he's pushing me away, saying, "Get offa me, get offa me."

I find his heart, the bullet holes making it easy, and I crush the fat, warm thing and I still fucking hear that *thum-thump, thum-thump*, and Collins moans, "Lie down, we're dead, we're dead," and the burning's only gotten worse, and I watch the light dying away, but the snakes don't come back, only the stars.

"You still awake, David?" Collins asks. I try to answer, but my jaw's blown off, so I only gurgle up blood.

"Reister," Collins whispers after a while, and the starlight glimmers just like the old man's eyes, and I can see fine, even though I'm dead. The burning's finally cooling, but the noise is getting worse with every second. It takes some work, some real fucking work, but I conjure up Reister's face—Reister's damned, damning face—and I remember. Even though it hurts, I remember.

Moving makes it a little better, even though the *thum-thump* is even louder out in the grass on the hilltop, but me and Collins are soldiers again, and even with my legs all dripping and soft I run so fast, so damn fast, it's like I'm swimming through the jungle. I can't hear anything but the heartbeat, coming from everything, from everywhere, getting louder and louder, and we find their footprints, and it's so easy, so many footprints. Collins says things, and I want to answer, but I can't, and "Besides," he says, "they'll be able to kill us for sure, definitely, fuckin' A."

Then the jungle stops, and the *thum-thump, thum-thump* is so loud my ears rupture and bleed, and Collins is screaming. Frank, big Frank never liked us much, and Collins is on him—heh, some guard—and Frank is screaming, too, as he drops his gun and falls under Collins.

Soldiers everywhere, flares blinding me all around, but the *thum-thump* is worse, so terrible it hurts more than any bullet. Then he's right there, all three hundred pounds of throbbing fat and muscle: Reister. I want to show him, to lead him down through the tunnels to behold sights unseen by living men, so he can know, so he can understand. But watching him trip as he turns to run, shoving one of his terrified men between us, I know he already does: better him than you, after all, eh, Reister? Loyalty? Courage? Honor? Bullshit. Survival. Blood, under their fingernails or yours. *Thum-thump.* We run together, me and Reister, and then I'm on him, and then he's wide open, his guts unspooling into my arms in the grass under the stars, and the heartbeat gets a tiny bit softer, and it's fucking glorious . . . .

BRAINBURGERS AND BILE SHAKES: A LOVE STORY

JIM C. HINES

WHEN I MET BISSA, SHE was selling brainburgers and bile shakes at horribly inflated prices.

I had more than blown my meal allowance from work, paying twenty-plus bucks for gray beef patties, a green milkshake, and watered-down ketchup. I didn't care. I kept going back to the counter, finding one excuse after another to talk to her, even if our conversation was less than romantic.

"Is something wrong with your brainburger?" she asked when I returned yet again.

I probably sounded like a zombie myself as I unknotted my tongue enough to stammer, "It's delicious."

She stared at me, waiting. Behind her, other employees of the Zombie-Land Snack Shack scurried about, swapping baskets in the deep fryer and wrapping uniformly gray meat products in wax paper. The man with the *Manager* badge even adopted an exaggerated limp, mimicking the slow shuffle of the walking dead as he went from table to table.

Of course, the Snack Shack was one of the few places in ZombieLand where actual zombies were forbidden. The health inspectors would shut down the whole park if a zombie came within twenty feet of the restaurant.

The employees all wore the same uniform, but only Bissa made it beautiful. A blue cap hid her hair, except for a long, sleek braid. The embroidered blood splatters on her shirt highlighted the green of her eyes. Her skin was smooth and tan. She wore no makeup. Her small mouth quirked on one side.

"Sir?" She gestured at the line behind me. "Was there anything you needed, sir?"

"Jack. Jack Young." I peeked at the backlit menu behind her. "Um . . . the ribs sound good. How large is your child's portion?"

She held her hands about a foot apart, and my stomach gurgled in protest. In the past hour and a half, I had already eaten enough for three men.

"That seems like a lot."

One plucked eyebrow rose. "Listen, Jack Young, I don't know how small children are where you're from, but here in Nevada, this is the width of an average child's rib cage."

I stammered something about how I wasn't that hungry and glanced back at the menu. Only then did she break into a grin. She reached over the counter to squeeze my shoulder. "Gullible, aren't you? The kids' meal is three pork riblets, a mini-shake, and a toy."

A more suave man would have replied with an amusing repartee, something to make her flash that smile again. I opened my mouth, hesitated, and mumbled that I would take the kids' ribs.

My meal came in a plastic bucket shaped like a human head. I popped the scalp off and removed the toy—a plastic green block with a gravestone at one end.

Bissa took it from my hand and set it on the counter. "Like this," she said, pressing the gravestone. A tiny, two-dimensional zombie popped up from the grass.

"Cute."

Another long silence. She seemed to be waiting for something. My face got hot again. An exasperated father tapped my shoulder before I could speak.

"Are you finished? My kids are waiting for their finger-on-a-stick treats."

"Sorry." I dropped the toy into my plastic head and retreated to my seat. There, I watched Bissa's hands move as she took the next order. She had long, graceful fingers with black nail polish.

I turned away, afraid she would catch me staring.

The whole place smelled like grease. It even overpowered the smell of rotting zombie that hung over the whole of ZombieLand.

Looking out the window, I watched a group of handlers lead a parade of zombies through the street, between lines of cheering kids and weary parents. Several zombies banged on bongos, their desiccated hands slapping the only instruments the walking dead could master. Two men with brooms and dustbins followed, scooping up fallen bits of flesh.

When I glanced at the counter again, Bissa was watching me. I managed to smile and prayed my teeth were reasonably rib-free.

Twenty minutes later, she came to my table and asked me out.

We met in the Mortuary Theater. I spotted Bissa sitting in an aisle seat in Row F. I handed my ticket to an attendant and hurried to join her.

"You're late," she said.

"I went to Sepulcher Stage by mistake," I said, still breathing hard from the run. I was sweating, and the sun beating down on the open theater didn't help. I hoped I didn't sweat through my shirt. "This place is a maze. How long did you work here before you learned where everything was?"

She smiled and tapped her temple. "Photographic memory. I memorized the map on my first day."

Feeling stupider by the minute, I nodded and pretended to watch the show. A zombie dressed in black velvet trimmed with gold thread trotted across the stage. A silver-hilted rapier hung from his belt. Not a real one, of course—federal regs, and all that.

A second zombie carried a shovel onto the stage and pretended to dig. The audience chuckled at the irony of a zombie gravedigger. The first zombie stepped forward and picked up a withered, blond-haired head.

"Alas, poor Yorick," a voice said. It was supposedly the zombie speaking in a cultured British accent, but that was impossible since his lips were missing and a poorly mended rip split his cheek. His mouth wasn't even moving. The prerecorded dialogue came from speakers mounted above the stage.

"The head used to play Hamlet," Bissa whispered. "His body got torn up in the riots last year, so they decided to use him for Yorick. Cheaper than paying disposal fees, I guess."

Yorick's mouth was in better condition. His lips moved almost in synch with the speakers. "Ach, Hamlet, you've caught me at a bad time. I was about to go to the head."

A collective groan from the audience.

Before Hamlet could reply, the speakers squealed and died. The audience muttered as a woman in black Kevlar walked to the front of the stage. She had a ZombieLand patch on her shoulder.

Behind her, similarly dressed men used steel poles to loop plastic rings around the zombies' necks and lead them away. In the case of poor Yorick, they used a shovel.

"Ladies and gentlemen, we apologize for the interruption." The woman spoke in a calm voice tinged with a hint of a Southern accent. "Federal law requires us to hold occasional drills to make sure ZombieLand is prepared in case of an emergency."

"What kind of emergency?" yelled a teenager. He wore a baseball cap with foam brains stuck to the top. "I thought zombies were safe!"

"Safety standards at ZombieLand exceed state and federal requirements," she reassured us. "The drills are a holdover from years ago, before zombies were brought under control."

She gave the audience a confident smile. "Everything is perfectly safe. As a representative of ZombieLand, I apologize for any inconvenience. You will all receive free passes to the next showing."

"How often do they do these drills?" I asked as we filed out of the theater.

Bissa shrugged. "I've never seen one before. But I've only worked here since March."

"Oh." I searched for something else to say, anything to break the silence. I'd never been able to talk to women. I worried too much, and it made me freeze up. Like I was doing now. She was watching me again, waiting for me to speak.

"I think you're beautiful," I blurted out.

She dimpled. "Yeah, sure. My hair's a frizzed mess, I've got ketchup on my shirt, and I smell like burger grease. What's not to love?"

But she twined her fingers with mine as we walked through the crowd.

❖   ❖   ❖

Bissa got us into the next show for free, which was a good thing since my wallet was running dry. We sat near the front row and watched a group of zombies in Army uniforms reenact the Firebombing of Fargo. Most of the seats were empty. A cardboard zombie outside the door had proclaimed that the show was *For Mature Humans Only*.

Up on stage, a lone woman—a human woman—sat in a mock control room, surrounded by blinking lights. The command station in Fargo, a small radio station where Linda Graystrom had condemned the town—and herself—to death.

"Tell me about yourself," whispered Bissa. "What do you do when you're not picking up women at ZombieLand?"

"I do field testing for the Department of Environmental Quality."

"A state employee? So you're halfway to being a zombie yourself." She chuckled. "Do your bosses know how you're spending your afternoon?"

Her laughter came from deep in her throat. And it was a real laugh, not the delicate tinkle some women affected.

At the control center in Fargo, zombies proceeded to break through the door, only to find Linda waiting. Even with leather mittens strapped over their hands and blue nylon stitches sealing their lips shut, the sight of attacking zombies still made many audience members shift uncomfortably.

Linda's pistol thundered again and again. Blanks, of course, but the zombies flopped backward as they had been trained to do. The biting smell of gunpowder drifted through the crowd. When the ammunition ran out, Linda attacked the last zombie with a foot-long knife, splattering drops of black blood across the stage. A plastic screen kept the audience from being splashed.

"What brought you to ZombieLand?" Bissa asked.

I turned away from the stage. "I was collecting water samples all morning." I had gotten lost three times before I finished. "I have test tubes from every drinking fountain, hose, sink, and bathroom in the park, all labeled and refrigerated in my car. I figured I'd relax for a bit before heading back."

"Spoken like a true state worker," she said. "So you're playing hooky? I hadn't pegged you for the rebel type."

"Once, I even stole a box of paperclips from supplies," I said, deadpan.

"Tell me more, bad boy." She squeezed my hand. "It makes me go all tingly."

We laughed again. I marveled at how natural it felt. I had started to relax enough to talk and joke, and she wasn't bored! She didn't even mention my initial awkwardness and embarrassment back at the Snack Shack.

On stage, Linda sat back in her chair. Her face was drawn and pale. Her sleeve was torn, bloody from the bite of a zombie. Historically, the wound had probably been deeper, but the blood dripping down her arm looked real enough.

She knew what would happen. She knew dozens of zombies were even now roaming the streets, and she knew what would happen if they weren't stopped. The speakers played the actual tape of Linda Graystrom's final orders, activating the contingency plan that wiped Fargo from the map. Then the actress set down the radio and raised her fake gun to her head. The curtains closed an instant before the gun went off.

The audience applauded politely.

I looked away, my cheerfulness gone.

"What's wrong?" Bissa asked.

"Nothing. I . . . can we go somewhere else?"

"How about the Hall of Dead Presidents? That's usually quiet. Too intellectual for most folks."

We had walked about a hundred yards when gunfire and screams from the theater cut through the afternoon air. I jumped, and Bissa glanced back.

"They must have added another act to the show. An encore, you know?" She touched my arm. "Hey, you look pretty shaken up. You're not one of those ZRA people, are you? If so, don't worry about the one who got knifed. They fix it up after every show. Staples, superglue, and a week in the dirt, and it's good as new. More or less."

"I'm not a Zombie Rights nut," I said, slipping an arm around her shoulder. "It's just . . ."

"You can tell me." Her voice was warm, and she looked up at me so openly that I kissed her before I realized what I was doing. It was only a quick peck, but she didn't pull away.

We kept walking in silence, our bodies pressed into one another like those couples I had watched and envied over the years. Now it was finally my turn. My turn to slip a hand around a beautiful girl's waist. My turn to pull her close and feel her do the same.

I was in heaven.

❖   ❖   ❖

"It's because of my brother, Sam," I said. "He joined the National Guard in college. When the first uprising hit, back before mandatory cremation, he was one of the guys they called in to protect Vegas."

Richard Nixon waved victory Vs at us from behind a wall of plexiglass. Tricky Dick was the healthiest zombie in the building, being the most recently deceased. The tip of his nose was a bit rotted, but overall, he was remarkably intact.

I wasn't impressed. Bissa had already explained how they had to implant steel rods to keep his fingers bent like that. When I looked closely, I could see the tip of one rod protruding through his index finger.

"What happened?" she asked gently as she pulled me along.

"They thought it would be easy. The zombies didn't put up much resistance, so the Guard herded them into the Luxor."

"That's the pyramid, right? The casino with the big spotlight on top?"

"Used to be," I said, then lost myself in the memories.

They sent a Guardsman to our house with the news. He arrived right before dinnertime. I still recalled the smell of my mother's chili simmering on the stove, and the overpowering scent of sage from the recent storms wafting through the house as my father opened the door.

Officially, Sam died battling zombies in the Luxor. Years later, I talked to a friend at the CDC and learned the truth.

Bissa gave my hand a squeeze and brought me back to the present. "So Sam was sent to the Luxor," she prompted.

I gave her a weak smile. "He was posted on the fourth floor, guarding the stairs. They had a few people on every floor, just in case. This was back before they knew how contagious the stuff was. I guess a group of zombies on the ground floor broke free and started feeding on anyone in sight. You know how they get when they're hungry."

"Yeah." She shivered. "You couldn't pay me enough to work as a feeder. One little slip, and . . ."

It was my turn to squeeze her hand. We waited while a group of school kids walked past, tapping the plexiglass to see if they could get a withered Harry Truman to react.

Bissa took a deep breath. "You said Sam was on the fourth floor."

"That's right. The Luxor is hollow on the inside. From the balcony, Sam could see everything that happened." I sighed raggedly. "The Guardsmen were outnumbered, and the zombies' sudden rush caught them off guard . . . ."

I relived it in my nightmares for months after I'd learned what happened. I could hear the rapid popping of gunfire, the shouted orders and panicked screams, and the crunch of shattering skulls as the zombies fed, splitting the heads of their enemies as easily as I might crack an eggshell.

"Sam rallied a handful of men," I said sadly. "They took up sniper positions and picked off zombies one by one."

"He sounds very brave."

"He was too late to save the men on the first floor, but he made sure the zombies didn't escape. I saw photos of the place. Real photos, not the sanitized stuff that made it into the papers. There was blood everywhere, red and black both. Blood on the statues, in the carpets, splattered over the slot machines and the roulette wheel." My voice caught. "Blood in the fountains."

Her grip tightened on mine.

"It got into the water supply," I said. "Sam must have taken a drink from a water fountain. Or maybe he needed to wash off after the slaughter, I don't know."

We stopped to watch Lyndon Johnson pace the length of his clear prison.

"They had to napalm the Luxor a week later. They caught Sam in Reno, eating his girlfriend's father. Sam had shot him in both legs to keep him from running."

Bissa's face was pale, and her lower lip trembled slightly. "I didn't know. I remember seeing the news—they said it was a minor outbreak, that a broken gas line caused the explosion. My God, how can you even stand to be here?"

"Years of therapy," I said. "That, and knowing Sam helped stop an outbreak. At least we never had to resort to nukes. Look at Taiwan or Sydney."

I concentrated on my breathing, going through the relaxation exercises my therapist had taught me. They didn't work.

"They told us Sam died fighting zombies, and that's what I choose to believe. He died a hero, as much as Linda Graystrom or anyone else."

"Sam *was* a hero," she said firmly. "And so are you. Driving all over the state to check the water and make sure nothing like that happens again." She kissed my cheek and, in a little girl voice, said, "My hero."

I thought about the samples locked in the cooler in my Jeep and tried not to feel guilty. I was no hero. In all the years I had worked at DEQ, I had yet to find a single contaminated water source. I had yet to do anything that mattered. My job was a joke. And every time I sent a test tube through the analyzer, it reminded me of Sam.

I didn't want my bitterness to ruin things with Bissa, so I smiled and said, "I guess so."

"Come on. Let's go someplace quieter."

Until she mentioned it, I hadn't noticed the screams outside. The Hall of Dead Presidents was sandwiched between the Pale Horse Water Ride and the Catacombs Coaster (guaranteed to scramble even the heartiest of brains). From the sound of it, the coaster delivered the promised terrors and more.

"What did you have in mind?" I asked.

Her eyes twinkled. "I know a place where nobody will bother us."

"They're calling it the Petting Zoo," Bissa explained. She passed her ID card in front of the lock, and the LED turned green. "It's not scheduled to open until August, but they've already got some of the exhibits set up."

The air inside was cooler. It reminded me of the hay and excrement smell of a barn, but the stench of death and decay overpowered everything else. Bissa gave me an apologetic half-shrug.

"It'll smell better once they get the ventilation hooked up. Come on—the far end of the building is all administrative offices and a gift shop. The stink shouldn't be as bad down there."

I glanced around as we walked through the corridor, our footsteps surprisingly loud against the cement floor. The zoo was laid out like the Hall of Dead Presidents, with individual rooms to either side, walled in by thick plexiglass.

In one cage a boa constrictor rested on a tilted two-by-four. Its middle segments were little more than bone, and its dirty skin flaked and peeled like a bad case of sunburn. On the other side, an otter banged a severed chicken's head against a rock, trying to get at the tender brains inside. In the next display, a squirrel scraped bloody claws against the cement, trying in vain to bury the half-eaten corpse of a mouse.

"You won't actually be able to pet them, of course," Bissa said. "I mean, they say animals can't infect humans, but you know how worked up people get about zombies." She bit her lip. "I didn't mean you. I meant . . . damn. That was stupid."

"It's okay," I said, with a hug to let her know I meant it. In truth, I was starting to like ZombieLand. I liked seeing them in cages or performing for their living masters. It was proof that we had won.

We moved on to a parrot that was flapping in vain as it tried to reach its perch. Its wings were featherless gray meat, the ends black with rot.

"They're trying to teach the animals tricks," Bissa explained. "I guess it's even harder than with human zombies. The handlers are always talking about how you can't teach a dead dog new tricks."

I smiled. "So where are the handlers?"

She shrugged. "I don't know. Ella's supposed to be on duty today, but she's a flake." She poked me in the side and grinned. "Or maybe she found a good-looking, intelligent, compassionate man, and they went somewhere they could be alone."

Even I could read a signal like that. Our tongues danced together as we pressed our bodies close. Her hands grabbed my waist and moved lower.

When she finally pulled away, it was only to gasp for air and lead me to the empty gift shop down the hall. We locked the door behind us. Bissa was right—the smell was less noticeable in this part of the building.

Soon we were rolling on the carpet behind an empty display case, little more than animals ourselves.

Hours later, we snuck out the back door of the Petting Zoo and into the chill night air. I glanced at my pager to check the time. Nearly nine o'clock. Two hours after ZombieLand closed.

Most of the lights were out. We stumbled along in the moonlight, giddy and giggling as we held each other.

I stepped in something sticky. Hard to tell in the darkness, but it looked like someone's spilled Snack Shack meal, complete with a finger-on-a-stick, sans stick.

Bissa sniffed in disgust. "The cleaning crew should have taken care of that. They probably left early, figuring the pigeons would clean up the worst of it."

She appeared to be correct. I spotted a pair of birds picking at something stringy on a bench. They looked big for pigeons. Then again, these pigeons feasted on fried food every night. It was a miracle they weren't too fat to fly.

"When do I get to see you again?" I asked.

She licked her lips. "How about tonight? You can swing by my place and pick me up after I change out of these disgusting clothes."

"I . . ."

"What's wrong?"

"I can't." A part of me was still thinking about Sam, and the water samples in my Jeep. Every time a sample tested clean, it proved we had won, that Sam hadn't died for nothing. "I should get those test tubes back to the lab."

"It's a waste of taxpayer money," she said, leaning her body into mine. "All of our water gets piped through Reno. We're as clean as they are!"

I sniffed, then regretted it. The smell of blood and rot was stronger without the crowds to overpower the zombie stench.

"I have to," I said. I thought of the zombies I had seen today, a far cry from the monsters of my nightmares. When I spoke, my voice was full of surprise. "ZombieLand is Sam's memorial."

She didn't answer.

"What's the matter?"

She pointed at a large man in a ZombieLand uniform up ahead. "That's my boss. I never signed out this afternoon. He'll kill me if he knows I bailed before the dinner rush." She tugged me toward a photo booth where you could get your picture taken with an actual zombie.

It was too late. The Snack Shack manager hurried to cut us off, still affecting the limp I had seen during lunch. That limp had been laughable under the fluorescent lights of the Snack Shack, but the night made it far more credible. His gait could have belonged to a real zombie.

"Relax," I said, pulling out my state I.D. "I'll tell him you were helping me on my inspection."

She smiled. "Look who's Mister Self-Confidence all of the sudden."

"It's you. And this place . . . ."

ZombieLand gave meaning to Sam's death, and to my life.

I glanced around, lost in thought as I approached Bissa's shambling boss. After today, I vowed to myself, there would be no more negligence, no more wasted afternoons or forgotten water samples.

My work was too important.

SCENES FROM A FOREIGN HORROR VIDEO, WITH ZOMBIES AND TASTEFUL NUDITY

MARK McLAUGHLIN

G RAINY, SWEEPING SHOTS OF SKYSCRAPERS, crowded metro sidewalks, hectic traffic, and a pale young woman entering an office building. The Daughter. Her thick black hair is piled high, and held in place with several large silver clasps.

Suddenly the camera sweeps up, up to a blazing sun, and shimmering blood-red letters appear: *Nightmare of the Watching Dead*. The words fade away, and then names, names, and more names appear, shimmer, and disappear. Then the camera sweeps down, down to a crow picking at a glowing eyeball on the hood of a black limousine.

The Reporter gasps as the bird flies away with its juicy prize. "Did you see that?" he whispers. "A terrible omen." He has deep, sullen eyes and gray streaks at the temples.

A passerby—a fortyish woman with maroon lipstick—laughs, though it sounds more like a bark. She is The Nurse. "I have seen worse," she says, matter-of-factly.

❖   ❖   ❖

The Heavyset Man cruises the Internet, clicking here, clicking there. He is wearing a stained bathrobe and is sitting at his desk in the middle of his cluttered apartment. A crow watches him from the sill of an open window.

"What is this?" the man says to no one. "A website about witches?"

The screen is filled with images of pale women with long, straight red hair. "They are pretty, these witches."

The image of an eyeball pops up in the corner of the screen. The eyeball begins to pulse with a greenish light. Intrigued, The Heavyset Man clicks on this link.

Instantly, a beam of green energy shoots out of the monitor. It splits in midair and hits the man in both eyes. He leans to one side, then falls out of his chair and hits the floor, dead.

The crow flutters into the room, settling on the man's neck. The bird leans forward, gently slides its beak around one of his eyeballs, then gives the orb a sharp tug, pulling it free.

The crow flies out the window, and the camera watches it disappear, up into the roiling clouds. When the camera turns to view the room again, the body is gone.

A tropical island at night. Too many animal cries—growls, hoots, monkey-shrieks, and crow-caws—echo at the same time.

In a pavilion swathed in mosquito netting, The Fat Witch hands a goblet to The Young Witch. Both are pale with red hair.

"Soon," says the fat one, "everyone will be screaming. No one can withstand the dead when they are instilled with the nuclear life-force." Occasionally, the movements of her lips match her words.

"Yes, it is a perfect plan." The young one drinks deep from the goblet, leaving a smear of red, too thick and shiny for wine, on her top lip. "But how shall we begin?" She wipes at the stain with the back of her hand, but only succeeds in spreading it along her cheek.

"The answer is easy. I have already begun the process. How the fools love their Internet computers." The fat one turns suddenly, pointing, and the camera zooms in the direction of her finger. A computer monitor sits on a makeshift altar of bloody bones and broken keyboards. The screen of the monitor is broken, and a decayed hand is pinned on some of the larger shards of glass. The hand softly glows with green energy.

"The Internet, yes." The Young Witch nods. "They do not know it is controlled by witches and nuclear power."

"We set sail in the morning," hisses The Fat Witch.

The hand twitches, fingers churning like the legs of an eager spider.

The morning sun shines down on The Businessman's patio.

Here, practically everything is white—the metal furniture, the tiles, the marble rim of the pool. The water is blue, but it is a pale, oddly milky sky blue.

The Daughter has finished swimming and is drying herself with a fluffy white towel. She is the pale woman who had entered the office building earlier. She looks up at the sky, lost in thought.

(*I've done this before. I know it. A hundred, a thousand times before.*)

She walks to a table where The Businessman, her father, is having breakfast with The Scientist, her boyfriend.

"Father," she says, "I saw a news program last night. They were saying terrible things about the Internet."

"Ridiculous. An outrage." The Businessman spears a sausage with his fork. "The Internet is good. My best investment yet. What lies were they saying on the television?"

"Pay them no mind—they are jealous," The Scientist says. He is very handsome, with boyish good looks.

The Daughter picks up and eats a sausage from The Scientist's plate. "They say the Internet has too many websites about witches on it, and that people are disappearing. And, there have been many terrible omens. In fact, last night I had a dream." She takes another sausage. "I dreamed that mother was not dead. I dreamed that she was a witch on an island, and that she was very fat and evil."

The Businessman turns to The Scientist. "These liars on the television are upsetting Miracula. Take her into the house and look at the Internet with her. See all the good things it has to show."

"I will do so immediately," says The Scientist.

"I do not like it when you two gang up on me," the girl says, pouting. "And I do not like it that you will not tell me about mother. You say she is dead, but even if that is so, I still have a right to know more about her."

The Businessman takes her hand. "Someday I will tell you everything." He then nods to The Scientist, and the young man leads her into the house.

Scenes of the young couple looking at the Internet, taking turns clicking on this and that.

Scenes of The Nurse examining ancient, leatherbound books in cobwebbed chambers.

Scenes of zombies stumbling through dark, filthy alleys, tipping over trash cans.

Scenes of birds and bats flying out of shadowed church entrances.

Scenes of crows, always crows, with eyeballs in their beaks.

A close-up of one of the glowing eyeballs. The voice of The Fat Witch is heard: "How much they see, my pretty pets."

Midnight. An enormous room filled with computers, monitors, cables. The very walls are lined with computers. Tiny lights of blue and white twinkle like stars.

This room is the mighty heart of the Internet. Over the door is a framed portrait of The Businessman.

A fly lands on the portrait. The camera zooms in tight on the insect, cherishing the repulsive details of its filthy, squirming mouth. The fly zips off and the camera follows it, up and down, all over the room.

The fly darts through a disk slot in one of the computers. The camera continues to follow it on and on, through a mad eternity of flashing lights, shifting geometric patterns, clouds of blue lightning, and everywhere, eyeballs attached to sparking cables. The eyeballs glow green with radioactivity. Crows fly in to add new eyeballs, popping them onto free cables, or to take away old ones that have lost their glow.

A cemetery under a full moon. Tombstones, dead trees, statues of angels with broken wings.

A young couple embrace, sitting on top of a large granite tombstone. A twig-snap echoes.

"What was that sound?" the woman says, startled.

"A stray dog. A cat. Nothing at all. Kiss me." The man has a gentle face and full lips.

"I tell you, I heard something." The woman looks around, then sees a faintly glowing figure, partially hidden by a tree, about thirty feet away. "My God. What is that?"

"You," the young man shouts to the intruder. "We see you. What are you doing there?"

Slowly the shape moves forward. It is The Heavyset Man, still in his robe, which is now even filthier. His body glows a faint, sickly green. He stares at them with his single eye as he advances. A thin line of green slime drips from the empty eye socket.

"Hideous," the man whispers.

"We must get out of here," the woman cries, tugging at her lover's arm.

"No. I want to see this. I have heard of these zombies." He moves a few feet toward the creature. "He is very slow. I can escape him easily."

"You are insane," the woman says.

"They say on the television that the Internet is responsible." The young man moves closer, even as the zombie inches toward him. "There may be a reward for finding one."

"Madness," the woman hisses.

The man turns to his sweetheart. "If I had a rope, then I—" While he is looking away, the zombie rushes forward and leaps upon him, digging his meaty hands into the man's belly.

The zombie then looks up to stare at the screaming woman. A green bolt of energy blazes forth from his eye, and splits to strike both of her eyes.

She falls to the ground.

A crow lands on her neck.

The press conference.

The Businessman and his associates are seated behind a long table. Each has his own microphone and glass of water.

Facing them, in rows of metal chairs, sit The Reporter and his colleagues from various television stations and newspapers.

"More and more witch websites are appearing," The Reporter suddenly shouts, standing up. "Plus, more zombies are being spotted. They have attacked many innocent people. You cannot deny there is a connection."

"That is not a question," The Businessman says smugly. "Are you deciding the news for yourself? Is that how it works? And you call yourselves reporters."

This enrages the media people, and many begin angrily shouting questions:

"What about the crows of death?"

"Do you realize that radioactivity is involved?"

"Can you explain the missing eyes?"

Suddenly The Fat Witch enters the room through a door behind the reporters, and The Businessman stands up. "What are you doing here?" he says. "Are you again trying to destroy my life?"

She smiles and nods, and steps aside as glowing zombies shamble into the room. They dig their strong hands into the throats and bellies of the media people. Green bolts fire from their eyes. Crows flutter gracefully into the room.

In the confusion, The Businessman slips away through a door behind some large potted ferns. The Fat Witch sees this and follows him.

Once she is through the door, she finds herself at the top of a metal framework staircase. She sees The Businessman on the landing below. The two regard each other.

"So you are behind all of this. I suspected as much. You and your witches, making my life into an insane delusion." The Businessman's face is beaded with sweat. "Why can't you leave me alone?"

"Fool," she cries. "Can you not see that together, we are unstoppable?"

"I once loved you," he says, "but I cannot live in a world of misery and death. You want to control everything."

"Admit it. My power excites you." The fat one moves a step closer to him. "I love you. I am your destiny. Together, we can rule the planet. Without me, you will be dead. Your corpse will provide food for my zombies and the crows. You will be nothing. Do you hear me? Nothing."

"You talk of love. What do you know of such a thing? To you, it is just another word." He turns and scrambles down the stairs.

The Fat Witch does not follow. "There is no escape," she whispers. "No escape." A tear glides down the powdered roundness of her cheek.

At the base of the stairs, The Businessman opens the door to the parking garage. Glowing hands seize his arms, his shoulders, his throat.

Scenes of The Nurse, rushing through busy offices, smashing computers with a hammer.

Scenes of zombies staggering down busy streets, into department stores and restaurants and hospitals.

Scenes of merciless hands tearing into soft flesh.

Scenes of glowing teeth ripping into gleaming innards.

A close-up of a beak, lovingly ripping an eye from its socket.

Twilight. A parking lot outside of a church.

"It is all so impossible," The Daughter says, wrapping her arms around The Scientist, crying on his shoulder.

(*Why am I doing this? I do not love him. He is boring. He babbles like a fool.*)

"I have learned the truth, Miracula," the handsome man says. "Witches have seized control of the Internet through the power of nuclear reactions. They are using radioactivity to reconfigure the brainwaves of crows, and to re-energize deceased human tissue. They can even download images through the eyes of the living dead. Their power is horrifying."

The Daughter points to the church. "Then why doesn't God help us?"

He shakes his head. "I am afraid even God cannot defeat the science of the witches."

The Nurse walks up to the couple. She is tired and breathing heavily. In the fading light, her maroon lipstick looks black. "Excuse me. We have not met, but I know much about you from an old acquaintance. I used to be a friend of your mother."

"My mother? Tell me about her." The Daughter grabs The Nurse by the wrist. "I have waited so long to learn her identity."

"You will wish you did not know," the older woman says. "The truth will break your heart."

"And what is the truth?" The Scientist asks. "Tell us now."

"Very well." The Nurse takes a deep breath and stares into the girl's eyes. "Your mother is The Queen of the Witches. She is the most evil creature to ever walk the earth. I was once her handmaiden, but then I learned I was going to have a baby, so I escaped and hid myself from her. I did not want my child exposed to her vileness." She strokes the girl's cheek. "A few years later, when you were born, your father had the same thought. He stole you away from your mother while she was asleep. I helped him to hide from her. Your mother has been waiting for the day when she can at last reclaim you. Our only hope now is to destroy all the Internet computers."

"I want to meet my mother," The Daughter says. "My love will make her good."

(*I do not believe that. Why did I even say it? Why am I inviting doom into my life?*)

"Impossible. You must hide," the older woman says. "I have looked in all the old books. You cannot win." Suddenly she sees The Young Witch at the far end of the parking lot. "There. That woman is spying on us. She is your half-sister. Her father was one of the living dead."

"The living dead? Then she is a demon." The Daughter looks with fright—and curiosity, too—at the slender red-haired woman. "But running away cannot solve the problem." She turns and walks toward her half-sister.

"We must stop her," says The Nurse.

"Let her go. She has goodness in her heart," The Scientist replies. "She will speak to the witches on behalf of humanity, and God." He looks from the older woman to the church.

A moment later, The Daughter and The Young Witch enter a black limousine, which drives off into the gloom.

Scenes of zombies ripping the clothes off of attractive men and women.

In some scenes, they simply devour the living. But in others, they drag their prey into the shadows, subjecting them to horrible pleasures of the flesh.

Close-up of a television screen.

"The situation is a catastrophe without end," says The Reporter. He is badly bruised, with scratches on his forehead and jaw. "The hungry dead continue to infect the world with their horror and radioactivity. The streets are filled with the torn bodies of the innocent. Plus, it has been revealed that the zombies are now forcing their victims to succumb to foul carnal acts. Authorities fear that these acts of abomination will result in grotesque cross-breed births. It is rumored that some of the resultant infants may grow to become Internet witches. Stay tuned to this television channel for further developments."

An enormous cave lit by blazing torches.

The Daughter's clothes are torn, and she is wrapped in chains. She has been placed on a bloodstained stone altar.

"So," The Fat Witch says. "We meet again, Miracula. I am your mother, The Queen of the Witches. Does that make you happy, my child? That means you are a Witch Princess."

"That does not matter," The Daughter says. "All I have ever wanted is your love. Forget your evil and be a good and kind mother to me."

(*This old whore is repulsive. I wish that she was dead. But I am trapped.*)

"I could not do so even if I tried," the fat one says. "I could never forget the thrill of my great and terrible vices. A simple life means nothing to me. You are the one in the chains, but mine is the greater prison. Join me in the exquisite hell of ultimate power."

The Fat Witch touches a finger to The Daughter's forehead. Her black hair slowly begins to turn red.

"I do not want your madness," The Daughter cries.

The Young Witch enters the cave, followed by a male zombie. It is The Scientist. Both of them are naked except for loose strips of cloth wrapped around their hips. The Young Witch fondles the zombie's face and well-muscled shoulders, and then leads him into the shadows.

The fat one touches the chest of The Daughter. Her plump finger is just a few inches from the captive's heart. A red glow spreads through the girl's body, and she screams.

"There is no escape, my sweet," The Fat Witch says. "Soon the world will be a radioactive wasteland inhabited by witches and the living dead."

The Young Witch, satisfied, emerges from the shadows. She takes the knife from beside the altar and, laughing wildly, thrusts it repeatedly into the chest of The Scientist. Then she jabs it into his empty eye socket.

The fat one smirks as the zombie falls to the cave floor. Then she turns back to The Daughter. "Waves of my energy are surging through you. Soon you will feel the power of my vast knowledge. And knowledge is simply another word for evil."

The Daughter begins to look around, and see—

(*Now I see why I cannot remember my childhood. Why sometimes words appear in the sky. Why there is a toilet in the bathroom, but I never need to use it. This is not life—it is a twisted fantasy, a nightmare born in some diseased brain. No matter what I want, what I wish, it will never change. Why doesn't my God help me? Why—?*)

"Why does God allow this to happen?" the girl screams.

The fat one throws back her head and laughs. "Perhaps your God finds this all very amusing. Yes, no doubt He is watching right now, enjoying this quaint little drama: the end of the world."

The Young Witch laughs as well. "Dear Miracula's hair is now red and her eyes—see how they glow with fire," she cries.

"But I do not want to be a monster," The Daughter screams.

(*But I do. I want to destroy this filthy world of lies.*)

She begins to cry. "I want to go back to my old life. I was happy then."

(*Inside, I have always been miserable. I want to die.*)

Suddenly a figure looms before them all. It is the zombie that had once been The Scientist. He pulls the knife out of his eye socket. With a roar of triumph, he lashes out, cutting through the pale throat of The Young Witch. He plunges the knife into the heart of The Fat Witch, releasing a torrent of black blood. He then begins to unwrap the chains that bind The Daughter.

"I—I love you," he croaks through his dead, dry lips.

"And I love you," she says, her smile suddenly hard and twisted.

(*You disgust me. But that is a small matter. I am just a puppet hanging from unseen strings, dancing for a God who does not care.*)

She takes the hand of the creature and leads him out of the cave, through winding passageways, into a world that they now rule. An endless domain of chaos, agony, and tears.

Names, names, and more names. Darkness. Static.

Rewind.

FADING QUAYLE, DANCING QUAYLE

CHARLES COLEMAN FINLAY

T HE TOP CIRCLE IN THE traffic light looked pink, faint pink, like a single drop of blood in a cup full of water.

Andy Quayle heard a voice, his own, say, "Red."

His leg twitched, his foot hit the brake, and the minivan skidded to a stop. The bumper slammed into an old man crossing the street and he went down hard. Andy leaned over the dashboard to see what had happened.

The old man stood up, stared at Andy with dead white eyes, and shuffled off, his arm bent akimbo. A jagged sliver of bone poked through a fresh tear in his windbreaker's sleeve. The windbreaker was pale blue, the color of veins under skin.

"Navy," said Andy's voice.

He watched the pale blue coat bob across the street. The old man tripped over the curb and crashed to the ground. He tried to push himself up, but the broken arm kept folding in half.

Something crawled in the road beside the old man, a small creature that was mostly head, and the head mostly mouth, and the mouth an open, hungry, toothless maw.

"Baby," said Andy's voice.

His head swiveled. A baby seat was belted in the minivan behind him. His hand fumbled at the latch. The door swung open. He staggered over to the baby.

The baby sat up. It shoved an old bone into its mouth, sucking on it like a pacifier.

"Slurpy, slurpy," said Andy's voice.

He lifted the baby and turned around. The empty van rolled slowly down the road away from him. Andy tucked the baby under his arm and lurched after it.

"Brake," said Andy's voice, and his free hand popped up to slap his forehead.

The van rolled through a pool of pale green transmission fluid and punched into the side of an abandoned car, making a slight hiccup as its headlight shattered. A woman in T-shirt and jeans climbed out of the wreck's back seat, an arm bone clutched in her teeth, and ran away.

Andy slid the van door open and fastened the squirming baby into the car seat.

"Safety first," said Andy's voice. "Gootchey-goo."

"Gah!" said the baby, swinging the bone at him.

He took the driver's seat, backed up, and continued driving down the street, tires crunching over broken glass.

He passed a house, a house, a house, a church—no stop. Corner—turn. Store, store, bank, store—no stop. KFC. Meat.

Meat—must eat!

His leg twitched. The van skidded to a stop. Andy smacked into the steering column.

He shook off the impact and looked more closely. Overturned tables straddled broken window frames. Empty paper buckets sprouted across the parking lot like mushrooms in the forest. The smell of old, cold grease hung in the air.

But no meat.

There was no more meat anywhere. Only hunger. Even his hunger faded, like washed-out colors, until it was hardly an itch worth scratching.

Andy heard his own voice sobbing.

The back of his hand rubbed at his eye sockets and ended up damp. His leg straightened and the van sped forward again.

Around a corner, he saw a school. He accelerated past the *One Way—Do Not Enter* sign, jumped the curb, and drove over the grass to park by the side doors.

"Work," said Andy's voice. "Late."

His hand switched off the ignition and tugged the emergency brake until it caught.

"Brake," said Andy's voice, and his head nodded.

He hopped out of the van and hurried over to the side door. The baby cried as Andy got close. Dull thuds emanated through the hollow core steel. With both hands he managed to depress the latch until it clicked.

The door swung open, spilling a mass of bodies in a moaning heap. Some stood up and began to wander away. Andy tripped over the rest to enter the building.

Andy wandered the halls. In the gym, a tall boy attempted to dribble a flat basketball. A very short man with a long beard stood at the front of one classroom, writing with a piece of chalk so small his nails scraped the word-covered blackboard in a steady, rhythmic screech. In the main office, a chubby woman hunched over the copier, flinching every time the machine whirred and the light flashed. Reams of loose paper carpeted the floor, all printed with the same thing. Her blank eyes fixed on Andy.

"You'll. Love. This. It's. Funny." she said, her pudgy fingers thrusting out a fresh copy. "Top. Ten. Things. You. Can. Do. With. A. Brain."

He jerked away from her. The stench of burned coffee leaked out of the teachers' lounge and filled the hall. He walked on until he came to the cafeteria, where two boys threw paper wads at each other across the tables.

"Hey, stop that," said Andy's voice.

The kids looked at him. "Uh, uh," they said, but they stopped.

Andy saw the art room and went to it.

Construction paper covered the floor. Big sloppy swirls of acrylic paint decorated the cabinet doors and desktops. The throwing wheel whirred in one corner. The kiln switch read *on* but Andy didn't see it glowing.

He untaped the pedal on the wheel to stop its spinning. He tried to wash the brushes in the sink, but the bristles were stiff and ruined. Sweat poured off his head. The kiln switch read *on* so he unplugged it. Then he scooped paper into the trash can until it overflowed. An empty trash can sat in the cafeteria. His body turned to get it.

He saw a girl skulking around a corner at the end of the hallway. Young woman. Girl. Young woman. Girl. She wore go-go boots, and a velvet skirt, and a sheer blouse that clung to her slender frame. The colors were all gray, like ash.

"Black," said Andy's voice.

She wore so much patchouli that Andy's nose couldn't smell anything else. She carried a large, bulging purse over her shoulder and carried two flat cardboard boxes in her hands. She wobbled slightly under their weight.

Andy lurched forward. "Can I help you?" he heard his voice ask.

The girl shrieked and dropped the boxes, which fell smack on the ground. Andy bent to pick them up as she jumped backward, pulling an aerosol can and lighter from her purse. "Stay back!"

"Your hair looks nice," said Andy's voice. Something twitched at his nose, hiding behind the powerful patchouli. A hunger rumbled low in his belly.

"Are you for real? Aren't you a—?"

"Art teacher," said Andy's voice.

"Like, shit. It's so hard to tell anymore." Her shoulders sagged and she leaned against the wall. She thrust the can and lighter into her bag, and tilted her head at the boxes in Andy's hands. "You carry those. Wait here—I'll get a couple more."

Andy stood rooted to the spot. She returned from the cafeteria store-room with three more cases.

"Extra's for you," she said, slipping it onto his pile. "I used to work in the school cafeteria, so I knew there'd be stuff here. We better get going before any of those zombies notice us. It's only three blocks away."

They walked out the exit and across the playground. When she stopped to shift the bag on her shoulder, Andy continued on. It was daylight, late afternoon, although it felt almost dark. Andy lifted his head to the sky. A car alarm blasted somewhere far away. A mourning dove cooed in a tree, just above the branch where a zombie squirrel gnawed on an empty walnut shell.

Someone screamed right behind him.

Andy pivoted. The boys from the cafeteria clutched at the girl. One held her arm, and she spun, pounding him on the head with a blackjack, using his body to block the second one's attack.

He set his cases on the ground and staggered toward them, grabbing the two boys by the hair and slamming their heads together. They made a hollow *clonk*, so he did it again. Then he grabbed their collars and pushed them toward the school building.

"Detention," said Andy's voice.

"Uh, uh," the boys mouthed in protest. But they went.

"Shit, shit, *shit*. You just saved my life, teach." She stood there, hands clutching her chest, head leaning forward. She looked at the ground, where the dropped boxes had split at the seams and cans rolled in different directions. "We can't carry these three blocks, not this way."

Andy's forefinger jumped out at the end of his arm, pointing toward the parking lot. "Minivan," said Andy's voice.

"Oh, good thinking!" Using a broken box like a basket, she gathered about half the cans. "Let's go. Before they come back."

He walked toward the van.

"Wait—aren't you going to get those boxes?"

Andy stopped, turned, saw that he'd walked past them. He picked them up and carried them over to the van. He pulled open the door and placed them on the seat beside the baby. Then he climbed into the driver's seat, turning the ignition.

The passenger door opened and she slid in next to him. "What an ugly kid," she said. Her eyes flicked back and forth from the baby to Andy. "Is it—?"

"Baby," said Andy's voice.

"Aw, I'm sorry, that must be so—whoa!"

Something bounced off the inside of the windshield and landed on her lap. She held it up near her chest. The buttons gaped open on her blouse, revealing the shy gray bra underneath. Beside it, her skin appeared almost translucent, like skim milk.

"What's this?" she asked.

"Breast," said Andy's voice. His eyes shifted back to the object in her hand. "Bone."

"Breastbone? Like, ewwwww!" She threw it out the window and wiped her hands on her velvet skirt. "I'd guess you know all that stuff 'cause of art. Like, anatomy. We want to go that way—" She pointed.

Andy's leg straightened. The van leaped forward, crashed through the fence, hopped over the curb, and scraped bottom on the road. He veered around an abandoned school bus. One of the tires flapped flat on the road. The van listed sideways.

"That's cool, just keep driving," she said. "Like, you forget to think of the most basic stuff, y'know, running all the time. I could have driven a car over to the school."

She directed him to an old brick warehouse just off the main street. A display window in front framed a big screen TV with a video camera aimed at the sidewalk. A large crowd had collected. Most stood there watching themselves wave at the camera, though a few aimed remote controls at the picture, their thumbs rising and falling with a range of vigorous arm gestures.

"Just keep driving," she said, ducking and shoving his head down to the dashboard. "Just go past them. Down to the next alley, and tuuuuuurn—" she extended the *ur*-sound until they reached it "—here!"

He turned there, the metal hub of the wheel screeching as it ground to a stop under a dead neon sign. Other vehicles lined the alley—an SUV, a sedan, a convertible—among a scattering of human artifacts and remains.

"We're downstairs in the club," she said, jumping out. "I better go tell them you're coming. We kinda hate surprises."

Andy got out and waited. At the open end of the alley, a bald man with a beer belly and a beaked nose shoved a recliner down the street toward the big screen TV. He stopped and stared at Andy. Andy stared back. The door creaked open behind him. The bald man stared at something behind Andy. Andy turned.

She gestured at him to hurry.

"Come on," she said. "Bring the boxes."

Andy piled up all the boxes. He went through the propped open door, put his foot out onto nothing, and tumbled down the steps. The door swung open at the bottom. Andy looked up.

An unshaven man in army fatigues, with skin the color of weak tea, stared down. He was covered in some cologne so strong Andy coughed. Behind it lurked the scent of something else, something almost familiar. The man pointed a shotgun at Andy's face.

"He's a zombie! He's a damn zombie!"

The girl slammed her hand against the barrel and the blast went wide of Andy's head. A can exploded and a shower of green beans fell on Andy.

"He's an art teacher, shithead. He, like, saved my life back at school."

Andy pushed himself upright and staggered past them both. Inside, lights spun and strobed. Music played, a driving techno drone with a bass beat so strong it vibrated up through the floor and into his bones. Something intense called to him. His body hurled toward the parquet floor, legs pumping, arms swinging.

"Well, he sure dances like your average white boy," the man in the fatigues said.

"I think he's kinda funky," the girl said.

"Dance," said Andy's voice. His body throbbed and jerked, a half-beat out of synch with the music but struggling to catch up. Drops of sweat formed on his forehead. The back of his hand rubbed at his cheeks and ended up damp.

Pounding came from an inside door.

Andy looked up and saw that the girl and the man in fatigues had stacked all the canned food atop one of the tables. The man in fatigues aimed his gun at the door.

"Who's there?" he shouted.

"S'Earl," the reply came.

Fatigues unbolted the lock. "Come on in, Earl. We've got something to eat now besides stale peanuts and chips."

Two new people entered the room—a skinny guy with wild hair and glasses, followed by a harried-looking, motherly woman.

"Who the hell's that?" the skinny guy, Earl, asked.

"New boyfriend," Fatigues said, jerking his thumb at the girl.

"Asshole," the girl said. Earl snickered, and the girl said, "You're both assholes."

"Ohmygod!" the new woman cried. "I know him. That's Andy Quayle. He teaches—he taught—at the school with me."

Andy's hand shot into the air and waved. "Hi, Marsha," said Andy's voice.

"Er, hi, Andy," she said in return.

He continued to dance. Something inside him thirsted.

"He's just, y'know, in shock or something," the girl said. "I mean, my God. Like, who isn't? Y'know?"

"Well," Marsha said, staring at Andy. She shrugged, and dropped her voice. "He's not exactly the brightest bulb in the socket. I have no clue how he survived this long."

"Sweet potatoes and green beans!" Earl whined. "Gimme that can opener. Where's the real food? Where's the frozen meatloaf?"

"Meat's the problem," the girl yelled at him. "Meat means murder—from now on we're all vegan!"

The man in the fatigues rolled his eyes.

"Aw, the hell with it," Earl said, spooning the dull brown mass into his mouth. "There's two dozen out front in the trap. We just checked."

"Maybe it's a trap for us," Fatigues said, scowling. "If this is all caused by that Chinese mind collective, the way I think, then they'll—"

"You're nuts!" Earl swallowed and wiped his mouth on his sleeve. "It's the silicon synapse transplants, the big brain bulk-up gone bad. I told you people, I warned everybody against it, because you can't get smart for nothing. At least the neural deterioration lets us overwhelm their senses, confuse them."

All of them but the girl glanced over at Andy.

Marsha waved her hands. "No, that can't be right. That just doesn't explain the feeding frenzies *or* the way it happened so fast *or* the zombie cats we've found—"

"That cat did nothing but purr," the girl said. "It was harmless, and there was *no* reason for you guys to burn it!"

Earl sneered, but Fatigues said, "It could have been contagious. Maybe that's the vector that introduced the plague!"

"There's no plague," Earl growled with his mouth full.

"Has to be," Marsha said. "It's some bio-warfare thing designed to provoke a simple stimulus-response reaction. Now that most of the brains are deprived of the original defining stimulus, they're rewiring themselves."

"Whoa," the girl said. "You go, science lady."

"Except for the fact that it doesn't affect those of us smart enough—" Earl looked sideways at the girl "—or dumb enough not to go for the brain bulk-up in the first place."

Fatigues snorted. "They could be alien parasites for all I care." He clutched a grenade on his belt. "They watch TV, we blow them up, God sorts them out. As long as *that* works, I like it. I like it a lot."

The music played on the whole time they argued, *thump-thumpa-thump-thumpa-thump-thumpa-thump*. . . . Andy heard a faint, muffled, arrhythmic banging that threw off his dancing.

"So, like, is there any hope for a cure?" the girl asked.

"If it starts evolving," Marsha said, "maybe it'll break down into something where we can be safe. We already see some evidence of that, with the—"

Earl slammed his fist on the table. "You think you know everything, but you don't! There's no cure, not until all those stupid people are wiped out!"

"I say it'll be over when we make it over," Fatigues said, shaking his gun. "So the sooner we get to work the better."

"Whatever," the girl said. She slumped in her chair. "I just wish it would end so—"

The outside door buckled and banged open. A dozen zombies poured inside, heads turning from side to side. The last one through the door carried a remote control at arm's length in front of him. The bald, pot-bellied man in the lead pointed toward the girl.

"Burg-her. Eat burg-her."

"Uh, uh," said the other zombies. They surged forward.

"I don't like this!" Fatigues screamed, kicking tables over. "I don't like this at all!"

Marsha dove for the other door, unlatching it and dragging Fatigues behind her. His shotgun blasted, knocking a few zombies off-balance and slowing their assault. Earl, rising from the fallen table, went down in a tangle of arms as he tried to follow them. He screamed, stabbing his spoon at their faces. Fluid spattered into the air.

Andy danced.

A bottle with a flaming wick flew from behind the bar and shattered on the pile. One of the zombies instantly became a torch, sizzling and popping, filling the air with the thick stench of burned flesh as he spun in circles, arms in the air. The girl stood behind the bar. She threw another bottle, and another. Zombies pulled the door open to pursue Marsha and Fatigues, or flee the flames.

And the vibrations pounded up through the floor into his legs, so Andy danced.

Sprinklers blossomed water, extinguishing the fires in a spray of steam and smoke. Andy lifted his mouth and swallowed as he danced, but his thirst didn't go away. Over by the bar, Baldy attacked the girl. She batted his hands away with the bottles, wicks hanging wet and limp in the necks.

Conduits sparked on the wall; the lights flickered and quit. The music shuddered, died.

"Aaaarggh!" screamed Andy's voice.

He jumped forward, picked up a chair, and smashed it into the last place he'd seen Baldy. He hit something hard—the impact shivered up through his shoulders—that fell with a *thump* onto the floor. Andy pounded it again and again, until the chair broke.

A hand gripped Andy's elbow and he spun.

"Come on!" the girl said.

She led him toward a light trickling in through the door. He followed her up the steps to the alley. Out in the sunlight, everything seemed blindingly bright. He squinted and looked at the long shadows. Even the little convertible had one. On the ground, in the shadow, beside pieces of a skull, he saw keys. His hand reached out to grab the ring.

"What're you doing?" the girl shouted. She waited halfway down the alley.

"Nice car," said Andy's voice.

He climbed into the driver's seat and shoved the keys into the slot. He looked over his shoulder as the girl tossed the baby into the little back seat. The baby sucked quietly on its yellowed thumb.

"Didn't want to forget your kid," the girl said, "y'know, even if—y'know, like . . ."

She climbed over the door into the passenger seat as the engine revved to life. Her hair was plastered to her head. Her clothes hung tight to her skin. The sprinklers had washed off the overpowering scent of patchouli and underneath the lingering odor he smelled something else. Sweat. Skin. Something danced in his belly, where that old and nearly forgotten hunger sat.

He shifted into gear, pulling out of the alley and driving down the street.

She reached into her purse and held a cigarette to her lips. It shook in her fingers. As she foraged through the bag, he punched the dashboard lighter in. When it popped out, he held it up for her. She sucked on the cigarette and exhaled a little puff of clove-scented smoke.

He noticed the dimple in her chin. The tip of his tongue would fit perfectly in that dimple. He leaned toward her.

"Uh, uh!"

"Hey! Keep your eyes on the road!"

Andy's head snapped upright. He steered the car back between the lines.

"You're looking a little stiff there, teach." She laughed, and took another drag on her cigarette. "Like, you saved my life. Twice. Thanks." When he didn't say anything, she said, "So where do we go now?"

Andy stared at her cheek. It blushed pink like the western sky above the highway. "Into the sunset."

"Sounds good to me." She exhaled a stream of smoke. "Let's do it."

He jerked the steering wheel to cut across the boulevard, accelerated through a yellow light, and zipped up the entrance ramp. In the rearview mirror, he saw Andy's mouth grinning like a happy man.

HOMELANDS

LUCIEN SOULBAN

SHANGHAI BURNED, GOD'S JUDGMENT AGAINST the Asian Sodom rendered . . . .

A gaily painted river of umbrellas and parasols drifted down Bubbling Well Road in a slow, lethargic ballet. Beneath the cloth canopy bustled yellow palanquins, leather sedan chairs, and bamboo rickshaws. British and American colonists streamed past, heading for the already crammed docks along the Bund, a picturesque stretch of road bordering Whangpu River. Most maintained an air of refined panic, fleeing as fast as propriety allowed. Such was the price of "civilizing" China: the facade of control. Others moved swiftly, gentility be damned.

Cedric Halston watched the crowd surge past white European-style colonial villas, a few of which coughed a steady pillar of black smoke from soot-blasted windows. A lanky six-footer and topped with an original tan Stetson, Halston held a commanding view over people's crowns, and he didn't much like the vista. He wanted to fire a gun, if only to move this herd even faster, though admittedly, he was an impatient man. Instead, he kept one hand tight on his holstered Army revolver and used the other hand to brush aside locks of black hair latched to his sweating face. His hands, rough and callused, bore the marks of his days in the Union's Dead Walker unit. Still, no Nevada heat could prepare him for the Shanghai humidity, which made walls perspire and plagued civilized folk with "unmentionables" like ringworm. The burning houses didn't help settle the heat either, and instead sent a frantic twinkle in his gray eyes.

A scream broke Halston's reverie. The skittish crowd moved and swelled, continuing the first cry with their own panicked shrieks.

"Move!" Halston shouted, gun drawn.

Two Sikh policemen, the red-turbaned Bulwan and Sohan, their shag beards and waxed mustaches framing grave faces, fell in at Halston's elbows, helping him push through the crowd. The mob surged forward, but Halston and his two escorts straight-armed their way through. Bulwan fired his rifle skyward once, splitting the herd like frightened sheep.

The trio burst into a narrow adjoining alley where a Brit spun and shrieked like a wild Moroccan dervish. A dead body, bloodied, lay at his feet. Halston raised his revolver and aimed; Bulwan and Sohan followed his lead with their rifles, hoping he'd venture the first shot—and thus take responsibility—for killing the Britisher. Halston paused, his breath suspended in the raucous, naked moment, waiting . . .

Waiting . . .

Finally, a rip appeared across the man's stomach. The clothing and flesh beneath parted, opened as though by the will of God. Blood sprayed out in a fan of crimson, painting *something* in the air. A lengthy red cord of internal organs unraveled from the Brit's wound. The man shrieked before his throat puckered inward and a fistful of flesh vanished in a ragged bite, betraying a floating set of teeth.

Halston fired at the unseen attacker. Bulwan and Sohan followed suit, their shots thudding into solid air that bled black ichor.

The Brit collapsed. His attacker fell atop him a second later, pressing down on him and creasing his clothes with its flour-sack bulk. Whatever it was, it was no longer moving. The dark-skinned and impassive Sohan walked over and emptied a bullet into the skull of the Brit and, after running one hand over the other, fired another into what he assumed to be the assailant's skull, punctuating both reports by reloading his single-shot carbine. Dismayed outcry moved through the crowd, but Halston swept his gun across the mob, parts of which lurched backward.

"Don't you folks have somewhere to be?"

Reluctantly, the onlookers moved down the street, but a few shot Halston poisoned looks.

"Well, *sahib*," Bulwan said. "Things aren't very tiptop."

"Not tiptop, indeed," Halston said.

The crowd drifted past, their contempt for Halston unspoken, but naked in their stares. Halston knew their thoughts: *Bloody indolent Americans. Damn Yank refugees.* That's what they thought of all Americans these days.

Now that America was no more.

"The Admiralty's blockaded the bay," Commissioner Lexington said, running his fingers through the frayed bush of white hair that rested above an equally impressive snowy hedge of eyebrows. He clipped his words in proper British military style. "They'll sink any ship leaving the docks."

"Tell that to them," Halston said, staring out the window of the Cathay Hotel. The docks below were lost beneath a sea of black hats, bonnets, and coolie caps, and a forest of arms waving wads of money at stevedores and captains, anyone who'd smuggle them aboard the next ship. It was like the Frisco evacuation all over again—parents holding up children, blindly offering them up for a chance at salvation; captains indenturing those who couldn't pay the suddenly exorbitant price for a passage. Halston fought the momentary onslaught of panic's echo, saw himself lost, looking for a ship.

He didn't want to lose everything again.

"They're frightened," Lexington said. "They remember the Admiralty's handling of that outbreak in Port Sudan and what."

"Well, if the city keeps burning, the Admiralty won't have to fire a single volley," Halston said.

"No," Lexington admitted, easing himself back into the velvet chair.

"Railways?"

"Blockaded by the blasted Chinese. Devils don't want our problem spilling into their districts."

"And the fire?"

"Spreading across the International Settlement and French Concession."

"It'll handle some of the dead meat. What about the Chinese districts?"

"Unaffected—for now. The flames haven't leaped across Soochow or Sillawei Creeks yet."

Halston shrugged. "It's sparing them a tarring, but the creeks are just funneling the fires and driving the dead meat here."

"Mr. Halston," Lexington said curtly, "we hired you for your experience in these matters. To handle them before they became inconvenient. They're now inconvenient. We were told you were the best the Americas had to offer."

"Don't get upset." Halston said. "I can handle any problem involving the walking dead. It's just I never met any invisible ones before."

"Perhaps the work of one of your infamous zombie masters? I should think we'd do well to round up all the Negroes."

"Don't waste your time."

"What then?"

"Leave Bulwan and Sohan with me. They're good. So far, it looks like the unseen zombies can't turn others invisible or even Lazarus them with a bite. That's all to the good. It means we don't have an epidemic. I'll figure out who's turning them invisible and nip this problem in the bud."

"Very well. We'll relocate to the Astor House Hotel in Hongkew and hold the bridges for as long as we can. If we have to raise anchor, we'll do so without you."

"I thought the Admiralty blockaded the city."

"Balderdash," Lexington said. "Not for us."

"Bulwan, Sohan," Halston said, elbowing his way down the hotel's crowded marble stairs. "You're with me."

"Are we killing more dead-*wallah, sahib?*" Bulwan asked. He fell into step behind Halston. Sohan followed, shouldering his rifle quietly.

Halston nodded. The crowds thinned farther down the street, and the dusk sun shone through rips in the rising smoke. Those who hadn't made it this far now sought refuge where fate dictated.

"We need ammunition," Halston said, checking his belt. Eight bullets, not counting the pills in his guns. "Lexington said he couldn't spare any."

"Of course he did. I'm thinking you're going to Lauza Police Station?" Bulwan asked. "They are pulling out, across the Garden Bridge. And many people are stealing ammunition for themselves."

Halston sighed. "What do you suggest, Bulwan?"

"The Sûreté."

"Frenchies got their own problems."

"Yes, *sahib,*" Bulwan said, "but they are employing Chinese detectives, from the Green Gang."

Halston nodded. The French hired local scofflaws from the Big Eight Mob, which ran Shanghai's underworld. The Sûreté turned a blind eye to their pirating, so long as they didn't prey on Europeans. In return, the Mob provided a ready source of agents and even gave the Frenchies access to their arsenal.

Yes, the Sûreté would have ammunition—for a price.

South of Nanking Road rested Foochow Road, the rapidly beating heart of Shanghai's entertainment district. Teahouses and pagoda-roofed businesses lined the street in a parade of bright colors. Adjoining the street were dozens of thin alleys called *li*, which were low on respectability and high on discretion. Tonight, however, the once-lively avenue lay forsaken. A few spilt sedan chairs testified to some panicked moments, but otherwise, the streets bore no witnesses. Fortunately, fire hadn't consumed any buildings here; instead, the blazes remained west of Thibet Road, turning the horizon into a burning crown.

Halston walked down Foochow Road with Bulwan and Sohan flanking him. Down each *li*, Halston saw the same scene: empty alleys and red Chinese lanterns burning above doorways. He stopped, sniffing the air.

"Smell that?"

"I am smelling many things, *sahib*," Bulwan said with a grin. "Fires, dead bodies, you."

"Funny. I thought the Brits trained you boys better?"

"They did," Bulwan responded. "But you are not being British."

Sohan grinned ever so briefly.

"Trust me, *sahib*. Not being British is a good thing," Bulwan said before sniffing the air. There was a sharp reek to it. "Opium," he noted.

"And lots of it," Halston said. The smell normally pervaded the alleys, but tonight, the vapors clung to the road's cobblestones.

Flickering red lanterns adorned the doorways of the colorfully named "sing-song" houses and nail sheds, where prostitutes plied their trade. Lanterns also capped the summits of the opium dens' doors, proclaiming they were still open for customers. Halston walked to the closest *li* and inhaled the smoke tendrils from the nearest lantern. His vision swooned, everything suddenly slippery.

"*Sahib*?" Bulwan asked. His voice echoed in the empty cavern of Halston's skull.

Halston shook his head, trying to jar the molasses cobwebs loose. "They're burning opium in the lanterns," he said, looking up and down the *li*. "Som' bitch. They all are."

"*Sahib*!" Bulwan cried, his gaze fixed on something a dozen yards away on the cobblestone street. Sohan aimed his rifle down the road.

Then Halston heard it—a low groan, part breathless exhalation, part effort. A sigh plundered of emotion. Zombie.

The groan grew louder, but the street remained empty. Halston's heart skipped a beat.

"Damn," Halston said. "Shoulder your rifles. Pull out those toothpicks of yours."

Bulwan and Sohan shot Halston strange looks, but followed his example as he pulled an eighteen-inch bayonet blade by the makeshift handle from his thigh sheath. Most veterans of the old Union forces were shy about using bayonets, but Halston recognized their usefulness in facing zombies; they threaded dead meat eyeballs and skewered brains easier than needle through silk. The invisible ones, though, would take more skill.

The two Sikhs unsheathed their ceremonial *khirpan* blades from their red sashes before drawing in, shoulder to shoulder, with Halston. The groaning bounced off walls and down alleys with a queer, rising tone. Halston estimated the dead man was within ten yards now and closing. He wanted to run, regroup, but he could be running into other zombies for all he knew.

The irregular swish of fabric and the sound of dragging feet grew more pronounced, shifting to Halston's left, then the right. Five yards or so now. An old, familiar fear awoke in Halston's guts.

"Shit," Halston said. "The bastard's weaving all over the place."

The groaning hit a steady, incessant pitch. Then, the stumbling rush of feet. It was three yards away now, close enough that Halston smelled the deep, pungent rot of earth and gangrene. An anxious Bulwan stepped forward, swinging his *khirpan*.

"Stop!" Halston said, but the command came too late.

Bulwan imbedded his blade deep into unseen flesh. At the same instant, Halston heard a second clatter of footfalls right beside the Sikh. The snarls and steps weren't echoes in the street. Two invisible things stalked them.

Before Bulwan could react, the second attacker hammered his shoulders with meaty fists. Bulwan's collar bone snapped, and the Sikh let loose a shriek. The zombie lifted the screaming soldier into the air, the broken clavicle a blind man's knife dancing in and out of his wound. At his partner's peril, Sohan rushed in, but the dead thing dropped Bulwan and backhanded him. The blow sent Sohan flying back several feet.

Halston reached out blindly and locked his fingers when they came in contact with what he figured to be the zombie's arm. He pictured his adversary in his mind and lashed out with his bayonet. The blow was perfectly aimed, the steel driving into the soft underside of the zombie's rotting jaw and up through the roof of its mouth. Halston's bayonet seemed to disappear, to vanish into the night air. But he knew he had struck true when the thing in his grip spasmed, then went slack. And when Halston pulled the blade back, its surface was thick and shiny with black ooze.

The first zombie, pig stuck with Bulwan's blade, thrashed on the ground and moaned. Halston kicked at the sound, catching the zombie full in the ribs, if he interpreted the noise of splintering bones correctly. Anger had motivated the blow, not fear. Halston could see by the feeble movements of the half-exposed *khirpan* that the dead thing was floundering, helpless. But he was furious with himself for the way the fight had gone, for getting

Bulwan hurt, for feeling defenseless—and afraid. He almost kicked the zombie again, but controlled his temper long enough to pull his revolver. Four shots cracked the air, splattering the ground black.

The doors to Saint James's Church burst open on the receiving end of Halston's brogan. His grip was full of splintering plank, on which Sohan and he carried Bulwan. A few startled cries echoed through the church, but most folks hunched or lay in the pews, serene or deathly calm. Some even slept.

An Anglican minister moved forward, his balding pate wet with Shanghai heat, his jowls bouncing with each step. His blue eyes puffed out like those of a strangled fish.

"We need help," Halston said, setting Bulwan down. The Sikh gritted his teeth against the jostling. The minister stared blankly at the three men.

"He's been wounded," Halston snapped.

A shadow of disdain crossed the minister's face, the same look Brits gave Chinese commoners when they accidentally brushed against them. The same look Americans received for begging alongside Chinese hobos. Halston didn't have time for intolerance. Pulling his revolver, he leveled it straight at the clergyman's forehead.

"Administer aid to him," Halston said, cocking the hammer. "Now."

"There's no need for that . . . ."

Halston turned to see a nun step through the crowd. His gun inched down, but he kept the hammer eager.

The nun stood a couple heads shorter than Halston; her black habit stretched over a well-fed body. She spoke with a New England accent, but Halston barely noticed. He was more interested in her eyes, which swam in a mist of opium languor. In fact, the bite of opium hung over the whole church, overwhelming even the smell of stale sweat. Before Halston could comment, the nun swished past him to tend to Bulwan.

Halston finally holstered his firearm, then gestured for Sohan to take watch at a broken stained glass window.

"Your friend should remain here a while," the nun said, satisfied with her examination.

"Can I talk to you, Sister—privately?" Halston said.

The minister, fish eyes struggling to focus on the stranger, interposed himself between them. "That would be improper," he slurred.

Halston ignored the clergyman. "Just us Americans."

The nun paused, on the brink of deferring to the minister's authority, but moved off with Halston anyway. The minister tried following them, but a sharp click drew his attention to the stained glass window. Sohan's gaze was still directed outside, but the rifle on his lap was primed and aimed conspicuously at the minister. The fish-eyed man took the point.

"Where you from?" Halston asked once they'd moved behind a pillar near the confessionals. He loomed over the nun, pressed close and lowered his voice to a rumble.

"Boston," she said, no more frightened of him than she was of her needy charges. "I made it out on the last boat."

"A lot of misery got spread around in those final days."

"It was as bad in Boston as it got anywhere."

Halston nodded and stepped back. His intimidation tactics wouldn't work on her. "In case you haven't heard, there are zombies on the loose. You saw firsthand what they can do; why isn't anyone keeping watch at the windows?"

"Oh, I'd heard, but we're safe here. This is God's house," she said, not entirely convinced or convincing.

"I've seen dead meat cross themselves before entering a church and tearing apart everyone inside."

The nun looked away.

"Listen," Halston said. "You know what'll happen if they bust down that door."

"But they won't!" she snapped. Her eyes were suddenly clear; anger or defiance had burned away the opium dreams.

"I'm figuring that out," Halston said. "I'm just not sure what it's got to do with opium."

The nun bit her tongue and offered nothing but a stare.

"Every opium den and nail shack on Foochow is burning the stuff like incense on Chinese New Year. Now I find this church reeking of it. The dead meat we tangled with came past here, but they left you alone. That's got to be why."

"Yes," the nun finally admitted. "Minister Parsons gave us the opium. He said it would calm folks—and keep the zombies away, if we burned enough of it."

Halston nodded. "How long you been chasing dragons? It doesn't affect you like the others. You're used to it."

"I don't want to remember everything I've seen," she said. "It's easier to believe in God that way."

Halston moved out from behind the column and stalked up to the minister. "Father," he said, draping his arm around the shorter man's shoulders, "who told you about the opium keeping the dead meat at bay?"

Minister Parsons blinked with a bovine slowness. "A Chinaman."

"What Chinaman?"

"I don't know his name." Parsons's words dragged across his tongue.

"Did he sell you the opium?" Halston asked.

The minister nodded.

"Some Chinaman you don't know tells you opium keeps zombies away, and you believe him?" Halston said. "Either you're a fool for trusting him, or for thinking I'd believe you."

He drove one hand into Parsons's pockets, searching. The minister squirmed, but Halston grabbed him in a headlock. Some of the parishioners moved to help Parsons. They sat down again when Sohan stood and leveled his rifle at them.

"You're supposed to protect us," a Brit cried out to Sohan. He pointed one trembling finger at Halston. "From riffraff like him!"

"Actually," Halston announced, "Sohan's been deputized by the Shanghai Municipal Council to help me however necessary. Ah, here we go . . . ."

He pulled a tin from the minister's pocket. It was decorated with faux gold leaf, with painted poppy plants and flower vines framing the rim. Raised black lettering identified the brand as *Persephone's Odyssey*. Below it was the stenciled logo of Nichols and Company.

"Thanks, *padre*," Halston said. "If you hadn't lied, I wouldn't have known who you were protecting."

Avenue Edouard VII was a thin no man's land separating the International Settlement from the more liberal French Concession. Escaping the law in Shanghai often meant crossing this or any of the dozens of similarly situated streets, where extraterritoriality rendered nations immune from each other's laws. Many Americans, however, had no such consideration in these sour times. Without a country to call home, they were subject to Chinese law until they could buy another passport or citizen certificate. Many came to Shanghai because local European counsels sold nationalities like a saloon sold whiskey. Business was booming and havens could be had, if you could afford to pay. Most Americans could not. They worked, like Halston, as mercenaries or found some cobblestoned patch of street from which to beg, huddled shoulder-to-elbow with native Chinese beggars. The Europeans hated the Americans for that. No sin could be as great as shattering the facade of white man's superiority.

Conditions were especially hard on women. They indentured themselves to ship captains for a ticket out of the embargoed zone and across the Pacific. The captains, in turn, sold their markers to labor contractors, dance hall proprietors, and bordello madams.

Halston and Sohan crossed the empty Avenue Edouard VII and made their way toward the brightly lit windows of the sing-song house known as the Delightful Flower Gardens. A gold pagoda-style roof topped the two-story building, while red strips of paper fluttered from the eaves, tastefully announcing the services offered within. The muted sound of piano music haunted the air like the fragrance from plucked flower petals.

Halston remembered seeing the club and its financial backer, one Detective Sun, mentioned in the local mosquito press, tabloids notorious for their stinging gossip. Sun Chen was a nasty piece of work, a hoodlum who headed the Sûreté's Chinese Detective Division.

Approaching the door, Halston smelled the opium. He motioned for Sohan to stand watch outside, and entered the building's dark interior. No use dragging Sohan along. The Chinese uniformly disliked Sikh policeman for their heavy-handed methods. Sohan would only hinder negotiations.

Blue- and tan-robed ghosts drifted through the opium mists. Some cast sidelong glances Halston's way, but few really cared enough to notice. Halston moved through rooms covered in silk curtains, past low blackwood tables and red benches and the occasional jade painting. Clients lay on their sides, cradled by satin cushions and the blessed lethargy of the poppy, while hostesses glided among them with serene purpose.

Halston caught the elbow of an Asian beauty bathed in green silk. "Sun Chen" was all he said.

With an unreadable, porcelain expression, the daydreaming ghost glanced to a darkened archway, then drifted away. Halston walked through the silk curtains and into a private room commanded by a carved and lacquered red table, around which sat four robed gentleman, each with a prostitute on his arm. The men's cuffs had been rolled up, exposing their forearms in a manner most Chinese considered vulgar. That alone marked them as individuals of dubious integrity.

"I'm looking for ammunition," Halston said. ".50 caliber centerfires and .44s."

One gentleman with slight features stretched across an oval, milky white face, leaned forward, smiling. "*Chinois* or Russian." His voice betrayed an odd French lilt, an unusual Franglais.

"You have Russian?"

"*Oui.*" The man shrugged as if the answer were obvious. "It's more expensive, but—"

"And the Chinese ammo?"

"From Kiangnan Arsenal. The best."

Halston scowled. The Chinese, desperate to bridge the gap between Europe's military might and their own, had hired thousands of dispossessed Americans to head the foundries and gunsmith shops at places like Kiangnan. Another betrayal of the West's vaunted superiority.

"Price?" Halston asked.

"Money means little to men like us, *Monsieur* Halston."

"You think you know me, *Monsieur* Sun?"

Sun laughed. "Not many cowboys like you in Shanghai. You're the Brit's Number One Boy."

The words stung. "I'm nobody's 'boy'!"

Sun sat back. "All Americans are *boys* now. No better than us *pauvre Chinois*—or the slaves who revolted against you."

Halston held his tongue. He needed Sun's help. "What's your price?"

"I heard you were quite the zombie killer in *les États-Unis*."

"And?"

"And, I want to know how you make them."

Halston blinked, stunned. "Make them?"

"*Oui*—alcohol, opium, *les filles*, weapons . . . zombies. Even you Americans are commodities these days. Only, those of you who know how to create zombies can make a fortune. Sell yourself or sell what you know."

"I don't know how they're made," Halston said, "and I sure as hell wouldn't tell you if I did. Damn things are dangerous. They spread faster than crabs in a whorehouse."

"*Mais non*," Sun said with a face-splitting smile. "Not anymore. Not if you know how to control the infection."

"Opium?"

Sun sipped his tea.

"How is it everybody knows about the opium?"

"Not everybody," a Chinaman at the table said. Everybody laughed, except Halston.

"*Monsieur* Halston," Sun said, "if you cannot help us, we cannot help you."

Halston might have argued, had he been in any position to do so. "Then you can't help me," he said at last. "But before I go, I got one question. Just between us. No bullshit."

Sun motioned Halston to continue.

"How does every nail shed and saltwater sister in Shanghai know about the opium?"

Sun sighed. "*Monsieur* Halston. . . . Very well, but no tricks, *oui*? You have no ambassador to protect you, and the British care little about your fate."

"My word."

"They know because somebody wants them to know. Somebody is creating a . . . as you say, monopoly, *oui?* For opium consumption. This brand above all others."

Halston showed Sun the tin he found on Parsons. "The locals are being told that only this brand will save them."

"It *will* save them. This Persephone's Odyssey is very effective for keeping at bay the zombies now plaguing Shanghai. Very fortunate for Nichols and Company, eh? But it is a tricky business. Politics prevent the other opium sellers from properly displaying their displeasure with the situation. And many of these other sellers are our friends . . . ." Sun paused and let that last comment hang in the air. Then he added, "Are you going to visit this Nichols, perhaps?"

"No choice now."

Sun muttered something to the girl next to him. She left the room, returning a moment later with a box of Russian .44 bullets on a wooden platter.

"What's this for?" Halston asked.

Detective Sun shrugged and smiled. "Good for business."

Halston took the box. He had no problem playing six-shot messenger.

The night sky released its burden in a thick downpour that doused the fires and turned the wet cobblestone streets into something reptilian.

Halston walked up to the Nichols estate alone. By the light of the windows, he could see refugees in makeshift tents crowded on the lawn. As Halston reached the gates, a tall man, his face sliced by a mean grimace, stepped forward. The slight bow of his legs revealed him as a born rider, and though he was dressed like a gent, he looked like he would be equally comfortable in jeans and a duster.

"Can I help you, son?" the man asked, his accent deeply Southern.

"I'm here to see Nichols."

"And you are?"

"The law," Halston said. "I'm with the Shanghai Municipal Council."

"Then you ain't the law here. We're nationals of Mexico City, subject to their laws, not Britain's."

Protected within a bowl of mountains and ruled by the iron general Porfirio Díaz, Mexico City had escaped the Americas' fate. It boasted the only functioning government on the continent, but remained besieged by dead meat trying to penetrate the enclosed basin. Rumor had it, though, that Díaz was turning the tide, thanks to the help of a zombie master of African and Indian parentage working for him.

Mexico's citizens were protected by the so-called Extrality Laws. Halston had no authority here. He cursed Sun Chen for not warning him about that.

"Fine," Halston said. "Then may I *please* speak with Nichols?"

"That's better," the man replied. "Sure you can."

The Nichols's estate was massive and covered with manicured lawns and broad-canopied plane trees. The refugees stared as Halston and his escort walked by. The grime on their fine clothes and the hollow expressions on their faces betrayed the strain of this unaccustomed hardship.

"Who are they?" Halston asked.

"Guests of Mrs. Nichols."

"*Mrs.* Nichols?"

"Mr. Nichols died during the evacuation of New York. Mrs. Nichols has been his estate's proprietor since."

They reached the front steps of the three-story mansion, which appeared from this vantage more Greek monument than home. On the porch, four impressive Doric columns supported a triangular and ornately carved overhang, while the straight-faced marble walls accommodated inset windows. A disheveled gentleman waited near one of those windows, his tan suit stained with grass and his bowler a touch battered.

The double doors opened and a fifty-something gentleman stepped out, clutching a bag to his chest. He looked broken, but muttered a string of British-dappled "thank you"s to the middle-aged woman escorting him out. A born and bred socialite, her dusty hair bled more toward the white than straw, and her skin resembled nothing so much as freckled alabaster. She wore tasseled boots that ran to the knees, black Kentucky jeans, and a dark blue Bolero-style jacket over a ruffled white blouse. She appraised Halston with a glance.

"Curran, dear," she asked Halston's escort, "who is this?"

Halston offered his name, but didn't bother to mention his sponsors.

"Ah. And whereabouts are you from?"

"Nevada," Halston said. "And you're Mrs. Nichols?"

"I am. What brings you here?"

Halston shot the waiting gentleman a sidelong look. Mrs. Nichols smiled and turned to the gentleman. As she did, Halston got a look at the papers he was holding. From the stamps and seals, he figured them for property deeds.

"Forgive me, Mr. Pennworth," Nichols said, "but I must attend to this matter. I shan't be a moment." She looked at Halston and invited him in with a restrained sweep of the arm. "In private, then?"

"If it's all the same," Halston noted, "I'd prefer to stay outside."

Nichols offered a civil smile, then turned to Pennworth. "Mr. Pennworth," she said, "why don't you go inside. The servants will bring you tea and cucumber sandwiches."

Pennworth thanked her profusely, with the eagerness of someone who hadn't eaten in some time, and vanished behind closed doors.

"To what do I owe the honor, Mr. Halston?" Nichols asked, stepping down to the manicured lawn.

Halston followed, his eyes slowly taking in the buildings surrounding the estate. He appeared impressed by the architecture, but was actually gauging which had the best sightlines. "Opium," he offered at last. "I'm here about opium."

"You don't strike me as the type."

"I'm not," Halston said. "I'm just wondering why your particular brand seems to affect dead meat."

Nichols studied Halston briefly before dismissing Curran, who had trailed them at a discreet distance, with a nod.

"Coincidence?" she asked after the servant had gone.

"Awfully lucrative coincidence."

"Opium distribution isn't illegal, Mr. Halston."

"Nope, but if it could be proved a merchant was creating a problem one of their products was solving—well, I don't think any treaty would shield someone like that. Do you?"

Nichols remained quiet a moment. "Mr. Halston," she said, as if examining the name for a watermark. "Are you the same Halston who works for the Shanghai Municipal Council? Rumor has it that you served with the Dead Walkers."

"I am, and I did. Are you avoiding my question?"

"Not at all." Nichols turned and walked slowly across the lawn, toward the back of the mansion. Before he followed, Halston again glanced at the roofs of the neighboring buildings.

"Please, indulge me a moment," Nichols said when Halston caught up. "Where'd you evacuate from?"

"Frisco."

"New York," she replied to a question never asked. "My husband and I were separated during the evacuation. He bought his way aboard another ship—one later scuttled by the British when they discovered it carried infected passengers."

"Sorry. But it's no sadder than the other stories I've heard."

"My husband could have prevented a lot of that sadness, had he been given more time. He served in a field hospital outside New York during the uprising, you see. He used a cornucopia of drugs—including opium cordials—to treat emotionally distressed patients. That's how he discovered that zombies disliked the . . . taste of these patients. They killed them, but never ate them.

"Unfortunately, his discovery came too late—for him and America. We had to evacuate, but dear Henry told me everything before we parted. The key was opium. So, when I arrived here, I continued his research, eventually buying some Indian poppy fields belonging to Jardine, Matheson, and Company. They were abandoning the business as beneath them," Nichols concluded. "So they had no problem selling to an American."

Nichols led Halston to a brick shed with a padlocked door. She opened the padlock and door, revealing stairs leading down into the rough and dark earth.

"It's called a *tykhana*," Nichols said. "I borrowed the idea from India's Mughals. It's a cooling room, intended to stave off the summer heat."

Halston caught the smell of rotted flesh wafting up from the depths, even as he heard the sound of rushing feet behind him. He reached for his gun, but it had not cleared its holster when a shot rang out. Halston didn't even flinch. He knew he was not the target.

A dozen steps from Halston and the shed, Curran collapsed, a coin-sized hole punched in his ribs. On a rooftop across the street, Sohan reloaded his carbine and turned his sights on Nichols. Halston, however, already covered her with his revolver.

"You were going to feed me to the things down there."

Nichols, saddened by the accusation, offered a melancholy smile. "No. We just wanted to speak with you—as Americans—and show you every-thing we're doing. But we thought you might injure one of the zombies," she said. "They're caged. Curran was only going to take your gun."

Nichols moved toward her servant, but Halston motioned her back with his revolver. "He's done for. If you don't want to join him, you best explain yourself—and fast."

"Do you know the legend of Persephone, Mr. Halston? No, I doubt it. Hades kidnapped Persephone. Her tormented mother, Demeter, created the poppy to—"

"I'm not here to listen to folktales. How'd you turn them invisible?"

Nichols sighed. "During my research, I discovered a Hermetic ritual. By soaking poppy seeds in wine for fifteen days, then drinking the wine for five days while otherwise fasting, you can make yourself invisible at will."

"And you got the dead meat to do that? I thought they hated the taste of the poppies."

"Of opium, Mr. Halston. There's a difference."

"Okay. You can step away from the door," Halston said. "We'll let the Brits handle you, extrat or no extrat."

"Don't! I beg you—reconsider. You're resourceful and you're American. That's why I want you in my employ."

"I won't ask again," Halston said, drawing back the hammer on his gun. "Close the door."

Nichols nodded, her countenance infinitely wounded, and moved to shut the door. Suddenly, distant thunder rippled across the silent night and reverberated through Shanghai's shallow canyons. For a second, Halston thought Sohan had fired another shot, but the noise was too deep. A rumble broke the stillness again, tripping over its own echoes, followed by the clap of another volley.

"Dear Lord," Nichols gasped. "They've begun."

"That's cannon fire!" Halston said. "The bastards! They don't have to do this!"

The first shells whined through the air with certain and deadly aim, and the stables at the Shanghai Race Club evaporated in a fiery blossom. The thunder was steady now, as the Royal Navy's battleships—two new Royal Sovereigns in the pack—competed to unleash their full horror upon Chinese soil.

The ground shook with each titan footfall of cannon fire. Two apartment buildings across the street from the Nichols's estate vanished, a well-placed shot ripping through their foundations. The structures collapsed like they'd been built of matchsticks, then exploded into flame.

Halston watched, momentarily stunned, before he waved at Sohan to escape. Then another whine rang in Halston's ears with a peculiar timbre that rose in pitch. He recognized the sound as the herald of an incoming shell, and grabbed Nichols's arm in a most unceremonious fashion. He pushed her through the door and followed, more leaping than running. An explosion up on the lawn collapsed the *tykhana*'s entrance. Halston's world went bright white from pain as he tumbled down the stairs.

Into the hungry dark.

Halston hit the floor hard, and blood filled his mouth. Nichols grunted from the pain, and tried moving, but Halston leveled his gun on her, fully intending to reunite her with her husband.

"They did this—the people you serve." Nichols's eyes glittered in the dark. Another blast shook the ground and rained debris inside the *tykhana*.

"The blasted Brits didn't unleash this chaos on Shanghai," Halston said, spitting blood. "You did, by creating the dead meat!"

"Perhaps. But the Brits have had a taste of their own bitter medicines now, haven't they?"

"Then all this . . . just for revenge?"

"No, Mr. Halston. This was both a lesson and a test. The British don't know what it means to be homeless . . . refugees. In fact, they derive no small pleasure from our misery. They keep us cowed and humiliated. And they've done nothing but remind us of how they saved us during the exodus."

Halston stood. "I was right the first time. This *is* about revenge. The Brits kill your husband, and you—" Another explosion shook the earth, interrupting him.

"Hardly. There are other considerations." Nichols retrieved a lantern still suspended from a wall hook. She lit it, casting long shadows down the corridor. "I'm consolidating power, for all Americans."

"Through opium."

"An opium monopoly won't last. Not if the Society for the Suppression of the Opium Trade has its way in London. No, I'm purchasing a homeland—here in Shanghai. In twelve years, land prices have soared from fifty pounds an acre to twenty thousand pounds. The chief buyers were Europeans, who then rented the property for profits of ten thousand percent, Mr. Halston. Ten thousand. That's what I'm after. Once I purchase Shanghai's available property, we can build a homeland for Americans. The Chinese have already promised us recognition as a sovereign nation, if we help them modernize."

"You think folks will just sell you their land?"

"But they *are* selling. Those refugees on my lawn—they're landowners who believe Shanghai is overrun by dead meat and figure that's a problem even the Admiralty's shells can't solve. They're more than willing to sell their estates, on my terms, and return to Europe. I already own a quarter of Shanghai."

"Then what?" Halston asked. "You run everything as some 'madame dictator'?"

"No. I only want to see my people returned home. What I have planned will take longer than my years can offer. I need men, like yourself, to help build a temporary homeland here, in Shanghai, where we will consolidate our forces. Afterward, we'll use our revenues from opium, property leases, and the sale of our technical expertise to retake the Americas. Díaz has already offered us Mexico City as a base of operations for military actions directed at retaking the continent. And we can succeed, now that we know how to corral the dead meat."

Halston tried saying something, but the complexity of it all stunned him to silence. And in that momentary quiet, he heard low groans floating through the *tykhana* like echo-winged ravens. The sound battered Halston's heart.

"The zombies," Nichols said with surprising calm. "They're loose. The siege must have damaged their pens. But—"

"The stairs to the lawn are blocked," Halston interrupted. "Is there another way out of here?"

Another explosion drowned out her first response. "Yes," she repeated. "But it's through the kennels."

Halston sighed, then motioned with the barrel of his gun for Nichols to lead the way. Their footsteps clattered off the walls. It was dark and cool, the stone path veering away into the shadows, no matter where they held the lantern.

Nichols hesitated, tried to speak, but Halston nudged her forward. They advanced cautiously, with Nichols's back to a wall. The moaning grew louder between the explosions; Nichols almost stumbled into an intersecting corridor, then stopped.

"You'll find the kennels ahead," she said. "To the left."

Halston listened intently. Slow feet dragged against the floor. Reacting on instinct, he pulled Nichols back, even as something grabbed his shirt. Halston whirled and fired.

The muzzle flash punched snapshot images in the corridor, but the shot itself only struck rock. Halston continued firing, felling one zombie, but there was another. He fired twice, blindly. His second shot caught something that grunted and sprayed the walls with a wet splatter of gore.

Silence, then another explosion above.

Halston reloaded one pistol and pulled a matching revolver holstered in the small of his back. He grabbed Nichols, pulling her down the left corridor. They reached another turn. The area beyond was rank with decay.

"The kennels," Nichols said flatly.

Halston moved quickly, pushing Nichols forward. Around the corner, the corridor emptied into a large room with metal cages lining the walls. Some cages were still closed, but the bombardment had broken three open. Halston left Nichols, who pushed herself flat against the nearest wall. He held his ground, waiting for the telltale sounds of the living dead.

And then they came at him, all at once, in a mad, stumbling rush.

Halston backed up, unleashing his own thunder, loud enough in the enclosed room to drown out the rumble of cannon fire overhead. Something dropped at his feet with a thud and grabbed his boot. Halston fired down once, to finish the thing off, then emptied his guns in a slow, steady sweep. But even after the shooting was done, one of the dead things remained. It clamped cold hands on either side of his face.

With the calm of one finally dead himself, Halston dropped the revolvers and pulled his bayonet. He stabbed, sometimes punching air, sometimes threading meat. Finally, he struck upward through soft flesh. The invisible zombie shuddered, then dropped to the floor.

Halston listened, but the only noise, a snarling hiss, came from the back of the shadow-draped chamber. Halston quietly reloaded his revolvers and motioned for Nichols to join him. She did, staying by Halston's side. Cage by cage, the pair advanced, until finally, they reached the last pen.

The zombie's cage was open, but the dead meat—still quite visible—wasn't going anywhere. Iron braces secured the thing to a wooden table. Its legs and arms had been amputated, leaving four gory stumps. Halston raised his pistol. That's when he felt the Colt derringer pressed against his temple.

"Our buck zombie," Nichols said. "I'd be foolish to let something like an infected stallion remain unfettered, not when his bite can create more zombies. By killing the others, you did us a service; we'll need the room down here for the refugees and supplies. But this one is still important to my plans. I'm certain you'll understand that I cannot allow him destroyed. Holster your weapons, please."

Halston nodded and did as he was told. "Your stallion's pulling back from you. Afraid of its torturer?"

"My clothes are treated with opium," she noted. "None of the zombies would have bitten me."

He snorted. No wonder she hadn't fought him when he made her lead the way through the tunnels. "Now what?"

Nichols sighed. "That's up to you. You know what your countrymen have endured—the brothels, the factories, the slums. Do you believe that's a fair alternative to what I'm offering? Do you believe we'll be anything more than second-class citizens, anywhere we go, so long as we are without our own country? We can do it without your help, of course, but I'd prefer not to kill a fellow American.

"What do you say, Mr. Halston?" Nichols asked, the derringer steady on his temple.

Shanghai burned, God's judgment against the Asian Sodom rendered . . . .

The British cannon fire continued, leveling the city with a cascade of hammer blows that sent a steady rain of dust plumes falling from the *tykhana*'s ceiling.

"I loved that house," Nichols noted, then set off through the room crowded with refugees, food stocks, and water barrels.

"How long will the Brits keep this up?" a woman asked.

"Till there's nothing left standing," Nichols said. "After that, we go up and rebuild." She tapped the metal strongbox filled with land deeds. "On our own terms."

Nichols slipped between the huddled refugees, offering blankets to some and a reassuring hand to others. She finally reached one corner of the room where two men sat.

"Saint James's Church has a strong cellar," Nichols said. "I'm sure your Sikh friend is safe there."

"Bulwan," Halston said sourly. "His name's Bulwan."

Nichols glanced at Sohan before asking Halston, "You believe you can trust this . . . gentleman?"

"With my life. Besides, way I figure it, they're both in the same boat as us with the Brits and all," Halston said. "And at least I know where I stand with Bulwan and Sohan."

Nichols nodded. "You are doing the right thing."

"I hope so," Halston replied, feeling more cold and numb than he'd ever felt before. "I hope this homeland of ours is worth the price we paid for it."

"That's for our descendants to decide, Mr. Halston. Such considerations are no longer our luxury."

NIGHT SHIFT

REBECCA BROCK

"**W**E GOT A PROBLEM UPSTAIRS!"

I didn't have to even ask. I knew what Sharon was talking about. It had to be Tina, one of the new kids who had been assigned to the shelter just a day before all this shit started. She was thirteen years old and already had a ladder of scars up both wrists. We were supposed to be keeping her on suicide watch, but all of a sudden we had a few more pressing issues to keep us occupied. The life or death of one emotionally fucked up kid wasn't quite the priority that it used to be.

I glanced over my shoulder to Sharon, but I couldn't get away from the door; at that moment, the only thing between us and about twenty or so screaming dead people was me. Of all the nights for me to come in early . . . .

"What happened?" I shouted as I worked on nailing a thick piece of plywood over the entrance. Thank God we'd been in the middle of replacing a section of the kitchen floor when all this started. I didn't like to think of what would be happening right now if we hadn't had plywood and nails lying around.

"Tina broke a mirror," Sharon said. She stared warily at the rotted hands grasping through the holes in the boarded windows, then moved closer anyway. I had to give her credit for that.

"And?" I missed my mark and slammed the hammer into the back of a gray-green hand. Bone crunched, but there was no scream of pain. Bastards didn't feel *anything*.

"And she slit her wrists," Sharon said, keeping her voice low so the other kids couldn't hear her. I doubted any of them would have cared anyway. Most of them were only worried about their own asses.

"Is she dead?"

Sharon nodded. I knew she was probably feeling guilty. She'd been a relief worker for a couple years longer than me, and she was the type of person who actually cared about the messed up kids we had to deal with, even the ones who threatened to kill her. If the world hadn't been ending all around us, she'd be torn up over Tina's death. All it meant to me was that we had to get the kid out of the house.

I looked around. Danny and Larry were taking care of the porch-level windows, using bookshelves they'd pulled off the walls for a makeshift barrier. Joanie was piling up boxes of canned food from the pantry. We'd decided to try to hole up in the attic for as long as it took for help to find us. *If* they found us. I wasn't holding out much hope for any saviors to arrive.

"Sean! Take over!" I yelled, tossing the hammer over to one of the bigger guys, a surly teenager who was now so pale his zits seemed to glow against his skin. He'd been placed in the children's shelter because one day he'd decided he didn't like the way his mother treated him, so he grabbed her hair while she was driving and slammed her head into the side window. I didn't like Sean and he didn't like me, but since I outweighed him by a good fifty pounds and stood a foot taller than him, he stayed out of my way.

"Sean! Now!"

He acted like he didn't want to get close enough to the door to start pounding nails, so I grabbed him by the neck of his T-shirt and held him close enough to get a feel of the dead hands reaching through the openings between the boards. "Get your ass going or I swear to God I'll throw you out there."

Sean got to work.

The entire shelter was in chaos. We'd been at full capacity when the trouble started: six girls and four boys, with four counselors—Sharon, Danny, Larry, and Joanie—to handle them until the night shift arrived. I made it five. Most of the girls had become either catatonic or screechy, useless for anything but attracting more of those fuckers outside. The boys were trying to hold on to their tough-guy attitude, but most had already pissed their pants once they saw what was just outside the door. A couple of them still thought they were badasses, Sean being the worst of the bunch. I could tell that they were just waiting for their chance to do something. I wasn't looking forward to the time when I'd have to give them some kind of weapon. They'd be more likely to use it on me than on the dead things.

We were between shifts when the first ones showed up outside the house. Sharon had called me before that and asked if I could come in a couple of hours early to help with some of the troublemakers. Like everybody else, I'd heard the news reports about weird shit happening in other parts of the country, but I hadn't paid much attention to it. There'd been so much of it lately that I'd tuned it out.

Goddamn it. If I'd just waited to come in, I would have been home when it started . . . .

But I couldn't think about home. I couldn't think about what might be happening there.

"What are we going to do about Tina?" Sharon asked. I could hear the panicky rise of her voice. She was close to losing it. I couldn't blame her if she did; she'd left her kids with a sitter and wasn't able to get anyone on the phone before the lines went dead. I was surprised she'd lasted this long.

"How long has it been?" I asked as I ran for the steps.

"I don't know—two, maybe three hours. I lost track of her once everything started." Sharon caught my arm before I could go into the girls' bedroom. "Eddie . . . what are we going to do?"

"We need to get her out of the house and—"

"Not that. The kids."

I didn't know what to tell her. What *could* I tell her? That everything was going to be all right? That we just had to sit tight and wait for the cops to come and escort everybody home? I didn't even know if we still had homes to go to. Whatever was happening was happening fast. We still had power, but I didn't figure that would last for much longer. The scraps of news I was able to overhear on TV made it sound like everywhere had it just as bad as what we were dealing with here. The world had gone to hell and there wasn't anything anybody could do to stop it.

But before I could say any of that to Sharon, I heard something thump against the floor on the other side of the bedroom door, a slap like raw meat hitting concrete. Sharon and I looked at each other. I think we both knew, but didn't want to believe it.

"I thought you said—"

"I checked her pulse. She'd bled out . . . ." Sharon took a step away from the door. "I *know* she was dead."

The door shook in its hinges as the thing on the other side threw its weight against it. Underneath the shrill screams, the grunts and groans, I could hear it scratching at the wood with its nails, like it could claw its way through to get to us.

Downstairs, glass shattered. A couple of the kids screamed.

"Shit!" I ran for the stairs. "Keep her in there!"

Sharon made a grab for the doorknob just as it began to turn. "Eddie! She's opening the door!"

Down below, the dead things were pushing their way through a broken window. One of them had already gotten halfway in, its stomach caught on a piece of jagged glass. Behind me, Sharon held onto the doorknob, trying to keep Tina from opening the door from the inside.

Fuck.

I ran back to Sharon and shoved her away from the door. "Get down there with the kids. Now!"

The door opened as soon as Sharon let go of the knob. I felt the impact of the thing before I even saw it launch itself out of the bedroom. I couldn't think of anything but keeping those teeth away from me. I grabbed Tina by the hair and yanked her head back, hard, turning it around as I forced her down the long hallway, toward the window at the far end. It didn't take much to throw her through the glass. Tina hadn't been a very big girl.

By the time I got back downstairs, the dead thing that had been caught on the glass had managed to get inside. It came at me. For a second I couldn't react. The guy's face looked like it had been ripped off and eaten. Its nose was gone, a gaping hole right in the middle of its face. Its cheeks were ragged and torn. Intestines hung from its slashed gut. It reached for me and I could see that chunks of its arms had been torn away. There were teethmarks in its skin.

Before the thing could touch me, I grabbed its arm and yanked it behind its back, putting it in one of the restraint positions we used on the kids, forcing it to the floor. It kept twisting its head around, hoping to take a chunk out of me, so I did the only thing I could do: I slammed its head into the floor as hard as I could, over and over again, until I could hear the bones shattering and feel its skull caving in beneath my hand. I didn't stop until it quit moving.

And then I realized how quiet it had gotten. I looked around. Sharon had gathered the kids together and was herding them toward the steps. Joanie looked like she was just about to break, twitching at every creak of the boards on the porch, a Bible clutched to her chest. Danny stood at the door, watching the dirt road in front of the house. The shelter was at the top of a hill, one road in and out. If we could get to the van . . .

No. No way that was going to happen. The kids couldn't be controlled. I'd already seen a couple of the boys palming kitchen knives when they thought nobody was watching. They wouldn't be thinking of anything but getting their own asses out of here. And I didn't particularly want to end up with a knife blade between my shoulders.

"What's happening?" Larry asked quietly. His voice sounded raw. It was the first time since it had all started that any of us had had a chance to think about it. "What *are* those things?"

"It's Judgement Day," Joanie whispered. "The dead are rising up from their graves to punish the sinners."

"Shut up, Joanie." I went to the door and took a look outside. There were five or six of the things shuffling around on the front lawn, moving in and out of the porch lights' orange glow. I moved to the side, pressing my face against the boards so I could look down the road. The moon was full, so I could see clearly enough to count at least seven more on their way. Shit . . . .

"Start moving the food and water upstairs," I said, not looking away from the advancing dead things. I knew they were dead. They had to be dead. Some of them had been torn up pretty bad—guts hanging out of their bellies, faces shredded, limbs missing. They were dead, but they didn't look like they'd ever been buried. I just couldn't figure out how it all started so fast. And why we never had any warning.

"What about the basement?" Danny asked. "We might be safer—"

"Fine. Go down to the basement." I looked away from the window long enough to stare hard at Danny. "But I'm getting my ass up to the attic when the time comes. I don't care what you want to do."

The rumbling of an engine caught us all by surprise. I looked out again, joined by Sharon and Larry. The dead things were gone. For a minute all I could see was headlights, then I recognized Bob Carson's pickup truck as it bounced up the rutted road. Bob worked night shift with me. I hadn't realized it was so late.

But why the hell was he coming in to work? Why bother, unless—?

I hurried to flip on the outdoor floodlights and then almost immediately wished I hadn't. I could see the look on his face as he stopped the truck just in front of the sidewalk leading up to the porch. The man was scared shitless. The grill of his truck was covered with blood and meat and bits of hair. I didn't want to know what he'd seen on his way in. He must have thought he'd be safer here.

Bob looked both ways, saw that it was clear, and moved to open the truck's door.

"Don't get out!" I yelled, knowing he couldn't hear me. I grabbed a hammer and started prying loose the boards so he could get inside. Just because he couldn't see any of those things didn't mean they weren't out there. Fuckers were probably hiding in the dark. Just waiting.

Bob jumped out of the truck and hit the ground running. And it was like he'd triggered some kind of alarm, because as soon as he was three steps from the truck cab they came at him, all of them at once.

"Help me!" I shouted to Larry and Danny. They didn't move, unable to look away from what was going on outside. Joanie was just as useless, spouting out prayers and bits of some godawful hymn, crying and singing and babbling all at once.

One of the boards finally gave way and I looked over to see that Sharon was prying out nails alongside me. I chanced another look outside. Bob was surrounded by the things. He pushed them aside and took the porch steps two at a time, just barely getting away from their grasping hands. He looked at me. I think he knew he wasn't going to make it.

"Let me in!" He threw his weight against the front door, rattling the doorknob, crying as he pounded at the wood. Behind him, five of the dead things closed in. One of them was a little girl holding a Raggedy Ann doll. I had the crazy thought that she shouldn't be out so late.

Two boards were down. Three left to go. We weren't going to make it. I looked around and saw that one of the porch windows was covered by a tabletop. Larry and Danny had used it to cover the hole where the thing had gotten inside earlier.

"Bob! Go to the left window! Now!"

I sprinted over to the window and managed to pull off the tabletop with my bare hands. I smashed out the rest of the glass with my hammer and leaned out. One of the things was on me in an instant. It grabbed me by the hair and yanked my head to the side, scraping my throat against the wood of the windowsill. I felt splinters go in. I swung the hammer and caught it in the wrist, shattering the bones with just enough force to make it let go of me. I swung again and buried the hammer's claw end between its eyes. It went down, stayed down.

Bob came barreling around the corner of the porch. He'd been bitten a couple of times. His T-shirt was soaked with blood. The things were right behind him, moving faster than dead people had a right to move—as if dead people had a right to move at all. I heard footsteps to my left and saw more of the bastards coming at the window. Fuck. There were probably fifteen of them on the porch alone.

"Jesus, Bob! Come on!" I reached for him and he made a lunge for my hand. I ducked back into the house, pulling him along with me. One of the things, an old woman with knitting needles sticking out of her throat, had grabbed him around the waist and was gnawing at his belly. Bob screamed. It was the worst sound I have ever heard in my life.

I think I was crying at that point, but all I could think about was getting Bob inside, away from the things that were biting and chewing and ripping at him. I pulled, but they pulled back, like it was a tug-of-war with Bob as the prize. One of the things bit into his throat and an arc of blood sprayed out, hitting me full in the face.

He was looking at me when he died. And I think Bob knew exactly when I let go of his hand and let them have him. In those last seconds, I don't think he forgave me.

"Help me," I said to someone, anyone. I lifted the tabletop and put it back into place, hammering one nail after another as quickly as I could, smelling Bob's blood on my hands. Tasting it in my mouth. The claw of the hammer was covered with something black and thick. Brains, I guessed.

Sharon had managed to snap Danny and Larry out of their shock, and they all helped me secure the window. The things outside were too preoccupied with their catch to worry about storming the house for a while. I don't know if the others had realized it yet, but we were fucked.

"I can't stay here," Danny said abruptly, backing away from all of us. He looked at me and I swear to God his eyes were just blank. They looked like the eyes of the things outside the house.

"Where are you going to go?" I asked, wiping my hands on my jeans, using the sleeve of my shirt to wipe Bob's blood off my face. I spat to clear the saltiness of it out of my mouth. "We've got to get upstairs—"

Danny shook his head. "I gotta get out of here, man."

"You can't—"

"You're not stopping me, Ed." Danny stepped forward, the hammer in his hand. He didn't raise it, didn't threaten, but I could tell that he'd use it on me, and happily, if I got between him and the door. "Come with me. We've got a chance if we stay together."

Sharon and I looked at each other. I could see that she was tempted.

"What about the kids?" I asked quietly.

"What? You're going to stay here and protect a bunch of punks and junkies? Fuck 'em, man." Danny shook his head. "I've got to get home."

Larry stood by the window, looking at the front porch through a small opening in the boards. "I think you can get to your car, but you've gotta go now."

Danny looked at me. "You coming?"

I wanted to go. Any other time I would have gone. I hated the job. Hated the night shift. Hated the parade of juvenile sex offenders and drug addicts and petty criminals that I saw walk through here on a daily basis. There wasn't a single damn thing to make me stay.

But they were kids. In the end, they were just a bunch of scared kids.

"I gotta go," Danny said. "Come on while they're distracted."

"You'll be safer here," I said, knowing it was probably not true. Danny began tearing down the rest of the wood covering a broken window, making a hole big enough to crawl through. "We can barricade ourselves upstairs—"

"And then what? Starve to death? Fuck that, man. I'll take my chances out there." Danny hesitated at the window, looking at us like he might have wanted us to stop him.

And then he was gone, through the hole and onto the porch. He jumped down the porch steps and made a mad run for the parking lot. I actually thought he might make it . . . until he dropped his keys at the car door. Even before the pack of the things moved, I could see them in the darkness, just waiting. Their eyes caught the light and glowed like cats' eyes. I think Joanie saw them, too, because she screamed.

And then they pounced.

I turned away from the window and closed my eyes for a second. Joanie's screams got the girls started again, but even underneath all their noise, I could still hear Danny crying out. And I could hear them ripping and tearing and . . . eating him.

I picked up a hammer and a board and propped it against the open space. "Somebody help me fix this hole."

The movies got it all wrong. The bad things didn't end just because the sun came up. By daylight there were even more of the dead people milling around the shelter. So far, by some dumb luck, the barricades were still holding at the doors and windows. It helped that they'd stopped banging on the boards so much, probably because they couldn't smell us anymore. We'd moved the kids and supplies up to the attic as soon as we finished plugging up the holes and reinforcing everything.

I spent the rest of the night sitting at the window, watching it all like I was God or something. I saw Danny rise up and take his place with the others. It looked like he was missing about ten pounds of flesh, most of it from his chest and stomach. Once I thought he looked up and saw me, but no way that could happen. Those things didn't think like that. They couldn't feel. They just attacked. And ate. They didn't have any human intelligence left. And despite Joanie's praying and hymn singing, I didn't think they had any souls, either.

The kids finally settled down at dawn, curling up in old sleeping bags against the far wall. I wasn't worried too much about the girls, but something wasn't right with Sean and his gang. I kept seeing nervous looks pass between them, kept hearing whispers. There were just four of them—all but Sean barely big enough to reach my armpit—but if they decided to pull a stunt while Larry, Sharon, and me were distracted . . .

"I hope it was quick."

I looked up. Sharon was standing beside me, staring out past the parking lot, past the milling crowd of dead people in the yard.

"You hope what was quick?" I rubbed at my eyes. It felt like someone had sprinkled ground glass into them.

"My kids." Sharon looked over at me and smiled sadly. "I know they're not alive. I don't think Abby would have known what to do to protect them."

The matter-of-fact tone of her voice bothered me. Her eyes were red and swollen, and I'd heard her crying quietly all night, once we'd gotten settled in the attic. But the fact that she'd actually accepted that there was no hope made me wonder if it wouldn't have been kinder to all of us to just open the doors and get it over with. Why fight so hard when there was nothing to win?

"I just can't stand not being sure," Sharon said, still staring out to the road, to the escape so close but so out of our reach. "I keep imagining all these different ways that it might have happened. And I can hear them screaming—" Sharon's voice, thick with sudden tears, trembled. "And I can see those things . . . tearing at them. Oh, God . . . ."

She covered her face with her hands and I could tell that whatever strength she'd once possessed had finally run out. As she sank to the floor, rocking back and forth, wailing loud enough to wake the kids, I thought I should do something for her. Put my arms around her. Try to comfort her. Something.

But I didn't. There was no comfort to be found anywhere, least of all with me. I had my own dead to mourn. I'd left a pregnant wife and my mother at home, all because my damn job needed me. I should have been there, protecting them, instead of here, with these strangers, these people I didn't even like.

I could have comforted Sharon, lied to her and told her that everything would be all right, but I didn't. Instead, I went over to the pile of supplies to ration out the morning meal.

It didn't take long for the kids' natural tendencies to kick back into gear. By darkfall of that first day in the attic, boredom overtook them, what with no Playstation games or MTV to keep their short attention spans occupied. To entertain themselves they stole food from each other, fought, made crude weapons out of jagged metal lids. Two of the girls came to blows over a piece of lukewarm Spam.

And then there was Sean.

He knew he had Larry cowed. Larry came from the "we just need to reach them emotionally" school of counseling and always wanted to know how the kids were *feeling*, what they were *thinking*. It was horseshit and I knew it and the kids knew it. There were dozens of nights when they had to call me in to settle down fights on Larry's shift because he didn't want to get in the middle of a couple of prepubescent punks.

Joanie was just as bad, only she used religion as her bludgeon. The kids had learned to steer clear of doing anything in front of Joanie because if she caught them it would mean two hours of Bible study and an hour and a half of preaching and sermonizing to hammer her point home. The kids despised her. None of them respected what little authority she managed to have. They knew they could get away with murder, as long as they paid lip service to God and prayed a little with her. Then she'd forgive them and they'd be free to do whatever the hell they wanted.

By full dark, Joanie and Sharon seemed to have switched personalities. Sharon couldn't stop crying and Joanie discovered that this was the moment for which she had been waiting and praying all her life: the Rapture. I tried not to listen to her ranting, but she had a couple of the girls mesmerized with her stories of Apocalypse and the dead rising up for their final judgment. I didn't care what she wanted to believe, didn't care what she wanted to do, but it was pissing me off to see her wasting our drinking water by using it to baptize the girls.

The situation was getting worse by the minute. I couldn't stop thinking about Beth and Mom. Like Sharon, I kept imagining what had happened to them, what they might have done when the dead came to our door. We live in a little house about five minutes away from the shelter; I know that whatever brought those things here would have brought them to my home, too.

Beth was six months pregnant. We would have had a little girl.

I knew better than to think that they were still alive.

But I had to know for sure. All through that first day, the thoughts kept eating at me. Even though I knew they were gone, could feel that they were gone, I didn't know for sure. And it was killing me. It felt like an itch right in the middle of my back. My hands and feet twitched with wanting to move, to go, to get away.

Instead, I agreed to take the first watch. Around ten or so, with nothing better to do, everyone else had finally gone to sleep. Sharon was edging past grief and into catatonia, curled up in the far corner of the attic. Joanie and her two disciples slept with open Bibles lying across their chests like shields. Sean and the others slept huddled together like wild dogs on the other side of the room.

This was what I had chosen over my family.

"You're going to go, aren't you?"

Sharon was awake, watching me from her corner. Until she said the words, I hadn't actually thought I could do it.

"Yeah," I said softly. "I am."

"Will you check on Jamie and Lisa for me?" Sharon smiled slightly and shook her head. Even in the darkness, I could see that there was something wrong with that smile. "I know they're probably up past their bedtimes. They love to stay up late."

I nodded, not really knowing what else to do. "I'll check on them for you."

"Good. And tell them Mommy's going to be a little late, okay? They worry about me if I don't tell them when I'm coming home."

I stood and quietly opened the window. From the attic I could climb right out onto the porch roof. Then it was just a few feet to the ground. I could make it, easy, as long as I had plenty of room between me and the dead things.

I felt for my keys. I'd have to get them out before making the drop. My car was just a few feet from the porch. I could make it. I know I could.

"And tell them Mommy loves them," Sharon whispered, already falling asleep again. She was sleeping more and more now. I guessed that was better; being asleep beat the hell out of being conscious.

I ducked out the window, hesitating with one leg out and one still inside. I felt like a coward taking off in the middle of the night and leaving them, but I knew that the downstairs was secure enough to buy them at least a few more days. There was enough food to last them if they were careful, and the kids had Larry and Joanie to watch over them. I wasn't leaving them high and dry. Hell, if anything, I would be helping them more by leaving. Maybe I could find the cops or the National Guard, get everybody out before the food ran dry or the barricades gave way.

That's what I was thinking as I climbed out. I almost had myself believing it, too.

It felt weird being outside again. Almost wrong. The smell of those things was overwhelming, like a slaughterhouse at high noon. As I made my way down the incline of the roof, I could hear their moans and gasps. It almost sounded like they were talking to each other. The thought of them being smart enough to communicate, smart enough to group together and hunt in packs, made my stomach feel hollow and greasy. I'd brought a baseball bat as a weapon. Now, as I got closer to those walking dead men, the Louisville Slugger didn't seem nearly enough. A fully loaded Uzi wouldn't have been enough.

I scooted down the last bit of roof. One jump to the ground and then a few feet to the right and I'd be at my car. By my count there were three of the things that might give me trouble. Otherwise, it was a clear shot.

I fished the keys out of my pocket and got ready. And then I jumped.

There were a dozen of them grouped together on the porch, and I think I surprised them as much as they surprised me. I was running for my car before they could move. I managed to duck two of the three I'd been worried about, but the third got close enough to touch me. Their hands aren't cold, but room temperature warm. And they feel wet—from the decay, I guess. When they touch you, you feel like you've been marked, tagged for them to get later. They had all the time in the world.

I tried not to think as I ran those few feet to the car. I had my keys in a deathgrip. I'd played out the scene in my mind: *Hit the door. Unlock it. Slide into the front seat. Close and lock the doors. Drive home as fast as you can.* All the things I should have done when the shit first started.

I dodged and weaved. Finally, the upper half of an old woman, which I'd missed from my vantage on the roof somehow, was the only dead thing between me and my car door, and I managed to jump over its grasping hands without it even touching me. I looked around as I shakily unlocked the door. The closest ones were still a good ten feet away. I had time. I couldn't believe how easy it was proving to be.

The door opened and I dove inside my car, locking up even as I made sure all the windows were up. Then I took a second to close my eyes and breathe. I'd been holding my breath since jumping down from the roof. My chest burned. My hands felt locked in a deathgrip around my keys and the baseball bat. I had to force myself to unclench my muscles. Unless the fuckers could chew through glass and steel, I was safe for a minute.

They surrounded the car, throwing themselves on the hood, smearing their gray flesh on the windows as they scratched at the glass. Their moaning was even louder now, and I had the feeling that they were calling others of their kind. Their strength was in numbers, and with enough help, they might be able to break a window or even flip a car. Then I'd be trapped, helpless, and they could just crawl in with me and—

That was all I needed to imagine.

The car started on the first attempt. I hadn't even considered that it wouldn't. I edged forward slowly at first, but the stupid things refused to move. They were deliberately blocking my way.

I floored it.

The dead things went down like grass under a mower. And God help me, but it felt good to hear their bones cracking beneath my wheels. I think

I was laughing as I plowed through them. Maybe I was crying. I don't know. There doesn't seem much difference between the two now.

I went home.

No one was there.

I cut the engine but left the keys in the ignition and the door unlocked. The house's front door was gone. All the windows were broken. Every light was on.

But nothing moved. Not even the dead things. They'd taken what they'd wanted and moved on.

I shouldn't have gone inside, but I couldn't help myself. I knew that there was no chance Beth or Mom was alive, but I had to be certain. I knew I'd never be able to sleep again if there was even a chance that I'd walked away and left them hurt or dying inside our own home.

I never thought about what I'd do if I found them any other way.

The house was absolutely still. I think that bothered me more than the splintered doors or the smears of blood and God-knew-what along the walls. I searched every room. The fuckers had been everywhere. There was nowhere Mom and Beth could have hidden. Even if I had been home, I don't think I could have made this place safe for us.

The only room I couldn't go in was the nursery. From the doorway I could see that there was blood on the walls, smeared into the rainbow-patterned wallpaper that Beth had loved. They'd died in there. And they were probably walking around somewhere right now. Beth and the baby still inside her. Mom.

Dead, but not really gone. I had no illusions.

I spent the rest of the night curled up in the hall, just outside the nursery, staring at the bloody splatters all over those rainbows, wondering which was Beth's and which was Mom's.

And after a while, like an idiot, I slept.

It was dusk when I woke up again. I think I'd half-hoped that the dead things would find me while I was asleep. They didn't. I was still alive. But now I knew what I had to do.

It didn't take long for me to find everything I needed. I boxed up all the canned food in the pantry, all the bottled water and juices and Coke that we had. I grabbed flashlights and batteries, my old camping gear, blankets and pillows, everything I thought I could use, and loaded it all in my trunk.

I slammed the trunk and looked back at my house. We'd only been living there a few months. Not enough time to create a bunch of sentimental memories.

So there was one more thing I had to do before going back up to the shelter.

I went around to the back, where I kept the kerosene grill. I'd just barbecued steaks for us a couple of nights ago, before the world began to end.

It was an old house. It'd burn quick.

I just wanted it gone.

The fire drew the dead. I sat in my car for a long time, watching the flames, listening to the static on the radio. No broadcasts. Not a surprise. I don't think I wanted to know what was going on in the cities.

The things stood as close to the fire as they could. A few of them got too close and went up like they'd been soaked in gasoline. On the far side of the house, just behind the ruined wall of the nursery, one of the things watched me instead of the flames. I stared at her for a long, long time. I remembered the pink nightgown and fuzzy houseshoes. The glasses hanging around her neck by a thick gold chain.

Mom. She'd come home.

I didn't want to stick around long enough to see if Beth had come with her.

By the time I got back to the shelter, it was too late.

Dead things swarmed everywhere, pouring into the front door, through the windows. And there were so many of them now. More than I could handle with my baseball bat or my car. I wondered where they all came from, why they were drawn to the shelter.

Then I saw the bodies.

And I knew what they had done.

The little shits had gone "Lord of the Flies" up in that attic.

Joanie had been nailed to the slope of the roof, crucified just out of reach of the things. Whether she died of blood loss or shock, it didn't really matter now. She'd come back as one of them, and she was still pinned to the roof, struggling against the nails in her wrists and hands and feet. I didn't think it was the kind of resurrection she'd always imagined.

I stared so long at Joanie's snapping, snarling corpse that I didn't even notice Larry's body at first. Sean and the others had tied a rope around his feet and dangled him out of the attic window, letting him dip low enough to be devoured by the dead. I'll never know exactly what they did to him, but I've thought about it every night since. I imagined them toying with Larry, who none of them had ever liked. I imagined them keeping him alive for a long time, letting the dead things tear chunks out of his body and then pulling him just out of reach, so his blood would drip and splatter and make the things even more frenzied . . . .

And then I saw the rest. They'd joined the walking dead gathered beneath Larry's corpse. Bob. Danny. And now two of the girls who had huddled with Joanie and her Bible. The girls dragged themselves on broken legs, their heads cocked at unnatural angles. I guessed that they had objected to Sean's fun and games and gotten themselves thrown out the attic window for their troubles.

I don't remember much of what happened next. I don't remember getting out of the car. I don't remember swinging the bat at any of the dead things that got too close. I don't remember opening the trunk and getting out the can of kerosene. I don't remember any of that.

I just remember looking up at that window and seeing Sean leaning out, laughing along with the other kids who'd stayed safe in the barricaded attic. And I remember the thing Sean held, dangling by its hair. I remember how its eyes still seemed to see, how its mouth still opened and closed and silently screamed. They'd killed her and let her come back. They hadn't even had the decency to let her stay dead.

I got close enough to splash kerosene on the front porch. Close enough to toss a match. Close enough to hear them screaming inside when the flames began to feed and rise.

I hoped Sharon had been sleeping when it happened, that she hadn't felt any pain. I hoped she'd been dreaming of her kids.

THE ETHICAL TREATMENT OF MEAT

CLAUDE LALUMIÈRE

RAYMOND AND GEORGE HAD NEVER thought much about religion. They'd tried going to services at their local church shortly after adopting the child—it seemed like the right thing to do—but the preacher said children weren't allowed. No animals of any kind. Only people. It had never occurred to Raymond and George that there was that kind of bigotry in the world. They shopped around and found a more open-minded church about a thirty-minute drive away from their home. It was more trouble than they'd bargained for, but they wanted to be good parents.

They weren't the first ones to adopt a fleshie as a pet child—almost a family member, really—but they were the first in their neighborhood. They decided to get a boy, hoping he'd fit in with the all-male character of their household. The agency said his name was Rod, but they didn't like that. So they called him Scott, instead. He was so cute.

They loved Scott like a son. It was biologically impossible for people to have children, and George had heard on the news that recent studies indicated that the lack of children was a probable cause of apathy and depression, an unconscious nostalgia for people's animal past. So, when George noticed that Raymond was maybe getting a little depressed, he suggested that they nip the problem in the bud and adopt a fleshie child. Even if it was expensive.

The mere idea of it had so lifted Raymond's mood that George had known it was the right thing to do. Besides, it wasn't like it was a long-term commitment or anything. Scott was already four years old; he'd only be a child for another ten years or so. Adoption was such a new fad that people didn't really know what they'd do with the fleshie children once they grew up. This was the topic of the preacher's sermon.

Scott was sitting between Raymond and George, with a gag in his mouth to keep him from shouting during the service and his hands tied to make sure he didn't remove the gag. George smiled when he noticed how affectionately Raymond kept his arm around the boy.

Most people thought that, once the children grew up, they should be sold so their brains could be used as food, or simply killed by their adoptive families, their brains eaten fresh. Fresh brains were such a rare— and delicious—treat. That packaged stuff was never as good. Too many preservatives.

But the preacher at this church was a radical. She loudly advocated animal rights, even human rights, for fleshies. George listened. He had never considered these ideas seriously before. He used to snicker at anyone so naive as to buy into that sentimental propaganda. Glancing at the boy, he pondered the preacher's words. He wasn't convinced, but he realized that he now needed to think about all this more carefully.

Food was a problem. Pet food came in two formats. There was kibble, which wasn't too smelly, but Scott clearly wasn't that enthusiastic about it. He loved the other kind, the moist food. But neither George nor Raymond could stand the smell of the stuff, those icky vegetable, leafy, and fruity odors.

They argued about it. Raymond was willing to try, for the boy's sake. Plus, the vet said that the moist food was healthier.

George, however, was far from convinced. "No! It's just too disgusting," he said as Raymond served dinner. They were having brain casserole with chunky brain sauce. The brain cake they were going to eat for dessert was baking in the oven. It all smelled so delicious.

He continued: "And who cares if it's healthier? It's not like he's going to have a long life or anything."

Raymond looked hurt. "Don't say that! You heard what the preacher said! We have to work toward becoming a more compassionate society! To stop thinking about these animals only as a resource, a source of food. I mean, look at them—they look almost exactly like us. Sure, their skin is kind of sickly smooth, without any rot, and you can't see any of their bones or anything, but, still, they almost look like people. They can talk. They walk on two legs. It's not their fault if they smell, well, alive or something. Sure, it's kind of revolting that they grow old and then just stop moving once they die. But what we do to them in those factory farms just isn't right!"

George waited before replying. There was a tense, uncomfortable silence—save for Scott's constant crying and yelling and pounding. The boy always had so much fun when they locked him in that closet. After a few minutes, George glared at Raymond and said, "Are you done? Can I speak now?"

Raymond crossed his arms and nodded reluctantly.

"First, where do you think this meal comes from? From dead animals— animals just like Scott. This is what these animals are—food. Meat. They're our only source of food. And we have to farm them, or else we wouldn't be able to feed everyone. Do you—"

"Farming's not natural. The preacher said so! And she's right. You know she is."

George was livid. "Don't interrupt me! I let you drone on. Now you listen to me."

Pouting, Raymond said, "Okay, I'm listening."

George wagged his finger, his mouth open, ready to bark his anger at Raymond, but instead he let his arm and shoulders drop and said in a neutral voice, "Oh, what's the use." He walked out of the house.

What was really irritating George was that he found himself starting to agree with Raymond and the preacher. But he didn't want to. He hated this kind of sentimental anthropomorphizing. Meat was meat. He was starting to regret ever adopting the boy. None of this would be an issue if Raymond hadn't become so attached to Scott.

He wandered around the neighborhood for an hour or so and then decided to go back home.

He heard the screams even before he opened the door. He walked into the living room and saw Raymond playing with the boy. Scott's screams were so loud. He must really be enjoying himself. George could see that the boy had shat and peed himself in excitement, tears and snot running down his face. Raymond and Scott looked so beautiful playing hide-the-maggots that George's anger melted away. He took a handful of maggots out of his mouth and joined the two of them at their game. Scott screamed even louder when George started pushing maggots up the boy's nose. What fun! George softened even more and gave Raymond a loving look. They kissed, the boy's screams making it all the more meaningful.

Basil and Judith Fesper were moonbathing on their front lawn when George stepped out of the house to wash the car. They waved at him to come over. Inwardly, he groaned. What were they going to complain about now? What had Scott done this time?

"Hello, Basil. Judith."

They were both smiling. Basil said, "I wanted to apologize for almost eating your boy last month."

That surprised George. "Huh . . . thanks." Scott had run away a few weeks ago, and George had found Basil Fesper about to pop the boy's skull open for a quick snack. But George had intervened just in time. Basil had said, "If I ever find that animal on my property again, he'll be a meal!" Since then, Raymond and George usually kept the boy chained up to keep him out of trouble.

Judith shook her husband's shoulder. "Ask him, Basil. Ask him."

Basil looked irritated for a second, but then recovered. "What the wife and I mean is that hearing all those screams coming from your house. . . . Well, it makes us yearn for the pitter-patter of little feet, you know? We're thinking about getting a little one of our own. We were wondering if you could give us the number of the agency where you got Scooter."

"Scott."

"Right. Scott. So, what's the number?"

The preacher led George through the church. George looked at the frescos depicting the seven-day meteor shower that, according to Scripture, released God's chosen from the ground and allowed them to inherit the Earth from the fleshie animals who had ruled it in prehistoric times. It was so hard for George to remember that chaotic age, centuries ago, when people first walked the Earth. All he could recall was an all-consuming hunger for fleshie brains. Scripture said the feeding frenzy before God gave people consciousness lasted another seven days, but who really knew? George had never really cared about religious dogma. He didn't see the point in arguing over details nobody could prove or disprove. Maybe people had simply been too hungry to think straight.

They reached her office in the back. She offered him a glass of brain juice. "It's organic," she said. "From free-range fleshies."

It tastes the same as regular brain juice, he thought.

Sitting behind her big desk, she asked, "Is everything alright with your family, George? How's Raymond? And little Scott?"

"Well, there's nothing wrong per se, but that is kind of why I'm here." George looked at the floor and shuffled his feet, not sure how to continue. The preacher waited patiently.

George plunged ahead. "I've been thinking a lot about all that animal rights stuff of yours. At first I was pretty dismissive of it, but now I'm not so sure. I think I might be starting to agree with you. Especially the part about how it's unnatural for people to live apart from animals. I mean, since we've adopted Scott, Raymond's happier than he's ever been. And even I have to admit that the boy's fleshie screams are soothing for the soul. They make me feel . . . I dunno . . . complete or wholesome or something. And even the neighbors, who were antagonistic when we first got Scott, have been adopting fleshie children, too." George was getting wrapped up in what he was saying, talking more rapidly. "For example, just next door, the Fespers have adopted three children. Three!" He shook his hand to emphasize his point, and a morsel of flesh snapped off his index finger and fell to the floor.

"Now, there's a real sense of community in the neighborhood. There never was before. People throw parties and invite the neighbors to meet their new children. That kind of thing. There's never a moment without at least some screaming on our street. And it feels so right, so natural."

"I'm very glad to hear that, George. But I don't understand what your problem is."

"Well . . . I've been thinking about the appalling conditions in the factory farms, and all that. And I—I think I want to do more. I want to help change things. Make this a better world for others like Scott, for the fleshies."

The preacher stayed silent, scrutinizing George.

He fidgeted in his chair. "Did I say something wrong?"

"No. Absolutely not. Have you gone crazy?"

George couldn't understand why Raymond was so upset.

"You're going to get arrested. And where would that leave poor little Scott, with you in jail and only me to look after him?"

"But, Raymond, I'm doing this for Scott, so that he can grow up in a better world. I thought you'd be proud of me. That you'd want to do this, too. You're always talking about this fleshie rights stuff. Arguing with me to see things your way. And now I do. I really do. And I want to do something about it. Talk isn't enough. It won't change the world without action to back it up."

"That doesn't mean that I condone this kind of—of terrorism. It's criminal, George. Plus, your first responsibility should be to your family. To me and little Scott."

George was getting angry and impatient. First Raymond fought with him because George didn't believe in animal rights, and now they were arguing because, more than simply spouting slogans, George actually wanted to do something to help the fleshies. Before he could stop himself, he yelled at Raymond, "You're such a hypocrite. Such a coward. You don't really want what's best for Scott, just what's best for yourself!" And, with that, he stomped outside and drove away, to the rendezvous point the preacher had given him.

The preacher said that they were going to hit a fleshie factory farm. Blow up walls and liberate the fleshies. Make the authorities notice that people really cared about this, that it wasn't just empty rhetoric.

There were nine of them altogether. George recognized some of them from church. They split up in three vans. One of the vans, not the one George was in, was loaded with explosives. They were going to aim that van at the wall of the farm. The explosion should blow a hole big enough to let the fleshies escape. In the confusion, they'd slip in and make sure all the fleshies were freed. There shouldn't be too many people at the plant. They'd chosen a religious holiday for their operation: the first day of the Week of the Sacred Meteors.

Well, that was the plan.

The first part went off well. They drove far out of town, to where the factory was. The driverless van hit the wall. It exploded. It brought the wall down. They waited a few minutes, but no fleshies ran out. In fact, nobody ran out.

Confused, the group advanced toward the factory. They walked through the damaged wall and into the building. Inside, they saw that the van had hit the security guard's office. His head had been torn off his body. It lay on the floor in the doorway to the corridor.

As the animal liberators walked by, the head said, "Hey! Who are you guys? What the flesh is going on here?"

The group ignored the security guard. George thought, *I sure hope that guy has good medical coverage. Recapitation's not cheap.* Then one of the guys kicked the head. The preacher got mad: "Ralph! There was no need for that!"

Ralph, who was so tall he had to bend down to walk through the doorway, looked sheepish and said, "Sorry. Got too revved up."

The factory felt empty, deserted. The corridor led to a number of closed doors. The preacher said, "The fleshies must be behind those doors. Come on. Let's do what we came here for."

The first door led to a broom closet. George opened the second door. Jackpot.

The room was huge. Naked fleshies were stacked in a big cage, pressed tightly against each other. Their arms and legs had been amputated, but they were still alive. There must have been hundreds of them. They were all covered in excrement. Their mouths were sewn onto transparent plastic tubes that led to a big vat above their cage. Some kind of liquid goop flowed from the machines and into the mouths of the fleshies.

George could never have even imagined these conditions.

Between the door and the cage, there was a long stretch of tables, on which were piled mountains of amputated fleshie corpses with their skulls sawn open. On the floor, there was a long and deep tub filled to the rim with unprocessed brains.

The smell of the raw brains was overpowering.

The group of animal liberators, George included, mobbed the big tub and started chomping away at the cornucopia of raw meat.

In less than an hour, the tub was licked dry. High on food, the activists approached the cage that held the live amputated fleshies. They tore the iron bars apart with their bare hands. They ripped the tubes from the fleshies' mouths. They cracked the skulls of the animals on the floor and gorged themselves on fresh brains.

They fed until they'd eaten all the meat stored at that factory.

George lay on the floor in a stupor, his body covered in blood, gore, and brain goo. He was roused by the police sirens. Around him, the other liberators were slowly starting to come out of their post-binge daze. George, alarmed by the sound, collected himself and hurried outside. A half-dozen police vehicles were on the road, driving fast toward the factory farm. He ran to a ditch and jumped in. He prayed that the police hadn't seen him.

From the ditch, George saw the police round up all of his cohorts and search the would-be liberators' two remaining vans. After a while, they drove off. He'd managed to escape. Raymond had been right. This had been a crazy idea.

They hadn't done any good for the fleshies. All they'd done was eat.

George got angry at the preacher for putting all these stupid ideas into his head. Eating was natural. Meat was meat was meat. And that's all there was to it.

George and Raymond invited the whole neighborhood to their backyard barbecue. The Fespers were the first to arrive, but soon dozens of people were milling about the yard, their children tied up and well-behaved, screaming and crying. Scott was tied to the fence, next to the barbecue.

Basil Fesper said, "I've never trusted preachers. All that holiness. It warps the mind."

Raymond said, "Basil, it was only that one preacher who was criminally insane. Not all of them!"

Basil harrumphed. "They're all trying to contaminate us with their subversive notions, I tell you. I'll breathe before you ever see me in a church!"

His wife giggled. "Oh, Basil! Like you need an excuse for not going to church! Honestly, if I hadn't insisted on a traditional wedding . . ."

Holding hands, George and Raymond left the couple to bicker with each other.

Raymond turned to George and said, "Darling, I don't know why I got so depressed before we got Scott, but, almost losing you because of that stupid stunt, it really put things in perspective. I love you, and that's all that really matters."

"I love you, too, Raymond. I'm sorry we fought so much. That I got so tense and angry all the time."

"And all that over an animal! Over a ridiculous fad! What were we thinking?" They laughed.

Raymond clapped his hands to get the guests' attention. "Okay, everyone, I guess we should get started!"

George fired up the barbecue grill.

Everyone grabbed their children. Raymond looked at George, "He's all yours, darling."

George dug his fingers into Scott's skull and cracked it open. He was looking forward to better and better times with Raymond, now that they'd worked things out. *But*, George thought, *I'll miss the screams.*

ONE LAST,
LITTLE REVENGE

ED GREENWOOD

THERE ARE TIMES IN EVERY life when dreams come crashing down. This was one of those times for me, and I just hoped I could make the crash as spectacular as it deserved to be.

The darkly gleaming, glossy boardroom table stretched away for a seeming mile from my fingertips. I'd never bothered with such fripperies when Prendergast Fireworks and Novelties had still been mine alone. My creation, all those years ago. My overgrown workshop, a place of dust and clutter and fun . . . until Dr. Martyn Stannergar had come.

I needed "the Doctor," of course, and all of the sly, gray-faced suits he brought with him. My clowning still delighted small children, but the dollars weren't coming in the way they once had. Computers and "adult" toys were the rage nowadays, and "Jolly" Roger Prendergast didn't do either.

I still don't. An ugly new building blocks the view from my office window, blotting out even the tiniest glimpse of the little valley and the stream that winds through it—and that building is full of young, unkempt people I wouldn't want to come within two blocks of, let alone have on my payroll. They stare into flickering computer screens all day long, playing endless games that all seem to involve gunfire and explosions and screaming death while they purport to be doing something that'll enrich us all at Prendergast. Their break-even point is only a year or so away, Stannergar tells me.

Still, it's his money . . . their money. I had none left. All they needed was my name and distribution network. Oh, and my reputation: the kindly old salesman in the clownish, wide-stripe mock business suit who drove from store to store, playing with toys, giving some away, and fixing broken ones. Prendergast's Warbling Spintops, Prendergast's Marching Martians, Wiley's Walking Spiders, and hundreds more. Heard of them? Of course not. They're *old* toys, from the "good old days."

Yes, the good old days, when men cared about their work and their good names—and the phrase "an honest day's work" didn't evoke a snigger from bankers and young suits alike.

Like Stannergar, the toadies ranged down both sides of the table smirked at me in open contempt. They'd got what they wanted, and now it was time to snatch Prendergast's company away from the old fool and show him the door. Still penniless, and with nothing to show for sixty years of one honest working day after another. They'd called their security goons already, anticipating a scene; I could see tall, menacing men in uniforms peering coldly in at the doors.

"This is a day none of us wanted to come," Dr. Stannergar was saying soothingly, unable to keep a gleeful smile entirely off his face, "but—"

I held up a hand in a *stop* gesture, and—wonders!—the Doctor fell silent. I gave him my best kindly old geezer smile, and said in as humble a voice as I could manage, "I knew all along this day would have to come too, Martyn—"

He winced, hating my wise father act as much as ever.

"—and I can see that I've not kept up with the times, and that what little I still do here is holding Prendergast Fireworks and Novelties back. I'd hoped you'd level with me as I used to, when I had men who just weren't working out, but that's all changing, too. So it's for the best. I'll go now, happily and quietly, so long as you produce one last toy for this Christmas season. I think it's my masterpiece."

There was a stir up and down the table, and a lot of side-glances. I kept the smile on my face and in my voice. "If I've misfired again—well, it's only one season, isn't it? You own this last little surprise already, lock and stock, you do. . . . I just want a chance to see it sweep the world. All right?"

The glances were exchanged openly this time, as I calmly adjusted my bow tie and then folded my hands on the table. Not a trace of a quaver or the trembling that sometimes came. Good.

In the end, Stannergar nodded reluctantly. "You plan to show it to us now?"

I nodded. "I'll just fetch it from my office. One of the men you've so thoughtfully invited—" I nodded at one of the doorways; Stannergar gave me a hard look, but I kept all trace of sarcasm or anger out of my voice "—can accompany me, and I'll bring it right back here. If you agree to produce it, it'll be handshakes all around, I'll give you my keys, and at long last I'll be able to go home and watch Desi and Lucy on my new television. It's got color, you know. I must have missed a lot of episodes by now."

They all smiled tolerantly; none of them bothered to stoop to the minor cruelty of telling me how long Arnaz or Ball had been dead.

"You go do that, Jolly," the fattest of Stannergar's suited sharks said, almost eagerly. "If you think you've got a masterpiece, I've got to see it!"

There was an awkward pause, and then a sudden chorus of enthusiastic and entirely false agreement, all around the table—except from Stannergar, who didn't bother joining in. He just sat there looking irritated that his self-scripted moment of glory had been disrupted. The great scene of power, wherein he smoothly and dramatically crushed the soul of an eighty-year-old man in a bow tie and a rumpled suit, and had him bodily thrown off the premises faster than a Prendergast Rushing Moon Rocket.

Dear, dear. He'd never be able to tell his grandchildren about it, now.

No less than four security guards accompanied me on my short, cane-assisted hobble to my office. They had the grace to look sheepish about it, however, and made no protest when I went around behind my desk into my back office, past the Singing Robots and the hanging cluster of Fly by Night glow-planes, and closed the door in their faces. The bolt was as large as my wrist, and well-oiled; they'd need a cutting torch to get through it in anything less than an hour. After I'd secured the lock, I went to the closet in the corner, opened the door, and embraced the shiny firepole within—hey now, what good is it being president of your own novelties company if you don't give yourself a carload or two of, well, novelties?

Two Screaming Eyes went off as they were supposed to, whirling past me in the shaft like tiny firebolts. Appropriate; I was going forth into battle at last. Years after I should have done so, but better late than never.

The gigantic flatulence cushion at the bottom made my landing as gentle as . . . well, I'll spare you the lame joke. It took me just two steps to reach the closet that opened only to the little key on the end of my keyring. We were right behind the furnace—excuse me, "HVAC unit"—and so it was amid the deafening thunder of burners and blowers and suchlike that the door yielded and I found myself staring at: me.

It smelled a little, yes, but who knows—maybe I did, too. There was a reason I'd worn the same bow tie and rumpled suit all this past year, as Stannergar's confident smiles grew ever wider. Project Nightstalk, in all its glory.

Six strong, now. All of them once men who'd worked for me, toymakers who'd have toiled for "Father" Prendergast right into their graves. The inventors of the Walking Spider and the Bubbling Aquarium on Your

Finger Ring and the Smacktail Dog; Dabble, the Dancing Duck; and dozens more. Great men, geniuses. Principled men, too. They'd refused to make the Doctor's cruel and rude adult "toys," and found no joy in the shoot 'em up video games the younger designers played. They were all past their eightieth or ninetieth year, so the computers themselves had been quite beyond them.

Stannergar had almost fallen over himself in his gloating rush to fire them. They'd barely shuffled back to their sagging old homes when he slapped them with unfounded lawsuits, accusing them of stealing "his" secrets—innovations they'd come up with down the years, and shared freely with me, as I had my inventions with them. Their only crime had been to live in the houses I'd built, around the factory. Right in the way of Stannergar's planned glass box of a building. They'd stayed on working because they loved it—but to Stannergar, they were just men to knock down and administer a good kicking to.

Red had come up with the gloop that kept cowhide supple and seemingly alive. Danged if it didn't work on humans, too, skin and flesh and all. Prendergast's Crawling Masks—later Prendergast's Haunted Masks—had come from that. Wiley had been the one to link the little car motors to batteries, and later to nerves, making a cat with paralyzed hind legs walk again. Later, he'd been the first *real* genius amongst us: He made Bob Jimry's shattered arm work again, the whirring little motor driving fingers and wrists and elbows to move as well as before the accident.

One by one, heartsick at all the police and the sneering lawyers and the gloating lawsuits, they'd died. I suspected some of these same security goons had helped Bob Jimry to his last breath—I don't see how he could have broken his neck falling *up* a flight of porch steps, the key to his locked front door still in his hand. Or hit himself three times on the back of the head doing so.

I paid for all of the funerals—and buried none of them. Wiley had made dozens of his little motors, and I worked for days in my cellar, next to the freezers that usually held moose from Red's hunting trips. Wiley was the first I managed to get standing. Then Red, and Bob Jimry, and Hallahan. Giving them a chance to get their revenge on the monster who'd hounded them to death. It was the least I could do.

My contribution had been the preservatives that kept them from collapsing entirely back to the earth that spawns us all. That and a little fiddling with the motors, which led to the creation of the small box that controlled their movements from afar. Years, that "little fiddling" had taken.

God knows I've never been a brilliant man, and even less a miracle worker—they were still dead men, their brains gone, their eyes empty and staring. But from time to time I fancied they were *looking* at me. I hoped, somehow, that wherever they might now be, they were aware of what I was doing to their bodies, and why. I hoped they were more enraged at Stannergar than at me.

I had six walking corpses in all, and latex masks for each, to make their skull-like, rotting faces into my own kindly collection of wrinkles, big nose and all. But only this one, staring back at me out of the closet, wore duplicates of my suit and tie.

I stared critically at its hair, ruffled it with my hand to more closely resemble what the mirror on the closet door was showing me, and steadied the cardboard box in its hands. *Prendergast's Special Surprise*, the box read, just to give them all something to think about, and beneath that label I'd written the comment: *Number 13. Not one of my best, but it does the job.*

I gave those words the crooked smile they deserved and took down the control box I'd spent so many years perfecting from atop Prendergast's Special Surprise. Switching it on, I watched the zombie unstiffen, turn its head to regard me, and open its eyes. Those eyes had been Red's once, but I tried not to think of that. Dust on eyeballs always looks a little strange, I think. I made it smile.

When it—Red—no, *it*—did, I smiled back and told it, "Break a leg, kid."

As it lurched past me to the service elevator, my zombie did not reply.

Hmmph. Kids, these days.

With a remote, I opened a door from the closet leading back to the hallways, a secret route that didn't pass through my office. Then I sat down in the big, comfy chair, sneezing at the dust, and switched on the bank of monitors. Spying is what screens are for, Stannergar, not playing games. Not nice ones, anyway.

The boardroom flickered into grainy, purplish life, and I pulled a rod and made that monitor slide out to hang in front of me. I was in time to see my own grand entrance.

Unspeaking, I went to my seat, set the box on the table, and started pulling out beakers and stoppered test tubes and little containers with oversized old radio switches and coiling wires trailing out of them. The men around the table smiled at the dust on things, and at the little show I made myself do, patting the heads of little lightbulbs that I'd painted faces on.

The Doctor surveyed the mismatched and moldering odds and ends, and managed an indulgent little laugh. "Really, Mister Prendergast—"

My double straightened, gave him a smile of triumph that the mask didn't quite convey, and brought its fist down hard on the test tubes.

I'd forgotten just how strong my zombies were. Stannergar's precious boardroom table split for quite a way down its length, and the sleep gas I'd meant to distribute around the room by tossing the test tubes boiled out like smoke. It was a mess. Just like my first three Prendergast's Pecking Penguins, who'd enthusiastically battered their little heads to shards breaking my workbench. Their stuffing went everywhere, too. We were finding it for months afterward.

Back in the boardroom there were shouts of alarm, and men shoved their chairs back and got to their feet in a hurry. Damn. I wasn't even sure the sleep-stuff still worked after all the time it'd been in storage. From the control room I made my double bow and thrust its hand down the front of its pants.

That made the security men—those that were left, that is; the others would still be sitting uneasily in my office—halt in their various charges forward, and peer at my double in amazement. Zombie fingers pulled the switch beneath the rumpled trousers.

I stopped watching, closing my eyes and turning my head away from the monitor just before the terrific crash came.

The room shook, a long, rolling boom that spilled more than one monitor to the floor, amid sparks and shards of glass and spitting, swaying wires. Around me, the lights all went out, and then came back on again, along with an insistent ringing of alarm bells. And no wonder. Most of the top floor of Prendergast Fireworks and Novelties was gone, along with all the glass windows of that nice new building full of computers. There would be fires.

Thankfully, my way out was all a matter of unlocked doors and level passages, right out to the old overgrown shed at the back of the warehouse Stannergar hadn't gotten around to bulldozing yet, along with all of its Prendergast's Patriotic Saluting Generals and Jimry's Singing Parachutes and suchlike. Hmmph. He never would, now.

Well done, Red. Useful things, zombies. A pity I'd had to blow my best one up. But up in the warehouse, there were still five of me left. All I had to do now was get all of us off the premises before—

No such luck. Sirens were wailing and tires screeching before my old legs brought me up the stairs into the warehouse's dusty gloom. Thankfully there was still one small, heavily barred window looking out across the parking lot.

Flashing lights, lots of them—and more arriving every moment. Police cars, not just ambulances and fire trucks. Not that there was much left of the old factory to salvage, anyway. As I watched, the blazing wreckage fell into the lower two floors, and there was a terrific explosion. Boilers and oil tanks and that new HVAC unit, no doubt.

As if in sympathy, Stannergar's new glass-box building collapsed, too. I chuckled. All I'd wanted was one last, little revenge, but these things have always had a habit of, well, getting away from me . . . .

There were men running toward me now. Of course they'd head here; this was the last building left standing, except for the gatehouse for the parking lot. I'd have to hide, or feign complete befuddlement, and somehow I didn't think I'd manage to fool any angry young policemen just now.

What to do, what to do?

There were thuddings on the doors, and shouts. "Is anyone in there? Hello!"

What to—ah, yes. Of *course.*

"Hello? Is anyone *in there?* Say something!"

I hurried to the locked cubicle at the end of the warehouse, fumbling in the dark for the right key. The same little one, at the end. Yes. *Yes.*

The door opened and I stepped inside and slid the bolt home—just as light flooded into the warehouse and brought more shouts with it.

The flashlight hanging inside the door should have died long ago. It gave me only a few feeble moments of amber flickering, but they were enough. I threw the switch that turned off the rat-frying field, shouldered past a Jimry's Hugging Doll that was almost my height, and clambered up onto the simple wooden shelf that held the rest of Project Nightstalk.

They were lying in a peaceful row, arranged like customers in the backroom of a morgue I'd once seen. Five moldering zombies, silent and intact, all of them wearing face masks to look like me. I crawled slowly over them all to the empty space at the end, and laid down, putting my hands at my sides. It wasn't so dark, after all; light was coming down from one dirty skylight, high above.

I was shaking. I was old, damn it, and this hurrying wasn't good for what was left of me. I lay still and stared up into the near-darkness, wondering how long I'd have to stay there. They'd probably put guards on the grounds, and bring in a forensic team. . . . God, I might starve waiting!

I couldn't just wander out of the warehouse, because they were sure to search it if I did, from end to end and cellar to rafters. And when they found my zombies . . .

I shuddered, there in the dark, and tried not to notice the sickly sweet smell of rotting flesh from beside me. *Close* beside me.

I ground my teeth. They were false, and it hurt, but I had to—had to—

The smell was growing stronger. Yes, it was.

I closed my eyes, shuddered again—and then felt something touch my arm.

Something thin and crumpling, that rasped like paper. I opened my eyes and looked down my chest. It was a piece of paper.

And it was being held out to me by—by the zombie lying next to me! I turned my head, heaven knows I didn't want to, and it was *looking* at me. There, in the dark, its dead eyes darker holes in the gloom.

I tried to scream, but only managed a whistling wheeze. The thing that had once been Bryce Wiley drew back the paper and then thrust it at me again, tapping my arm and chest. I tried not to remember the boardroom table splitting under the force of a zombie fist . . . and failed. I felt in my pocket for my little box, dragged it out—and saw that it was shut off. Dark, its switches all down. I rattled it. Nothing.

The zombie slowly shook its head.

How could this be? It was moving, without any goading from my control box! Had I made a better toy than I could ever have dreamed of? Or—or–

The paper scraped insistently across my chest again.

God save me! Quailing, I reached out for it. There was writing on it, but damned if I could read it in the gloom.

I spread my hands, helplessly, as flashlight beams played across the ceiling high above and police snapped sharp challenges at each other. They sounded disappointed at the lack of immediately apparent criminals or stored drugs or lurking gangsters, and their voices faded. But I knew they'd be back. Back to search, and find.

There was a bad taste in my mouth now. Fear. I didn't want to die in a cell after months of being dragged from courtroom to police van to interrogation room and back to jail.

"It would have been better if I'd been in the boardroom," I whispered to myself. "Carried my own explosives."

The paper was snatched away from me, and there were scratchings. I turned my head, fascinated. Yes, the nearest zombie was writing something—and I could see the heads of others now, raised to peer over their fellow.

At me. I swallowed, fighting down fresh fear, as something metallic was passed down the row of zombies and held patiently out to the last one. It finished its writing, held the paper out to me again, and accepted the metal object: a watchman's flashlight.

The flashlight clicked on, held low above the page so as not to spill excess light where anyone wandering the warehouse might see it. I read the words caught in its beam: *No, Mr. Prendergast, your death wouldn't have made anything better. We need you. Children who love good toys need you. Stannergar must die, and every last one of his young idiots. All the sick games they've created. All computer games. We must do the smashing and slaying, to make sure. Clear across the country. Every man, and every game. All. Revenge!*

The undead hand turned the paper over to show me the older writing on the other side: *It's long past time we discussed working conditions and wages. We can wait forever, but we won't.*

I stared at the paper for a long time, and then turned to look into those dead eyes again and mimed writing something. The flashlight clicked off and a pencil was thrust at me. I was pleased to see that my hand trembled only slightly when rotting fingers brushed my own. Then I took the pencil and the flashlight snapped back on. In its small, bright circle I wrote carefully: *Yes. Revenge. Agreed. After, I'll be delighted to make you all full partners in the company, if I have one left. My equals. I might have some difficulty in doing anything for a time: Police.*

That hand reached out, took the pencil from me, wrote something, and then held the flashlight again for me to read: *Understood. Agreed. Give me the box.*

The box? Oh. I reached back into my breast pocket, took out the little control box, and handed it over. The zombie cradled my masterpiece gingerly, held it up where all of its fellows could see—and then curled its fingers together, ignoring the brief flurry of spitting sparks and falling knobs and springs. What it gently handed back to me was a crushed, wrenched sculpture.

I was wet with fear now. Trapped. Helplessly I watched the hands that had just crushed metal set pencil and paper aside, and then rise to its chin.

The zombie turned its face toward me as it peeled the mask. Most of its flesh came away with it, baring yellowed bone beneath, but it rolled the latex back only to its nose, and I realized suddenly that it—that Wiley—was trying to show me a smile.

Then it reached out for me.

I tried to scream again, but only managed a gasp. It extended its hand again, insistently . . . like a salesman who's tried to shake your hand and been ignored, and is trying again.

Oh. Wiley had once refused to shake my hand because I was his employer, and "'twouldn't have been right" to do so. A sign of disrespect.

I cleared my throat. It took me three tries before I could manage the words. "Is it 'right' now, Mister Wiley?"

That dark, rotting head nodded, slowly, and tried to smile again.

Wonderingly, I extended my hand.

With infinite gentleness the cold, cold flesh touched mine, matched its grip to mine, and we shook hands, there in the darkness.

There are times in every life when new dreams come leaping up, and this was one of those times for me.

SHOUTING DOWN THE MOON

MYKE COLE

M UMBI'S HANDS WERE ON HIM, and she was beautiful, beautiful, and beautiful. He filled his hands with her and she called out his name as softly as she could.

When they were finished, Nkosi rose and picked up his spear. He looked at her for a long time, memorizing the contours of her face.

"What if you don't come back to me?" she asked.

Nkosi smiled. He plucked a flower from a nearby sugarbush, stringing it to her necklace. "I will come back."

Mumbi sniffed the blossom. "They will kill you."

Nkosi's smile did not waver. "Ah, my love. I will still come back."

When Nkosi opened his eyes, he was alive again.

No, not alive, but standing and seeing. A quick glance at his body and he wished that were not so. His skin was pitted and withered like rotting tree bark. Moss hung from the gaping spear wound that had killed him.

"It isn't pretty, I know." It was a harsh whisper.

At first, Nkosi thought the speaker was a ghost. He was tall and robed in black. Gold bangles wreathed his thin arms. The ash paste on his skin glowed white in the firelight.

The man snatched a burning twig from the fire and thrust it into Nkosi's belly. It hissed out a tendril of gray smoke.

Nkosi felt nothing. The man grinned. "It has its advantages, my *makeri*. You can't feel pain."

Nkosi shuddered. *Makeri*, a walking corpse. The man was a sorcerer. Nkosi tried to reach out for him, but could not move his arms. He shook and groaned.

The sorcerer's face was painted with the same dotted pattern worn by the Kaonde warrior who had driven the spear into Nkosi's side.

"You'll move when I decide. How do you like that, *makeri?*" the sorcerer asked. "Now you fight for the Kaonde."

Nkosi found he could turn his head. Beyond the crackling campfire, he could make out the small jumble of fetishes the sorcerer had used to pull him from the graveworld: a decapitated bird, some rattles, a bundle of small bones. Farther out, the black waters of the Uele raced along, stripping away the soil and laying bare veins of gold. Though he could not see them from here, Nkosi knew his fellow Zande tribesmen sifted the earth for the gold quietly, casting wary eyes about for roving bands of ravenous *biloko*. The sorcerer must have dragged his body from the banks of the Uele to raise him here.

Nkosi tried to speak. It sounded strangled. "Piss on you, Kaonde."

The sorcerer laughed. "Piss on you, Zande. You should be happy. You're going to see your beloved tribe again."

The sorcerer couldn't know that Mumbi was among the Zande. If Nkosi's heart still beat, it would have quickened at the thought of her. He turned his head again. The Zande fires could still be seen a little way off, along the banks; the tribe hadn't yet moved. That meant he had not been dead more than a fortnight.

The sorcerer leaned in close, wrinkling his nose at Nkosi's rotted face. "I don't think your Zande brothers are going to like you very much now."

Mumbi scratched in the ground, filling the basket with roots as quietly as she could. The *biloko* combed the savannah, blending in with the tall grasses, eating all in their path. Mumbi hadn't believed that the monsters were more than legend—until she saw them for herself. The size of a leopard, they had round bodies that were mostly mouth. Stubby claws propelled them through the savannah faster than any man could run. That speed was used in the hunt that consumed their every waking hour. No man had even seen a *biloko* sleep. Even the Kaonde feared them.

Since they'd arrived, the Zande worked day and night without pause, sleeping in shifts, the faster to be away from the *biloko* runs and out of harm's way.

The silence was as complete as the darkness blanketing the plain, broken only by the muffled ringing of a cloth-wrapped shovel scraping the earth and the soft glow of the hooded candles lighting the ground.

Standing beside her, Njanu nervously hefted his spear and sniffed the night wind. The air smelled clean to Mumbi. Filling her lungs with it helped shake off some of the fatigue of their work's breakneck pace. The quicker in and out, the quicker they would have the gold home—gold that would buy metal for spearheads. Gold that would hire Chokwe mercenaries.

Gold that would save them from the Kaonde.

She glanced at Njanu. The tall warrior looked strained, his dark skin waxy in the moonlight. She hadn't seen him sleep since they'd arrived on the Uele. He'd been either digging or guarding the entire time. She took another deep breath before standing and picking up the basket.

She stopped. Another smell rode the air now. The breeze felt thick.

She whispered a warning to Njanu, but he was already moving cautiously out into the darkness, waving her back with a callused hand.

Despite his fatigue, Njanu moved carefully, his powerful legs parting the tall grasses. Mumbi caught a glimpse of the lion pelt draped about his waist before he vanished into the night.

Mumbi froze. With Njanu gone, and the rest of the Zande back panning gold, she was alone. The darkness swallowed her. Only the dim light of the moon and the feel of the basket at her hip reminded her that she had not fallen into the graveworld.

She took a step backward.

The smell grew stronger, cloying. She heard the tall grasses rustle.

A tide of relief washed over her. Njanu was returning. But the relief soon curdled in her gut. No man moved that swiftly.

The moonlight revealed the *biloko* driving arrow-straight toward her. The low form was bent, and plains grass sprouted from its hide, blending it seamlessly into the surrounding savannah.

The only indicators of its presence were lines of movement, eyes, and row upon row of teeth.

The mouth was horrendous.

And the smell . . . even at this distance, the stench was stifling.

Mumbi began to walk backward, not daring to shriek and risk bringing more *biloko* down upon them. She bit her tongue until the copper taste of blood filled her mouth.

The *biloko* picked up speed. The mouth snapped once, experimentally. The sound was lightning rending a tree.

Mumbi threw her load at it. Another lightning crack, and she watched as basket, roots and all, disappeared into the giant mouth. The creature darted forward, the stink blotting out all her senses.

Mumbi stopped moving backward. It could not be outrun.

She kicked at it, once, but the *biloko* knocked her foot aside with a quick swipe of a stubby claw. The mouth opened wide.

Then Njanu was upon it, leaping on the creature's back and sinking his spear deep into the gaping maw. The *biloko* let out a strangled cough and clamped its jaw shut, snapping the spear shaft in two and throwing Njanu off. It ran in tight circles and clawed at its throat. It flexed its jaw once, twice, trying to howl. Each time, the spear point protruded farther from the wound and all the beast managed was a hissing choke.

Mumbi snatched up a rock and hammered on the monster. Njanu stood stunned for a moment before he joined her. The *biloko* slowed under the rain of blows. Finally it stopped, twitched once, and collapsed.

Mumbi and Njanu stood completely still, barely daring to breathe, waiting. The night wind whispered in the long grass. Somewhere in the distance, a sunbird let out a mournful call.

Nothing.

Njanu let out his breath. "It must have sniffed out your basket of food, or perhaps this—" He patted his lion pelt. "We are fortunate it foraged alone."

Mumbi nodded. She looked back to Njanu, his strong frame ropy with muscle. He was as strong a warrior as any could hope for, but she would not feel safe until her Nkosi returned. Njanu returned her glance and she felt the heat of his eyes. Mumbi almost went to him, but he was not Nkosi. It would do no good. The moment would pass and her trembling would subside, and he would still not be Nkosi. Nkosi would still be out on the Uele, fighting the Kaonde scouts who had come to sniff out the gold for themselves.

A few more nights here and the carts would be loaded with enough gold to make the Kaonde the smallest of worries. In the meantime, there were men to feed, water to be drawn, carts to be loaded.

There were *biloko* to hide from, and a lover to pine for.

Nkosi would come back to her. Mumbi stroked the dried sugarbush blossom she wore around her neck. Even after all this time, it emitted a faint scent of mountainsides far from *biloko*, Kaonde, and suffering.

Nkosi had sworn that even death couldn't keep them apart.

Mumbi believed him.

There were few Kaonde after all. The sorcerer had hired Chokwe mercenaries to do his work. They crouched in the grass, the Uele dark and brooding at their backs. Some clustered around Nkosi where he stood with two other *makeri*, both Zande warriors killed along the river. Rare was the man who had seen a *makeri*. One of the Chokwe came close to Nkosi and lifted his beaded mask. "Does it hurt?" he asked.

"I feel nothing." Nkosi's answer was mumbled, his lips thick.

The Chokwe repeated the answer to his fellows in their own dialect. Nkosi thought it sounded like the croaking of frogs. The Chokwe leaned into one another, whispering through their masks and leaning on their spears. After the hushed conference, they asked him what the graveworld was like.

"The sky is the bottom of a thousand graves," Nkosi said, "and the rest is cold vastness." He did not tell them about the wandering, calling out Mumbi's name, scrambling for an exit back to her.

"Did you see your father? Your mother?" the Chokwe asked.

"No. You know they are there, but it is dark and there are many voices crying out. You cannot find anyone."

Nkosi had been completely alone. Faintly, he had smelled the dried petals of a sugarbush blossom and had nearly gone mad running after it. But he had always known that it was beyond the graveworld—and his reach.

Another round of whispers, and Nkosi suffered them thrusting their spear points into him until the sorcerer shooed them away. The other Kaonde came forward with him, distributing ankle rattles, drums, wooden whistles. The Chokwe took them, muttering about warriors reduced to playing music.

"Why waste your lives in a battle you can have the *biloko* fight for you?" the sorcerer asked. The Chokwe fell silent at the mention of the monsters. "Make certain that you upset the ore carts; leave the Zande no way to move the gold. Most importantly, drum and cry out! Shout down the very moon! Bring the *biloko* down upon them."

Nkosi turned to the Chokwe beside him. "They will kill you, too. The *biloko* do not care who they take."

The Chokwe shrugged. "They aren't hyenas, *makeri*. They won't touch dead flesh. You have nothing to fear."

"And as long as you are with us," one of the Kaonde cut in, "we have nothing to fear either. You will protect us, won't you, *makeri*?"

Nkosi could feel the Chokwe smiling behind his mask. The Kaonde paid in gold. For a Chokwe, gold was second only to a woman in its power to make men brave.

The sorcerer ushered them into reed boats assembled along the rocky riverbed, prows tossing gently in the rippling water. A Kaonde warrior led each party, a host of Chokwe behind him and a *makeri* at his side. The sorcerer stood on the bank as they pushed off, gesturing encouragement. "Remember the noise," he whispered as loudly as he dared. "Shout down the very moon!"

Nkosi had seen the *biloko* at work when his people had first come to the Uele. One of the men had gone gathering grass for his belt and had barely made it back to the caravan before a lone *biloko* caught up with him. They had killed the creature, but not before it had a chance to take a single bite.

A single bite had been more than enough.

Nkosi gazed in horror as the Chokwe shook the rattles experimentally. He turned to the Kaonde next to him, hoping his rotting face could convey the hatred that burned in his dead heart.

The Kaonde smiled, showing white teeth. "You hate it now, *makeri?* Wait until we make you fight."

Nkosi reached for him, but the painted patterns on the Kaonde's face seemed to swirl and spread, and at once the strength fled from his arms. The Kaonde laughed again.

Nkosi felt a sob rise in his throat, but he could not bring it out. So he stood silently as the Chokwe pushed against the river, poling the boats off shore until the current took them.

Mumbi pressed the sugarbush blossom to her nostrils and inhaled. Amidst the dry smell of the savannah grasses and the faint odor of the *biloko*, it was an oasis of sweet air.

The Zande smelled like fear. It was a sharp, intense odor borne on the sweat running in rivulets down their straining backs. They cast nervous glances over their shoulders, searching the horizon for *biloko* with each toss of their muffled shovels.

The smell threatened to overwhelm her. Mumbi brushed her lips with the dried blossom and again thought of Nkosi. He had been many things—impetuous, bull-headed, sometimes even childish.

But he had never been frightened.

And so she hadn't been either.

Her need for him was a needle in her belly. Njanu could hold her, but he could not be Nkosi.

One of the scouts came trotting in, his cloak woven with long grass to blend him with the savannah. The light of the hooded work candles shone dully on his chest. Njanu raised a hand in greeting, and the scout stepped lightly over to them, shaking his head to show that he had seen no *biloko* on his patrol. The less words the better. Every breath carried potentially death-dealing noise.

In the short time she had been on the Uele, Mumbi had learned to speak without words, keeping the silence that had become almost sacred over the last weeks. She made her eyes large and fixed the scout hard with them.

He looked at her and shook his head again. Once. Firmly.

No sign of the Uele party or of her Nkosi. Mumbi recognized the shame the scout felt in telling her, and put out a hand on his arm to steady him.

The scout looked at her, his eyes pools of sympathy. Then the pools abruptly emptied, his eyes rolled up in his head, and he collapsed.

A brightly painted spear protruded from his back.

The silence split apart in a thunderclap of beating drums and shrieking reed whistles. The sudden din washed over the Zande, a wave of confusion and alarm. For a moment the whole camp could do nothing but stare in disbelief.

The grass about them rustled into life. Dozens of Chokwe stood in a line of throbbing sound. Their masks dripped beads and stringed shells as they beat their instruments and threw back their heads, shouting down the moon. Three Kaonde warriors ran out before them. Beside each was a black and shriveled form that could not possibly be a man.

The Zande were desperately silent as they advanced to meet them.

Mumbi covered her ears as if shutting the sound from her hearing could shut it from the world. It did no good.

The Zande ignored the quieter Kaonde and made for the drum-wielding Chokwe. But the mercenaries made no attempt to fight; they faded backward into the tall grasses, blowing their whistles for all they were worth. Njanu and a few others realized they could not catch them, and turned their attention to the Kaonde.

As they did, the Chokwe concealed in the grass suddenly ceased their harsh music. A few took off running toward the Uele. A small group broke off, as if only then remembering their mission, and made for the gold-heavy ore carts.

Mumbi watched Odiambo, her tribesman, engage one of the black, shuffling things protecting the Kaonde. It shambled forward, swatting at him as if he were a troublesome insect. Odiambo leaped at it, burying his spade deep in the thing's chest. It merely shrugged and slapped at him again.

"*Makeri!*" Njanu called to Odiambo. "Leave it and come on!" But Odiambo, desperate to keep a weapon in his hands, pulled on the spade's handle, trying to wrench it free. The creature grasped the spade with one hand and Odiambo's throat with the other.

Mumbi looked away as Odiambo emitted a choked gurgle.

Njanu scrambled after the Chokwe, hoping to protect the carts. He darted wide and herded them against one another, feinting and waving his spear when they made to move past him. A few of the other Zande—those not dueling with the *makeri*—took up the chase. But there were not enough to shield the carts for long. Too many of their fellow tribesmen had run off into the night, thinking it better to take their chances with the *biloko* than the raiders and their dead servants.

Seeing the terrible price the dead things exacted upon the Zande made Mumbi wonder if the others had been right to flee. The few tribesmen battling the Chokwe for the carts were bloody, but still standing. Those who attacked the Kaonde and their *makeri* fell one by one, until their corpses ringed their enemies. No warrior could stand against the dead men; they shrugged off spear thrusts and brushed away deadly blows from even the heaviest of picks. The *makeri* were slow, but they were tireless. The initial desperation of the Zande soon dwindled to resignation, until Mumbi thought the warriors resembled tired dancers, going through the motions of combat for the benefit of some expectant audience.

Mumbi cursed the withered plain as she crushed the sugarbush blossom to her breast. As if responding to this, one of the *makeri* looked up, sniffed the air, and began to move toward her. The Zande leaped on the undefended Kaonde warrior, hammering him with their pans and shovels. He called after the creature, his voice shrill and desperate until it was cut short by a shovel's edge.

Mumbi watched the *makeri* close the distance between them, each unsteady step throwing its rotten body forward. She opened her mouth to call for help, but found it suddenly dry.

The *makeri* reached forward, dead lips working silently. A sound escaped its ruptured throat—an almost musical groan of longing.

Mumbi's ears filled with the buzzing of terror. The wind, the shouting, the crooning of the *makeri* were all reduced to the same low hum. The scent of sugarbush rose in her nostrils.

Through the hum, she could hear Njanu call her name. The warrior was charging toward the *makeri*, but he would not reach the dead thing before it reached her. Mumbi retrieved the spear from the fallen scout; she would have to defend herself.

The *makeri* groaned again and lurched forward. As it neared, the smeared remains of the war paint on its dead face came clear.

They were Zande patterns.

Mumbi could remember painting them.

The spear became heavy in her hands; she could barely raise the point toward the walking corpse. It reached for her throat, fetid hands brushing the flower that hung there.

Njanu howled and let fly his own spear. It arced gracefully and buried itself, haft deep, in the *makeri*'s shoulder.

Mumbi continued to stare into the empty eyes. A rank stench replaced the smell of sugarbush, bullying the lighter fragrance from her nostrils.

The *makeri* turned as the tall grasses about them seemed to dance and grow—and finally erupted into scores of charging *biloko*.

The few remaining Chokwe abandoned their assault on the ore carts and fled for the Uele. A dozen or so *biloko* chased them. The rest plunged among the Zande, their massive jaws working feverishly. They came low, snapping up running legs, grass, earth, and stone—everything in their path.

The *makeri* worked to protect their Kaonde masters, buying them time to join the Chokwe in flying for the river.

Most of the Zande ran, as well, but a few men recalled that a *biloko* could outrun a frightened antelope. Those men turned to fight.

Mumbi could see there were too many. The *biloko* crashed over the camp, scores of darting, snapping mouths. Though the *makeri* struck at them, the *biloko* ignored the dead men in favor of warmer flesh. The *biloko* were hunters, not scavengers. Mumbi heard a low cry and the sound of splintering wood as they fell upon the oxen, gulping down their harness and most of the carts in their frenzy.

One of the *biloko* separated itself from the pack and charged toward her, only to be intercepted by the *makeri*, which snatched the creature up in its arms and flung it away. Mumbi again heard Njanu calling her name as he struck about him with a fallen shovel at the snarling *biloko*. The shovel rose and fell, rose and fell, each time more slowly, as the circle of creatures about the warrior grew. Before long, there were only *biloko* and she could not see Njanu or his shovel at all.

Two of the monsters raced toward Mumbi. The *makeri* tackled one, wrestling it to the ground and driving its clawlike hands into the beast's side. The other neatly sidestepped the dead man and leaped at Mumbi. She threw herself to her right, striking the creature's back with the spear's butt and sending it sprawling. She leaped to her feet and threw her weight behind the weapon. The head tore clean through the *biloko* and into the earth beneath it. The beast howled, then fell still. Mumbi tugged on the spear, but she could not pull it free.

A shriek rose in the back of her throat as she wrenched at the shaft, hauling it back and forth, cursing the hated tree from which it had been carved. She only succeeded in shifting the *biloko*'s corpse.

It was then she noticed how silent the plain had become.

No drums, no whistles, no screaming. There was only a faint rustling of wind, the distant murmur of the river.

Mumbi looked up from the spear shaft and met the eyes of dozens of *biloko*.

She was completely surrounded. Only the three *makeri* stood, black sticks in a sea of monsters and gently shifting grass.

The *biloko* moved slowly forward. They examined her, relishing her fear, lightly snapping their huge mouths as if her terror were a thing to be eaten.

She backed up, turned around. The *biloko* had formed a ring. Horrible, piggish eyes stared at her from all sides.

Mumbi raised the dried blossom to her face and breathed deeply. The smell calmed her, the sweet tendrils of scent reaching into her lungs and gentling her heart.

Defiantly Mumbi threw back her head and cried out, longer and louder than she ever had before. She sang out to her Nkosi, letting him know that she loved him, that she was sorry, that she would miss him terribly.

But it wasn't Nkosi who answered. It was the *biloko*. They howled and gnashed their jaws, eating up her screams.

Then they were upon her.

Nkosi threw the *biloko* aside, but it didn't matter. Seeing that there was nothing left to eat, they scattered, streaming out of the camp.

They had even eaten the bones. There was nothing left but mud, broken shovels, and piles of crude gold scattered amidst the splintered remains of ox carts.

There was no sign of Mumbi at all. Not a scrap of cloth, not a spot of blood.

Nkosi shifted and moved toward where he believed she had last been. A passing *biloko* paused at the movement and sniffed at him. Finding nothing worth eating, it moved on to join the rest of the departing pack.

As quickly as they had come, they were gone, and the camp was left to the dead.

The other *makeri* stood still, looking at their feet, waiting for word from their Kaonde commanders.

A cry rose in Nkosi's throat. The sound welling within him was one to rival Mumbi's defiant final shout, which still echoed in his ears, but nothing would come out. He stood like the other *makeri*, looking at the ground.

The heavy stench of the *biloko* was gone. The night breeze swept it away, replacing it with the clean smells of the Uele and the shifting dust of the plain.

And something else.

The faint wisp of a sugarbush flower, petals dried and broken by time and wear.

Nkosi lifted his head. He sniffed the air experimentally.

There was no doubting it. The smell was faint, barely perceptible, but it was there. It danced on the wind and tickled his upper lip.

He turned his head this way and that, seeking the blossom. The *biloko* had devoured it along with every other shred of his lost love, yet its fragrance rose from everywhere at once, whispering on the wind.

Nkosi found his voice. "Mumbi," he rasped.

The air around him vibrated. At the edge of his hearing, a gentle voice sighed his name. The voice came from somewhere in a dark emptiness, beneath a sky of graves.

There was a thud. Nkosi turned to see one of the *makeri* drop. His task complete, the magic binding his soul to his corpse was broken.

Nkosi sniffed the sweet air once more—and smiled.

The other *makeri* closed his eyes, then fell backward into the grass.

Nkosi could no longer move his arms. His body had begun to feel like an old cloak, in need of replacement.

The corners of his mouth curled further.

The graveworld was vast beyond counting. It was dark, and millions of voices screamed in fear and wonder. It was impossible to find another soul in the midst of that maelstrom.

Unless you had a trail to follow.

Nkosi sniffed the air again, filling his dead lungs with the scent of the blossom, and went into the void with a glad heart.

DAWN OF THE LIVING IMPAIRED

CHRISTINE MORGAN

"**W**ELCOME BACK TO *DAYBREAK COAST to Coast*, with Elaine Kristin," the pre-recorded announcer said.

Elaine turned her megawatt smile into Camera One, her impeccably coiffed caramel locks falling over the shoulders of her rich turquoise blouse.

"In just a while, we'll be joining home styles consultant Frances Meade, who'll be showing us how you can decorate your house for the holidays with the contents of your recycling bins! But first, in our continuing effort to keep you up-to-date on events here and around the world, we have two special guests with us to discuss perhaps the most controversial issue of our time."

Elaine shifted her gaze to Camera Two, knowing that an inset screen would now be showing scenes from some of the choicer news segments and home video clips they had on file. Nothing *too* icky, of course, nothing to put the millions of viewers off their breakfast. The sponsors wouldn't appreciate that.

So instead of the infamous and grisly footage of what had happened at last month's gala Entertainment Achievement Awards—a bloodbath that had made Elaine Kristen *almost* forgive them for snubbing her in the morning show host category for a third year running—the booth ran the ones of the disinterred milling aimlessly outside of a closed mall like impatient shoppers before a big sale.

"Since the first of them rose and walked away from their mortuary slabs and caskets six months ago," Elaine went on, ignoring the small sound of pained disapproval from her left, "their numbers have increased drastically, in an epidemic that has affected nearly every nation. Each government has taken its own steps to combat what is seen as both menace and health risk. Solutions have primarily taken the form of military action, violent eradication and disposal."

Camera One panned back to include Elaine, her comfy dove-colored chair, and the fake windows that looked out on a photo mural of a sunswept, smog-free cityscape. It was no place that could ever be seen in reality, consisting as it did of computer-melded snippets of New York, Los Angeles, Seattle, and Chicago.

"Here in America, the land of the free," Elaine chirped, "the efforts of the military have run into a roadblock. I'm speaking of the so-called 'zombie rights movement.' With me today to discuss the movement are General Jason Gillespie, recently retired member of the U.S. taskforce organized to deal with the situation . . . ."

Gillespie, sitting to her right, nodded brusquely into the camera. His steel-gray hair was cropped close, his dark eyes both hooded and piercing. A sort of stern charisma, all iron and resolve, radiated from him, despite the knotted white scar that scrawled from his eye to his chin, and the obvious prosthetic that replaced his left arm.

"Good morning, Elaine," he said with a voice both deep and harsh, the sort of voice that belonged shouting orders from the top of a trench while bullets stitched the air.

Elaine nodded pertly and continued: "And Doctor Karen Wyatt-Anderson, noted psychiatrist and president of NALI." Elaine shifted her position to face the other woman. "Doctor Wyatt-Anderson, we'll begin with you. Can you tell us a little about your organization?"

Karen Wyatt-Anderson was a cool winter-eyed blonde in a severe navy-blue suit and silk blouse. Her features were aristocratic and patrician. Her spine was even more rigid, her shoulders more stiffly held, than the general's.

"Yes, Elaine," she said. "To begin, I must object to your use of the term 'zombie rights.' NALI stands for the National Alliance for the Living-Impaired, and we are dedicated to correcting the damaging misconceptions revolving around our clients."

"They *are* zombies," rumbled Gillespie, rubbing fitfully, absently at the prosthetic as if he could feel sensation in the phantom limb.

"That's like calling those with a mental illness 'nuts,'" Wyatt-Anderson countered sharply. "It is a hurtful term. NALI would like to see it stricken from popular usage. Along with several others."

"What others?" Elaine asked.

"The frequent and derogatory or belittling phrases involving the word 'dead,'" the doctor replied. "Whenever someone refers to someone else as 'dead meat,' or claims to be 'dead on their feet,' it reflects poorly on our clients."

"Your clients dig themselves out of their graves and eat people," Gillespie pointed out. "It's a contagion, it's spreading, and it needs to be dealt with. Decisively, and soon."

"That's the very attitude NALI is seeking to change." Wyatt-Anderson returned her attention to Elaine, seeking sympathy. "These people—yes, *people*—are our friends and neighbors, our families. They deserve to be treated with the dignity and respect they had in life. They should not be feared, reviled, or hunted down."

"But haven't they changed, Doctor?" Elaine said.

"They're not the same as they were, no. But neither is someone who has suffered a debilitating brain injury, or fallen into a coma, or been stricken with a mental illness or decline in cognition. Yet in those cases, the afflicted are still cared for. Their basic needs are still met."

"Basic needs!" The general leaned forward. "Lady, the only basic need a zombie's got is to chow down on human flesh! I've *seen* these things in action. I was in New York during the big July breakout. I saw one bunch of them overturn a busload of kids and dig right in!"

"How did you handle the July breakout?" Wyatt-Anderson shot back. "By gunning down thousands of the living-impaired, in direct violation of their civil rights."

"Damn straight! They're not people anymore. They're corpses. Their civil rights went out the window the minute they pulled themselves out of the ground and started helping themselves to brain take-out!"

Elaine knew there was a time to intervene and a time to sit back and let the interviews take their course. This was the latter. She discreetly picked up her coffee cup—emblazoned with the sponsor's logo, naturally—and sipped as the studio audience enjoyed the argument.

"It has been consistently proven that the living-impaired retain rudimentary memories of their past lives and habits. They are able to recognize familiar faces—"

"And bite 'em off to get at the gooey bits," snarled Gillespie. "They need to be wiped out."

"Destroying them is not the answer!"

"What is? We could have had this country cleansed by now, if you people hadn't come along whining about tolerance. What would you rather do? Get 'em all in a circle, hold hands, sing 'Kumbaya'?"

"With proper treatment, the living-impaired can be brought to a reasonable level of functioning."

"What sort of treatment?" Elaine interjected smoothly.

"Primarily therapy and medication—"

"God bless America," the general muttered as a curse, rolling his eyes. "Therapy!"

Doctor Wyatt-Anderson ignored him and went on speaking to Elaine, who was nodding encouragingly. "Their desire for flesh, which is simply another form of addiction, can be treated with a patch."

"A patch?" Elaine urged.

"The Necroderm C-Q," she explained. "It's a time-release appetite suppressant combined with a craving inhibitor."

"Does it come in a gum?" someone from the audience called snidely.

"No," Wyatt-Anderson said, "but there is a liquid form that can be injected in stronger doses. We use that to stabilize clients in crisis."

"Suppose that you can control their addiction," Elaine said. "What then?"

"Then we enroll them in a series of programs. Anger management. Coping skills. Job training. We help them and encourage them to manage their symptoms and compensate for their condition, with the goal of being able to exist in a non-restrictive environment."

"Non-restrictive . . . you mean on their own?"

The general muttered a comment, but it was lost as the doctor continued her explanation.

"Yes, Elaine, but to get them out on their own involves a slow, tedious process. At the moment, we have over six hundred of the living-impaired placed in residential facilities, and thousands more in more intensive hospital-style settings. But millions more are out there, desperately in need of our services. The hardest part of our job is outreach, getting help to these people. Thanks to the efforts of those like the general here, most of the living-impaired are afraid to come forward."

Elaine nodded sagely. "Recent statistics have shown that the living-impaired population now outnumbers the homeless and the mentally ill," she said. "When even those people couldn't receive adequate help, can NALI realistically offer their services to everyone?"

"Sadly, Elaine, we can't. NALI just doesn't have the staff or resources to extend all the help we'd like. Funding for our programs is practically nonexistent. We depend almost entirely on private donations from families who have been touched by this tragedy. But you mentioned the homeless and the mentally ill. The living-impaired population hasn't so much outnumbered them as it has absorbed them."

"Yeah, they feed on the ones they can catch," Gillesp
street people, winos, loonies. If they leave enough meat
those sorry bastards get up and start walking, too."

The doctor swept him with a scathing look. "With t
in those populations, one would expect that there would
funding left over. Money that had been going toward m   ....u
housing rehab programs could, and *should*, be funneled into ours. Yet that's
not happening, Elaine, and it needs to be."

"What about the Center for Disease Control?" Elaine asked. "What's
their stance? I had heard that this was being treated as a communicable
disease . . . postmortem infectious necrivorism, I believe was the term. Lots
of people are concerned about how to keep themselves safe."

Gillespie nodded, eyes glittering. "One bite, and they've got you. Don't
I know it! All they have to do is break the skin and there's not a damn thing
anyone can do. When they had me and were pulling me out of that evac
chopper . . . ."

Elaine shuddered in genuine sympathy. She'd argued bitterly with her
producers over whether or not they could show *that* clip, the one in which,
to avoid being dragged down or bitten by the trio of gray-green corpses
clinging to him, Gillespie had given the order that had cost him his arm.
Little wonder he was having trouble holding to the military's usual polite,
but firm stance on the subject. Then again, the general was retired and thus
removed from the control of handlers, and a notorious hothead—both of
which helped make him such a flashy guest.

The general was rumbling, with an almost cheerful grimness, through
his war story, but Wyatt-Anderson was intent on spoiling it for him. "The
key to containing the spread of the illness," she interrupted, "is to avoid
exposure." Her icy tone made it clear that she believed that the general
had cost himself his arm, and nearly his life, by provoking the attack. "The
use of universal precautions, to prevent the introduction of the infected
material—"

"Zombie spit," said the general. "The thing to do is eliminate the *source*.
If there were no goddam zombies, no one would have to worry about
catching it. We find them, shoot them, burn what's left, and there you go.
End of story, end of danger."

"Is that how you'd handle other contagious illnesses, General?" Wyatt-
Anderson asked. "AIDS, hepatitis, TB? This isn't the Dark Ages, and we will not
treat patients like condemned criminals! They are victims of a terrible, terrible
disease. We owe it to them to *help*, not draw plague circles around them!"

Elaine, responding to increasingly urgent signaling from her producer,
cut in with another of her brilliant smiles. "We have to take a short break for

portant messages, but we'll be back with General Gillespie and Doctor att-Anderson in a few minutes to take questions from our studio audience. And we'll also meet Barb and Danny, two of NALI's success stories."

The sign switched from ON AIR to OFF, and canned elevator music issued from the speakers over the audience. A couple of crew members came onstage to check and fiddle with this and that, and Elaine motioned for a refill on coffee.

"You're bringing some of those things out here?" asked Gillespie. His face had reddened, making the pale scar stand out in vivid relief.

"Don't be afraid, General," Wyatt-Anderson said condescendingly. "The counselors have everything under control."

"How *do* you keep them under control?" Elaine asked. "It's fine and well to talk about universal precautions and not getting bit, but when you're dealing with a new . . . a new client, how do you even get close enough to slap the patches on them?"

"Some direct methods are necessary," the doctor admitted. "They can be stunned or subdued by an electrical charge. Before the effects wear off, we get them under restraints to begin treatment."

"Waste of time," growled Gillespie. "Waste of money. You think you're going to rehabilitate zombies, put them back in regular society? That's crazy, that's all it is. Crazy."

"Thirty seconds," warned one of the production assistants.

Elaine thanked him with a nod, and got up. She smoothed her skirt— white with a tropical floral pattern in shades of turquoise—and took the handheld microphone.

"And . . . we're live in three, two, one!"

"Welcome back," Elaine said brightly. "We've been listening to some rather opposing viewpoints on today's topic. Doctor Karen Wyatt-Anderson, president of NALI, supports compassionate caregiving and treatment for the living-impaired. Retired General Jason Gillespie feels that zombies are a threat and must be handled with extreme prejudice. Now let's see what our audience thinks."

She held out the microphone to a clean-cut young college boy in a cableknit sweater. "Hi, Elaine, hi. I'm Jeff. My question is for the doctor. Do you, person-ally, work with the zombies? Er . . . with the living-impaired?"

Wyatt-Anderson gave Jeff a cool, lofty look. "In my capacity with NALI, I work very closely with the staff of several hospitals and facilities. My main function is in training and education."

"So that's a no?" he pressed. "You don't work personally, hands-on, with the stiffs? You don't have to look at them, smell them, worry that they might take a chunk out of you?"

"I have seen several living-impaired clients," she said.

Jeff looked straight into the camera and hoisted one eyebrow knowingly. Elaine thanked him and moved on to a portly man possessing the jowls and the sorrowful eyes of a basset hound.

"Albert Lawry here," he said, gaze fixed on the microphone. "I just . . . my wife Helen. . . . She died a year ago. . . . I was wondering, Doctor, if you could help me find her? She was buried in Oregon, with her parents, and when everything started I went to the cemetery, but she wasn't there. Do you have a list or something?"

"I'm sorry, Mr. Lawry. Most of the time, our clients have no identification. We try to track down their records, but it's a slow process. If you call NALI, at 1-888-555-3323—"

"That's 555-DEAD," Jeff announced, drawing a laugh from the audience and a flush of chagrin from the doctor.

She regained her composure, but if telepathy were real and could kill, there'd be one attractive twenty-something laid out on the floor. "If you call NALI and leave your name and information, we can contact you should we locate your wife."

Elaine moved to the next waving hand, which belonged to a teenaged girl with intricately beaded and cornrowed hair. "General Gillespie, my dad is in the Marines, and he says that zombies can only be killed if you blow their heads off or burn them, is that true?"

"I hardly think that's an appropriate question!" Doctor Wyatt-Anderson snapped.

The general faced the girl. "As near as we've been able to tell, the only way to stop them is to take out the brain. Fire might do it eventually, but in the meantime, they'd still be running around. And I'll tell you one thing . . . may be hard to believe, but a fried zombie stinks worse than a regular one."

Karen Wyatt-Anderson's lips had drawn together in a line so thin and tight that they'd almost disappeared. "I must once again object to your choice of language. These are *people* we're talking about. Wives, husbands, sons, daughters, mothers, and fathers! You demean and degrade them by referring to them in those terms!"

A thin, almost frighteningly intense woman with long dark hair popped up beside Elaine, pushing aside an anxious grandmotherly type. "They're *dead*! Can't you get that through your politically correct skull?"

"They've come back. Not all the way, granted, but they've made the effort."

"Effort! Some alien germ or solar radiation makes the corpses walk, that's all it is! Not God, not their own free will! Who would want to come back as something like that? Who'd want to live like that? I say that putting them out of their misery is doing them a favor, not sending them to some twelve-step program!"

Savage applause, not the least of which was from the general, greeted the woman's remarks. Mixed in were cries of "You said it!" and "All right!" and one man chanting, "Bring out your dead! Bring out your dead!"

"Why don't we?" chirped Elaine in her most vivacious talk show hostess tone. "Let's bring out Barb and Danny, and hear what they have to say!"

Jeff and the man who'd been chanting the Monty Python dialogue both cupped their hands around their mouths to make megaphones and called, "Braaaaaaaiiiiiiiinns!" in slow, dragging imitation of the undead.

The good doctor stood up. "I will not have them subjected to this blatantly hostile abuse! NALI's purpose is to increase public awareness and help our clients."

"Maybe it would help for everyone to see the progress they've made under treatment," Elaine suggested. "Instead of the negative, sensationalized images of their kind most of us have seen."

"Progress!" Gillespie snorted. "Couple of zombies, hosed off and put in clean clothes. Maybe you can train 'em like animals, but they're still flesh-eating monsters. Suppose you bring them out here and they decide it's an all-you-can-eat buffet?"

"Barb has been flesh-free for eight weeks," Wyatt-Anderson said huffily. "Danny for almost as long. They're proof that the patch and the treatment are effective, two of our most compensated clients."

Elaine caught the eye of one of the backstage crew, and he responded with a nod.

Moments later, a small group emerged from the side door of the set. Three men and a woman, all in pristine white lab coats, ushered in two shuffling figures.

An appalled, fascinated "Ooooh!" came from the audience, accompanied by a shifting rustle as they all leaned forward to get a good look at the necrivores.

The larger of the two, introduced as Barb, must have been a huge woman in life and hadn't diminished much since. A drab mustard-colored sweatsuit neither concealed nor flattered the drooping swell of her belly or the pendulous melon-sized breasts that bobbled like loosely filled sacks of gelatin. Her behind was truly mythic in its proportions, and with her head bent down against the glare of the studio lighting, her chins descended to her chest in a series of mushy folds.

They'd obviously made an effort to get her presentable. Her skin was doughy and blue-gray, but she was clean and not visibly maggot-ridden.

What was left of her brown hair had been drawn neatly back in a scrunchied ponytail. She had the sadly sweet face of so many hopelessly obese women, hinting at the beauty that might have been hers had her life taken a different turn.

It would have taken about eight Dannys to make up one Barb. The smaller of the pair couldn't have been more than ten years old when he died, and the evidence of his death was present in the form of a malformed dent in the side of his head. It was the sort of injury one might expect to see when a kid disregarded the helmet law and came to grief with one of those zippy little scooters.

The ghost of an impish smile lurked around his slack, dry lips. He wore jeans and an oversized football jersey and high-top sneakers like any other kid. Yards of spice-scented wrappings might have suited him better, for he appeared wizened and dry, more mummified than rotting. His dark skin had taken on a hue and texture reminiscent of ash-coated beef jerky.

General Gillespie made a sound somewhere between a moan and a snarl as the two zombies shambled closer. Their attendants stopped them at the center of the stage, Cameras One and Two zooming in for close-ups.

Both of their patches were in plain sight, pasted to the sides of their necks just below the ear. In a final bizarre touch, the patches were for some reason the gleaming plastic pink-tan that used to be called "flesh" by the crayon people, a color that didn't match the skin of any race of the living, let alone the dead. On Barb and Danny, it was as hectic as a clown's vivid red cheeks.

Doctor Wyatt-Anderson crossed her arms smugly and threw Gillespie a silent "Told you so!" as the nervous tittering and revolted gasps of the audience gave way to murmurings of pity.

Elaine was surprised to find that she understood their feelings, for there was something unspeakably tragic and solemn about the pair. They stood slouched by both in the poor posture of death and the inescapable defeated hopelessness of their circumstances.

Danny goggled at the nearest camera. One of his eyes was milky but otherwise normal; the other was distended from the socket as if it had been popped out and replaced without true concern for the fit. That orb was roadmapped with broken veins, and a purpled corona engulfed the pupil.

The bleak incomprehension in their stares changed as they took in the sight of the studio audience, dozens and dozens of healthy humans. The glint put Elaine in mind of reluctant dieters confronted with a bakery window.

What must we look like to those glassy gazes? the host wondered. *A parade of meaty limbs and delectable torsos?* She thought about the old saying—you can't help someone who didn't want to be helped. What was the treatment doing to the living dead? As far as she knew, as far as anyone knew, they came back with only one driving impulse: to eat. And now that had been taken away from them. What did that leave?

"My God," Elaine heard herself say. "This is terrible!"

"The growth rate of the living-impaired population," Wyatt-Anderson said, "has leveled off thanks to the increase in cremation as a form of funerary services. But there are still millions of them out there, and they need your help."

Gillespie shook his head. "What they need is to be sent back where they came from. That one lady was right—this is no way to be!"

Barb swiveled slowly in the general's direction. Watching her move was like watching the gaseous atmosphere of Jupiter rotate, bands of flesh shifting and sliding at different rates. A whiff of her odor reached Elaine. Mostly soap and talcum powder, but underneath was a faintly rancid, wholly repugnant reek of spoilage.

The general realized with evident, utter horror that he was the focus of three hundred-plus pounds of zombie attention, and took an involuntary step back.

"Deaaad," Barb said, forcing the word sluggishly through liquefying vocal cords.

"Dead," Danny seconded, his voice more clear but raspy as a file on sandpaper.

"And they should stay that way," said someone from the audience. Elaine recognized the intense brunette without needing to look. "Dead things should stay that way. This is wrong. Can't you see that? Wrong!"

Doctor Wyatt-Anderson stepped forward to argue, but Barb's chins tripled and then receded as she nodded. "Rrrrrrronnng!"

Her pudgy, sausage-fingered hand floated up as if tied to a helium balloon. It wandered aimlessly around her head for a moment, pulled strands of hair from the scrunchie to hang lank in her face, and then found the edge of the patch. Two of her fingernails peeled loose as she dug at it.

"Barb, stop it," said one of the attendants.

Danny squinted up at his behemothic companion, some dim understanding welling in his muddy eyes.

Barb's patch came unstuck with a grisly squelching noise, tearing away a spongy mat of flesh with it. "Dead!" she shrieked. "Dead-dead-dead!"

The attendants rushed in, bringing heavy-duty tazers out of concealed holsters. Elaine, rooted to the spot, was buffeted as the audience yielded to instinct and thundered for the exits.

"Dead-dead-dead!" Danny parroted, and ripped the patch from his own neck so vigorously that he nearly beheaded himself. The ivory knobs of his vertebrae poked through like stepping stones.

"Stop her!" Wyatt-Anderson ordered above the din. Then, incredibly, "We'll never get funding like this!"

It was, Elaine would later think, a pretty crappy set of last words. Barb lumbered forward with the force of a charging rhino, and crushed the doctor's rib cage with one swing of her massive arm.

Still unable to move, hypnotized by the spectacle, Elaine observed with detached marvel the way the impact sent ripples through the zombie's flab.

Barb seized Wyatt-Anderson, pulled her close as if going for a kiss, and clamped her jaws on the doctor's shoulder. Elaine, in a space beyond terror now, batted at Barb's face with the microphone and squashed her nose into a soggy ruin. Barb let go of her victim.

An attendant grabbed for Danny as Doctor Wyatt-Anderson's body was hitting the ground. The dead child writhed snake-fast and got a mouthful of muscle, eliciting a scream that was more fear than pain. And it was a lot of pain.

Barb stepped mostly over but partly on the fallen psychiatrist, cracking bones like twigs underfoot, and reached for her next meal. Elaine thrust out the microphone in a defensive effort and Barb chomped into it, masticating furiously at the spongy black covering before spitting it aside.

Someone dropped an iron safe onto a solid hardwood floor. Or at least that was what Elaine's first thought was as a colossal *boom* resonated through the studio. It wasn't until the side of Barb's skull blossomed out in a pulpy yellow and gray spray that she realized what had happened. The giant body went down so hard that it should have set off car alarms in the parking lot outside.

Elaine very nearly went down with it, as Barb's flailing hand snared the front of her blouse. She was yanked backward to safety by the college guy in the cableknit sweater—Jeff.

General Gillespie, his uniform jacket all askew and a holster tucked into the rear of his pants, was waving a gun roughly the size of a small cannon. He squeezed off a wild shot just as Frances Meade, *Daybreak Coast to Coast*'s answer to Martha Stewart, came rushing onstage to see what all the fuss was about. She went flying back in a crimson spray that clashed horribly with her pale green outfit.

Elaine saw that even though the cameramen had fled, the lights and the ON AIR sign were still working fine. Camera One had been knocked aslant and was getting nothing but stampeding feet. Camera Two, however, was getting everything.

Electricity leaped and sizzled as the attendants tried to tazer the ravenous smaller zombie into submission, but Danny was having none of it. The taste of hot blood and warm meat was in his mouth for the first time in weeks, and he was not going to be denied.

Elaine, knowing that this show would either make her career or destroy it, tore away from Jeff and rushed at the general. He was yelling incoherently, blasting away. It was a pure miracle that more of the panicked studio audience hadn't been hit. She snatched at the gun—wincing, but not pulling away from the touch of the hot barrel—and wrested the weapon away from him.

Danny was atop the bitten attendant. Grisly snacking and slurping noises could be heard even above the rest of the cacophony.

Elaine slammed her dainty turquoise-blue pump down on Danny's back, set the barrel of the gun to the back of his head, and with a grimace that she somehow knew resembled the way her mom looked when fishing around in a turkey for the giblet packet, pulled the trigger.

The recoil was instant and tremendous, slamming up her arm with such force she thought she had dislocated her shoulder. But the bullet plowed through Danny's small and already cracked skull, out the other side, and lodged in the thrashing attendant's face, saving him from the basic fate worse than death.

Only one NALI attendant remained, the other two having remembered pressing appointments elsewhere. In a total loss of sanity, he pointed his tazer at the morning show hostess. General Gillespie, wanting his toy back, had the bad luck to interpose himself in time to take the volts. He collapsed, twitching and jerking.

"It's all right!" Jeff yelled, pointing at the motionless bodies of Barb and Danny. "They're down! Both down!"

His words took the edge off of the furor, but it all went to hell again a split second later.

With a sudden convulsive lurch, Doctor Wyatt-Anderson pushed herself upright. She held herself awkwardly, with half of her ribs caved in and one arm dangling crazy-jointed and limp.

The remaining attendant, Jeff, and Elaine all shouted a word that would have been edited out or bleeped on tape, but they were still live, still rolling.

Wyatt-Anderson's gaze fell upon them. Formerly haughty and cold, it was now filled with a mindless hunger. Her lips drew back to expose a view that would have been right at home in a toothpaste commercial. She darted forward and swiped a handful of manicure at them.

On raw reflex, Elaine fired again. The shot hit Wyatt-Anderson between the eyes and took most of the top of her head off. The doctor cartwheeled in a tumble over the gore-splattered dove-gray chair that Elaine vowed never to sit in again, and came to rest in a heap at the bottom of the window with its fake cityscape.

"Wow," said Jeff shakily. "I guess she wasn't just president of the National Alliance for the Living-Impaired . . ."

It was the insanity of the moment, or the reek of blood and decomposition that made them take leave of their senses. But the rest of the surviving trio came in with him on the end.

"She's also a client!" they chorused, and finally someone in the control room had the good sense to go to commercial.

NAKED SHALL I RETURN

TOM PICCIRILLI

DECKER FOUND HIMSELF ON CAMPUS without knowing how he'd gotten back from the hospital.

His hand hurt like hell and he wondered what they'd done to him—needles? Cauterization? Maybe not that bad. He hoped he still had his thumb. But wait, it really hadn't been about him at all, now had it? There was something else. He looked down to see himself clutching his fist so tightly that his fingers had turned a bluish-purple.

It took a solid thirty seconds and all his willpower to force his hand open again. Decker held a crushed ball of white tape.

That's right, he thought, *my mother is dead*.

The slow, forced rhythm of his mom's chest had become pure torture, her body mechanically heaving as if in continuous death throes, the machine in control. It had been a long battle, but they didn't know with what. Cancer? Poison? Infection? The four dripping IVs of antibiotics looped around the room, tangling together.

The heart monitor began to squeal as her pulse dipped below the line of no return. They had told Decker that would happen. The respirator continued with its hateful regularity, IVs still pouring a flood of worthless medications into her. The lights on the machinery flashed, an abrupt beeping growing louder. Her pulse staggered on for another moment, fighting for the last second of life. He would've screamed but was afraid that, if he opened his mouth, nothing but unstoppable laughter would've come out.

The screens flashed numbers that faltered and skipped, her heart finally giving up as she flatlined. The respirator continued to force her to breathe even after she was gone. They turned off the machines and left him in there alone to say his final goodbyes.

With only a slight hesitancy, Decker had leaned over the bed, smoothed his mother's matted graying hair aside, and kissed her brow, which was moist from the last of her sweat.

He murmured for a moment, saying words that had no meaning, before he realized she was dead but staring at him—blinking—trying to talk.

"Ma?"

She was unable to speak because the respirator was still sealed over her mouth. He removed the tape and drew out the tubes, and then, with an alarmingly clear and mellifluous voice, she told him something he did not want to know.

He didn't remember what it was, but realized it would come to him, eventually.

The funeral was well attended.

She had been a beloved professor for twenty-five years and it looked like many of her students from the last two decades had shown up. So had the dean of science and most of the biology department. Decker's professors stared at him as he stood beside the casket; they touched his shoulder, muttered condolences. He tried to recognize their faces but was unable to differentiate one from another. These people barely held any specific identities now, and he couldn't decide if he enjoyed the change or not. They moved like water and shadow around him.

Someone grabbed his wrist, as if in a gesture of care or friendship, but Decker felt strong fingers pressing into his pulse. Checking his heart rate.

They're worried about me.

Perhaps it was true. But why?

Music, light, and laughter spilled out of the house and into the street. His roommate, Herbie, was throwing another party. Herbie weighed in at about two hundred and twenty, mostly muscle with just a jiggle of beer belly—surfer's tan, beatnik goatee that had come back into vogue, blond hair just an inch out of a crewcut. He'd been a senior for three years, thanks to a carefully orchestrated and constantly shifting series of majors. The latest was Renaissance poetry but next semester he planned to switch to chemical engineering out of the appalling fear of actually graduating.

Herbie just didn't give a damn yet and probably never would. He used any occasion to get girls over, booze himself into oblivion, push the macho valve wide and hold it open. These kind of nights always ended in a couple of fights, some overturned furniture, and busted glass. Without even knowing why, Herbie liked to piss off campus security. The house was north of Main Street, officially off school property, but in reality they were only fifty yards from the Science Building and night classes were in session until ten. Herbie pushed because he knew—had always known—he could get away with it thanks to Decker. To Decker's mom.

Now that she was gone, though, nobody was sure exactly what might happen next. It didn't slow the party down any.

This might just lead to somewhere new. Decker walked in, grabbed a bottle of gin, and took three long gulps from it. The heat quickly worked down his throat and into his chest, until something inside felt like it had slid out between his ribs. Faces whirled by at high speed, horse teeth at all angles, people calling him by name, asking him question after question as they pawed at his neck, his arms.

Swarming, they carried him along. The hard ridge of his shoulder muscles tensed further. He felt buoyant, oblivious, and ephemeral, but worried just the same. A strengthening current ran through the house. Planting his feet, he fought against its increased pull. A girl with a high-voltage smile pressed her tits into him and he let out an absurd giggle before backing up the staircase, step by step, and heading toward his bedroom on the second floor.

Holding court, Herbie sat in the middle of the hall, surrounded by five freshman. He was talking animatedly and playing well to his audience. That kind of quicksilver chatter had a way of hypnotizing the kids. He kept feeding them alcohol, god of the minute, eyeing every girl and making his final choice on who he planned to hunt down into bed. This little redhead in the summer dress, her pale knees flashing as she sipped from her beer and answered a question he'd put to her. The current was even stronger up here and Decker had to lean back against the wall and brace himself. Herbie listened thoughtfully and made a comment that broke the rest of them up. You could almost pluck the energy out of the air. Herbie drew magic from the crowd.

Tracy, Herbie's last girlfriend, had already been kicked loose. Decker had liked her a lot—shy, with an embarrassed grin that always hit him in the right way, witty and just self-effacing enough to show you she had a lot of confidence. She'd only been around for a couple of months when Herbie had come, pretending to be humble, with his hand out. He needed money for an abortion; Decker had given him the three hundred bucks, then watched through the blinds as Tracy silently climbed into her Honda and pulled away from the curb into angry traffic. Decker hadn't seen her since, anywhere, but he thought about her more than he probably should have.

Sometimes it happened like that.

The redhead leaned forward and whispered, smiling drunkenly, flashing a pierced tongue, and Herbie bent toward her until their foreheads were touching. Plucking his chin, Herbie cracked wise, which brought up a befuddled giggle from her pink throat.

Decker slid by without a word and let the drag sweep him into his room, flopped face down on his mattress.

The dead kid he'd been seeing the past few days peeked out from beneath the bed again: pale with intensely dark circles beneath his eyes and around those dry blue lips, coarse brown hair with a cowlick that would never flatten out. His nostrils were crusted, teeth almost a glowing green. One small hand appeared and the kid waved at Decker.

Decker waved back.

He laid on the bed and listened for some noise coming from under him—malicious titters, threats, hisses promising further horror—but the kid mostly kept quiet, murmuring to himself on occasion. Decker slept.

In the morning, the little redhead made breakfast and cleaned the place up some. She seemed equally excited and mortified as she scurried around with rags and a sponge, bagging trash and hauling it to the curb. Decker introduced himself and she told him her name, which he couldn't hold onto. He asked her to repeat it, which she did, and again it slithered away even while he tried to grab hold.

Herbie read the sports section and paused in his meal to occasionally grunt at Decker or the girl. Her voice was so soft that Decker thought she wasn't responding until he looked up and saw her lips moving. When he was finished eating, she took his plate away and washed it, left everything in the drain board, waited for Herbie to kiss her goodbye—he didn't—and flitted out the door to class.

"Nice girl," Decker said.

Herbie had used up all his personality last night and wouldn't recover it for another day or two. "Yeah."

"What happened to the last one?"

"Which?"

"Tracy, I think. I don't know."

"You almost sound judgmental."

"Maybe I almost am."

That got a laugh from both of them. Herbie shrugged and cracked his neck, patted down his stomach and said, "Hell, no—not you. That's why this is the perfect set-up. You're the best roommate I've ever had. No gripes, no arguments, no fighting. We ever have a fight?"

"No."

"See? That's friendship in action. Impeccability." He yawned, went to the fridge, and took a pull from a bottle of beer. It made him gag but he went in for a second sip, then poured the rest down the sink. "Good thing she took out the garbage. I think we've got rats. They're bold, too. Last night one was scurrying around in my closet. You heard 'em yet?"

Decker told him, "I need to get to the lab."

Warm noon winds swept down through the pines, washing the scents of car exhaust and ponderosa over him. He used his mother's keys and let himself through the locked biology department wing and into her lab. They'd cleared out her research, experiments, controls and trials, and cleaned the desk of her computer and notebooks. Decker wasn't worried; he'd find everything again.

Opening the blinds an inch, he looked out at people walking across the quad, all the jubilant activity and customary sounds tugging at him. Something remained missing. He still had trouble recognizing some faces. The dean—he thought it must be the dean—stood on the sidewalk so stately and imposing, an embodiment of such energy and force, that Decker couldn't even remember the man's name anymore.

The breach in his memories hinged on some trauma—perhaps the death of his mother, perhaps something else. Decker started to tremble wildly before the window, agitated but enraged, trying to ride out his frustrations as far removed as he could be. The planes and angles of the dean's features drifted even while Decker watched, until the man was faceless. It was so odd to see only a void left where the man's eyes should be, that black vortex drawing daylight itself into the depths, until Decker nearly began to hyperventilate.

He shut the blinds. Sometimes the dean would talk to him but Decker couldn't hear anything, only a humming that filled his mind and caused lapses. He'd ferret out the anguish later, when he had more time.

Why didn't they care that he still had the keys?

Jesus, his hand hurt. This time he didn't have to look, but simply loosened his grip on the ball of tape. Control could be learned. We all must adapt.

Scanning the room he saw that Professor Mason had been moved into Mom's lab. He'd set up a few trials and tests that appeared just nasty enough to be bio-warfare and used by the military—bogus assortments of

Nerve, Blood, Blister, and Incapacitating agents, including cholinesterase inhibitors. The schmuck didn't think far enough ahead to bother keeping any of the atropine and pralidoxime chloride antidotes on hand though. Bad fake out. So what were they really hiding?

Decker opened two vials and poured their contents into his palm: saline solution, plankton, some brine shrimp and simple agar, a waxy mix of protein and hydrocarbons. Made for a weak implication toward ecological attack, a cut-link in the food chain. Would some assembly of generals in D.C. buy Mason's treatise on manipulation of benign microorganisms genetically altered to produce toxins and pathogens?

Sure, why not?

Okay, Decker thought, *let's start with him and see where it goes.*

Mason stood about 5'4", a gnat of a septuagenarian whose high-pitched, whiny voice did a fair impression of incessant buzzing. Decker had taken Mason's algorithms for computational biology class in sophomore year. The class had focused on RH-mapping as a Hidden-Markov Model, programming algorithm for constructing phylogenetic trees from quartets, and clone intersection matrices and interval graphs. General study of the natural growth and spread of life.

The guy really didn't know much. Maybe he was merely a front for whatever was going on, a nonessential and expendable instrument.

When Mason walked into the office, clutching a cup of tea in his tiny white fist, Decker was seated at the desk. He sat with one heel on the edge of the bottom drawer, tilted back in the chair the same way his mother always did. Campus noises wafted in: bicycle wheels spinning, soft tramp of footsteps on the quad sidewalks, and girlish laughter rising on the breeze. He'd replaced the vials and sat as if inspecting them, thoughtful, inquisitive, somebody really putting all the pieces together.

Mason said, "You shouldn't be here."

"Why not?"

"It might be dangerous."

That was sort of a cute answer, with just a touch of threat to it, or perhaps a warning. "For who?"

"All of us. Any of us."

"Where are my mother's notes?"

"I don't know."

Professor Mason's lack of creativity had a certain genius to it—you just couldn't get a guy into a corner with answers like that. "Are you working with the dean on your latest project?"

"Project?" Mason said, sipping the tea, really rolling it around in his mouth. "The dean? No, not really."

It almost made Decker smile. The power of stupid. Except Mason wasn't actually stupid, he simply projected dull.

"What the hell are you people up to?"

"Ask your mother," Mason told him.

With a growl, Decker rose. He would've broken the bastard's jaw for the quip except, no matter how hard he tried, he couldn't make a fist.

Signs and portents ruled everyone's lives. If you could understand the symbols you could figure out the larger picture, the sphere you had been placed into, the path you walked.

If you could understand the symbols.

Decker couldn't be sure how important any of this was to them. So far, it looked like not much. He had to make some sort of play and see if they were willing to try to stop him.

It took only a couple of minutes to come up with something natural enough that would still provide him with a chance to learn what he needed to know. While Herbie sat in front of the TV with a pizza box on his lap, watching a four million dollar a year runner get tagged out at third, Decker handed him a printed list and said, "Let's throw another party."

"Sure." Herbie picked a drying piece of pepperoni off his chest and perused the names. "The hell is this? Sending out invitations?" He flipped through the three pages. "You want to ask our professors? The dean? You've got the entire science faculty here."

"And graduate teaching assistants."

"Why?"

"I'm trying to prove a theory."

Herbie had considered a biology major once and realized the power a word like *theory* held over scientists. "What kind?"

"It's sort of involved."

"Military shit, right?"

Decker was genuinely surprised. "What makes you say that?"

"Maybe I'm just paranoid."

"Or not."

"I mean, who the hell knows what they make in there. The army relies on dweebs like Professor Mason to dream up ways to slaughter nations nobody's ever visited. Mason couldn't get laid in high school and he's still pissed about it, thinking up ways to kill all the chicks who laughed at his scrawny chest. Nerve gas, toxins. I bet that fucker has a hand in it all, and plays with himself every time he gets a new batch of plutonium."

"You might be right."

But that was the end of the rant. Taking a bite out of another slice of pie, Herbie sort of deflated. "Hell, they'll never show up."

"It'll be nice if that's the case, anyway."

"What do you mean?"

"Nothing."

Herbie gave Decker the slow once-over, squinting, the hinges of his jaw tightening as he ground up the cheese and sauce and swallowed hard. "You've gotten really weird lately, man."

"Invite the little redhead, too."

"Who?"

"The girl who made us breakfast a couple of days ago and took out the trash."

"Oh, her. Why?"

"Why not?"

"I never called her back." Perhaps it made him feel bad, a hint of chagrin crossing his face. "You actually gonna be around for this one?"

"Long enough to see who shows up," Decker said.

By now Herbie had started to like the idea, glancing through the oil-spotted pages again. "I wonder how rowdy these science fucks will get after a keg."

The evening of the party Decker sat at the top of the stairs and made them all come to him.

One after another they ascended the steps and took his hand, thanking him for the invitation. They swelled around the living room and spoke to the other guests but not to each other. The dean, without eyes, brought bean dip. Carstairs had made a salad. Beyond them, the others offered their gifts and set them on the counters and tables around the apartment: Harrington, Devaul, Lowry, Wilson, Remford, Reece, Connelly. He knew the names and knew the faces, but wasn't certain he was matching them up correctly. It didn't matter, for his purposes they were only parts of one entity. Mason brought five pounds of shrimp and cocktail sauce in an ice-filled bucket.

With five beers in him, Herbie was in a playful mood, actually dancing a little and hugging just about everybody. He eventually pounded up the steps and sat beside Decker so that they were wedged tightly between the banister and the wall. Ruminating aloud about his fears of possible graduation, Herbie sprang up and returned several times. He commented on the women he'd slept with and those that had so far avoided his charms.

But his voice changed harshly, as if he'd been speared in the guts, when he cried, "*Jesus.*"

"What?"

"That lady." Herbie jutted his goatee, indicating the front door. "I know that lady. She's a doctor—but—"

"Lisa McGivern," Decker said. "She teaches experimental microbial genetics and metabolic biochemistry."

"No, man, she's a doctor, I mean . . . I took Tracy to her. To have an abortion. She did the abortion, man."

Without reason, Decker began to tremble again, the anger coming on much too fast and strong. Somehow, he understood that she was connected to the symbols that defined who he was. God damn it, his hand hurt. The tape. What did the tape mean?

"What are you saying?" Decker asked.

"What do you mean what am I saying? At the clinic, in town. It was her. She did the operation."

The rest of the night sped into a black blur of motion. Herbie ate most of the shrimp, threw up, and passed out at around midnight. After six shots of Jack Daniels, the redhead had come out of her shell. She took off her top and ran through the halls with nipples thick enough to break somebody's rib. A friend finally got her under control and put her to bed in Herbie's room while he dry heaved on the kitchen floor.

Decker sat up there and stared down, and they watched him from below, silently.

Curtains billowing, almost swaying around the room, like the skirt of his mother when he was a child. She walked him around the yard because he was too sick to play with the other children. Nauseous, fingers always quivering, the lethargy and infirmity so hard to overcome.

A couple of hours before dawn, the dead kid tugged at Decker's ankle. By the spatters of moonlight Decker watched the boy crouching at the foot of the bed, now pulling lightly at the sheets. Another figure hunkered there, as well—a dead little girl, maybe three or four years old at most. Her blond hair lay silver threaded in the dimness, but he could see she was smiling. She crept forward, bent over him, and placed her cheek against his knee. The iciness of it was searing but also comforting, like the cold compresses his mother once used to swab away his fevers.

"Hello," Decker said.

"Hi," she answered.

"Who are you?"

A sweet smile, showing that she had all her teeth. "I'm your sister."

"I don't have a sister."

"Uh huh," she sang. "Yeah you do, lots. Yuh huh, and lots of brothers, too."

The dead boy let out a soft chuckle of acknowledgment.

"Take me home with you," Decker said.

"This is our home. You're our home."

"Show me where you were before you came here to stay under my bed."

She cocked her head at him and pursed her lips, thinking it over. She laid her cheek against his leg again and nodded. "Okay."

My brothers and sisters.

They each stood and took one of his hands and led him into the corridor and down the stairs. They walked past Herbie, still unconscious and curled next to the oven. The boy bent and stroked Herbie's hair, and whispered in his ear.

Decker remembered what his mother had said to him, after she was already lying there, dead, in the hospital bed: *Take care of your brothers and sisters.*

They walked across the street to the science building. Every door of the biology department was open now, even the ones that Decker had previously needed his mother's keys to unlock. So he was expected. Good. Maybe it would make things easier for once. They swept farther and farther into the bowels of the building, until at last he didn't recognize his surroundings anymore. He'd spent six years of his life here and had stood inside this place a thousand times before, but only at this moment did he understand how ignorant he'd always been.

Of biology.

Of his own mother.

The kids soon ushered him into a factory of rotting flesh.

The machinery around them beeped and pinged and hummed, more alive than any of the expecting women in their beds, readied to give birth. His professors walked up and down the aisles with mechanical efficiency, wearing light blue scrubs and rubber-soled slippers. Their faces switched from one body to another, the ebony whirlpools of their empty eye sockets still pulling at him. No one spoke and Decker knew why—the ward was a tomb.

He counted fifty pregnant corpses before he gave up, unable to handle the overwhelming image before him. His knees weakened and he nearly toppled over. Dead women with lifeless gazes, mouths drooping a little, some of them chuckling softly. Decker turned to see blackening wrists strapped to the rails of hospital beds, most of the corpses with their legs spread and affixed in gleaming stirrups. The same kind of tangled IVs that had coiled around his own dying mother encompassed the ward like webbing.

No respirators this time. No respirators because they didn't breathe. Maybe that's why he'd held onto the tape for so long, because it proved his mother had once been alive, before this current phase of responsibility and permanence.

She was there along with the rest of them, with distended belly wobbling, roiling, and stewing, stuffed full. She stared blindly at him and he stared blindly back. He'd always believed life to be a bloody proceeding—red and wet and sanguine, loud, full of laughter and weeping. But they'd washed the bloated women down, cleaned the fetuses—rendering them cold, naked, and fresh—then replaced them with ease into the surgically widened birth canals. His teachers were busily re-implanting the fetuses taken by Lisa McGivern at the abortion clinic.

And what the dead boy—Decker's brother—had said to Herbie when they walked by him curled up and passed out next to the oven—yes, now it came into focus and made sense. The kid had said, "*Daddy.*"

If you could understand the symbols, you could figure out the larger picture, the sphere you had been placed into, the path you walked.

If you could understand the symbols.

So the boy had eventually come home after Herbie and Tracy had gone for the abortion. He knew his home. He knew his father.

Mason zipped up beside Decker and stood there almost buzzing, carrying files and notes that he thrust forward. He quivered with impatience and expectation. "We're going to die as a race—"

"Shut the fuck up."

"—but this ensures that we'll live on even after we're extinct. As a neoteric species."

Decker couldn't help himself. His vision grew too bright at the edges and he swooned for a moment, had to hold himself up by reaching out and grabbing onto one of the bed railings. A corpse woman tugged at her bonds and her fingers fluttered against his own, but he didn't draw away. Both of them had the same bluish-purple tint to their skin. "You crazy bastard."

"It was your mother's idea."

"I don't believe that," Decker said, but of course he realized it was true. "This isn't—" He couldn't even say the word.

"This is the highest form of science. She developed the serum. The entire process you see, actually, including much of the technology whereby the dead could live on in this capacity. She saw the potential and extrapolated the full usage of terminations. The walking dead, this new breed, will carry on when the earth is uninhabitable for the rest of us."

"Terminations?"

Buzzing louder, an insanely trapped insect battering wings against Decker's chest, Mason asked, almost begging now, "Don't you understand? Don't you? The world is becoming increasingly toxic to us. The impurities, contamination, pollution, radiation, and poisons are annihilating us. We can't survive much longer under such virulent conditions. Recent pathogens include streptococcus S23F, a newly discovered naturally occurring strain of—"

"Pneumonia," Decker said. "Resistant to at least six of the most commonly used antibiotics."

"Yes. And the flourishing awareness of new biological epidemics and pestilence prompted the Centers for Disease Control and Prevention to publish *The Journal of Emerging Infectious Diseases*. Ingenuously occurring biological hazards that threaten humanity are increasing and growing more varied every day. Our latest projections have us completely dying out within the next six decades."

Algorithms for computational biology. Decker took his mother's files and checked the pages, running some quick statistics. Mason still didn't know shit. Mom had worked in a frenzy for a reason. She gave them thirty-five years, tops, before mankind died out.

"My mother—"

"She—they—can only perform in this capacity for six months or so after primary expiration, before final stage organ failure and total cessation of body functions."

So what was his mom now—merely necrotic tissue? "What of the flora, the fauna? What happens when every other living creature dies off?"

"That's all superfluous. The new breed can survive consume, ingest, and subsist solely on themselves."

Decker tried to think it through. Humans were heterotrophs, their diet included organic molecules of carbohydrates, proteins, nucleic acids, vitamins, minerals, and other macro- and micronutrients. His mother's serum was heavy on polymers of monomer sub-units: starch, proteins, triglycerides, amino acids, nucleotides.

She had been making humans more nourishing and digestible to themselves.

"Oh, Jesus Christ," Decker groaned, clutching his belly, fighting not to hunch over and fall to his knees. "You're creating a vacuous biosphere that devours itself."

"Out of necessity. No food chain, just . . . food."

Not birth at all. No. No. Parasitic symbiosis. "And the gestation period for the . . . the new breed?"

The words brought a sorrowful smile to Mason's lips. "Very brief. Twenty-two, twenty-three days."

"The same as rats," Decker said.

The machinery continued to bleat while the women panted. Mason looked at him with pity, compassion, and condolence until his gaze was so heavy on Decker that he nearly buckled. Mason took Decker's pulse, and not finding any said, "You were the prototype, our exemplar specimen. She was healthy when she was re-implanted back then, injecting herself with only small doses of the serum. It's not nearly as efficient as when the host is already exanimate." And grinning now, his little insectoid face humming with glee, he added, "It took you four months to come fully to term. Your brother and sister rats don't fight this existence the way you did. They're eager for it."

And so he sat at his mother's side again.

Control could be learned. We all must adapt.

Signs and portents ruled everyone's deaths. If you could understand the symbols, you could figure out the larger picture, the necro-sphere you had been placed into, the dark path you stumbled upon.

Her hands clenched spasmodically, reaching for something to hold, and he placed the ball of tape into her right palm and folded her fingers over until she crushed it in her fist.

The other dead kids—his younger brother and sister—and all the many others now moving from all the shadowy corners of the room, giggling, climbed up and sat on his lap and gathered around him, and together they waited for the demise and birth of a new world emerging.

THE LAST SUPPER

SCOTT EDELMAN

W ALTER'S MIND WAS AT ONE time rich with emotions other than
hunger, but those feelings had long since fallen away. They'd dropped
from his being like the flesh, now absent, that had once kept the wind
from whistling through his cheeks.

Gone was happiness. Gone greed. Gone anger and love and joy.

Now there was but hunger, and hunger only.

As Walter, his joints as stiff as his brain, staggered through the deserted
streets of what had been until recently one of the most heavily populated
cities in the world, that hunger burned through him, becoming his entire
reason for being.

Hunger had not been an issue for him at first. During the early weeks
of his rebirth, there had been enough food for all. The streets had teemed
with meat. The survivors hadn't all evacuated at once. There were always
plenty of the foolish lingering, which meant that he had little competition
for the hunt. Those initial weeks of his renewed time on Earth had been
about as easy as that of a bear smacking salmon skyward from a boiling
river during spawning season.

Those days were gone. Now, not even a faint whiff of food remained
to tease him from a distance. The streets were filled with an army of the
hungry, devourers who no longer had objects of desire upon which to
fulfill their single purpose. For weeks, or maybe months, or perhaps even
years—for Walter's sense of time had been burned away along with most

of his sense of self—walking the streets was akin to wandering through a maze of mirrors and seeing reflected back nothing more than duplicates of who he was, of what he had become: a bag of soiled clothing and shredded flesh, animated by a dead, dead soul.

Staggering through a deserted square that lay in the former heart of the city, stumbling by shattered storefronts and overturned buses, he sought out flesh with a hunger grown so strong that it was less a conscious thought than a tropism born out of whatever affliction had brought him—and the rest of the human race—to this state. His senses, torn and ragged though they were, reached out in search of fresh meat, as they had every day since he had been reborn.

Nothing.

No scent filled his sunken nose, no sound his remaining ear. Yet he surged forward, sweeping the city, borne fruitlessly ahead by a bloodlust beyond thought. Until this day, when what was left of his tongue grew moist with saliva.

Blood. Somewhere out there was blood. Something with a pulse still radiated life nearby.

Whatever called to him was barely alive itself, and hidden, and quiet, but from its refuge its essence rang like a shout. Drawn by the vibrations of its life force, he turned from the square onto a broad avenue and then onto a narrow side street, knocking aside any barriers blocking the path to his blood—*his* blood now. He righted an overturned trashcan (but his promised meal was not hidden there), kicked up soot as he walked through the remnants of an ancient bonfire (but no, nothing there, either), and moved forward until he arrived at a large black car with its roof split open, flipped over on one side against a light pole.

He pushed his way through a carpet of broken glass and peered down through what remained of the driver's side door. He touched the steering wheel and a charge of energizing bloodlust coursed through him. Though the wheel's leather skin had long ago peeled away, he could feel the blood that had blossomed there right after impact, still feel the throbbing of its vanished presence. But he knew, if he could be said to know anything, that ghostly blood could not alone have sounded the call that he had heard. The tug on his attention had to be more than that. Something was here, waiting for him.

Or hiding from him.

In the back of the tilted car, a rustling came from under shredded remnants of seat stuffing. Confused eyes peered out at him. Walter filled with a surge of lust, and dropped atop the creature. A dog yelped—only a dog, and not a man, a man whose scream would strengthen him—and exploded into frantic wriggling, but there was no way the animal could escape the steel cage of Walter's hands. Seeing the nature of his victim's species, the lust vanished. There was no longer anything appealing about this prey.

But his hunger remained.

The dog whimpered as Walter shifted his fingers to surround its neck and cradle its head in his hands. Its bright eyes pleaded and teased, but Walter had learned that the promise of satiation there was pointless. He slowly tightened his grip anyway, and the animal split in two, its head popping off to drop at his feet. He held the oozing neck up to his lips, and drank.

The blood was warm. The blood was salty.

The blood was useless.

His hunger still raged, his needs unsatisfied. What he required could only be provided by the blood of human, not animal, intelligence. He let the dog fall, where it was immediately forgotten.

There had to be something more left on the face of the Earth.

Walter moved on, clumsy but determined, his hunger once more an all-consuming creature. It wasn't that he needed flesh to live. Its presence in his leaky stomach had never powered him. The strength of his desire was unrelated to any practical end.

He hungered, and so he needed to hunt. That was what he did. That was what he was.

He returned to endless days and nights spent walking the length and breadth of his island, but his prowling proved useless. Though he sniffed out the life of other dogs, and rats, and the last few surviving animals that had somehow not yet starved to death at the zoo, nothing human called to him. The city was empty.

One day, much later, he paused in the harbor and looked west toward the rest of his nation, a country that he had never seen in life. He listened for the call of something faint and distant, waited as the evidence of his senses washed over him. In an earlier time, he would have closed his eyes to focus, but his eyes no longer had lids to close.

The static of the city's life, quivering nearby, no longer rose up to distract him. There was no close cacophony muffling him from the rest of the continent, just a few remaining notes vibrating out from points west. He began to walk toward them, pulled by the memory of flesh.

He dragged his creaking body along the shoreline until he came to a bridge, and then he crossed it, picking his way past snapped cables, overturned cars, and rifts through which could be seen the raging river below. He had no map, and needed none, any more than a baby needed a map to her mother's breast or a flower needed a map to the sun.

Concrete canyons gave way to ones born of rock, and time passed, light and dark dancing to change places as they had since the beginning of time. Walter did not number the days they marked. The count did not matter. What mattered was that the sounds he heard, the stray pulsings in the distance, increased in volume as he moved.

His trek was not an easy one. He was used to concrete jungles, not the forest primeval, and yet that is where he was forced to travel, for life, if it wanted to stay alive, kept far from highways, as well. As he slipped on wet leaves and tumbled over fallen logs, he could feel an occasional beacon snuffed out, as another life was silenced, another slab of meat digested. Walter was not the only one on the prowl, and somehow he knew that if he did not hurry, the hunt would soon be over for him forever. As weeks passed, he could hear what had once been a constant chorus diminish into a plaintive solo. As Walter could pick out no other competing song, perhaps it was the final solo.

Its pull grew yet stronger, and as the flames of its sensations flickered higher, rubbing his desire raw, he moved even more quickly, stumbling lamely through a hilly forest.

Until one stumble became more than just a stumble. His ankle caught on an exposed root, and he then felt himself falling. He fell against what appeared to be a carpet of leaves, which exploded and scattered when he hit them, allowing him to fall some more.

From the bottom of a well twice his height, he looked up to a small patch of sky and saw the first face in an eternity that was, amazingly, not like looking in a mirror. The flesh of the man's face was pink and red, and as he breathed, puffs of steam came from his lips.

Then those lips, surrounded by a beard, moved, and a rough voice, grown unused to forming the sounds of human speech, said wearily, "Hello."

Walter had not heard another's voice in a long while, and that last time it had been molded in a scream.

Seeing the man up there, looking smug and seeming to feel himself safe, filled Walter with rage; it was the first time in ages anything but pure hunger had filled him. He slammed his fists wildly against the muddy walls of his hole, unconsciously seeking a handhold that could bring him to the waiting feast above, but there was nothing he could grasp. As he struggled to tear out grips with which to climb, his flesh grew flayed against sharp stones and splintered roots. Yet he did not tire. He would have gone on forever like that, a furious engine of need, had not the man above begun dropping further words to him down below. They were not frightened words or angry words or begging words—the only sorts that Walter was lately used to hearing—so their tone confused him. He wasn't sure what kind of words they were, and so he paused in his fury to listen.

"I've been waiting for you," said the man, his head and shoulders taunting Walter in the slice of sky above. "We have a lot to talk about, you and I. Well . . . actually . . . *I* have a lot to talk about. All you have to do is listen. Which is good, because I have learned from others of your kind that all you are capable of doing is listening, and barely that."

The man extended his arm over the hole. He rolled up his left sleeve, then used his right hand to remove a large knife from a scabbard strapped to one thigh.

"This should help you to listen," he said.

Walter could understand none of the words. But even he understood what happened next. The blade sliced the flesh of the man's inner forearm, and bright blood flowed across his skin, spilled into the crook of his elbow, and finally dripped in freefall. At the bottom of the pit, Walter tilted his head back like a man celebrating a spring rain, the stiff muscles in his neck creaking from the effort. He caught the short stream of drops on the back of his shredded throat.

"That's all I can spare you for now," the man said, pressing gauze against his voluntary wound and rolling his sleeve back down. "You don't like to hear that, do you?"

Walter had no idea what he liked or didn't like to hear. All he knew was the hunger. That brief taste had caused it to surge, multiplying the pain and power of his desire. He roared, flailing wildly again at the walls of his prison.

"If you can only shut up," said the man, "you'll get more. We need to come to an agreement, and then, only then, there'll be more. Can you understand that?"

Walter responded by throwing himself against the earthen walls, but this response gained him nothing. As he battered his fists against the side of the pit, three of his fingers snapped off and dropped to the uneven floor. He struggled more franticly, and those body parts were ground beneath his feet like fat worms.

"This isn't going to work," muttered the man above, who began to weep. "I must have gone mad."

He crumpled back out of Walter's field of vision. Though Walter could still sense the brimming bag of meat above, its disappearance from his line of sight lowered his rage, and he subsided slightly. His hunger still overwhelmed him, but he was no longer overtaken by the mindless urge to flail. He howled without ceasing at the changing clouds above, at the sun and at the moon, until his captor reappeared—suddenly, it seemed to him—and sat on the lip of the hole. The man let his feet dangle over the edge. Walter leaped as high as his dusty muscles would let him and tried to snatch the man's heels, but he could not reach them. He tried once again, still falling short. The man snorted. Or laughed. Or cried. Walter couldn't quite tell which.

"You can't kill me." The man peered down through his knees. "Well, you can, but you shouldn't. Because once you kill me, it might be all over. Can you understand that? It's been years since I saw another human being. Do you realize that? I may be it."

Walter growled in response and continued to batter against the sides of his prison.

"Damn," moaned the man. "What do I have to do to get your attention?"

Walter saw him bring out the knife again. The man looked at the line on his arm, which had now become a long, thin scab, and then gazed down into the pit, to where Walter's shed fingers lay crushed. The man shook his head. After a moment, he pulled his upper body back so that all Walter could see were dangling feet.

"This time," the man said, "I've got to do whatever it takes."

Walter heard a dull thud, one accompanied by a sharp intake of breath and a visible jerking of the man's legs. When the man leaned forward again, a handkerchief was wrapped around one hand. He used his good hand to dangle a bloody finger out over the pit.

"Listen to me now," the man said. Walter, frozen, stared at the offered digit. "I may be your last meal for the rest of your eternal life. I may be the last human left on Earth. Try to get that through your undead head."

The man let the finger drop.

Walter leaped and caught it in midair. He had it in his mouth before his feet hit the ground. He chewed so fiercely that he ate his lips away, and many of his teeth popped from their sockets. If the man were continuing to speak, Walter would never have known it, as the sounds of his feasting echoed deafeningly. Silence did not return until after the digit had been devoured, and only then did Walter look skyward again.

"I want to live," said the man. "I don't want this to be the end of the human race. We have to make some sort of peace, you and I. We have to reach some sort of an agreement. That's why I moved out here and filled these hills with pits like this one. I knew that your kind would eventually sweep out from the cities and find me even here in the middle of nowhere, and I wanted to be ready for you.

"You have to tell the others. You have to let them know. Know that I'm the last. That if you just pluck me off the face of the Earth, there will be nothing left, only eternal hunger. Is that something you can understand? Is that something you can communicate to the others? If so, they'll let me live. Let the human race live."

What the man said was meaningless to Walter. He knew the word *hunger*, and plucked it from the forest of words being dropped on him. But that was about it. He could not comprehend the man's message, could not possibly pass it on to others. In fact, as far as his consciousness allowed, there were no others. There was only Walter—Walter below and his food above. And the food was not getting any closer.

The man pulled his legs up from the hole, and for a moment it looked to Walter as if he were leaving, but, instead, there was another thud. Then the man poked his head into the pit, even closer this time, since he was lying on his stomach rather than sitting on the lip. The man brought his hands around to show another dangling finger. Walter leaped unsuccessfully, impatient for the flesh to be dropped.

"I can see that this is the only thing you will understand. Do you see now? If you eat me, it will all be over. Eternal hunger, with nothing more—*ever*—coming along to quench it. But if we can make a deal, I can help you feed for a long while. I can give you blood, and even some flesh from time to time."

The man dropped his finger, and this time, Walter caught it directly in his mouth. His teeth began crunching on it immediately, but, unlike before, he did not take his eyes off his captor. Walter looked up at the blood soaking through the handkerchief in the man's hand. The man noticed Walter's gaze. Loosening the cloth, he dangled his damaged hand down into the pit and shook it. The discarded handkerchief slowly and softly lofted down. Walter caught the cloth and tossed it into his mouth. He sucked on the blooming stain, the corners of the handkerchief hanging out of his mouth and down his chin.

"Do we have a deal?" asked the man. His eyes were wide, and he was so caught up in his hope that he did not immediately pull back his extended hand. Filled with lust at the sight of the wet wounds hanging there, Walter ran to the wall and leaped up toward them, wedging his feet in the damp mud before the man could yank himself back. Walter's remaining fingers intertwined with his captor's remaining fingers, and with his dead weight, Walter started pulling the man, sliding him forward so that more of his body hung over the edge.

"No! I'm the last man on Earth! You can't do this! Without me, you'll have nothing! Don't you understand?"

But Walter did not understand, not really, and the man's screaming and scrambling did little to slow his descent into the hole. Walter pulled him down mercilessly—for he had no mercy, only hunger—and at last, after far too long, the hunger was allowed to run free. Walter began with the man's lips, silencing the urgent pleas. Then he gnawed his way deep into the man's chest, cracking his ribs and burrowing into his heart. Walter's face grew slick with blood as he gorged. It had been far too long since he'd fed this well, and even though he remained trapped at the bottom of a pit, he had no concern for tomorrow, no thought of putting anything aside for another day. He savored the flesh and sucked the bones, and then . . . then it was all gone, much too soon.

Momentarily sated, Walter looked up at clouds. He sniffed out the universe, listening for the pulse of the planet—and discovered in that instant that his jailer had been correct: He had been the last man on Earth. Walter could sense no blood moving in the world. No food remained.

All that existed for Walter now were a few square feet of ground, his dirt wall, and the sky above. Time passed. Walter could not say whether it passed quickly or slowly. He only knew that the opening above him regularly darkened and lightened again. During the days, his view was occasionally altered by a bird flitting by, and at night there was the occasional flash of a falling star. Hunger returned and was his constant companion, but there was no longer any point in raging.

Mud and leaves and the detritus of time slowly filled the pit. As he paced from side to side, Walter rose a little each day, his ascension so gradual as to be almost imperceptible. He never realized what was happening, merely found himself one day high enough to peer over the lip. Only then did he pull himself up to the surface and stand, seeing the world again for the first time in ages as something other than a tunnel-vision picture of the sky . . . though the difference didn't really matter. For whether he was trapped in a hole or free to roam the land, nothing had changed. His only companion for now and forever more would be his hunger, and since he could no longer sense anything out there with which to quench it, it mattered little where he spent eternity.

Walter moved on without a destination.

Strangely, the sky now seemed filled with falling stars. And yet, they did not behave the way such things were meant to behave. Instead of vanishing quickly, as had the living human race, the bright spots crisscrossed the sky, like embers that refused to die. During the day, the stars still shone, another anomaly Walter no longer had the brain power to consider.

He wandered the world aimlessly, but only until the stars themselves were no longer wandering aimlessly. The stars were suddenly on the move in a purposeful manner, and as he gazed into the sky, he sensed where they were heading. With the flavor of the last man on Earth forever branded on his lips, he followed the path they made, moving back east across a country that was continuing to crumble, that was transforming from civilization into debris.

The bridge into the city, when he saw it again after what had been hundreds of years, had collapsed into the river. He had to pick his way over floating rubble, still bound together by cables, to move from shore to shore. He walked the city streets once more, watching the sky, until so many stars hung overhead that it seemed impossible to fit any more. Then their trajectories shifted, and they set about carving concentric circles in the sky. Walter's hunger positioned him beneath the heart of them. Others of his kind joined him.

As he watched, a single star dropped, pulling itself away from the carefully choreographed dance, becoming more than just a speck, gaining dimension as it fell. By the time it reached the buckled pavement on which Walter stood, it had grown into a globe several stories high. The fact that it floated there, sprouting legs on which it came to rest, had no effect on Walter. He sensed only dead machinery and felt nothing, not even curiosity. But when the outlines of a door appeared and then opened, that all changed. Walter could feel again the old familiar tingling that had been missing for so long.

A walkway eased its way out from the opening to touch the ground. A tall, attenuated creature walked down the ramp, followed by a hovering cylindrical machine half again as tall. The visitor, its two arms and two legs garbed in soft silver, stepped off the walkway into what, for it, was a new world. With alien eyes, it regarded Walter and his brethren.

Walter, agitated by a humanoid form stinking of the raw stuff of life, rushed forward—only to thud against the invisible wall surrounding the grounded star and its passenger. Flesh was close, so close, and Walter was enraged. He could not comprehend why his remaining teeth were not even then tearing the thing apart.

Walter roared, and his deafening anger was soon echoed by the keening of the other zombies that ringed the ship. The being removed a helmet, revealing a face that, though off in its proportions, contained all the right elements—eyes, nose, mouth—that signified humanity. This only served to fill Walter with a further fury.

The alien surveyed the crowd, looking at the crescent of the undead with all-too-human eyes. It then held a slender hand out toward Walter, who suddenly found himself able to surge forward, ahead of the others. Arms outstretched, he raced toward the flesh—*his* flesh—but stopped short in front of his meal, frozen as if encased in metal bands. Walter struggled to close that final gap, but could not.

Suddenly Walter found himself floating a few feet off the rubble. He tilted back, both alien and globe vanishing from his field of vision, to be replaced by the sky. He could see the moving stars pause in their flight. The alien stepped closer, and Walter was overcome by the need to open his mouth, to gnaw, to rend, but his body no longer followed the command of those needs. The metal cylinder, which had trailed closely behind the visitor, tilted on its side and floated to Walter's feet. It slid over Walter, engulfing him, encasing him from head to what remained of his toes. He was trapped once more. This time, he was unable to even bang against the sides of his prison.

The patch of metal before Walter's face cleared to transparency.

"Hello," the alien said, in a voice unused to forming the sounds of human speech. It leaned in close. "We have traveled a long way in search of our ancient cousins."

It waved its thin hands over the exterior of the cylinder, and sequential lights flashed, a rainbow coursing over Walter's mottled skin. He struggled to escape their glow, but, regardless of his rage, he moved in his mind only. When the colors ceased, that rage remained.

"How sad," said the alien. "Our cousins are still here, and yet . . . they are gone. They are all gone."

The words were meaningless to Walter, barely even heard over the angry urges in his head goading him to feed. Then the cylinder pulled away, and Walter found himself upright again, his muscles once more his own. He started to bound forward, but at the height of his leap, the strange creature waved its arms and Walter teleported back with the others. His momentum still carried him to complete his trajectory, and he slammed against the invisible shield.

The visitor walked back up the ramp, the cylinder floating by its side, and the metal path retracted back into the ship. The creature paused in the doorway. It was still looking toward Walter as the door closed and the force field died. Walter rushed the craft, but it rose effortlessly back into the sky before he could beat himself against its glittering sides.

The bright stars that had up until then formed circles in the sky vanished, but Walter barely noticed the emptiness above. So great was his lust for flesh that he was driven to return immediately to his hungry wandering, where he found nothing but that his hunger increased. His hunt through the rubble of humanity would prove fruitless, for his senses never again tingled to tease his immortal desire.

The sun and the moon continued to trade places, but no stars ever returned to move through the sky, and Walter's hunger, which left no room for any other emotions, never faded—at least not until, eons later, Earth's close and constant star expanded to fill his world with fire and finally erase his hunger forever.

CONTRIBUTORS' NOTES

By day, REBECCA BROCK is the director at a small rural library, but at night she works her second job and writes horror (and the occasional romance novel). Her first collection of (mostly zombie) horror stories, *Abominations*, is available at Amazon.com. Pearlsong Press will publish her first romance novel, *The Giving Season*, in November 2009. Brock has also contributed to several horror anthologies, including *History is Dead*, *Cold Flesh*, and *Decadence of the Dead*. Visit her blog at horror-hack.blogspot.com.

LANA BROWN is a high school English teacher and history buff living in Tulsa, Oklahoma. She is currently at work on her second novel. WARREN BROWN is married to Lana Brown. He has published stories in *Omni*, *The Best of Omni Fiction*, *The Magazine of Fantasy and Science Fiction*, *After Hours*, *Amazing Stories*, *Tomorrow*, and scifidimensions.com.

TOBIAS S. BUCKELL is a Caribbean-born writer who grew up in Grenada, the British Virgin Islands, and the U.S. Virgin Islands. He has published stories in various magazines and anthologies. His *New York Times*-bestselling novel *Halo: The Cole Protocol* and his three Caribbean SF novels—*Crystal Rain*, *Ragamuffin*, and *Sly Mongoose*—were all published by Tor. He is currently working on his next book.

JESSE BULLINGTON is the author of the novel *The Sad Tale of the Brothers Grossbart*, as well as assorted articles, reviews, and short fiction. Physically he can be found in the fine state of Colorado, and more ephemerally at jessebullington.com.

MYKE COLE was a top finisher in the Writers of the Future contest and has had stories published in *Black Gate* and *Weird Tales*. He also writes non-fiction on counterterrorism and related topics for *Small Wars Journal* and *CounterTerrorism*. Cole is a reserve officer in the U.S. Coast Guard and a civilian employee for the Department of Defense.

KRIS DIKEMAN lives and works in New York City. She is a graduate of Clarion West and was a finalist in the Million Writer Stories Contest. Her stories have appeared in *All Hallows, Lady Churchill's Rosebud Wristlet, Strange Horizons, The Many Faces of Van Helsing*, and *Year's Best Fantasy #9*. She is currently working on a zombie novel set in the building where she works, where people who in no way resemble her co-workers die screaming. Read more of her work at krisdikeman.com.

SCOTT EDELMAN has published more than seventy-five short stories in magazines and anthologies, and a collection of his zombie fiction will be appearing from PS Publishing in early 2010. He has been a Stoker Award finalist four times, in the categories of both Short Story and Long Fiction. Edelman currently works for the SCI FI Channel as the features editor for *SCI FI Wire*. He was the founding editor of *Science Fiction Age*, which he edited during its entire eight-year run. He has been a four-time Hugo Award finalist for Best Editor.

CHARLES COLEMAN FINLAY is the author of *Wild Things*, a collection of short stories, and four novels, including *The Prodigal Troll* and (writing as C. C. Finlay) the historical fantasy trilogy Traitor to the Crown, which is about witches fighting in the American Revolution. *The Patriot Witch*, the first volume in the series, includes zombies. He lives in Columbus, Ohio, with his wife and sons, and can be found online at ccfinlay.com.

ED GREENWOOD is a Canadian writer, editor, game designer, and librarian, best known as the creator of the Forgotten Realms fantasy world. A co-winner of multiple Origins and ENnie Awards, he was inducted into the Academy of Adventure Gaming Arts and Design Hall of Fame in 2003. His *New York Times*-bestselling fantasy novels have sold millions of copies worldwide in over thirty languages. Ed has judged the World Fantasy Awards and the Sunburst Awards, and been a guest of honor at more than fifty SF, gaming, and library conventions.

The latest book from JIM C. HINES is *The Mermaid's Madness*, the second in his series about butt-kicking fairy tale heroines (because Sleeping Beauty was meant to be a ninja, and Snow White makes a bad-ass witch). He's also the author of the humorous Goblin Quest trilogy, as well as more than forty published short stories in markets such as *Realms of Fantasy, Sword & Sorceress*, and *Turn the Other Chick*. You can find him online at jimchines.com. As always, Jim would like to thank his wife and children for putting up with him. Living with a writer ain't easy.

BARRY HOLLANDER knows zombies. He teaches journalism at the University of Georgia, where the stares of students often resemble those of the undead, especially on Monday mornings. His fiction has appeared in a number of magazines and anthologies, though of late he writes more non-fiction than fiction, all while sucking down cups of coffee. Hollander believes that a decaffeinated life is not worth living.

MICHAEL JASPER has published over four-dozen short stories in *Asimov's*, *Strange Horizons*, *Polyphony*, *Writers of the Future*, the *Raleigh News & Observer*, and other fine venues. His most recent novel is *A Gathering of Doorways* (Wildside Books, 2009), which *Booklist* called "a finely nuanced blend of fantasy and horror." He lives in North Carolina with his beautiful wife and two amazing sons. His website is michaeljasper.net.

MICHAEL LAIMO's publications include the Stoker-nominated horror novels *Atmosphere* and *Deep in the Darkness* and the dark SF-suspense novel *Sleepwalker*, which was published in limited edition hardcover by Delirium Books. He's written and published over one hundred short stories, many of which have been collected in the books *Dark Ride*; *Demons, Freaks, and Other Abnormalities*; and *Dregs of Society*. His short story "Anxiety" was filmed as a feature by Burning Grounds Motion Entertainment. Michael can be contacted through his website at laimo.com or through myspace.com/michaellaimo.

CLAUDE LALUMIÈRE (lostmyths.net/claude) is the author of the story collection *Objects of Worship* (CZP, 2009). He has edited eight anthologies, including the Aurora Award nominee *Tesseracts Twelve: New Novellas of Canadian Fantastic Fiction* (Edge, 2008). With Rupert Bottenberg, he's the co-creator of lostmyths.net.

ROBIN D. LAWS is the author of six novels, various short stories, web serials, comic books, and a long list of roleplaying game products. His novels include *Pierced Heart*, *The Rough and the Smooth*, and *The Freedom Phalanx*. Robin created the classic RPG *Feng Shui* and such recent titles as *Mutant City Blues*, *The Esoterrorists*, and the newly redesigned *HeroQuest 2*. Google his name to find his blog, a cavalcade of hobby games, film, culture, narrative structure, and gun-toting avians.

As an editor, JAMES LOWDER has directed book lines or series for several publishers and has helmed more than a dozen critically acclaimed anthologies, including *Worlds of Their Own* and *Hobby Games: The 100 Best*. He's authored several bestselling dark fantasy novels; short fiction for such anthologies as *Shadows Over Baker Street*; comic book scripts for DC, Devil's Due, and Moonstone; and a wide array of reviews and feature articles. He's been a finalist for the International Horror Guild Award and the Stoker Award, and has won five Origins Awards and a silver ENnie. Online at jameslowder.com.

MARK MCLAUGHLIN's fiction, non-fiction, and poetry have appeared in hundreds of publications. Collections of his fiction include *Motivational Shrieker, Slime After Slime, Pickman's Motel, At the Foothills of Frenzy* (with co-authors Shane Ryan Staley and Brian Knight), *Twisted Tales for Sick Puppies*, and *Raising Demons for Fun and Profit*. With collaborator Michael McCarty, he has written the novel *Monster Behind the Wheel* and the poetry collection *Attack of the Two-Headed Poetry Monster*. To find out more, visit myspace.com/monsterbook and myspace.com/phantasmapedia.

CHRISTINE MORGAN divides her writing time among many genres and forms: fantasy, horror, children's stories, thrillers, roleplaying games, erotica, even the sordid world of fanfiction. She writes for the *Horror Fiction Review* and has tackled editing 'zines and convention anthologies. She works the overnight shift in a psych facility, which gives her a lot of time to pursue her various projects. Her interests, apart from zombies, include pirates, superheroes, Britcoms, and cheesy disaster movies. Her husband is a gamer/living historian, and their surly Goth teenager recently sold a zombie story of her own.

SCOTT NICHOLSON is author of seven novels, including *The Red Church* and *The Skull Ring*, as well as two story collections. He also writes screenplays and comic scripts, adapting the Dirt series from his short fiction. His articles and more can be found at hauntedcomputer.com.

TOM PICCIRILLI is the author of twenty novels, including *The Cold Spot, The Coldest Mile, A Choir of Ill Children*, and the recently released *Shadow Season*. He's won the International Thriller Award and four Bram Stoker Awards, and has been nominated for the Edgar, the World Fantasy Award, the Macavity, and Le Grand Prix de L'imagination.

LUCIEN SOULBAN lives in beautiful Montreal and spends his days writing. His novels include *Desert Raiders* and *Renegade Wizards*. He's also penned scripts for such videogames as *Rainbow Six: Vegas, Warhammer 40K: Dawn of War*, and *Deus Ex 3*. Lucien has contributed to the horror anthologies *Blood Lite* and *Horrors Beyond* II, and you can find his non-fiction in the upcoming *Butcher Knives and Body Counts*, a collection of essays from Dark Scribe Press celebrating the slasher film. Visit luciensoulban.com for more information on Lucien's past, present, and future works.

Having gotten zombies off his brain—mostly—SHANE STEWART has moved back to Kentucky. He has also added a ninety-odd-pound dog named Jake to his definition of "normal life," a beast whose sole purpose is to keep him on his toes. It's a job the canine excels at. When not wondering what exactly he's gotten himself into, Shane continues to pursue a writing career, slowly but surely.

JEREMY ZOSS spends much of his time writing about video games and geek culture. He's traveled the world as a staff writer for the popular gaming magazine, *Game Informer*; interviewed comic book artists for *Wizard*; blogged for Village Voice Media; and otherwise spent too much time being a nerd. He is a member of the Horror Writers Association and his fiction has appeared in numerous anthologies, magazines, and online outlets. The story in this volume, "Electric Jesus and the Living Dead," inspired a song by an LA-area death metal band. He is pretty sure he's not a zombie.